DESTINIES DIVIDED

A World War 1

Romance of the Chinese Diaspora

Mee-mee Phipps

SERIOUSLY RED BOOKS
16 Kingfisher Grove, Greenhithe
Auckland, New Zealand

Destinies Divided: A World War I romance of the Chinese Diaspora

ISBN e-book: 978-0-473-27300-2
ISBN print: 978-0-473-27298-2

Acknowledgements: My thanks to Roshani Sengupta, Lesley Walker and Alan Patterson for their comments as readers, my editor, Steph Dagg and finally, Bev Robitai for the cover design.

Also by Mee-mee Phipps:

MEMORIES IN THE BONE: He Who Pursues Revenge Digs Two Graves (1st book in the Trilogy of the Chinese Diaspora)

THE MING ADMIRAL: A Chinese Odyssey. The story of two of the greatest men in Chinese history, the Emperor YongLe and his favourite, ZhengHe, warrior, poet, diplomat and Grand Admiral of the Treasure Fleets.

My ancestors gave me life, but destiny chooses my path.
It is not life I fear, but the destiny shaped for me by evil men
unknown.

Author's Note

I had never heard of the Chinese Labour Corp in World War One till I lived in France twelve years ago. There, an English friend and French resident asked me whether I knew the most popular name on the war graves headstones. Smith and Jones came straight to my mind, only to be corrected by CHINAMAN.

Thus began my fascination for this part of recent history that is unknown to most people. It forms the basis of this book because I wish to bring to public knowledge the suffering of so many in a war not of their making...

The newly formed Republic of China wanted to be rid of the yoke imposed by the Eight Foreign Nations, Japan amongst them. China hoped that by the end of the war, her contribution would be recognised and she would be able to have her territories and ports returned to her. She hoped that her sovereignty as a nation, stripped from her after the Siege of Beijing by the Boxers, by the foreign powers, would be recognised.

Another reason I wrote and am still writing about the Chinese Diaspora is because with the economic rise of China this century, I wish the non-Chinese world to know what the Chinese have gone through to be where they are today. In doing this, I hope to dispel the prejudices that sadly, still persist about a people who form a quarter of the world's population and who are only people who want to do the best they can in an ever changing world, regardless of politics.

I am not a historian, therefore I use the novel form to bring to you, readers, the recent history of the Chinese as I know it, as I see it. Forgive me if I intrude on your sensibilities in doing so. But I do hope you will enjoy reading this book and its precursor, **MEMORIES IN THE BONE,** also available in the e-book format and paperback.

The final book in this trilogy, **THE LIFTING OF THE SUN** is work in progress. It follows the fortunes of Zhou Yu's descendents and politics in New Zealand, China and British Malaya. It begins with the Great Flu Pandemic of 1919, goes through the Second World War and may possibly end with the Cultural Revolution in 1966. Who knows?

Mee-mee Phipps, March 2014

Chapter 1

1881: Dunedin

They had come on the new train from Oamaru only six months ago. On her deathbed, the old *kuia*, Auntie Ngaire, had a feast made of Horowhai's mother, Arel. As it was, Auntie Ngaire did not even live long enough to eat her properly, taking her last breath with her first mouthful of Arel's steamed flesh. Afterwards, the Reverend Pita Hohepa had honoured his word to Arel, a slave raised in their tribe, to let Zhou Yu take Horowhai away from the village that had been her home since she was born – a place which she now loathed and everyone in it, including the Reverend himself.

But for Horowhai, who had never been to a city before, Dunedin was too strange, too frightening, too large. Her entire life had been spent in Pita Hohepa's *papa kainga,* that village on the banks of the river outside Oamaru. And what a tiny village it was, she had soon realised when she first arrived in Dunedin. Her mind was like an embryonic egg, compared to Zhou Yu's.

Zhou Yu had taken her out several times when they first arrived and introduced her to his Chinese friends who had gaped at her in disbelief, before transferring their gaze to him, nodding in silence. Some even ventured a smile and a short 'hello' in English. Zhou Yu told her she could do the shopping once she got used to the streets around them. But she lacked the courage to go out alone. No, she was more than happy to let him keep doing that.

This noon, Horowhai gazed into the opened shoe-box.

"I'm only his slave wife, Mama. He won't want this child."

The blackened, shrivelled head of Arel faced upwards in its calico lining; the eyelids sunk deep into the sockets, the lips drawn back in a grotesque grin against brown teeth. The hair, matted and dried like black straw, was sparse on the small head. The *tohunga*, the village holy man, had tied it up roughly into a topknot with twine.

Her tears dropped onto the head as she bent over it, the box on her knees. The desiccated cheeks glistened. She wiped them with the hem of her skirt.

Her lips moved in prayer. "Show me how I can tell him, Mama. He will be so angry with me, I know it." The tears flowed copiously now. She continued kneeling on the mat he had woven out of flax leaves when they first moved into their house.

The door in the kitchen opened and shut again, his footsteps already moving about inside. She heard him fill the kettle. Hurriedly she replaced the cover on the shoebox and, standing on tiptoe, pushed it well back on top of the old oak armoire, out of view. Then she wiped her face with her apron and re-arranged her skirt. *He mustn't know, not yet.* He must not see her tears. Yet she was already in her fourth month and he would have noticed the change in her body, if he bothered to look at her properly.

Zhou Yu nodded with a smile when she emerged from their bedroom.

"I'm making some tea, would you like a cup?"

She nodded in return as she inched past him towards the sink bench. She had not done the breakfast dishes yet. She was grateful that he did not comment on it. *I'm not a good slave wife,* she said to herself as she started to stack them ready to do when the water boiled, if there was enough left after he'd made the pot of his Chinese tea. Oolong Cha, he had said it was, a tea priced for its beneficial effect on the digestion.

Now she looked at Zhou Yu quietly pre-occupied with his little tea ceremony, pouring the boiling water onto the cups both to clean and heat them after he had made the tea. She could see he had used up all the hot water.

As if reading her thoughts, he said, "Don't worry, heat up another lot. I'm sure we can afford the coal." Frugal though he was, she was even more so. He was pleased with that aspect of her; that she knew.

She peered at him from under her brows. He was taller than most of his Chinese friends and much more handsome. He held himself upright, his head high when he walked about, but she had seen it bend in what she could only assume was sorrow when he thought he was alone. Then his eyelids would droop over his sloe eyes and his wide lips would compress, and quiver downwards. She had come upon him once in the backyard wiping his face as if he had been crying.

They sat and drank their tea in silence. Even after six months she could not bring herself to raise her eyes to him and he had not encouraged any intimacy. They had coupled only a few times after their first month together.

"You've put on weight," Zhou Yu said with a slight smile as he now appraised her.

Horowhai nodded, not looking up. It was true; she was eating much better in her new life, especially when he cooked, which was nearly every evening. She loved his Chinese cooking. He always served fresh vegetables briefly stirred in oil and there was usually some fish or chicken with dinner. And at every meal a mouth-watering clear soup made from pork bones and vegetables would wash everything down with delicious warmth. She knew he got their green groceries from the small Chinese shops around their neighbourhood. He was building up his connections in Dunedin.

As she sat opposite him sipping tea, she darted him a look and realised that he was losing confidence in her. She had never gone out of the house on her own and he was still buying all their necessities. Because she did not expand her world, she had nothing to talk about when he returned home. The silences between them had grown longer and more frequent. And she was now with child – his Chinese child. Last night she had felt it stir.

Horowhai knew that apart from his good food, the reason for her weight gain was her pregnancy. She had seen how the women in the *papa kainga* grew fatter even as their bellies grew. Should she tell him now? He was in a congenial mood.

"I'm going to have a baby," she said, still with averted eyes.

A long silence followed. It seemed to echo in every part of the room. She felt his steady eyes on her, probing her face, and was embarrassed. She knew her long curly hair, tied with a strip of calico behind her back, was too unruly. Her fingers, surprisingly knotty for someone her age, and calloused from hard, physical work, clutched the cracked cup of steaming brown tea.

"I see," he said, unruffled.

She looked up and saw that his eyes were beginning to grow distant and knew he was thinking of someone else and she looked away again, feeling the gulf between them, feeling the depth of the abyss sucking her in.

*

Zhou Yu's thoughts travelled to that other child, the son left in China; to that other mother waiting for each letter with a New Zealand postmark on its envelope which she had told him she kept in her pillow box together with all the others. His eyes remained on Horowhai, vaguely taking in her unruly hair, her forever-scared, round eyes and full mouth that he had once found so appealing. His gaze travelled down to her midriff, then further down to her belly. Yes, he could see it now. *Yung*, he thought, *how I have betrayed you, my poor wife.*

He looked down at his hands holding the teacup, feeling its heat warming them as he grew aware of the chill in his body even though the wood burner was on in the room. It had been on all morning as he was the one who lit it. *How good I am at hiding myself,* he thought. *I should not be here, fathering another child, and by a native who's not my wife when Yung and little Hongyun are already there, waiting for our reconciliation. Yet when can that ever be possible? Meantime, what is a man to do, a man such as I?*

She felt no anger from him. Only a gentle stillness. She finally looked up and met his stare.

"You are not angry?" she asked.

"Why should I be angry? It's not your fault. It's mine equally."

She nodded and bowed her head again; relieved.

She felt his eyes still on her, felt his pity, and knew he understood her aloneness, her fear. After a while, since she would not respond further, he drained his cup and made to leave the house.

"I shall try to bring a fish back for dinner," he said.

Besides his good food there was not much for her in the house. The water was on tap in the backyard where the toilet was, in a proper little shed, and the floor of their dwelling was wooden. After her life in the village where she was occupied from sunrise to sundown in her numerous duties as tribal slave, there was nothing much for her to do in Dunedin. The house was small, consisting of just two rooms and the kitchen and there was only him to serve. He was easy to serve; he did not demand much and he was out most of the day.

*

From his warehouse on the other side of the street, William Faulkner looked up at the quiet click of the latch. He watched Zhou Yu close the gate and start to walk towards Wharf Street, about a mile away from his cottage in the poorer part of town. Faulkner owned that cottage, whose garden was growing weeds around the front and back as it developed a loose plank or two.It was far from the centre of town and was leaning towards Buller Street, making it even less desirable. When Edward Hats approached him to rent it to the Chinaman, he was happy to play landlord.

Faulkner was glad of the five shillings a month from the Chinaman and his Maori girl. He hoped they would keep it tidy and shipshape. He anticipated the Johnny would make a vegetable garden out of the front and back yards, coming as he did from a race good at gardening. Most of the vegetable gardens in the area were developed by the Johnnies after their unsuccessful stints in the goldfields.

Edward Hats had given the Chinaman a good recommendation backed by the Reverend Don. And so far his new tenants had given him no trouble, though there was no sign of a vegetable garden as yet. He saw Zhou Yu regularly going about this part of town, but he had only seen the Maori girl once, on the day they moved in. He wondered how she kept herself occupied, though it was none of his business. He heard from Edward Hats that the Chinaman was going into the business of importing tiles from China via Melbourne, where he had once been in the same business. Good luck to him.

Now, from the shadows of the warehouse, Faulkner watched him leave his rental, observed his quiet movements –

the click of the gate latch barely audible, the footsteps light as he lifted his feet in his walk, unlike the other Chinese who shuffled flat-footed. He, Faulkner, could not read his face. He had seen the Chinaman several times with his sloe eyes travelling from article to article, place to place, studying and appraising all in his view, but the only time he had shown anything akin to emotion was when he thanked him for the cheap rent of the house.

*

Zhou Yu walked with an even pace. He gave his upright stance a humble air; he sloped his shoulders forward slightly, bent his head down a little, kept his arms swinging just that bit more gently – anything to avoid being held up or taunted by any unruly, impolite member of the white community. But damned if he was going to be the kind of 'ratty, chinky, chonky Chinaman' that he had heard some young louts call out as he passed by. He was Zhou Yu, the son of Zhou Fengyi, a scholar and gentleman farmer of Suzhou, the most beautiful canal city of east China. He was part owner of a successful import/distribution business in Melbourne and about to open a branch here. So he made sure to deport himself with dignity and always dressed well in his Melbourne-bought clothes.

Arriving in Buller Street, Zhou Yu entered Chew's Boarding House, now grandly renamed Sunrise Hotel. During Zhou Yu's eighteen month sojourn at Pita Hohepa's village, Chew had managed to obtain a license to sell liquor and felt the new name more suitable.

"The only difference is that it is now legal," old Liew, the hotel factotum, told Zhou Yu upon his return from Oamaru.

But before being granted the license, Chew had had to do a considerable amount of tidying and cleaning to bring the establishment up to the standards required by the Council's Licensing Trust. To cover the cost of the upgrade and to uphold the standard, the price of alcohol sold at Sunrise Hotel rose by three percent.

The regulars staged a boycott.

"Three percent!" they had yelled. "You can easily recoup the expenses with one percent over a year, surely. What are you, Chew? A leech on your countrymen? Three percent indeed!"

6

In the end Chew settled on one and a half percent and the hotel was soon full again with all the Chinese in Dunedin seeking solace in each other's company at the end of a hard day, playing fan-tan and mah-jong for small change as they spat mightily into spittoons under each table. Spit, splat! The globs would glide down the inside of the spittoon or, if they missed, would land on the wooden floor to be cleaned up by the cussing factotum. And in a secret back room, up to six men at a time could squash down on a platform bed to smoke the opium that, for a few hours at least, banished the forlorn loneliness endemic amongst them.

The hotel was also a place of business dealings amongst the Chinese. Today Zhou Yu was going in to interview two men to help him in his fledgling business. The first shipment of ceramic tiles was on its way; trans-shipped from Melbourne, and paid for out of his account there. He had enough money to sign a lease for a suitable warehouse near the docks at Dunedin's port. The wooden shed reminded him of the one in Melbourne that had roared up to the heavens in a mighty conflagration one dark night more than four years ago. He had trepidations about another wooden building, but all the sheds in the port were wooden and owned by the port and local government, reassuring him. He did not think the local authorities would be burning them up for the insurance money as he suspected the Melbourne landlord had done.

Zhou Yu walked to the back of the bar room. Two men of early middle age were already sitting at a back table under the stairs leading up to the rooms for rent, with a pot of tea between them. They were dressed in faded Western clothes – grey wool jackets, grey flannel shirts over dun-coloured drill trousers, brown leather boots, and felt hats planted firmly on their small heads.

Chapter 2

1889: Dunedin -- Eddie

The dark boy walked rapidly away from the small school, his head down, a wavy lock of hair over his forehead. Out of the school gate spilled a horde of children, shrieking their delight at the close of another day in front of the blackboard and Mrs O'Brien. They skipped and ran, determined to put as much distance between themselves and their place of incarceration as possible. A group dashed past the boy, swiping him on the head and shoulders with strong brown hands. "C'mon, Ching Chong Chinaboy, stop clutterin' up th' street!"

He ignored them but the scowl on his face deepened as he watched their receding backs from beneath his brow. He slowed his steps as the last sounds of his schoolmates died out.

*

His mother's voice rang through from the kitchen as he let himself into the dark corridor of the cottage. His young sister pounced on him, happy that her adored companion was home at last.

"You remember the milk, Eddie?"

He slipped his sister's arms from round his neck, sighing.

"No Mama, I'll go out now for it."

He felt the coin in his pocket, still there, thank goodness.

"Take me, take me!" demanded Emily, hopping up and down, flouncing her calico dress.

Horowhai came through from the kitchen, her hands coated up to the elbow with flour. He noticed the white on her face and hair. She was not good at baking, being untidy in her motions and uncertain still in her method though Mrs Hats had taught her to make bread over a year ago. He knew it was still a hit and miss result each time, though the hits were becoming more frequent lately.

"You not lost the money, Eddie?" she demanded, her voice shrill in its tiredness.

"No, Mama, I got it," he replied, looking at her burgeoning belly. He had heard his father grumble about "Another mouth to feed," when told six months ago of the third addition to the family.

He took his sister's hand and shut the image of his mother behind the peeling front door. Emily skipped beside him, elated to be let out, her chatter intruding loud and rude into his sombre reflections.

*

The tiny kitchen was warm that evening, suffused with the smell of freshly made bread overlaid with the onions and garlic of stir-fried vegetables and deep-fried fish. Since Horowhai took up bread-making, their meals were a mixture of Chinese food and bread and butter. She cooked rice only when the bread did not turn out.

"I've found us a bigger house," Zhou Yu announced, glancing at Emily and Eddie on both sides of him. He looked across to his common-law wife, seeing her incomprehension slowly replaced by a look of joy. "It's not too far from here, actually, three streets further along – towards Hill Street. It has three extra rooms, so there will be space for me to have an office."

"Is it far from my school, Pa?" Eddie asked, hoping it would be, hoping for the possibility of a change of school.

Zhou Yu looked at him and smiled, indulgent. "No, Eddie, it's actually a little closer, so it would be more convenient, wouldn't it?"

Eddie nodded without returning the smile. The year after next Emily would also be going to that school. Eddie hoped she would have an easier time of it, being a girl and all.

Zhou Yu studied his New Zealand-born son with his round face the colour of liquid honey, his large sloe eyes fringed by thick lashes and the flattish nose inherited from his mother, whose curly hair had also been passed on, though in loose waves that she kept short around his ears. The wide, chiselled mouth was definitely from him. The boy was unhappy yet Zhou Yu felt powerless to help. Eddie was the only boy of Chinese

9

blood in the native school; the odd one singled out by the boisterous Maori boys for their pranks, the one they could call names. He had not made any friends in the year he had been there. Yet no other school would admit a Chinese-Maori child. Zhou Yu doubted the other native school on the peninsula would be any better, even if it were closer. He took his son's hand, gave it a squeeze and was rewarded by a grateful half smile. Little Emily's gaze glided around the table; solemn, steady, digesting inwardly all the nuances that outwardly manifested themselves between her parents and her brother.

"How much rent?" her mother now asked.

"Mortgage," replied her father. "I am buying that house. I have put down the deposit already."

Zhou Yu smiled at the light that came on in Horowhai's eyes. He knew she did not understand the words 'mortgage' or 'deposit', but she knew what buying meant. *Now she'll go and tell that bit of news to Arel,* he thought, looking back at the children. He wondered if they knew of their grandmother's head in that shoebox.

"When we move out?" asked Horowhai.

He noticed how pretty she actually was, now that she had grown into maternal plumpness again. She was taking more care of her appearance of late, under the tutelage of Mrs Hats and one or two of her *Pakeha* friends.

"Next month, when the present owners move out," he replied, turning to Emily's growing excitement. She clapped her hands and whooped. Eddie smiled wanly.

*

A week later, Zhou Yu returned to the house to find Horowhai howling, hysterical. Emily was cowering under the kitchen table, her little arms bearing the red welts of a caning, her eyes swollen with weeping. Eddie was nowhere to be seen.

"*Tien de!* What in heaven's name is going on?" he demanded as he knelt down to pull his daughter out. The little girl's sobbing renewed.

"They found out! They found out!" Horowhai screamed. She stomped towards them, lifting her right arm to hit Emily again. The child ducked and hid her head in her father's coat, mewling.

"Found out what?" Zhou Yu demanded as he grabbed Horowhai's hand in mid-strike.

"My mother! They found her head! I told them not to play!" Horowhai now started pacing the small kitchen, tearing at her skirt and her hair, tears and mucus flowing freely.

"Oh God, oh heaven preserve us," Zhou Yu muttered. He kept his clutch on the trembling Emily who seemed intent on melding her little body into his. "Where's Eddie?" He felt Emily's little head shake against his hips, her muffled reply indiscernible.

"I beat him, he ran away," Horowhai replied.

"Clean her up, I'm going to look for him."

Zhou Yu released Emily's grip around his waist and pushed her towards her mother. He noticed Eddie's coat on its hook in the passageway. *The boy will be freezing*, he thought as he left the house with it under his arm.

He scoured the surrounding streets in the fading winter light for an hour before retracing his steps home. He had called at every corner, looked behind every fence. Nobody had seen the boy at his usual haunts. As he approached their cottage, he saw a slight movement behind the back of Mr Faulkner's warehouse and found Eddie. The boy was shivering, his arms clutched tight round his body, his eyes red with crying.

"Come on, son," Zhou Yu said quietly in Chinese. "Let's go home."

He gathered the boy in his arms, feeling the desperation of the child's clutch round his neck.

"You okay?"

The child nodded into his shoulder. He lifted the boy up and walked back across the street to their house.

Both Horowhai and Emily had calmed down. Zhou Yu noticed the cane welts on Eddie's arms and legs. He sat him on a stool and proceeded to clean his face with a wet cloth. Then he rubbed a green balm of comfrey into the wounded areas of both children's limbs as they sniffled. Horowhai looked on, the wildness in her eyes betraying the sternness settling into her face. He put the children to bed in their small bedroom.

"You must not beat the children so hard," he told her as he got into bed.

"They deserve it," she replied, defensive.

"No, they don't. The beating was far too severe. We are a small family, we must love each other."

He studied her turned back. She started to cry. *Not again*, he groaned inwardly, but she would not cease. He turned away and tried to block out her sobs. Sleep finally came.

*

The move had been traumatic for Zhou Yu as he struggled to fit the family's possessions onto the dray from his own warehouse. He had planned the move on a Sunday so that his partners in the business could afford him a helping hand. As he loaded the armoire onto the cart, he noticed that Horowhai had wrapped the shoebox with her mother's head in the quilt from their own bed. He shuddered, but felt helpless against the hysteria that seemed now to be part of Horowhai's daily behaviour. He would not occasion another outburst, not if he could help it.

The children seemed to have recovered from that fateful evening though they refused to enter the parental bedroom from then on. Their attitude towards their mother appeared more reticent, more polite. They had taken to spending their time together playing outside in the cold back yard, rather than be in the warm kitchen with her. Their care of each other pleased Zhou Yu, though he worried for them. Horowhai seemed oblivious of this change in her children.

It took the men two trips with the well-packed dray to move the Zhou family into their new home. Once the large pieces of furniture were situated in the correct places, the men departed, taking the horse and dray with them and refusing the offer of a cup of tea. Zhou Yu knew they were uncomfortable in Horowhai's presence, as were most of his Chinese friends.

Alexander Zhou was born a month after, blasting his lungs out into the world and looking every inch a stranger. As Zhou Yu and the children stared at this new addition, he was aware that he had not managed to pass any of his Chinese looks to this third child. The large round eyes and curly hair in an inordinately big brown infant's body, along with the hysteria with which his mother bore him, estranged the poor baby from his father.

Chapter 3

1891: A Wedge of Fantasy

Zhou Yu's business expanded with the city. As bigger buildings went up, the orders for his tiles and slates increased. It grew in spite of the racism rampant amongst many in the community. Their Sinophobia had not been strong enough when the Chinese tiles proved to be as good as those they could import from the old country and were much cheaper.

Edward Hats dropped by Zhou Yu's warehouse late one afternoon when Zhou Yu and his employees were in the process of finishing up for the day. Hats hung his derby on one of several hooks by the door and took the proffered chair, his short stocky frame awkward on it. His blond walrus moustache bristled with congeniality; his blue eyes twinkled in their folds as he accepted the tea Zhou Yu handed him.

"And how are you, young man?" he asked, as he sipped the lukewarm brown brew.

"Well as can be, I hope, Mr Hats." Zhou Yu gave his friend an awkward smile.

"I can see you ain't, though. You are not as inscrutable as you think," Edward Hats said. "Mind telling me?"

Zhou Yu hesitated, wondering how he could confide his worst fears to this European friend. It would be such a loss of face. It was bad enough that his own community suspected his troubles – he had heard the whispers, felt the sympathetic glances in his direction each time he went into the Sunrise Hotel. Hats waited patiently, sipping the oolong tea in a white mug stamped NZ Rail as he watched Zhou Yu. Beyond them, Chinese workers, all former gold miners, were moving and stocking the pallets of ceramic ware. The occasional clanking was followed by cussing as metal rollers turned renegade beneath the heavy loads.

"Horowhai lose her mind," he confessed at last, as he turned round to face Hats, his honey-coloured cheeks reddening with shame.

Hats raised an eyebrow but said nothing. He had heard from his wife, the good and reliably solid Emily Rose, about Horowhai's erratic behaviour which would unexpectedly manifest itself regardless of time or place.

"Even at the butcher's where I took her the other day," she had said, "when you were out at Lawrence, she just started yelling because the apprentice couldn't quite understand her order. She acted like it was the biggest insult in the world! And she would still carry on, though I tried most hard to placate her. I feel so sorry for her wee bairns, what they must be goin' through."

And he had tutted in sympathy, seeing the picture in his mind's eye.

"She not able let go of her mother's death," Zhou Yu continued. "She talks each day to her head, sometimes many times day. Children dare not go near her. Emily says bread burning in stove one day; so long she stayed in bedroom, talking to Arel's head. Poor Emily. She too young to take on burden of household and Alex too." He sighed and took a sip of his tea as his eyes turned to the cussing from the other side of the warehouse.

"How old is Emily now?"

"Soon she be eight," murmured Zhou Yu.

"You are sending Eddie back to China, aren't you, back to your aunt's mission school in Shanghai?"

"Yes, I feel best thing to do. He not be happy at school. He outgrown bullying, but he not got good opinion of himself. Aunt Meng suggest she take him under her care, while she still strong." More sips of tea, noisy Chinese chatter unabated in the background. "Of course, that incident of grandmother head three years ago completely upset Eddie. He very moody and I feel anger in him."

Hats listened to Zhou Yu's broken English patiently. By now, after all these years of socialising with the Chinese, he had grown accustomed to their brave attempt with the intricacies of English grammar. Articles, for example, being absent in their language were not usually taken on board, nor the past or present perfect tenses. Zhou Yu's English had deteriorated somewhat since his return from Pita Hohepa's village in Oamaru with Horowhai. And he could only deduce it was because he was under stress.

Now Hats said, "Yes, Shanghai seems to be the answer for all its advantages, and probably distance from his mother would be chief amongst them. But why don't you send Emily too?"

Zhou Yu stared at him. *Of course, why not?* Aunt Meng's school took both boys and girls. The foreign children in Shanghai started their education there before they were old enough to return to their own countries for higher schooling. And the wealthy Chinese children followed the pattern of going off to America to the church schools there. Yet... a girl's place should be with her mother as her help and companion. But Emily was terrified of hers, and there seemed little connection between mother and daughter since that evening of punishment. In her early troubled days while settling into the city, the emotionally bereft Horowhai had not bonded with her two elder children. All her frustrated love was now poured into Alex who resembled her wholly, at least in appearance.

Edward Hats noted Zhou Yu's change of countenance. "I know. You think she should be here to help her mother. But Zhou Yu, anyone in the Maori community can be paid to do the housework. Emily needs to be looked after. She's bright. Don't dim that star."

Zhou Yu nodded. He would write to his aunt and would make enquiries for a passage to China for himself and the two children. He also must pay a visit to his first family in Suzhou, something he had put off year after year until the accumulation of time had widened the gap too much for any more excuses. He hated thinking about it. How would he be received by the wife and son he abandoned so long ago, and had broken his promise to in every way but the monetary one?

*

The children had been very seasick at first. The crossing of the Tasman saw them confined to their bunks, not being able to keep any food down. Just as Zhou Yu was beginning to despair, they suddenly came right. Soon after the cargo cum passenger ship docked at Sydney, they had sat up and asked for congee, the rice broth fed to most invalids amongst the Chinese. After that, their sea legs improved from day to day and they started to enjoy the voyage, playing cards with their father and all three studying English from the books he brought with him.

But the idyll was not to last. The voyage proved too long and they relived the entire gamut of their initial emotions at leaving home for the unknown – excitement, relief, and finally sadness. On the Dunedin dock Emily had hugged little Alexander tight as she sobbed into his curly hair, reluctant to release him. Horowhai had stood behind them, her face registering nothing as she looked on, arms folded. Now at sea, one or the other would take turns in displays of negative moods, irritating the other passengers and wearing their father's patience thin. But by the time they reached Shanghai, sailing in through the mist of dawn, the ship's foghorns sounding off the smaller craft crowding cheek by jowl in their path, they had worn themselves out. A new fear then set in as they gazed at the enormous city rising to meet them in the cool of the September morning.

*

Shanghai, twelve years from the last time Zhou Yu saw it, was much changed. The city was even more cosmopolitan, and motorised vehicles were much more numerous. Trams were now commonplace but the rickshaws had not decreased in number. Zhou Yu started to notice beggars and the multitude of poor eddying along the street. They were still going around plying their various trades, shoving carts ahead of them or carrying their goods in baskets dangling at the end of bamboo slats, still wearing rags. Monks in grey robes and shaved heads peddled herbal medicine and healing plasters from shop to shop. Beggar women in the dirty black trouser and top combinations favoured by labouring women still carried scab-covered babies slung on their backs as they pushed their outstretched palms in the faces of passers-by. "Please, master, some cash for my baby's breakfast," Zhou Yu heard them cry. But he had no spare change; the purser on board ship only had larger notes. He had to turn his face – there were too many of them. Eddie and Emily stared at them, then at him, their eyes soft with understanding and he felt shamed before them.

Zhou Yu waved down a multi-passenger cart. It had just off-loaded six people in front of them. He put their cases in before helping Eddie and Emily on and instructed the weary puller he need not pick up other fare, but to take them directly to the mission. Now, sitting together in the cart, the children clutched hands, open-mouthed and apprehensive.

"You will love it here," Zhou Yu smiled at them, speaking in Chinese. "The mission is lovely and the friends you make there will stand you in good stead later."

Emily returned his smile and replied in his tongue. "You said our older brother is there already. Since we've never met, will he like us?"

"What is there not to like, Emily? You are kin. He will look after you both, I am sure," Zhou Yu replied.

He studied her with a mixture of pride and wistfulness. Her long wavy hair framed a gamine face under a fringe. Large brown trusting eyes stared at him, slanted but with her mother's long eyelashes. Honey skin slightly darker than his. *I hope to God they won't face discrimination here,* he thought, as his eyes passed from one to the other.

"What is his mother like?" Eddie asked quietly.

For the first time, Zhou Yu felt obligated to explain Yung to these foreign children of his brought back to his native soil.

Sensing his hesitation, Emily asked, "Is she like Mama? Is she mad?"

"Where did you hear that about your mother?" Zhou Yu exclaimed.

"Everyone says so," the child shrugged.

Eddie remained silent, and stared out at the noisy crowd, chattering and hoiking to the start of their day.

"She is kind, and not at all mad," Zhou Yu answered, glancing in Eddie's direction. "You can go back to our farm for your holidays with Hongyun and enjoy the country air. You can help her work on the farm; you'd like that, wouldn't you?"

Yet even as the words were out of his mouth, he felt his heart constrict. *Really?* He smiled at them. They studied him, small hands clutching each other, saying nothing.

*

The mission school and its surrounding streets at least had not changed. The cart dropped them off at the back entrance and Zhou Yu led the children through the black wrought iron gate into the dark corridors going towards Aunt Meng's quarters. As he passed the busy workrooms, the kitchen hands stopped to stare at them. Just as he thought he knew none of them from his time before, an old woman approached, drying her wet hands on her grey apron. Surprise and joy showed in her snaggle-toothed face.

"*Aiya*, is that you, Zhou Yu? *Huanying, kuanying,* welcome. Your honoured aunt told us you would be coming home." She bowed low before him as others clamoured around.

Embarrassed at forgetting her name, Zhou Yu returned her bow. "Thank you, *Ayee,* Auntie, I am glad to see you are well."

"Your children from *Xin Xi Lan,* I see. Ahh, welcome, little ones," the old woman crooned, putting out her hand to stroke Emily's hair. Emily flinched at such close quarters to her overwhelming odour of garlic and old unwashed clothes. She pressed her face into the side of her father's jacket.

"Well," a nonplussed Zhou Yu said, "we shall see you presently, *Ayee.* Now I must find my aunt."

As he walked the children away, he asked, "How much of that did you understand?"

"Hardly any," Eddie replied, grim.

Zhou Yu could see his son would have trouble settling in. The boy seemed to have made up his mind about a whole lot of things in his usual way, not being prepared to give anything new much of a chance.

"We must learn proper Chinese really quickly, mustn't we, Pa, to live here?" Emily asked, as she lugged her small bag behind him.

Precious child, he thought. *Mr Hats was right, she is a bright star.*

*

Aunt Meng's door was also the same. The paintwork had not been retouched in the intervening years. His stomach fluttered with excitement as he set down the two large suitcases and knocked on the door.

"*Jing jin*," answered a soft, crackly voice.

How old she sounds! Sorrow filled his heart.

He opened the door slowly, afraid of what he might see.

"Aunt Meng, we are here." He ushered the children in, leaving their cases outside.

Aunt Meng turned from her desk. "Oh, oh, nephew! Oh, how wonderful to see you. And the children! Oh, come!" She reverted to English.

Eddie and Emily relaxed in the presence of the familiar language and allowed themselves to be stroked by their great-aunt. A sad sense of déjà vu swamped over Zhou Yu; the same painting and erhu had hung unmoved on the wall in all the years he had been away.

Aunt Meng got up to pour tea for everyone. Zhou Yu saw she was hunched over, her frame upright no more. Her hair was now completely white and all the vicissitudes of old age now sat on this once beautiful, loving woman.

As if reading his thoughts, Aunt Meng said, "So, as you see, I am now truly old, nephew. I am nearly eighty, you know."

"But you are still working, though, Auntie?"

"Not the way I used to. Certainly, I no longer teach, but I still supervise the kitchen and other domestic staff. As you know, the Bishop in America has allowed me to remain here for the rest of my days. No, nephew, I am less than half the woman I was, but, fortunately still strong enough to see to the next generation of our family." Supported by her cane, she handed the tea around, one cup at a time.

The children sat side by side on her bed, Emily's feet barely touching the floor. They accepted their cups silently with both hands and helped themselves to the tin of sampler biscuits she offered, their eyes large and intent on her every word, as they bathed in the comfort of her kindly smile. Aunt Meng did not want to discuss Yung or Horowhai in front of the children, so after a few minutes of light chit-chat she went outside to call the porter. "Please fetch Master Hongyun. His German class should be over by now."

The children understood the simple Chinese spoken. They looked at each other, then at their father. They shuffled closer together, hands seeking out each other's. Zhou Yu smiled at them, understanding.

After a while the knock on the door announced the visitor. He entered. For the first time since he was a three-month-old baby, Hongyun looked at his father. His face was set tight, his eyes expressionless. Then, very slowly, he clasped both hands together on his chest and bowed.

Chapter 4

1892: Shanghai --The Abandoned Son

Zhou Yu shot to his feet, speechless. The air hung for the slightest moment before streams of animosity emitted from Hongyun, felt by everyone. He straightened from his bow but made no move towards Zhou Yu who stared at him, his initial smile frozen on his face. Aunt Meng looked from one to the other. Eddie and Emily gaped at this unknown elder brother, their fear finally seeming justified. Hongyun's unblinking eyes pinned Zhou Yu in place. After a long while, as Aunt Meng moved to break the silence, Zhou Yu found his voice.

"Son," he whispered.

No response came from the rigid thirteen-year-old. As Zhou Yu relapsed into silence, Hongyun turned his head slowly towards Eddie and Emily sitting shoulder to shoulder on the edge of the bed. The younger children's goggle-eyed perplexity produced the flicker of a smile though his eyes remained still. Then he turned back to his father.

If Zhou Yu were able to say what was in his heart at this first sight of his eldest, it would have been, "How you've grown, my son. How handsome you are in your school uniform and how proud I am of you. Me, the father who has neglected you, has given you everything a boy needs but time and companionship and the proximity of my love. For love you, I do." But he was stilled from the onset by the mute hatred from eyes so like his and contempt from the compressed lips that could have been his own. He let his hands fall to his side.

Aunt Meng said in English, "Hongyun, as I told you, your brother and sister are here to have an education. I trust them into your care. Take a seat."

She indicated the space beside Eddie. The boy obeyed as his siblings shuffled a little aside for him, a perfunctory movement as the extra space created was no more than a couple of inches. Aunt Meng smiled at Eddie and Emily.

"You can understand Chinese, can't you? Our Suzhou dialect? Well, outside of class, you can keep that up. You will also learn to read and write Mandarin, yes indeed, and speak it. Your brother Hongyun will practise with you and I'm sure his English will increase in fluency in return."

She looked from one to the other, her little smile hovering under anxious hooded eyes.

*

Hongyun had known about Zhou Yu's second family in New Zealand since he was ten years old. Until then his mother, Yung, had been ignorant of the reason why his father had not returned to China. To the wife and son he left behind. To the farm he abandoned for an unfathomable life in a raw country where he had admitted early on he was unwanted. But when the fateful letter arrived one spring day informing her of the impending birth of his third son and his secret life with a native woman, her longing for him convoluted itself into such fury that she spared her young son no bounds. This sudden reversal of feeling, this hatred so much the sharper because of the enduring love that had been so consuming and forgiving, had speared the young boy's psyche into the realm of such darkness that at every mention of his father, his remembrance of his mother's suffering would surface. Now as he stood in the quiet of Aunt Meng's room, the loathing for this man, this older image of himself with his two dark devil's spawn, overwhelmed him. He struggled under a demeanour of practised calm. He clamped his mouth tight to prevent the invective that was boiling up in him, demanding to be spat out. He had no intention whatsoever to obey his grand-aunt.

*

Zhou Yu remained in Shanghai a week to reconnoitre the city, staying in a small hotel in the Chinese section a few blocks from the mission school. Eddie and Emily were put into dormitories with other Chinese children, separated by gender. They had been tested and put into classes of their own level. Zhou Yu visited them at the end of each day in Aunt Meng's room. At each visit, Hongyun was required to be present, silent and unwilling, and it was clear to the adults that he had kept himself a stranger to his siblings.

"I will be taking you three to spend the next weekend at the farm," he informed them one evening.

They started at this news. Hongyun's eyes flickered with concealed joy, but the younger children accepted the information with anxious looks between them. They seemed afraid of their older half-brother.

After Hongyun had excused himself, Emily said, "Must we go, Pa?"

"Yes," he sighed. "It is my duty to see my wife, and check on my property.'

"Mama is your wife," Emily spoke for both of them.

Zhou Yu exchanged a glance with Aunt Meng.

After the children had gone to their dormitories, Aunt Meng poured tea for Zhou Yu and herself.

"Yung hates you, you know. Is it fair to expose the children to her on this first visit?"

"It has to be done, Aunt, and the sooner it is over with, the better." Zhou Yu sipped his tea with a grim face.

"Hongyun will have nothing to do with them, and indeed, I cannot force him."

Zhou Yu nodded and rubbed his eyes, feeling the weariness created by repressed fear of meeting Yung after all these years. "I suppose I should not expect anything else. But fool that I am, I was hoping she would have the children when Hongyun goes home for the holidays. It would be a safe place for them and they could graft onto the Chinese part of themselves."

"Well, they can stay with me during the holidays as long as I am able enough," Aunt Meng said, her eyes on her mother's erhu hanging on the wall opposite. "They are quite foreign in their ways. I hope that will be advantageous and that they will accept their Chinese part. Certainly, as Hongyun stands, it will be difficult for them to feel anything but foreign."

"Any idea how they are faring with their classmates?"

Aunt Meng sighed as if he had just loaded the world on her shoulders. "It is too early to say, nephew, but I have a feeling not so well, with Eddie at least. He is strange to the other boys, being foreign yet not European. He falls into the space between.

Emily seems to accept it with better facility. After all, there are still only a few Chinese girls at school here. She's a resourceful little thing, isn't she? But poor Eddie, he seems moodier by the day. However, we shall see. I can only hope Hongyun will relent and take him under his wing."

*

Zhou Yu and the children took an ox cart from the Suzhou train station back to the farm. The city seemed brighter to him, and a few Western-style buildings had replaced some older ones in the centre of the city. But the countryside had not changed. The rice fields lay green in their still waters. Buffaloes sat chewing their cud under willow trees and peasants toiled according to their ancient agenda.

All during the train journey, Hongyun spoke only when spoken to by his father. He had kept his face resolutely turned towards the window of the train, his small suitcase balanced on his knees, his arms over them, hands loose over the sides. The younger children's query about his intentions over the weekend was answered with a curt look. They stopped making conversation after that. Zhou Yu stopped after the fifth attempt.

*

Yung was not outside the gate to meet them though the cart driver had clanged his loud bell on their arrival. Hongyun leaped down and ran through the courtyard, scattering the chickens pecking the ground around as Zhou Yu helped Emily and Eddie down with their luggage. Zhou Yu paid the driver who then whipped his ox into a slow saunter back from where they'd come.

Zhou Yu looked around him. The fields looked the same, but closer to the house stood a large, open, solidly-built shed with signs of woodwork industry. Long pieces of timber lay stacked along one side; shavings littered the outside of the building. It looked like it was several years old in its place along the outer wall of the courtyard. A couple of carpenter's saw benches stood by the doorway. *A workshop,* he thought. *What is going on here?*

Before he could go any further, he was aware of Yung standing with arms folded by the door to the house watching him, Hongyun behind her. Zhou Yu turned slowly to her, a small

24

smile on his lips as Eddie and Emily hid behind him. He walked towards her, carrying his suitcase, studying her as he approached. She stood still, impassive, her expression unreadable. Her arms remained folded across her chest.

She has aged, as I have. The years have not been kind to her, he thought.

Yung had put on weight; not the flaccid weight of indulgent fat, but the weight of a body used to hard physical labour. The fresh bloom that he remembered was gone, and in place of it, a countenance made forlorn by worry and unrequited desires. Small folds in her eyelids half hid her slanted eyes. Her once mobile mouth was now set in a rigid angry line which emphasised the roundness of her full face.

"Wife, how are you?" he asked softly. He laid down his suitcase with a sideways bend, keeping his eyes on her.

She continued staring at him, vanquishing his small smile by a look as impassive as the stone wall surrounding them. So they continued thus, standing awhile as he gathered his thoughts, rearranging his face to what he hoped she would accept. She gave him no harbour. He turned to the younger children to find them where he had left them, twelve paces behind by the gate amidst the chickens since placated by no further rude human interruptions. He motioned for them to join him. They approached, holding hands, each clutching a small tote of belongings.

He turned back to see her watching them, then she marched into the dark interior of the home he had left behind thirteen years ago when he had vowed to return often, and hence had proven himself a liar.

*

The house had been redecorated. His father's study had been turned into a workroom, with a hand-turned sewing machine in one corner and a long table on which lay neat piles of different coloured cloth and other accoutrements of dressmaking. The rose-wood chairs and table in the living room were the original ones he remembered but the kitchen had been modernised with a newer wood stove and wash basins. Newer pots and pans hung from their hooks on one side of the stove. But it was in his old bedroom that he felt most uneasy.

The red quilt that was a wedding gift from her aunt had been replaced by a blue and white cotton one. But most disturbing was the bed itself. It was not the one they'd had. Instead it was bigger, having the width of two and a half pillows and boasted a carved spruce headboard and end. And there were two pillows side by side.

Zhou Yu dropped his suitcase at the entrance as he stared at it. Then he noticed the armoire that had never been there before – and a single bentwood chair beside it. He turned round and caught the heightening colour in Yung's face.

"I sleep with Ma when I'm home," came Hongyun's voice behind them both – the most words Zhou Yu had heard him utter.

Zhou Yu nodded. "Where shall I put the children?" he asked without turning.

Silently Yung marched off to what had been his father's bedroom. Fengyi's marital platform bed with its kapok mattress was already made up with a fresh quilt rolled up at the end of the mattress and two straw-filled pillows, the covers crinkled from the laundry.

Eddie and Emily followed behind them. They had not spoken a word since their arrival. They put down their tote bags.

"Please make us some tea," Zhou Yu told his wife.

She marched to the backdoor and called outside. From the yard, a middle-aged serving woman entered, wiping her hands on her soiled apron. On seeing Zhou Yu and the children, she smiled awkwardly with a bow and a brown-toothed welcome, "*Huangying, kuanying,* Lao Yeh," and she proceeded to stoke up the stove with kindling and put the kettle on to boil.

*

After dinner, Zhou Yu prepared himself for bed. Yung had taken herself outside without explanation and came in only when he was half asleep. He turned over to her as she slid quietly in between the sheets, his hand outstretched. He sensed her reluctance even as he was aware of his own. His lovemaking was hurried. When he was done, he rolled over onto his back, staring at the ceiling, noticing the lace of cobwebs at the corner above the armoire. Yung lay sullen, her top undone, her lower half naked. Slowly, she took a hand cloth from the drawer beside her and wiped herself.

After some consideration, Zhou Yu said with controlled calm, "I feel you have been with someone else."

Not a sound from Yung. She snuggled lower into the quilt, pulling it up to cover her shoulders as she turned away from him.

Zhou Yu moved towards her. "Who is he?" Silence. "Is he the one who works in that shed outside?" He felt obstinate anger emanating through her rigid back. "Where is he now?"

She refused to answer. He kept staring at her back till, weary, he returned to his side.

So it was that neither Zhou Yu nor Yung were able to sleep that first night together. The unvoiced foment between them splintered into sharp wedges, settling into a pattern that would, from then on, be their relationship.

On the other side of the wall, the New Zealand children slept fitfully, their arms round each other. They had heard the animal sounds which they recognised from their earliest cognition and the voice of their father – quiet yet demanding – before the eventual lull that closed their eyes and their awakening psyche to this strange world of which they were now a part.

The next morning, Yung refused to accompany Zhou Yu as he investigated the farm. Neither could he persuade Hongyun to show him and the younger children around. So he himself took them down to meet the farm labourers working in the fields. Two had grown old with the Zhou family and three of the new men were of early middle age. To a man, they showed inordinate surprise at seeing him, at being introduced as the overseas *laoban*, further strengthening his suspicions that there was someone else, another boss, in Yung's life.

After an hour walking around explaining the tempo of rural life in southern China, he said, "Do you think you could like it here?"

Eddie kept mute as he surveyed the distant hills with squinted eyes, but Emily said, "It doesn't matter, Pa, she doesn't like us."

He nodded. "Give her time. She will learn to like you and I shall talk to her. You two will come back here to spend your school holidays with Hongyun."

But Yung refused him this quarter. "I have one child, my son. None other, and I refuse to care for some native woman's offspring! How dare you hoist them on me?" She spat at him.

"Nevertheless, they are my children and Hongyun's brother and sister. I demand you care for them in my absence. You will find them helpful around the place as they are used to helping my... their mother. I shall send more money for their upkeep," he told her rejecting back, then added softly, "Please, Yung, do this for me." He put his hand on her arm but she shrugged him off.

*

For the next two days, Hongyun was present only at dinner time after which he would take himself off till late.

"Where does he go?" Zhou Yu had asked Yung on the first night.

She had shrugged, but said nothing.

Her attitude to Eddie and Emily was one of scornful avoidance. In her small world, they were their father's pet rodents, to be got rid of as soon as possible.

On their final day, as Zhou Yu loaded the children back onto the ox cart for the railway station, Yung appeared in the courtyard. "I meant what I said: I will not have them here. I will not have them contaminate my son's ground." And she stalked off into the house.

The outburst was too rapid for the New Zealand children to understand, but Hongyun's smirk told the story.

On the train, Zhou Yu realised he had not managed to find out who had replaced him in Yung's bed. The man was not seen anywhere and none of the servants would talk.

*

Zhou Yu left Shanghai for New Zealand ten days later. He planned to stop in Melbourne on the way to visit his old friends Chan and Ling, whom he had not seen for several years. Each man had visited him in Dunedin on separate occasions but it had been four years since the last reunion. Emily had wept inconsolably on their last night together when he hired a rickshaw cart and took them and Aunt Meng to dinner at a restaurant close to the mission. Hongyun had excused himself, making a formal bow to Zhou Yu when he bade him an early goodbye. Eddie had sat with passive rigidity throughout the dinner, barely touching his food. At this final hour, Zhou Yu had not known what to say to his children. He felt immensely sorry for them, looking so forlorn and strange and, somehow, very un-Chinese in this very noisy Chinese environment. His own despondency grew.

"They will be all right, nephew," Aunt Meng had commiserated, watching their distress.

"Please let me know their progress," Zhou Yu spluttered, close to breaking down. "And you promise you will write often, children? Eddie? I know Emily will, but I want you to also."

And the child had nodded with quivering lips, fighting back his tears.

As Zhou Yu took his leave at the back gate of the mission, Emily handed him a small packet from her tote bag. "Read this on the ship, Pa," she said as she hugged him, her tears soaking into his jacket front.

"Do I have to grow a pigtail?" Eddie asked as he was hugged in turn. "Hongyun said I must or the authorities will cut off my head."

"No," said his father, "you look foreign enough and the school will give you a letter to say you are indeed a foreigner from New Zealand. And *that* you must carry at all times with you."

*

As Shanghai receded into the horizon, Zhou Yu remembered Emily's packet in his jacket pocket. He found a bench on deck and opened it. Inside, in a little notebook brought all the way from New Zealand, was a pressed pansy, still fresh in its delicate purple – her attempt at remembrance of Dunedin. "Picked with Alex," he read. On the next page was a more recent flower; a tiny pink rosebud, which he recognised as amongst the ones she had picked during their wanderings around the Suzhou farm. "A memory of your Chinese home."

On the following page she had written in her round child's hand, "Dear Papa, please don't worry about us. We will try to be

Chinese. But that will then make us neither one nor the other. Which really do you want us to be? We miss you already, and Alex and Mama. Please be kind to her. Emily."

The rest of the notebook was filled with pencil drawings of the farm. Zhou Yu sat there a long while, hunched over, revisiting each page several times, as tears dripped onto his trousers.

Chapter 5

Dunedin: The Growing of Children – Alex

Alex moved about the empty house, overwhelmed by the silence.

"I shall be taking Eddie and Emily to China, Alex," his father, crouched down to his level, explained to him, as he stood beside his mother on the dock. Eddie and Emily were weeping. Mama was weeping and growing into one of her moods as she clutched his hand too tightly in hers. "They will go to school there. When you are older, you will join them, right, son? You will look after Mama while we're away, won't you? Like Eddie has done? That's my boy, eh?"

Papa had hugged him tight. Had given him a soft, warm kiss.

Alex watched as Zhou Yu and the two older children ascended the long gangplank onto the big, noisy ship. He felt suffocated by the many people around him, all talking, shouting, crying, all saying goodbye and wiping their faces with handkerchiefs. Then he saw his departing family high up, waving, calling his name. Eddie and Emily were jumping up and down to get his attention. Mama by now was really bawling her head off. The ship made huge tooting noises, belched piles and piles of black smoke and then slowly slipped away from the dock. The band kept playing till the ship had gone quite a way off. It would have been like a fair except so many people were crying. He, too, had cried and waved and jumped about till he could no longer see them. Papa. Eddie. Emily.

Then Mama had taken him home – to a dark, cold house. And silence descended.

*

He asked Mama each day, "Where's Papa? Eddie? Emily? When will they be home?" Till in the end she started screaming at him. And then she started slapping him each time he asked until he stopped. She had then wept and clutched him close, so close he felt his breath squashed out of him. After that, she took him to her bed – to keep the bad *atua* from coming to him in his cold, dark bedroom with two empty beds, in that quiet, still house. Bad spirits, bad *atua*. Who made him wet his mattress.

China was an obscure place, unfathomable to his three-year-old mind. "It is Papa's country," Mama had said. "Papa is a Chinaman, like old Wong Kiok who sells vegetables down the road." But Alex could not see much likeness between that man and his tall father, what with Wong Kiok's wobbly teeth, and his gnarled hands from working too long in the goldfields, then too long digging the earth growing veggies. And unlike Papa's, old Wong Kiok's speech was all funny. Poor old Wong Kiok. Pa said he was from a different part of China. That's why he couldn't understand him. *No, he's not like Papa. Oh, when are they coming home? When? When?* And Mama kept shutting herself in her bedroom during the daytime, shutting him out.

Poor Mama. What's the matter, Mama? He stood listening outside her door, his chipped wooden horse on its wheeled platform beside him, tethered to the grubby rope in his little hand. *Please stop crying, Mama. Please open the door.*

*

Zhou Yu watched his youngest child playing with some broken tiles on the warehouse floor. With surprising manual dexterity, the boy had built a row of tile houses and now he was pushing a small carved horse alongside, making neighing and galloping noises, absorbed in the game.

Zhou Yu had arrived back in Dunedin six weeks previously to find Alex deep in his little world of silence, insecure and over-clingy to his mother whose mood swings were more severe than he remembered. He could see she was unsettling the child and decided to take the boy with him to work as much as possible. Soon Alex had transferred his dependency from his mother to him and seemed content to play quietly all day while he conducted his business or went around with him to the Chinese shops. Zhou Yu was heart-broken, missing Eddie and

Emily much more than he expected. The house was so empty without them.

Now Zhou Yu looked up to see the slim form of the Reverend Alex Don standing in the doorway, smiling at his little namesake.

"Hello, Zhou Yu, hello young fella," Alex Don said as he removed his hat and made his way into the room.

The child looked up and ran to him and was rewarded with an upward swing in the clergyman's arms. He gurgled joyfully. Then he started screeching as he was swung further and further up. This was the first time he had shown any joy since Zhou Yu returned. *I must play with him more often,* Zhou Yu thought as he watched them with a tinge of wistfulness.

"Just thought I'd drop in as I was passing. How are you, Zhou Yu? Are the children settled in Shanghai now?"

Zhou Yu got up to offer the only half-decent chair in the warehouse to Alex Don.

"Yes, I received letter from my aunt and they both wrote – came in same envelope."

"And?"

"Well, they well can be, I think. Eddie's calligraphy and grammar improved even in this short while. Emily doing very well." Zhou Yu's unenthusiastic response made the reverend's ears prick up. He waited for further collaboration. "Truth is, Reverend, I don't know if it best move after all. Eddie just traded one form of bullying for another. This time it by Chinese, my eldest son amongst them. Hongyun caught and my aunt had to chastise him." Zhou Yu rubbed his tired eyes as he watched little Alex resume his solitary game, happier now.

"I'm sorry to hear that. I suppose it's natural Hongyun would resent them. Hopefully he will get used to the idea of having his siblings around, eh?"

Zhou Yu shook his head. "No chance of that. His mother very strong that she will not have them on farm in their holidays. Hongyun takes cue from her, I afraid. Can't blame them." He looked out the dirty window and paused as he watched his partners load up a dray of tiles for delivery.

The Reverend Don followed his eyes. "How's Emily taking it all?"

"Thank God for Emily. She her brother's carer. Amazing, her, younger one. I glad I took her. She came out fine, she coping well."

"Will you send Alex when his time comes?"

The child looked up at mention of his name, and smiled at them both.

"His mother begs me not to. She needs her favourite around, one child for consolation. Besides, he so Maori-looking he won't be bullied here. And he large for his age."

Both men studied the little boy as they lit their pipes.

"Neigh, clop, clop," Alex enunciated.

"Well, tell you what, Zhou Yu, I'll take him under my wing if you like – stretch his education a bit more than that native school can give him."

Zhou Yu could not contain his joy. "Oh Reverend, I be so grateful if you would."

"Well, needless to say, I would add that you teach him Chinese? Not just speaking, but reading and writing? Shame not to have both cultures in his education."

"Yes, yes! You enlightened man, you, Reverend, and good one. Thank you, thank you." Zhou Yu felt his eyes tearing up with relief. At last, the solution for Alex had presented itself.

The older Alex smiled. He had plans for his namesake in the foreseeable future. Little did Zhou Yu know what an asset he had in the little boy playing on the cold concrete floor.

*

Horowhai plunged her hands again and again into the lump of flour, muttering under her breath in English. "Why I do this? Why? He takes my baby every day from me. Why I feed him? Why I feed him? Alex don't love me no more." She kneaded the pale gooey lump with the strength of her body weight behind her arms. She thumped it again and again, stopping to sweep her hair off her face, whitening both. Then her mutterings turned into Maori. The tears ran down her face. She went back to English. "Eddie, Emily, Alex, my children, my children." Back to Maori.

The flour was going everywhere now; all over the table, onto the floor, smearing her tear-streaked face. She started howling, swiped the lump of flour onto the floor and ran into her bedroom. Standing on tiptoe, she brought down the shoe box and opened it to the grisly head. She knelt on the floor, swaying as she cried, "Mama, Mama..."

Zhou Yu came through the front door with Alex sitting on his shoulders. As he strode down the corridor, he saw the disarray in the kitchen and his mouth set into a hard line. *God, what now?*

Alex felt Zhou Yu's tension ripple up through his own body. He gripped his father's hair tighter, his young heart constricting with anxiety.

"Get down, son," Zhou Yu said as he lowered Alex to the floor. He then walked to the back door, retrieved the rush broom from behind it and started sweeping up the floury mess. Alex stood by watching as he cast nervous glances towards his parents' bedroom, listening to the sound of his mother's indiscernible moaning behind the closed door.

After wiping up the flour from the table, Zhou Yu put the kettle on the cook-top. He took a jug of milk from the larder in the back wall and poured a small cup of it for Alex. Then he gave him a ginger nut from an old sampler tin.

"Get this down you while I see to Mama," he said as he lifted the little boy onto a chair.

Horowhai turned when he opened the bedroom door, her face drenched in tears, her eyes wild, her hair a mass of black curls. She spat at him as he stopped short at the sight of her. She quickly closed the shoe-box and clutched it to her chest, but remained kneeling, glaring at him.

"Horowhai, please. Alex is home now. Don't terrify him," Zhou Yu pleaded quietly.

She spat again. She stood up to put the shoe-box back on top of the armoire.

"You take my son! You take my Alex from me!"

"No, no, Horowhai, I only thought he would enjoy playing in the warehouse. He's built a little town down there with all the broken tiles." Zhou Yu closed the door gently and sat on the bed. He looked up at her, standing dishevelled against the wall. "I thought you'd like time without him, to do your own things," he lied. *What can I do about her? She's getting worse by the day.*

Her sobbing quietened as the silence between them grew. Sniffling, she said, "I'll finish making bread," and made for the door.

"Don't worry, I'll cook dinner tonight. I bought a piece of good pork and some vegetables from old Wong Kiok. Why don't you spend some quiet time with Alex, eh?"

She nodded and went back to the kitchen.

*

Shanghai

Emily sat on a low stool in front of Aunt Meng, holding a skein of blue wool stretched between her arms. Aunt Meng was winding it into a ball and the young girl's arms moved in slow motion – down and around then back up to chest level to allow the wool to unwind from the skein. Down, around and up, down, around and up.

Eddie lay on his stomach on the narrow bed, reading an English text by the light of a kerosene lamp. This was always his happiest time: between dinner and bed, when he could be himself with the two most precious people in his Shanghai life. He knew Aunt Meng was knitting the pullover for him, and he felt moved and loved. He knew it was not so easy for her, what with her failing eyesight.

A knock on the door announced Hongyun's arrival.

"You wanted to see me, great-aunt?" He bowed. He was always polite to her, at least in her presence. Eddie and Emily stiffened. He glanced at them without recognition.

"Yes, grand-nephew. Now, I have told your mother that your brother and sister are to accompany you home for the Spring Festival next week."

"I am aware of that, great-aunt," he replied stiffly.

"I know neither you nor your mother are happy with this particular arrangement. But this is your obligation to your father – and to Eddie and Emily. Please be civil and try to make it a happy time for them. Promise me?"

A protracted silence. Underneath her brusqueness, her eyes were pleading. Hongyun's own sloe eyes remained expressionless. She knew she was asking too much.

36

"It will only be for ten days. Your father has assured me they will be useful around the farm. So, Hongyun, come for them here at nine. I shall have your train tickets ready."

Without a word to her, without a look to the younger children, he bowed and closed the door behind him.

"We don't mind staying here for the holidays," Emily said with a look at her brother, who nodded, miserable.

"It's not fair that you should. Besides, Yung does owe your father a duty of care for you. That you are here is not of your doing. The innocent shall not suffer." *And children should not be made to pay for their father's misdemeanour,* she could have added.

*

Hongyun ignored his siblings from the onset of the short journey to Suzhou. He was stern and silent and they were obliged to follow him, unquestioning. It was made difficult as he walked unusually fast. Their relief at finding themselves in the same cart with him from Suzhou train station and not left abandoned on the tracks was only supplanted by their fear of meeting his mother again. And she met them head on – with the same contemptuous silence as before.

Their bed sheets had not been changed since their last visit four months previously. Dinner was unannounced. The first evening they had to follow their noses to the dining area – to see a strange man sitting next to Yung. He gave them an awkward smile as he glanced at Yung. Hongyun greeted them with a smirk. Dinner had already begun but there was no place set for them – no chopsticks, no bowls.

"Eat with the servant," Yung ordered.

And in the kitchen, the old servant, Lao Ma, told them, "We wait for the left-overs, but here, look, I have saved some extra for you." And she gave them each a bowl of hot rice with some stir-fried vegetables and a few slivers of pork.

Only a few scraps swimming in congealed fat were left of the meat dishes that came back. Lao Ma ate her rice with these. At least there was some hot soup.

*

On the first day of the Lunar New Year, Hongyun paraded around in brand new clothes: a quilted red brocade jacket and thick padded black trousers. His queue sat neatly under a new black silk cap. He showed them several red packets of money gifts and gloated. They were still in their shabby New Zealand woollens. The red packets Aunt Meng had given them were still in her room and the set of new clothes each from her remained in their suitcases.

"We should wear them for today, at least," Emily had cajoled her brother.

"What? In this stinking place? I'd rather save them for when great-aunt takes us out. How I hate these people!"

"Yes, Eddie, and how they hate us. But I will try to like it here."

"Yah? And how?" Eddie retorted, obdurate as he stuck his hands in his pockets.

"Well, I shall help Lao Ma and learn to cook Chinese food. I like her steamed rolls, especially. Then maybe I can go down to the rice fields and learn how plants grow down there. Oh Eddie, please, let's. At least that will give us something to do and be away from them."

"Who do you think that man is? He sits where Pa should be sitting."

Emily grew quiet. She knew, somehow, who this man was. He was the one in the wood shed, the one making the strange animal noises she heard last night. The same noises she had heard Papa make when they were here last time, and also through the thin walls of their cottage back home in Dunedin where he slept with Mama. Now her homesickness smacked her in the face.

"I miss home so much," Eddie whimpered, bringing her thoughts out loud.

She said nothing, but took his hand and snuggled up close, the two of them sitting on the platform bed in their given room. Not even when Mama was in her tantrums had she ever felt as lonely as now, stranded in a house of belligerent strangers, marooned in the Chinese countryside so far from home.

*

Two days later, Eddie and Emily walked past the wood shed just as the man emerged. He held them in his steady gaze awhile and smiled.

38

"And what are you going to do today?" he asked, slowly enunciating the local patois that the children had come to understand.

They paused, taken aback by this unexpected friendliness. Seen away from Yung and Hongyun, the man looked kind. Emily studied him as he stood in front of the open shed, a piece of smoothened wood in his hands. He was much older than Pa, was smaller and had soft eyes in a sad, creased face. He wore a cloth cap over his greying pigtail and a dusty blue cotton quilted jacket and trousers. His padded cloth boots were also covered in sawdust, the pleasant smell of which now assailed their nostrils. As he continued looking at them, she sensed he wanted to make conversation and glanced at Eddie, who stood holding her hand, his face set in defiance and definitely not forthcoming to this overture of friendship.

"We're going down to the fields," she now replied, and attempted a small smile as she gave Eddie's hand a squeeze.

"My name is Feng Wen Kai," said the man. "Do you have Chinese names?"

"Zhou Hong Ling," replied Eddie, still unsmiling, though his hand in Emily's relaxed.

"Zhou Mei Ling," added Emily. "But we never use them back home. We only use our English names."

"Well, then, I shall call you by your English names," said Feng Wen Kai. "And you may address me as Uncle Feng."

They stood about awkwardly.

Eddie then said, "What are you doing in there?" He indicated the interior of the shed with his chin, still po-faced.

"I make furniture," Uncle Feng replied with a smile. "Would you like to come in and see?"

He led them into the shed. The smell of fresh wood brought sudden tears to Emily's eyes. Images of forests on the peninsula, images of the family, of summer picnics – the occasional one becoming a series in her memory. *So long ago, so far away. Oh Mama, Pa, Alex.* Behind Eddie's back, she wiped the tears away.

Uncle Feng chose to ignore her sadness and was now explaining what wood was used for what type of furniture.

"Will you teach me how to make a table?" she heard Eddie asking.

Uncle Feng chuckled. "Well, you are welcome to watch, and when you are bigger you can try to make one. But wood is expensive, you understand, I can't risk you spoiling any right now. You are still too young. But certainly, you can watch for as long as you want, and I shall explain the process as we go along."

Emily watched Eddie's face light up. A smile grew over his white teeth and spread to the rest of his face. *He's happy! At last, he's happy!* And she felt warm towards the usurper of her father's place.

The ten days of the Spring Festival holiday passed contentedly in the wood shed for Eddie. He seemed to have found his calling, learning to anticipate which tool was necessary for which bit in the making of furniture and becoming a willing sweeper of floors and fetcher of wood and tools. By the end of their stay, he was straightening bent nails with a small hammer. Emily spent her time in the kitchen with Lao Ma.

On their return to Shanghai, she told Aunt Meng proudly, "I'm able to make eight buns a minute for the steamer. Lao Ma said that's a lucky number to achieve."

From Hongyun there was only a stony silence.

Chapter 6

January 1898: Tsingdao County, Shandong Province,

The morning mist had cleared over the dry yellow earth, baring rocks scattered amongst fallowing fields. The few trees dotted here and there in the winter landscape had been denuded of leaves two months back. Now they stood, grey-trunked, spindly-branched, against the clear blue sky. From a cluster of low-brick houses, closely set together behind crumbling brick and stone walls, people emerged in small groups. Clad in faded padded jackets and trousers, dusty and musty through lack of washing, the hamlet dwellers hurried into the paths leading towards their village two miles east.

"*Kwai lai, kwai lai,* please hurry, Xiao Hua. We must see your father before it's too late," a young woman sobbed, dragging her six-year-old son who trotted beside her, frantic to keep up. Several other neighbours of this Li Tun were running past them, anxious to get to the public execution to be held that late morning in the clearing on a hillock overlooking the river.

The event had been advertised in the village bulletin board the week before, had been read out loud by those who could to those who couldn't. A band of rebels had been captured and the German occupiers of their province had ordered the execution to be a public event as a deterrent to all Boxer rebels.

"Ayahh!" the little boy cried out as he stumbled into a pothole and lost his grip of his mother's hand. He started bawling. "I hurt, Mama, I hurt! I can't walk." He clutched at his ankle, his little dust-covered face red, and now tear-streaked.

Li Tun helped him up, whispering, "Climb on my back, son, I'll carry you."

They were left behind. As she watched her group recede into the distance, Li Tun's desperation grew immeasurably. By the time she reached the village's stone walls, her exhausted wails were loud enough to attract others' attention. Others who had gathered to watch the bravest of their men folk exterminated that day.

*

Six rotund German policemen were leading their horses down the hill. Their red faces, moustachioed under pith helmets, looked grimly satisfied. Their necks strained under the tight high collars of their blue-grey tunics. As they arrived at the tramped dirt street, Li Tun heard their guttural conversation before they mounted their mares and cantered out of the village in the direction of the port of Tsingdao, six miles east.

Li Tun's cousin, Li Quang, who ran the small sundry shop, dashed back down to meet her. He, like everyone else descending that fateful hillock, was weeping.

"It's over," he told her.

At this, Li Tun screamed, prompting the same reaction from her son who was still clutching her neck. Li Quang took him off his mother's back and put a comforting arm around her shoulders. Now the muttering of the villagers grew loud around them. Li Tun unknotted the red cotton scarf from her head to wipe her face. She felt close to fainting, clutched at Li Quang to stay upright, and put her other arm around the boy.

The small contingent of soldiers, sent to execute the rebels, arrived from the killing ground with the village headman. They muttered to each other, angry, ashamed at the act foisted upon them by the German imperialists, and fully aware of the resentment towards them. The sergeant looked around the crowd, his hooded eyes guarded under stress.

"Good people," he said, bowing, "today we were forced to commit a crime against our own. We, my men and I, apologise profusely, deeply, to you and to our ancestors. But know this, we are of your sympathies and one day, we shall play a hand in throwing out the foreign scum from our holy province, indeed, from all China. No more will we let their missionaries taint our ancient beliefs; no more will we allow the rape of our resources. We will fight to obliterate the opium that is drugging our nation. But for this heinous act we performed today, we beg your forgiveness." He turned to the headman. "Lao Kong, please allow us to burn joss sticks at your temple to atone for our sins."

The crowd parted and followed them to the small temple on the perimeter of the village where the soldiers paid for joss sticks which they lit as they prayed before the shrine and then stuck them into the bronze urn. Then they bowed again to everybody surrounding them before marching east towards Tsingdao. Everybody paid their small cash for a clutch of joss sticks and followed the age-old method of worship and obeisance.

At the end of this ritual, the village folk gathered gunny sacks and hemp ropes from the rice warehouse. Li Tun left Xiao Hua with her old aunt and joined the more able-bodied men and women as they went back up the hill. Having cried her tears dry, she now surveyed the blood-soaked execution ground, searching for her husband's body. The other women started wailing afresh, but Li Tun resolutely took Li Quang's hand and they made their way across three other bodies to Feng Xin's headless corpse. She saw his head nearby which she picked up by his queue with trembling hands. Now her tears streamed down, copious but silent. Feng Xin's sightless, half open eyes stared at her from his once attractive face, caked with blood and the yellow soil of their region. Li Quang passed his hands over to close them. Together they wrapped Feng Xin's head and body in several gunny sacks which they bound tightly with rope. Around them, the relatives of the young executed men performed the same duty. Then they carried the shrouded bodies down to a shed used for animal feed storage and left them for the interim.

Armed with shovels, Li Quang and the other men crossed to the cemetery half a mile south of the village. Here they worked through the night, breaking up the hard, frozen yellow earth to make a grave deep enough for nine men. It was too difficult to dig proper graves for each; they would be dug up in three years' time, their bones washed before re-burial. Then they would have proper graves as befitting men of courage and honour. Then their grave stones would announce the fine patriotism for which they died.

*

As the sun rose, the villagers tied pieces of tiles painted with the names of the departed on each dead man before laying them, one on top of the other, on the communal cart, and trundled it down to the temple. All gathered here, men, women and children, old and young, to say prayers for the deceased. Robust weeping ensued. They lit joss sticks and chanted over the bodies, kowtowing incessantly. Then the stronger men dragged the tumbrel across to the cemetery, followed by the mourners, all wailing loudly to the heavens, with their clutches of smoking joss sticks and bags of funerary paper money.

As he watched his father being buried, little Feng Hua stood motionless, dry-eyed and grim-faced. He knew enough of bad foreigners robbing their country, and yesterday had seen a posse of them. Fat as pigs, sweating even in the cold winter's day, rich in their blue-grey uniforms and with fine horses. He knew enough to know that from now on he would not see his father ever again, never hear his vibrant voice, see his alert eyes, or watch his muscular body practising his *wushu*, self-defence skills, in their small family field. He knew enough to know that one day he would take great pleasure in killing foreigners such as those.

Chapter 7

Shanghai: Alex in Shanghai

In late January 1898, Hongyun, Eddie and Emily stood on the wharf watching the black steam ship being guided into berth by the pilot boat. The docks were busier and noisier than the time when Eddie and Emily arrived. The three young people felt swamped by the relentless activities around them. It had been a very hot, humid summer beset by countless torrential outbursts of the monsoon season. Shanghai had been flooded again and again. The sewers, unable to cope with the torrential rains, had turned the streets into odorous brown rivers, washing away the detritus of daily street life. Today, however, the winter air was calmer, the streets cleaner, and the gentle sun warmed them.

There were many foreigners in the waiting crowd, standing in groups in various forms of clothing from their different countries, ready to greet friends and relatives. Shanghai had its separate foreign enclaves and feminine clothing styles differentiated them from each other. Emily took note of the European women in long gowns fanning themselves, their faces turning a deep pink under their hats. Here and there, stood groups of Japanese men, quiet and composed, in grey western suits and bowler hats, their entire concentration on the looming black ship with many Japanese on board.

The young trio were studying French and German in their mission school. Emily was especially good at French and Hongyun had won prizes for his German. Eddie ambled along steadily in both. Now the boys stood, shoulder to shoulder, as they picked up snatches of conversation around them. Hongyun had his hands in the trouser pockets of his school uniform. Eddie slouched slightly, not knowing what to do with his own hands and ending up putting them behind his back.

Emily stood upright under a waxed blue parasol painted with pink plum flowers. The imminent arrival of her father and brother drew her thoughts back to the cool waters of Aramoana beach. The memories of this beautiful stretch of Dunedin, of water lapping around her ankles, calmed her. Since she and Eddie arrived in Shanghai, she had trained herself to regress into memories of home as the way to cope with separation from their family and to remove herself from the unpleasant present.

The thud of the docking ship snapped her out of her reverie. She looked at her brothers gazing intently up at the passengers at the railings. Hongyun, with his large sloe eyes and wide lips, his long queue incongruous with his Western clothes, cut a dashing figure. Eddie, with his short-cropped wavy hair and rounder eyes, was darkly attractive.

At fifteen, Emily was taller than most of the Chinese girls around her. Her bodice, under a pert bosom, was slim and her large eyes complimented her mobile mouth. The Maori nose had not passed to her. And crowning it all was her thick wavy hair, which, when coiled up into a topknot, as it was this morning, gave her appearance one of startling maturity.

*

Hongyun seemed to have warmed to them in the last two years.

"He's maturing, I guess," she had confided to Aunt Meng when discussing her brothers a week prior.

"I believe his change of attitude owes more to his impending trip to college in America," Aunt Meng had replied, surprisingly cynical.

Now Emily squealed, her composure gone as she pointed upwards to the bank of passengers looking down. "There! There they are, can you see?"

The boys followed her pointing finger and, sure enough, on the lower deck, was their father waving at them with a red handkerchief, then pointing them out to the young boy beside him, who started jumping up and down. The boy called out, waving, frantic. "Eddie! Emily! It's me, Alex!" over and over till his father quieted him with a joyful hug.

The brothers turned to see Emily wiping away tears. Eddie fought to keep his own at bay.

Hongyun smiled at the sight of his father. Now he would be able to complete his plans to go to America; he intended to extract from the old man all the money he would need to live there in the style he envisaged for himself. He glanced at his siblings. Their eyes were riveted on Zhou Yu and Alex descending the gangplank from the second class deck of the ship in their New Zealand clothes, clutching their cardboard suitcases. They did not see his smirk.

*

Aunt Meng had acquired an old armchair since the last time Zhou Yu visited. In it she sat, fragile and shrunken at eighty-five, wrapped in a thin blue and white cotton patchwork quilt. The printed roses in the cambric of the high-winged chair, the only piece of brightness in the corner of the sombre room, framed her in a background of cheer. Everything else was as it had always been – the bed and armoire in their old places, the erhu on its hook on the wall – and a film of grey in the air covering the entire room.

"How wonderful to see you again, nephew, and Alex! Come closer to your old great-aunt, Alex, my eyes are not so good now," Aunt Meng cackled softly.

Alex, shy in this strange environment, approached slowly. She took hold of his hand and peered at him through her steel-framed spectacles. "You speak Chinese, of course? Your father tells me you read and write it very well." She shook his hand, chuckled. Then she turned to the older children crowding behind the newcomers.

"Emily, please send for tea and ask Lao Tai to allow us more of her sweet dumplings. The travellers must be hungry. Oh, and more cups," she added to Emily's retreating back.

The New Zealand brothers sat on the bed as Zhou Yu took the chair by the desk. Hongyun lounged by the door, his hands in his trouser pockets, his eyes on the new arrivals. Alex was already up to his father's chin. Hongyun studied this most foreign-looking sibling with impassive eyes. The boy's shoulder-length hair was a riot of curls, his round eyes had not the slightest slope in them and the flattish nose above full lips, in a much darker complexion than the other two, made him distinctly unusual. *Just as well he's not staying*, thought

47

Hongyun, *he would not be in a happy place. Still, he has a placid look about him, not like bloody Eddie.* He continued gazing at Alex till Emily opened the door followed by Lao Tai with dumplings and tea.

After serving everyone, Emily sat between her brothers on the bed, but could not keep her eyes off Alex. She stroked and kissed him incessantly till at last he grew bashful and inched away from her.

"At last you're here, Alex. I've missed you so, and Mama. How is she?" She aimed the question more at her father than Alex. Zhou Yu shifted his gaze from one to the other. He exchanged a long look with Aunt Meng before he turned back to them.

"Not as well as we would hope, Emily," he said, looking at Alex, with a pleading expression.

Alex took him up. "Mama has been sick for years now, Emily. Got worse after you left," he added.

"You said nothing in your letters," Emily said, looking at her father. "How sick is she and what with?"

Aunt Meng's wrinkled old hands, transparent in their skin, quivered as she studied her teacup.

Hongyun could not prevent the derision showing on his face as he watched everyone in the room. *Fine lot they are; now what's up with that native bitch? Let's hear it,* he thought. He took pleasure in his father's discomfort. Zhou Yu seemed to crumple before his eyes. *That should teach you. Whatever it is that's wrong with your whore, whatever it is, I hope it really hurts. You bastard.*

Zhou Yu's despair showed on his wan face. His eyes passed between the three New Zealand children as he wondered how to impart the bad news to the two older ones.

"We had to put Mama into a hospital before we sailed," he said softly. He looked down at his hands.

Aunt Meng sat silent, her eyes closed.

"Why?" Emily now demanded.

"She might harm herself while we are away, Emily. It is for her own safety."

"In what way? From what, Pa? What is she sick with?"

Zhou Yu sighed. He took time to find his voice. "You remember how she used to lock herself in the bedroom talking to her mother's head?" Emily nodded. "Well, that preoccupation grew steadily worse, much worse after you left. She also took to wandering around town, along the beach. One time we found her on the Peninsula, on Te Rauone Beach, suffering from hunger and hyperthermia. If the people from Kai Tahu village hadn't found her, she would have died."

"Tell them about the fire, Pa," Alex prompted.

"Then last winter, whilst alone in the house, she set fire to the kitchen," Zhou Yu obliged. "Luckily the neighbours were able to break in and extinguish it before too much damage was done. She burnt herself quite badly."

"She was in hospital for a whole month," finished Alex.

"And that's why we had to put her in hospital for the time we're away," Zhou Yu finished, taking Emily's hand. He squeezed it tenderly. "I'm so sorry, Emily, Eddie. It was all I could do to keep her from harming herself."

"It's not a normal hospital, is it?" Emily asked.

Zhou Yu took a long time to answer. "No, Emily, it isn't."

"It's a hospital for mad people, isn't it, Pa?" Eddie now found his voice, stifling a sob.

"Yes, son, it is," Zhou Yu replied. His face reddened with the shame of it: the commitment of their mother, his common-law wife, to the madhouse was more than he could tolerate. He hung his head. He could not tell them what Alex didn't know, how he had found Horowhai on one of the whaling ships at port late one night after one of his Chinese friends had seen her boarding it with a drunken sailor and had run to inform Zhou Yu.

The news stupefied everyone into a heavy silence. Emily wept softly.

Watching their grief, Hongyun gloated with satisfaction. *At last, we are avenged, Ma and I. I wonder if madness is hereditary. Wouldn't it be wonderful if these bastard children all just went raving mad?*

*

As the ox cart carrying Zhou Yu and the four children ambled towards the farm, he saw Yung standing by the front door waiting. He had intended them all to spend the Spring Festival holidays together in his childhood home during which time he wanted to try a reconciliation with Yung. In all his years away, he had been torn by the longing for the home where his ancestors were buried, and his other one in New Zealand where his children were born, but where there were no spirits of ancestors to warm him. Where there were no voices to succour him in his moments of insecurity and loneliness. Where, despite a growing business with its accompanying material comfort, there was an emptiness lying beside a woman who had no understanding of his past and who was careless of his present. When he committed Horowhai into Seacliff Mental Asylum, he had made up his mind to return to China once Eddie was old enough to run his importing company in Dunedin.

But now, as he looked at the looming figure of Yung, her expression and body language stifled any hope he had harboured in his heart.

The cart dropped them off at the stone wall. Ignoring his father and the other children, Hongyun strode briskly towards his mother, his luggage firmly in hand.

"*Ni hao*, Mama, are you well?" He dropped his case to kowtow to her. "The whole catastrophe is now brought home to you," he added with a backward indication of his head.

"Humph! We shall see about that," Yung replied as she looked over his shoulder. "Go refresh yourself and tell Lao Ma to boil up more water for tea."

Zhou Yu and the New Zealand siblings were approaching, uncertainty on the faces of the children, a grim settlement on Zhou Yu's.

"Would you bother?" Hongyun asked.

"I have my reasons," replied his mother as she kept her gaze on the advancing visitors, her expression unchanged. Hongyun disappeared into the house.

Zhou Yu put down his suitcase and bowed. "Wife, how are you?"

She said nothing.

After a moment's hesitation, he turned and ushered Alex forward. "My youngest son, Alex." Then in English, he said, "This is Mother Yung, Alex. Kowtow to her now, good boy."

Yung watched, unimpressed, stony faced, as Alex obeyed, fisting his hands together, right over left, as he bowed.

"He's even wilder looking than the other two," she said to Zhou Yu in her deliberately broad Suzhou accent.

"He takes more after his mother, it is true. But he's not wild, Yung. He's a very gentle boy."

Emily and Eddie were inured to Yung's hostility from all their holidays spent at the farm. Now Emily moved towards Alex, defensive. Her kowtow to Yung was curt. Eddie bowed likewise. When he straightened up, he could not help but look towards the wood shed.

Yung smirked when she saw his anxious search for Uncle Feng. Eddie could be her weapon against his father.

Chapter 8

Shifting Winds, Drifting Sands

After Uncle Feng had befriended the New Zealand children outside the wood shed on their first Spring Festival, he had persuaded Yung to let them eat at the family table, and not with Lao Ma in the kitchen.

Eddie and Emily had grown up to understand Uncle Feng's relationship to Yung. He had been the softening influence in Yung's attitude towards them and he had made subsequent trips to the farm bearable. Her vindictive attitude had changed to one of ignoring them. As long as they did not intrude into her space, she could pretend they did not exist. She conducted every meal in silence, never including them in her conversation and treating remarks from Uncle Feng to them with disdain. They had traded left-overs and the discomfort of eating in the kitchen with a sympathetic servant for better food in an atmosphere of icy hatred.

This evening, Uncle Feng did not appear as he always did at the dinner table. In his place their father now sat.

Hongyun was next to his mother. The three New Zealand children clustered together at the opposite end of the round table that could seat ten, closer to their father, leaving four seats' spacing between them and Hongyun. There were two dishes more than the usual stir-fried vegetables, tofu and soup. A chicken casserole with ginger and mushrooms and a platter of tomato omelette made the meal look opulent.

How loud this terrible silence is, Emily thought during dinner. It seemed only the sound of their chewing could be heard. Towards the end, Zhou Yu began to ask Yung about the farm. To the children their conversation seemed forced; short, polite sentences in between awkward silences. But Hongyun's participation surprised Emily. His unusual friendly interjection into his parents' stilted exchanges reminded Emily of Aunt Meng's cryptic comments. *He is cultivating Pa's interest,* she thought. *He must want something. Yes, he wants Pa to help him go to America. But Pa's paying for it anyway. So what does he really want?*

*

On the second day, Eddie took Alex around the lower part of the fields. The farm hands were all at home in the cluster of low brick workers' cottages, resting on the only real holiday in the year for them. The fields lay in shallow water, fresh and green with winter rice. The farm buffalo were curled up asleep under a willow tree, oblivious of the boys as they passed.

"What do you think of this place, Alex?" Eddie asked, still marvelling at the size of his younger brother.

"It's fine, Eddie. What about you, do you like it?"

"It was hell at first, but later I got to like it more," replied Eddie. *Away from those racist bastards at school.*

"Papa warned me about Mother Yung; said she might be strict. But why must we call her Mother?"

"Because she is his wife." Eddie's answer was terse as he strode on.

"Isn't he married to Mama?" asked the ten-year-old.

"No, Alex," Eddie replied, angry at having his thoughts interrupted. "We are what Hongyun kindly calls bastards."

Alex burst into tears. "That's not fair! Pa is so good to Mama. Why didn't he marry her?"

"That's because he can't, Alex. Not under New Zealand law. Here in China it would not have mattered. They take several wives here. But in New Zealand, men are only allowed one wife. And Pa was already married and Hongyun born before he went to New Zealand."

They reached the cottages. Several occupants, attracted by the approaching foreign voices, were already peering outside their doors, the lintels of which were pasted with red paper brushed with good luck characters.

"Ahh, *Xin Nian Kwai Le,*" a worker greeted them, recognising Eddie.

"Happy New Year to you too, Lao Fong," replied Eddie in dialect. "No, thanks, we won't come in," he added to Lao Fong's gesture of welcome. "Have you seen Uncle Feng?"

Lao Fong's grin widened. "Wah, well, he has to surrender his place to the proper master, hasn't he? And who is this strange *gweilo*?" Lao Fong indicated Alex.

"My brother, he's here for a short visit with my Pa. He's only ten," replied Eddie.

"Only ten? Wah, he's a big one. Only ten. But he doesn't look that much like you, Eddie-ah."

"That's because he looks like our mother," Eddie replied, a bit more reticent.

"Ah, the native woman. We heard. Are all natives in *Xin Xi Lan* like him?"

"More or less. Tell me, Lao Fong, where has Uncle Feng gone? Who has he got to spend Spring Festival with?"

At this Lao Fong grinned even wider. He pointed to a smaller shed two doors down and went back into his cottage with a wave. His neighbours, satisfied with this latest addition for their gossip, shut their doors.

Alex, who managed to understand some of the conversation, asked, "What did he mean about surrendering to the proper master?"

Eddie ignored him and walked on towards the shed. At the door he knocked.

"*Lai,*" said a familiar voice inside.

"Uncle Feng, it's me." Eddie opened the door and went inside. Alex followed.

Uncle Feng was sitting on the *kang*, the boxed bed heated by a coal fire underneath. The room was warm, smelling of coal. Coal dust hung suspended in the air. His bedding was rolled up against the wall at his back. Sheaves of rice paper and a brush and inkwell lay in front of him. On seeing the boys, he hastily put these aside and moved to make space for them.

"*Xin Nian Kwai Le*, Eddie-ah. Happy New Year. How is your father? Ah, and this is your *Didi*, eh?"

"Yes, this is Alex." Eddie gestured to Alex, who was eyeing Uncle Feng with curiosity.

Eddie looked around the shed. Apart from the *kang*, the tiny space was bare. He felt a deep wave of pity sweep over him. "Don't you have any family to spend New Year with?"

Uncle Feng shook his head with a sad smile. "My widowed mother died years ago. Two of my three children died of typhoid and the surviving girl is married to a farmer in Tsingdao. Too far for me to visit. But hey, young man, you are not to worry about me. I eat with the Fongs, so I am fine. Don't fret yourself. And anyway, your *tieh* will be returning to New Zealand soon, yes?"

After some more polite talk, Eddie took his leave, Alex following with a bow. This made Uncle Feng laugh, "Your *Didi* has very good manners," he called out.

As they retraced their steps, Alex asked, "Who is that man? You two seemed to like each other a lot."

"Uncle Feng is Mother Yung's pretend husband," Eddie replied, stern. "Like Mama is Pa's pretend wife. He's there because Pa's here to visit."

Alex was stunned into silence. The intricacies of the big people's relationships were proving too much for him to understand. As they approached the house, he found his voice. "If Uncle Feng has only that place to live now, where will he go when Pa returns?"

Eddie stopped. He turned slowly to face his brother. "What do you mean, 'when Pa returns'? You mean, return for good?"

"Didn't he tell you?" Alex bit his lip.

"No, nor Emily, I'm sure. When?"

"When you go back to Dunedin. He will leave the business to you and come back here."

"But I may not go back. I hate it there. Mind you, China's not that wonderful either. But I haven't made up my mind to return to New Zealand."

Alex hung his head. "He wants you to, Eddie. He wants to leave you with a livelihood. It is a good one, he says. You will make a lot of money."

Eddie stared at the farmhouse, hating that Yung filled that space and had done for so many years, since Pa was his age. Then his thoughts flitted to Dunedin, to the native school, to his mother becoming more deranged as he was growing up. And the memories of being bullied at that school by his mother's type of people, not accepting him, laughing at him. The tension at home. The beatings from his mother when she was in one of her moods. That head in the shoe-box. And, above all, the withering, scornful indifference from the Europeans. His features turned dark. He became aware of Alex sobbing.

"Please don't tell anyone I told you," Alex whimpered.

"Don't worry, I won't. But it's good that I know." Eddie put an arm round his young brother's shoulder and walked him back to the house.

Emily came out to meet them. One look at both boys filled her heart with foreboding. She took their hands and led them inside to their communal bedroom to wait till lunch time.

*

On the third morning, Zhou Yu came to their bedroom. He had not slept well the previous night. His drawn face and slouched body told the children all they needed to know, that together with what they had heard during the night through the walls of their bedroom. What had kept them awake.

Yung's strident voice: "How dare you infer I have a lover? How dare you? What right have you to judge?"

Zhou Yu's moderate one: "I am merely asking, Yung. I can see that wood shed is well used. He must be here, someone of the house."

"I rent that wood shed out," she shouted.

"Then why isn't that rent in the ledgers?"

Silence.

"Well?"

"I take cash, to avoid paying more farm tax," Yung's voice came through the walls, hesitant now.

"I don't believe that, wife. The last time I was here, there was an extra dental cloth at the wash basin that went unused all the time I stayed. Not yours, not Hongyun's."

"It was a spare!" She was shrill now. "I used it to clean my gold jewellery."

"I don't believe that, Yung. It was too clean to have been used for such. Besides, I could tell the farm workers and Lao Ma were embarrassed. I sensed their shame when I was around. Lao Ma's behaviour towards me is still strained."

An object hit the wall. It smashed on the floor tiles with a loud splintering noise. Emily clutched Alex. All three children were awake. All three waiting, barely breathing, eyes wide open. Yung's sobbing became uncontrollable. More screaming.

"Yung, I demand to meet this man. Where is he?"

"No! You are not fit to wipe his shoes, not fit to take his place here."

"HERE?" Zhou Yu shouted, something none of the children had ever heard him do. Not even when Mama was in her worst moods. "Whose house is this? Who kept you all these years? Whose revered father took you in when your family were killed, gave you a home, GAVE YOU HIS LAST SURVIVING SON TO MARRY! Tell me, you... you... WHORE!"

Sounds of smashing furniture, splintering china.

"He is not a killer! Not a rapist! Not like you!"

A loud smack resounded. A shrill yelp of pain pierced the wall.

Alex had started whimpering; had clung to Emily, his face buried in her shoulders. Eddie was on his back, his head under folded arms, mouth tight, listening intently. And for hours into the night, the sound of Yung's weeping prevented them from sleeping.

*

Now Zhou Yu made to sit beside his New Zealand children. They moved to make room for him on their wide platform bed. It was the bed Zhou Yu and his two elder brothers had shared growing up all those years ago, before they were swallowed up by the Taiping Rebellion. The rebellion that had taken them over most of south China – that had destroyed over twenty million people, and had finally killed them. Leaving him.

"Did you manage to sleep?" he asked softly, not looking up at them.

"We heard you fighting," Alex replied, his eyes reddening, tearing up.

"I'm sorry. What did you hear besides?"

"She called you a killer, a rapist. Say it's not true, Pa!" Emily begged, her hand clutching Alex's.

57

Zhou Yu sat a long while, bent over his knees. From time to time, he shook his head. Snuffled. The children then realised he was quietly weeping. Emily, seated closest to him, started rubbing his back as she sobbed. No one spoke.

Then Zhou Yu straightened up. He took a handkerchief from his jacket pocket, wiped his eyes and blew his nose. "Let's all of us take a walk, shall we? Put on your coats."

*

Zhou Yu walked them beyond their own farmland, over the stream that meandered its way past other holdings in the district, each with winter rice growing in neatly divided shallows of water where young carp swam, to be fished out later as supplementary food. They followed its route into the small town where his father Fengyi had married his mother Wu Lan in its best restaurant. The restaurant had been very dilapidated during the Taiping Rebellion. It had closed and reopened several times, depending on the course of the war, but now, after years of settled peace, had finally regained its prosperity.

The town itself seemed better off than before too. Zhou Yu and Eddie strode silently on in front. Emily held Alex's hand as his curious eyes followed the activities around them. Of the people, most were peasants and small traders in the streets, dressed in shabby padded jackets and trousers of blue, grey or black. Most had not had a bath since the summer. They looked as dusty as the muddy streets and the unpainted two-storey shop-houses that lined them. But here and there, splashes of bright new colours adorned the children of the better-off as their parents treated them to candied fruit on sticks and other titbits. Stalls hawked trinkets, bamboo flutes, cymbals and bells, small articles of silk clothing, herbal teas and all types of hot snacks popular in the nippy weather. Alex strained to understand the fast, broad dialect of the countryside as he trudged beside his sister.

Now his father addressed them. "Are you as hungry as I am? Let's go into that restaurant and have a proper breakfast, eh?"

And he led them through the line of stalls to a fine-looking tea house with painted red doors. The ubiquitous good luck characters, black on red paper, were pasted on its doorframe.

*

The place was warm and crowded with noisy patrons enjoying the breakfast of the region – steamed pork buns, rice congee with chunks of black preserved duck eggs, steamed dumplings of various sorts called dim sims – little hearts – for which southern China was famous. Waiters shouted across to each other. One led them to a table at the back, its deep red lacquered screen giving the semblance of privacy from the rest of the restaurant. Another waiter immediately fetched up with steaming hot rolled towels that he dispensed with a long pair of chopsticks, and a third poured fragrant green tea into the cups already set. And before they were quite settled, hot bamboo baskets with small dishes of various morsels started appearing. Following their father's example, the young people used their chopsticks to pick up the choice titbits which they dipped into saucers of soy and chilli sauces. They ate in silence.

On his third morsel, Zhou Yu started recounting his long-hidden past. It was painful, soft and slow in the telling – an agony he forced himself to relive. A punishment to go through that these innocent young people should now understand. They stopped eating, open-mouthed, as they listened. He motioned for them to continue.

"It's a long story, and you must eat, otherwise they will throw us out. See all the people waiting at the entrance? So eat as I talk."

And so they had, slowly, their jaws scarcely moving, as they hung onto every word. Emily, Alex and finally Eddie succumbed to silent tears as they chewed their way through their father's secret past. Zhou Yu was conscious of the attention they were drawing from the neighbouring tables but was beyond caring. Anyway, their neighbours were more curious about the English he used. They did not understand the content. Now was the time his children knew the truth. And he did not spare himself.

Chapter 9

Aunt Meng

"I suppose you already know Hongyun has set his mind on *Lao Jin Shan*, California. He wants to go to the university in San Francisco," Aunt Meng whispered to Zhou Yu three days after his return from his farm.

Aunt Meng had caught a bad cold during the Spring Festival, which had quickly developed into pneumonia, and she was confined to bed, her shawl round her shoulders. The room smelt of medicine. Lao Tai, from the kitchen, had kept her fed with rice congee cooked with slivers of fish or eggs and pumped her full of medicinal teas. Her frailty had shocked Zhou Yu and the children upon their return to school. Zhou Yu's heart shrivelled upon seeing her. She was his recourse, the only surviving relative of his father's generation. She had been his succour in all the years he had been away, had nurtured and kept his hopes alive in his darkest moments. Had retained faith in him. And was the only one in China who knew of his New Zealand family, but now she was on the way out.

Today, Eddie and Emily had gone to class. Hongyun was extending his stay on the farm as his studies were over, but would return to Shanghai in a fortnight to take up temporary employment at Swire's till it was time for him to leave. It was an internship offered by that powerful English company to graduate Chinese students from the mission school as a way of recruitment.

Now only Alex remained with Zhou Yu. The young boy sat in the armchair and watched his father and great-aunt confer in barely audible voices. Zhou Yu was sitting on the bentwood chair, drawn up close to the bed, inclined over his aunt.

"How did it go with Yung?" Aunt Meng asked.

"Badly, as you might know, aunt. She had replaced me soon after she knew I had a family in New Zealand."

"The cabinet maker," she nodded, her lungs whirring deep inside her.

"You knew! Why didn't you tell me?" He straightened himself away from her, and let her hand drop.

"Nephew, I guessed... from little bits Hongyun let drop each time he returned from the farm. Awful as it is for you, can you blame her? She loved you so desperately. She was so loyal all those years, so lonely yet so brave, bringing Hongyun up on her own."

"Then why?"

"Revenge? Who knows? She needed someone. He is a decent and kind man, I hear. I suppose they helped each other along." She stopped to blow her nose. "What have you decided? Did you meet him?"

From way down the corridor a pot fell with a clang. Distant expletives followed, breaking into their line of thought.

Zhou Yu looked down at his hands, glanced quickly at Alex's impassive face. *Poor Alex, he has not spoken much since that breakfast in the tea house.* Since then, it was as if he had become a stranger to his own children. All three had lost their conviviality and trod gingerly when around him.

"I... I made Eddie take me down to the workers' cottages. He was staying there during my visit. Apparently he has no family living nearby. You know, aunt, even Eddie likes him. He's been good to Eddie, and Emily. He's made their holidays on the farm tolerable."

"And you... do you like him?" she coughed.

Zhou Yu pondered awhile. Slowly he raised his head and looked her in the eye. "Were he not in my bed, I would," he confessed. "As it was, after my fierce insistence on meeting him, I actually found nothing to say... I mean, what could I say?"

"So what is your decision?" Her eyes half-closed, the effort of speaking was exhausting her. She knew of his plan to return to China in the near future.

He shook his head. "I don't know. Eddie may not want to return to Dunedin. I just can't sell up. The family needs the business still."

"Eddie has very little to stay in China for either, nephew. He has been bullied here too by the Chinese boys and the European children treat him with curiosity and not a little scorn. Perhaps, with some effort on your part, he may be persuaded to return."

"Then what? How will I resolve the situation with Yung and this man? Must I drive him out? She prefers him to me, you know. If he goes, I am sure she will follow. And from what I know, he has been around since Hongyun was a baby but only moved in when the boy was ten years old."

"When they learnt of your New Zealand family."

Zhou Yu glanced again at Alex. The boy seemed to have incredible powers of concentration for one so young. Zhou Yu had expected him to doze off, yet here he was, wide-eyed, taking in every word. He smiled fondly at his youngest. Alex returned it with a twitch of his sensitive lips.

*

Hongyun returned to Shanghai with a confident stride. He had enjoyed his mother's indulgence for two extra weeks. Uncle Feng had been invited back to the house as soon as Zhou Yu and the other children had departed. Life, as he liked it, had returned to normal on the farm. He was due to sail for California as soon as his papers were ready, which would be around September. The mission school had given him half a scholarship and he and Yung had decided on the University of California in San Francisco. It was on the other side of the *Tai Yang,* the Pacific Ocean – closer to home than anywhere else on the American continent, and his American sponsors were there.

Now he came to Aunt Meng's room where his father was already seated. Eddie and Emily had taken Alex out for a bit of shopping in Nanjing Tong Lu. Emily had insisted they buy something for Mama, for when she got out of hospital on their return to Dunedin. Aunt Meng, feeling slightly better, lay propped up on her pillows in bed, her knitted shawl enshrouding her frail torso.

Zhou Yu sat in the armchair sipping tea and Hongyun sat well back on the bentwood chair beside Aunt Meng, his legs crossed, his manner relaxed.

He's comporting himself like a Westerner even before he gets there, Zhou Yu thought as he observed his first born. But he was, nevertheless, impressed by Hongyun's charm. Ever since he arrived, the young man had gone out of his way to be attentive. This new attitude both pleased and unsettled Zhou Yu. It was out of character. Despite putting it down to the boy's maturation, he felt the easy smiles and attentive glances to be a little too quick. He now listened to Hongyun talk of his plans for the beautiful country – *Mei Guo.*

"You wouldn't have me travel steerage, would you, Pa? That's down below, right above the boiler room with all the peasants? Please, say you'll pay the extra. Let me travel second class at least."

"Of course," Zhou Yu replied. "What about living expenses?"

Now Hongyun got really enthusiastic. "Well," he smiled, leaning forward in his chair. From his jacket pocket he took out a small notebook. He opened it to the required page and showed it fleetingly to Aunt Meng. Before the old woman had time to register it, blinking at the swift motion, it was gone. She sighed and slumped back on her pillows.

Zhou Yu studied the well-formed writing in English. He noted the subsidised cost of the lodgings in the home of a Mr and Mrs Sarginson in Berkeley, the half of college fees to be paid, the estimated cost of books, bus fares, meals at the university cafeteria and several other minor expenses, including pocket money. It was calculated to the last dollar to a total of thirty-five American dollars a month. He sighed. It would take a lot of tile sales in Dunedin to have this much more to spare. He sat back in the armchair, tapping the notebook on his chin as he went over the sums.

There was still Eddie and Emily's school fees at the mission school. And Eddie's further education to think of if he refused to take over the business. If he did, a course in accountancy and book-keeping would suffice. Emily had yet to choose her preferred occupation before, hopefully, a good marriage. Then there was Alex, but that was some years to go yet. Yes, it would be tight, but do-able. Involuntarily, he nodded.

"Oh, thank you, *Tieh*. I knew you would agree," Hongyun almost shouted. *Yes! Now I can live the way I want to in California!*

California had been his utopia since he heard some American boys in the school talk about it. The rest of what he had heard didn't matter – the bit about the hard, dangerous and underpaid labour of the coolies who went over, nor the racism, official or otherwise, towards them. All that didn't affect him. He was a student on half a scholarship from the biggest mission school in China, and a gentleman. His mother had promised to send him five American dollars each month, a princely sum for her, but that was none of his *tieh's* business. For the last six years, since Eddie and Emily arrived, Hongyun had decided that his relationship with his father would strictly be on an inform-only-when-necessary basis. And with that, he had also decided there was very little that Zhou Yu needed to know.

Now Zhou Yu broke into his daydreams. "And what have you decided to study?"

"Well, medicine is my first choice, but failing that, engineering. It depends on how they grade me when I go over."

"That's excellent, son, I hope you can make it to one or the other. China is in need of modern doctors and engineers. Well done. Try your best, for your mother's and my sake."

Hongyun smiled at his father, but his eyes were cold, unblinking.

As he looked into his son's clear, sloe eyes, Zhou Yu was overcome with a strange sense of presentiment that chilled him to the bone.

*

Three days afterwards, Aunt Meng took an inexplicable turn for the worst and passed away in her sleep. A moving service was held for her in the school chapel, with mourners spilling into the grounds. All the staff, both American and Chinese, and many pupils, past and present, turned up to honour her. She was buried in the Chinese part of the Christian cemetery in Lujiawan outside Shanghai, beyond the foreign enclave, on Chinese land.

Eddie and Emily were inconsolable. She had been their safe harbour against the harsh reality of life in a country where they belonged to neither side – where they were regularly discriminated against by both.

Eddie's moods darkened, and his attitude towards his father manifested itself in outbursts of anger.

"For goodness sake, Pa, leave me alone!" He had shaken his father off one evening when Zhou Yu put a consoling hand on his shoulders. "Just go back to Dunedin and get Mama out of that hell-forsaken asylum, will you?"

And neither would he admit his sister into his pool of misery. He beat away her outstretched hand, ignored her grief, and returned her nothing for loving him. Only Alex was unaffected. He stood around, helpless, as he watched his family's anguish over this old woman whom he knew so little of. But he felt left out, forgotten, and longed to return to Dunedin and to his godfather, Alex Don, his namesake and mentor.

*

Two weeks after the funeral, Zhou Yu and Alex were at the wharf ready to board the *SS Tsing Kwai*, one of Swire's ships, bound for Melbourne. Zhou Yu intended to spend a few days there with his old friends, Chan and Ling, and catch up with all their news. Their Melbourne business had now expanded to Sydney, and his shares in the company he had helped start before the fracas that ejected him to New Zealand so many years ago, had grown.

Hongyun accompanied Eddie and Emily to see them off at the wharf. He needed to cement his father's trust and money for the New World. An afternoon away from his internship at Swire's was little sacrifice.

Emily hugged Alex tight. "Please give Mama all my love, Alex darling. Please, tell her I shall be home as soon as school is over."

"Promise?" Alex demanded.

"Promise," she said, wiping her red eyes. Then she looked up at her father.

Zhou Yu stared at her. *So, I shall have her with me. My refuge, my strength where Horowhai should be. Oh, sweet daughter, thank you, thank you.*

Eddie stood stone-faced and silent. As Zhou Yu and Alex picked up their luggage to ascend the gangway, he suddenly clasped the boy tight.

"Goodbye, young fella, you'll be good, won't you?" he sobbed. "Goodbye, Pa, take Mama out of that hospital, promise me."

Zhou Yu nodded, his tears welling up even as his face set into rigid lines.

Hongyun smiled as he shook his father's hand. "Goodbye, Father, a safe journey and please write often. I shall keep you informed of proceedings."

He ignored Alex. Who stared at him, his young eyes all seeing. Who said nothing, but started climbing the gangway ahead of his father.

*

As Zhou Yu gazed at the receding figures, he knew it would be many years before he would see China again, if ever. The newspapers had been virulent with news of the rampaging Boxers, the Yinhetuan Movement, whose tentacles of influence were spreading day by day. They had now begun killing missionaries in the countryside in ways so cruel that the entire foreign population was demanding blood and retribution from the Emperor. Two years ago, a German was murdered in Tsingdao, a stronghold of the Boxer Rebellion, and the Kaiser had ordered extreme reprisals. The newspapers had reported the execution of nine Boxers in Tsingdao, Shandong Province, in January.

Apart from the Boxers, Shanghai was abuzz with the problems of the much disliked Empress Dowager Cixi – how she vacillated between support of the Boxers and the foreign powers, which were bending her to their will. Her co-ruler and nephew, the Emperor Guangxu, had no heirs. Now the strength of the anti-monarchists was growing.

Zhou Yu remembered the old axiom: "China will be destroyed by a woman." *This woman?*

The much hated opium was spreading through the country like the plague, and she was helpless in the wake of its progress. *China is on its knees; sick, a beggar nation. It's good that*

Hongyun will live in America for the next few years, and good that Eddie and Emily will come home. I can't wait.

Chapter 10

1902: San Francisco --
Many Eyes Watching, Many Fingers Pointing

Hongyun strolled through the leafy campus of the university clutching his leather bag in his right hand as his left straightened his tie and collar. He was on the way into town, where, in half an hour, he would be meeting Virginia Lawson for dinner at the Chinese restaurant off Durant Avenue. He didn't mind being early as he enjoyed window shopping in town.

On Durant Avenue, he slowed his stride to inspect the goods and also his new haircut in the shop windows. Two months ago, he had gone to the barber to have his queue cut off and the hair on the centre part of his head styled as well as possible.

Joe, the Negro barber had said, "I cain't do much here, Chinaboy, till th' rest grow out. There ain't nothing there to style right now."

Hongyun had sighed as he stared at them both in the mirror. The patch of strong, black hair stood up like stiff matting. Joe had given it a very close cut.

"Yeah, come back in eight weeks. You should've a decent patch by then, and I cain trim th' rest t' match."

And Hongyun had paid his dime, put his hat on and emerged from the spartan shop in a spartan lane, hiding his new look although no one was watching.

From the newspapers and what his host parents, the Sarginsons, had told him, the Manchurian Qing Dynasty was in its final days, threshing to stay alive. Their control over the Han Chinese and their way of life would soon be over. The queue was the last remnant to be shucked. Hongyun and most privately funded Chinese students in universities on the Western seaboard were chopping off their queues. Unlike the ignorant coolies labouring outback, the students felt no loyalty to this dynasty, still considered foreign after four hundred years. Anyhow, a short haircut would help assimilate them more into American life now and beyond.

He approached Hap Choy's eatery and looked about for Virginia, but she was late as usual. He wondered if it was a habit of American women to keep people waiting. Tardiness was impolite by Chinese standards, but this was America. Fleetingly, he wondered if her lateness was secretly a weapon against his race. But he dismissed the thought. She worked in a dental clinic and had to be there till the last client was finished.

"Good evening, Hongyun," she called now as she crossed the quiet lane. He turned and once more thrilled at the sight of her. Her auburn hair, tugged under a dark green cloche hat, flattered her oval face. She wore a matching woollen coat of a lighter green under which her russet coloured dress peeked. As he waited, she picked up her long skirt to avoid tripping on the pavement. "And how are you?" Her green eyes sparkled as she took his sleeve.

"Fine, thank you, Virginia. And you?" he answered formally, suddenly made shy by her forward ways. A girl in China would never take a man's arm, not even her brother's, but then again, this was America. "Shall we go in before the workers come?" He opened the narrow door.

The pungency of garlic and soy sauce assailed their nostrils in the closed atmosphere. It was just on five-thirty but already four of the eight tables were taken by students, both white and Chinese. The restaurant was as noisy as any in Shanghai, and none too clean. But the prices were very friendly so it was well patronised by Chinese students and workers alike, and some white friends on a budget. There was usually a line waiting outside. Hongyun and Virginia always managed to get a table immediately because he was able to get off class a period early on Wednesdays and Virginia's dental clinic was just round the corner.

Now they were seated with a stained white tablecloth between them. A small bottle of soy sauce and a pair of pepper and salt shakers by the wall propped up the menu. A young waiter, Charlie, still with his queue intact, walked up with a side plate of bread and butter. He knew the regulars and greeted Hongyun and Virginia with a toothy grin, looking like a rabbit with jug ears. The bald part of his head glistened, oily. His apron was none too clean.

"And what you have?" he demanded in English, staring at Virginia whose red hair fascinated him. He was not sure whether to congratulate Hongyun or commiserate with him for having a woman like her, who looked like her head was always on fire and whose face looked like she had dipped it in rice flour – so white she was.

Virginia gave him her dazzling smile, white teeth glistening, dimples deep in both cheeks.

"My usual corn soup and egg foo yung, please, Charlie," she replied.

"*Nay neh?*" he asked familiarly in Cantonese to Hongyun.

"And I shall have my usual fried noodles with pork and a bowl of hot and sour soup," replied Hongyun crisply in English without looking up. "And make the soup a big one."

"Okay! Quick come soon," said Charlie and walked away to shout his order to the kitchen before returning with a pot of tea and twin white cups.

Even after three years, Hongyun found it difficult to be the first to start a conversation with Virginia. So he began with the usual question, "And how is your mother?"

"As always," Virginia replied, smiling.

*

Virginia's mother was the younger sister of Mrs Sarginson, Hongyun's host mother. The Sarginsons were teachers in Aunt Meng's mission school before they retired when Hongyun was sixteen. They had both taught Hongyun and had encouraged him to apply for a scholarship, promising to board him in the event he was selected.

Virginia and her widowed mother were introduced to Hongyun within a week of his arrival in San Francisco. Virginia had been instructed to show him the campus and take him round the city on her days off from the dental surgery.

"Must I?" she had protested. "You know I need that time to myself. And what about David?"

"And what about David?" Mrs Lawson had replied archly. "You know what your father would have said about David, were he alive."

"It's only till he settles in, Ginny," her aunt had coaxed. "And he will do so quite quickly if you make a good fist of it. Then you can see more of David."

"Now don't you encourage her with that young man," scolded her sister. And Mrs Sarginson had given Virginia a sly look.

Virginia knew the reason behind her mother's opposition to David. It was because he was working-class Irish Catholic and they were staunch, educated, middle-class Methodists. Mrs Lawson lacked the racial tolerance of the Sarginsons whose years in China had imbued in them an acceptance of the "lesser, but most relevant children of God". And Virginia figured if her mother could allow a Chinaboy with pigtails and slope eyes in her close proximity, David's differences might soon not matter. So she had agreed to this onerous duty with dramatic moans of martyrdom.

The first sight of Hongyun had filled Virginia with temerity. He was so timid he would only speak when spoken to. He could not raise his eyes to her face. He seemed as tame as a caged mouse.

Virginia reported back to the Sarginsons after the first expedition into the campus: "He's easy enough to manage actually, like a child."

"Don't underestimate him, Ginny, just wait till he adjusts. He's got sass enough," replied her uncle from behind his newspapers.

*

The second weekend Virginia took Hongyun to town, David O'Malley joined them at the ferry terminal at Oakland Point. The tall Irishman ignored him but took off his derby, and gave Virginia a peck on both cheeks, his curly black hair spilling over her cheeks.

"And what shall we do today, Ginny? With Chinaboy?" His blue eyes looked Hongyun up and down. Hongyun was enraged

71

by the casual scrutiny, felt himself measured and found wanting. He felt a growing hatred for this arrogant foreigner, and felt slighted as Virginia took O'Malley's arm.

"This is Hongyun, David," she said, with a nudge against O'Malley's ribs.

"Howdy," said the Irishman, his eyes twinkling.

"Howdy," replied Hongyun, to which O'Malley had roared with amusement. Virginia giggled.

They had taken the ferry across to San Francisco. Hongyun had pretended not to notice O'Malley's arm around Virginia's waist, nor his frequent nuzzling of her ears. It seemed she had totally forgotten about him. His bad mood grew. He hated the trip into Union Square, ignored the beautiful shops in buildings that would have reminded him of those on the Bund, the coastal street along the Huangpu River on which Shanghai was built. He walked behind them, his hands in his trouser pockets, his derby firmly set over his queue, seething with rage and hating all tall American men with blue eyes and cavalier attitudes.

*

With time, Hongyun settled into the Sarginson household. His grammatically correct, accented school English gradually took on some American aphorisms, but he had not grown at ease in Berkeley as his hosts had hoped.

In Shanghai the foreigners he knew were kindly teachers at the mission school. His dormitory mates were all Chinese boys. The foreign children were separately schooled so his acquaintance with them had been distant. But in America, he regularly found himself racially targeted, especially away from the university and the Sarginsons' immediate environment. Apart from Virginia and the Sarginsons, he counted no Americans amongst his friends.

He made no mention of this to his letters home to Yung and Uncle Feng. But to Zhou Yu, he allowed his unease to slip, knowing his father would understand. However, he soon learnt to use it as a tool to extract more money from Zhou Yu. The only way to overcome racial prejudice in America was to succeed on their terms. And he intended to do so with funding from Zhou Yu; payback for the years of neglect.

*

"And what have you decided to do in graduate school?" Virginia now asked, looking at his close-cropped black hair with approval.

"Well, it depends on how good my grades are, Ginny. I still would like to study medicine, because doctors are highly regarded in China. If not, second is engineering. That too is a respectable profession." He stopped as Charlie approached with the soups.

"See, I tol' you, come quick time," said Charlie as he set down the soup a bit too hastily, causing a little spill of Virginia's.

"Watch it," Hongyun snapped.

"So solly, so solly," responded Charlie with a quick wipe of his soiled napkin.

"Don't worry, no harm done," replied Virginia. "Nothing's spilled on me."

During dinner, Hongyun made up his mind. They usually wandered through the small park towards Virginia's house off Parker Street before proceeding towards her house, three streets further north. Tonight he would suggest they linger awhile. He intended to propose to her. She was twenty-six to his twenty-four, and he knew that even by American standards she should be married by now. That cocky David O'Malley had somehow disappeared from her life six months earlier. Virginia had not explained and he had not asked. She had spent weeks vacillating between tears and anger but finally had emerged a more subdued and considerate person, especially towards him. Now he wanted to maximise the opportunity and hook her up before somebody else came on the scene. An American wife would steer him through all the pitfalls in this new land.

*

Virginia stared at the small diamond ring sparkling in the street-lamp light in its red box, his close proximal anxiety discomforting her.

"Please say yes, Ginny," he whispered.

She shook her head, incredulous. "Oh, Hongyun, I didn't... I never thought you felt this way. I like you very much, Hongyun, but... but not like that."

"Like what, then?" he asked, his hurt breathing though every pore.

"Well…" She looked up at him, unsure of how to tell him, then across to the further side of the park, conscious of curious glances from evening strollers. "Hongyun, I can't marry you."

"Why not?" he demanded, and when she could make no answer, he accused her, "Because I am Chinese? Ginny, I thought that doesn't matter to you."

He sidled to the other end of the wooden bench, rubbed his forehead, tears brimming in humiliation, his breath short and sharp.

"It doesn't matter as long as we are just friends, Hongyun… but I can't marry you," she whispered, closed the box and handed it back to him. "I can't." She stood up.

He stared up at her as he felt his life collapsing. She put a hand out to his shoulder, but he shook her off. After a while, he stood up, straightened his jacket and wiped his eyes.

"Can you excuse me, please? I will not be able to walk you home." And he strode off in the direction they had come, holding himself stiffly erect.

"I'm so sorry," she cried out. Passers-by eyed her, thinking, for a moment, the apology was for them before looking away.

Chapter 11

1902: Dunedin—Redeeming a Soul

Zhou Yu, Emily and Alexander stood staring at the baronial mansion set in its vast, well-tended grounds before them. Around the fringe of the formal garden, behind hedges and tall trees, clustered several minor buildings and adjunct cottages all painted white, clean and tidy, looking like servants' quarters for the main house. Seacliff seemed more like the home of a duke than a mental asylum.

The bitter cold wind blew in from the south, chilling the three visitors through their heavy woollen coats. The collars of the men's dark blue jackets were buttoned up, covering their ears. Their caps were pulled low over their foreheads, though Alex's unruly curls peeped from underneath, fringing his collar. Emily wore a red woollen cloche and matching scarf which covered her up to her chin, contrasting strongly with her long, deep green coat dress. They stood separate from one another, each harnessing his own strength for the ordeal ahead.

"Well, shall we go through then?" Zhou Yu asked softly in Chinese. He looked at Emily, her face tight in apprehension, her nose red over quivering lips. She nodded imperceptibly.

Zhou Yu had wanted her to settle back for a while before visiting Horowhai, but Emily had been impatient to see her mother from the moment she stepped off the steamer from Auckland.

Now Alex took her hand. At fourteen, he stood half a head taller than her and was shoulder to shoulder to his father. His soft eyes focussed intently on his sister as he gave her hand a squeeze. The trio walked purposefully up the long drive.

*

As they approached the mansion, a handsome Maori nurse in his mid-twenties emerged from the main entrance.

"*Kia ora,* good day," he greeted them, his eyes travelling between the three distinctly different-looking people. He knew Zhou Yu and Alex from previous visits, but Emily was new. *Half-Maori and half-Chinese, what a beauty!*

"Good day, Wiremu," Zhou Yu responded. "How she today?"

Wiremu hesitated somewhat. "She had treatment yesterday, so she isn't too bright today. Won't eat." He kept his eyes on Emily.

She returned his gaze, a small frown wrinkling her brows. Still Wiremu stood his ground.

"Oh, my daughter Emily, home from China." Zhou Yu was obliged to introduce them.

A rakish smile spread wide over Wiremu's face. His large eyes crinkled. Satisfied, he nodded several times before venturing, directly to Emily, "P'raps I take you to your mum, eh?"

"Thank you but we know way," Zhou Yu butted in, guiding his daughter away by the elbow.

Alex giggled. He could see the effect his beautiful sister had on Wiremu. "Your second day home and you've got a suitor already," he commented in Chinese, glancing back at Wiremu, still standing there looking after them. They exchanged a wave.

His father and sister strode on purposefully towards the information desk. The nurse on duty gave them the ward and room numbers with a worn-out look.

They walked down the long cold corridor, their footsteps resonating, till they came to a white door marked 121. A European orderly got up from her corner seat and approached them. Zhou Yu had not seen her before.

"Are you visiting Horowhai?" she demanded, her voice strident. They all nodded. She took a key from a bunch on her belt and unlocked the door. "She's not over the treatment from yesterday. Hadn't eaten for some days." She huffed back to her seat.

"Why they give her treatment this time?" Zhou Yu called after her.

"She was violent, wasn't she? She can be a handful, that one. Had to keep her strapped down for days. So the doctors decided to cool her down." And she returned to her knitting.

"Are you ready, Emily?" Zhou Yu asked in Chinese before opening the door.

*

Emily burst into tears at the sight of her mother lying prone on the iron bed, shivering, covered by a blue sheet and blankets up to her chest. Horowhai's head was a mess of tufted hair. Her cheeks clung to bones, showing lips shrivelled against teeth. She looked much older than Emily could ever imagine in her nightmares. Her sunken eyes gazed at them, unseeing.

"Mama," Emily sobbed as she slowly approached the bed, Zhou Yu and Alex close behind her. "Mama," she repeated.

She took Horowhai's wrinkled hand. She gently caressed it as she knelt beside her mother, and tears coursed down her own face.

Horowhai looked at her. Slowly, her eyes widened in recognition. She attempted a smile, ghoulish in her ravaged face. Her hand disengaged slowly from Emily's and up to stroke her daughter's cheek.

"You come home?" she croaked.

Emily nodded. Zhou Yu and Alex had stopped at the end of the bed, their hats clutched against the metal railing of the bed end. Alex was crying quietly.

"What did they do to her? What is this treatment the nurses talked about?" Emily demanded of her father.

"A new way, using ice. They think it calms the brain."

"That's barbaric! It's not helping, is it?" She sat down on the side of the bed.

"She was worse before the treatment, Emily, so it must work, at least for a while," Zhou Yu whispered, still in Chinese. "We can only rely on the doctors' expertise..."

A hysterical cackle from somewhere outside cut him short. Emily shuddered. She looked round the stark, white room, containing few personal belongings. A narrow cupboard stood in one corner, and a table and chair by the only window in the room.

"Is she always kept here?"

"Normally she lives in the women's section in the north part of the building," Alex told her. "She lives there for a few months at a stretch. But she regresses from time to time, and then she comes back here for the treatment."

"Does that mean she'll never get better?" Emily asked. She blew her nose onto a pink cotton handkerchief, bought in Shanghai, hand-embroidered by some poor woman in a side street. Sold for a pittance.

Alex said nothing.

Zhou Yu nodded. "It seems that way, Emily. It's something we have to face. Quite often she doesn't even recognise us... and she can be violent. Today is an exception. The treatment gives her periods of calm."

Horowhai remained silent, her eyes fixed on Emily. Her momentary joy at recognition of her daughter was now replaced by an intensity in her eyes, dark pupils in corneas of yellow. Her hand clutched Emily's with surprising strength.

Nothing could be said, nothing could be done. So they continued this silence for what to Emily was an age.

Finally, Zhou Yu took matters into hand. "It's late. Buses are not that frequent in the evenings." He moved to the other side of Horowhai. "We come again soon, Horowhai. You soon be transferred back to your friends, eh?" He clasped her frail shoulder for a quick moment, then released it as if it burnt him.

Horowhai turned to look at him. Alex moved up beside Zhou Yu. He bent down to kiss his mother's forehead. "Bye, Ma. See you soon."

The trio moved to leave.

"I want Mama's head!" Horowhai screeched suddenly. She began to thrash about.

Emily and Alex stopped abruptly at the door, stabbed to the quick by the outburst. Zhou Yu returned to the bed.

"It's in your room, Horowhai, remember? Soon you get better, you go back to your room."

And he hurriedly ushered the young people out.

*

The traffic passing outside their home had increased tenfold in Emily's time away. Trams and the occasional motor car now clattered past, as well as the clip-clop of draught horses towing their rumbling carts.

That evening, over the dinner that he had prepared, Zhou Yu said, "Emily, there is no real hope for your mama. Please try to be reconciled to it."

He looked at her picking at her food with her chopsticks, her tears welling up again. She had not been able to stop weeping for long since the first sight of Horowhai.

Zhou Yu continued. "What she suffered was too severe. Having that head with her all these years added greatly to the stress. The doctors say she's too far gone; they use new words... severe psy-cho-lo-gi-cal trau-ma-tic syn-drome. They can't really cure her, Emily; her case is hopeless." He stretched out his hand to comfort her.

"So she'll never come home," she finished for him.

"No."

Alex broke the long, ensuing silence. "What will you do now that you are home, Em?"

Emily sighed. "After seeing Mama today, I will become a nurse – at Seacliff."

"A nurse? That would be hard work, daughter." *And demeaning labour for one such as you,* he wanted to add, but held his tongue.

"I don't care, Pa. At least I shall acquire some knowledge to understand and look after Mama. It's very useful work, don't you think? So much of the world needs nursing. That's one thing I've learnt in China. All those sick people, all those horrible diseases – at least I can try to help."

"And you can work with Wiremu!" chortled Alex.

"I should hope not, Alex. I think your sister's much above that Maori boy from the Peninsula."

"Pa, Mama's Maori," Emily reminded him sternly.

"He's only half Maori," Alex added. "His pa's a whaler from one of the American ships. And look at me."

Zhou Yu felt Alex's remark like a punch on the nose. He frequently forgot his New Zealand children's maternity.

Alex continued. "We share the same distinction, but at least he doesn't get teased as much as I do."

Zhou Yu continued shuffling rice to his mouth. No, he would not countenance his precious daughter taking up with a Maori, pure or half-caste. He hoped she would marry one of the more prosperous Chinese merchants in Dunedin or a younger member from amongst his old friends' circle in Melbourne. Or one of Hongyun's connections in China or California. There were enough to choose from, surely. No! No Maori for Emily. She was too well-bred, too educated, too beautiful.

Watching him, Alex asked, "Why did you take up with Mama, Pa?"

Zhou Yu turned silently to him, then to Emily on the other side as he continued to eat. At the end of the meal, he said, "Make some tea now, Alex, and put more coal into the stove. What I have to tell you two will take a long time."

*

Through that long night, Zhou Yu recounted his experiences in Pita Hohepa's village outside of Oamaru. In his earlier confession in Suzhou four years previously, he had given a grinding story of his time in the Taiping Rebellion under Hong Xiuquan, the man who called himself God's Chinese Son. He had described the horror at the fall of Nanjing, and his brave older brother's ultimate death. He had ended with himself going to Australia before finishing up in New Zealand. He had explained his marriage to Yung and the birth of Hongyun, but not his real reason for not staying with Yung. He had given the poll tax as the excuse he had to return to New Zealand and how he ended up with Pita Hohepa's people in Oamaru. The children had been told he was given Horowhai when he left but he had not dared tell them the reason. It was not relevant then. Now it was.

Horowhai was his self-imposed penance, his punishment for his rape and murder of innocent women during the rebellion in China. He told them of Mun Fook, the scar-faced man he was obliged to kill in self-defence and the reason for Mun Fook wanting his death.

By the end of his narration, the room had turned cold, the coal bucket empty. The tea pot had been refilled several times. Emily and Alex were stultified by the tale of their slave grandmother, Arel, sacrificed in a long-dead tradition: a cannibal feast for an old dying Maori princess. Now they

80

understood why Horowhai kept Arel's head. And her obsession with it which eventually stripped her of her sanity. They sat a long time together on the couch, holding each other under a woollen blanket, their fingers so tightly entwined that they hurt when released.

"So now you know," Zhou Yu finished softly.

"Poor, poor Mama," Emily whispered.

"Poor all of us," Alex added.

They looked across at Zhou Yu, drooped and forlorn in his armchair. Simultaneously, they rose, kneeled before him and all three hugged each other tight, their anguished tears intermingling. Somewhere outside, a neighbour's rooster crowed in the dark winter morn in the silent city.

Chapter 12

September 1901: Beijing -- A Country Made for Plunder.

General Adna Chaffee of the US Army stood with his aide-de-camp as he looked up at the American flag still flying atop the partly destroyed thirty-foot high wall. Rubble piled all around them. This part of the wall was deserted of people; the stench of death still clung to the air as bits of Chinese body parts remained buried underneath, rotted, waiting to be cleared. The foreign armies had tacitly decided that the clearing of the mess they had made since June the year previously was to be left to the local inhabitants.

"Whatever you may say about them, the Chinese certainly know how to build, Lieutenant."

"Yessir, they have the manpower, sir," the young man beside him said, his nose crinkling with the pungent miasma wrapping them over. He was sweating under his hat. The collar of his uniform already bore the damp line of perspiration and his shirt stuck to his back and chest.

The general was suffering no less. He turned to his aide. "Looking forward to clearing out?"

"Oh yessir. Can't wait to leave this stinking city."

"Well, it was us that created the stink. If we'd let them alone all this would not have come to pass. We made a mistake, Lieutenant, when we rode on the backs of the British trade. We made this mess. So I hope you are not leaving with too much booty. You know what my orders are: the American military should not debase itself with plunder."

The lieutenant made no acknowledgement as he stood silent, po-faced. He had in his saddle bag a well-wrapped jade figurine looted from a shop in one of the *hutongs,* the many lanes near the moat surrounding the Forbidden City, as well as small cloisonné hair pieces for his mother and sisters. And silk fans. And an ebony-handled dagger. And... and...and... But they were minor items. Not like what the other foreigners were taking with the approval of their superiors. Beijing was an open treasure throve of gold, jade, lapis; you name it, the city had it. So much treasure, so much jade, so much exotic refinement, and the conquerors were stealing it all and shipping it back to whichever countries they came from. *Especially the Ruskies, and the Krauts, and the Jappos. No, they were the shameless ones. And the Brits, the main culprits who started it all in the first place. And we Americans had to come and rescue them, our China Relief Expedition. Don't mind saving the missionaries, they are doing God's work, but the rest? No sir, we are not like them, we certainly are not.*

And his mind went back to the aftermath of the siege, the massacres, the appalling beheadings. What a bloodbath that was, much worse than even the outright fighting. So much blood was let, so much damage done to the beautiful old Celestial buildings. His architect brother, Andrew, would condemn such callous destruction.

"Well," the general was saying, "after tomorrow, it will be truly over and we can sail back to the Philippines, back to the other duty, eh? I pity the Chinese. There'll be hell of a retribution to pay."

"How much, sir?"

"The Eight Nations are going for three hundred and thirty-five million dollars."

"Would we even have that kind of money, sir? Us Americans?"

"I don't know about that one, son. But what I have learned from all this is the greed of nations who consider themselves superior."

"But the Japs are amongst the eight, sir, and they look like Chinks."

"Ha! They are every bit as rampant, if not more so," the General snorted grimly, recalling the fast swinging swords of the Japanese through Chinese necks.

He thought back to his Indian wars. Those were different. They fought for territories to build a nation on. They had not looted... well, the Indians had nothing to loot anyway. But what had been happening in Beijing sickened him and he wanted to leave as soon as the treaty was signed.

*

The next morning in the Forbidden City, Prince Qing and the Viceroy of ZhiLi, Li Hung Zhang, sat at a long gilt-edged table with the heads of the Foreign Legation and their conquering generals. They signed away three hundred and thirty-five million dollars to be paid over the next thirty-nine years with compounding interest and were forced to pledge the destruction of all fortresses and their walls in every part of north China. And ten other minor clauses besides, all of which served to invalidate China as an imperial power in her own right.

*

April 1902: Tsingdao

Peasant farmers spread bamboo baskets of vegetables on the ground. A few of the better-off ones had theirs in shared communal drays that they had pulled in from the surrounding countryside. The bamboo baskets were carried in on poles, a couple on each end. The farmers now squatted behind their vegetables, live chickens and yellow-skinned sweet potatoes for which the region was famous. They had trudged miles from their tiny farms since sunrise and were now too exhausted to yell out their wares. But the sun would climb to its zenith before too long, and though they welcomed the rest, they were going to soon wilt in the heat, as would their perishable goods. Which meant lower prices. So they adjusted their conical bamboo hats and began to call out to passing customers.

Eddie Zhou and Ranjit Patel, his Indian friend from Delhi, stepped off the coastal packer to begin their exploratory holiday in Shandong Province. Eddie had resolved to visit the State of the Saints before leaving China and Ranjit, his fellow clerk at Swire's Shanghai, had been eager to join in. The plan was to climb that holy of holies, Tai Shan, the head of the five sacred mountains of China, as well as visit Qufu, the birthplace of Confucius, or KungTze to the Chinese. Now the young men wandered off the main street from the wharf in search of a

84

place to stay for a couple of days before traipsing off into the wilds of Shandong, which had been crawling with Germans for years.

Since 1897, the Germans had extracted a concession to the port city of Tsingdao and the coal-rich Jiao Zhou region. German railroads ploughed through the countryside, bringing the product into Tsingdao for shipment to Germany and other trading ports. The Chinese coolies worked the coal seams, built the railroads, the train stations, the port, and the churches. They worked and watched as their land was being plundered.

The Germans then put up a brewery to provide beer for themselves and the rest of the foreign legations along the entire coast. This they branded after the port.

They built an enclave of brick and stone houses reminiscent of those back in Bavaria, Hanover, Frankfurt – wherever they happened to have come from. And they put in German supervisors to police this exclusive section of Tsingdao from marauding eyes and thieving hands and the last remnants of the bloody Boxers. They transported ornate, black iron street lamps from Europe and used the coal gas to light the streets they widened. They built mansions to house their efficient administration offices. And as surely as each brick was added to such growth, as surely as each lump of coal was forced from the ground, the hatred of *Shandong ren,* the Shandong people, grew to fill their hearts and souls. This vicious hatred also encompassed all Chinese Christians they saw as supporting the foreign invaders.

*

As Eddie and Ranjit wandered along the narrow side-streets, they tried to ignore the hostile attention from the crowd. People hissed "thieves of coal", "rapists of our holy state", at Ranjit, whose Chinese was too elementary to understand the Shandong dialect, though he felt the hatred burn through him sure enough. Eddie tuned quickly in to the dialect, a close cousin to the official Mandarin.

"They will never forgive the defeat of the Boxers, Ranjit. Every foreigner is an enemy."

"But why can't they consider the improvements made here, Eddie, surely it is for the betterment of all," Ranjit protested.

"How can you say that? After what happened in India? Your country has suffered as much as China under the British." He strode on ahead, exasperated.

"Well, I suppose," Ranjit, trounced, replied. "But, Eddie, there are also great advantages under the British." To Eddie's unrelenting back, he added weakly, "Great advantages."

Eddie shook his head, not easing up, one hand in his trouser pocket where he kept his wallet, the other on the strap of the rucksack on his back. As the restlessness in the streets went unabated the deeper they walked into the untouched Chinese part of Tsingdao, he started having misgivings about the journey. Going to Qufu or Tai Shan – many miles away from German military protection – could prove disastrous, and from reports in the Shanghai papers, the Boxers defeated in the Siege of Beijing were not the last in the province. Pockets were still hiding out in the countryside, sheltered by their fellow peasants.

What on earth was I thinking? I'm putting our lives in danger, especially Ranjit's.

Then a roar of voices behind turned him around – in time to see a boy wearing a red kerchief on his head stick something into Ranjit's back. The Indian's face contorted in pain as he began to slump to his knees. The boy, no more than ten or twelve, stood his ground, unwilling or unable to flee, the blade red in his hands, his face impassive as stone.

"Ranjit!" Eddie yelled, as he dashed back to stop his friend from falling. He shouted in Chinese, "Bastard! This man has done nothing to you! He is not of them!" He saw the fear of the onlookers. "Help me get him to a hospital! Get a trishaw, a barrow, something!"

No one moved. Then the boy fled down an alleyway.

With Ranjit's arm around his shoulders, Eddie tried to retrace their steps. Ranjit grew heavier by the minute.

He moaned, "How bad is it?"

Eddie glanced down. He could see the red patch widening between his friend's shoulder blades. "I honestly can't tell. How do you feel?"

"Burning in hell."

Eddie pleaded again to the crowd. "We're strangers to this town. Please, help me get him to hospital. Please, someone. I will pay."

A vendor moved forward from his dray. "Will you pay for my sweet potatoes to be abandoned? Then I will take your friend to hospital."

Thank God! "Yes, yes, please hurry."

"Pay now, I want twenty cash."

Eddie pulled out a twenty cash note from his breast pocket and flung it to him. Immediately the man and his son, a boy of twelve, quickly started emptying their dray, swiping the sweet potatoes onto the street which were hurriedly retrieved by his neighbours. Then they helped Eddie lift Ranjit onto the dray and the three started pushing it into the wide main street. They ran the dray another five hundred yards. Then the farmer stopped outside the gate of a western-style building.

"We don't go in, you take your friend from here," the peasant said as he and his son started to pull Ranjit off the cart.

A Sikh security guard quickly came forward and, between the two of them, half lifted, half walked Ranjit through the door of the German hospital.

The portly doctor examined Ranjit's body as he lay face down on the white-sheeted gurney. He had a young Chinese orderly strip the shirt off, revealing a short, bleeding wound. His red face grim, he prodded gently round the wound with his thick fingers. Parting the flesh, he made a close examination and finally stood up with a grunt.

"Your friend is very lucky, *mein herr*, the knife did not go deep enough to do too much damage. It is a flesh wound which I shall disinfect and stitch up. Yar?"

Eddie practised his school German with the doctor as he watched him work.

"Well, if I were you, I would clear out of here, *unmittelbar*. This place is definitely not healthy, not good." The German looked at him over his glasses.

"I didn't think he would be a target," Eddie said lamely.

"You joke, yar? The Indians are also big opium traders. And the British use them in the army in many places. Even we Germans employ them. See our security guards? Who, otherwise, can you trust, yar? So," he pointed his needle at Ranjit's back, "your friend here can be so easily kaput, yar? Out in the alley? Ha! Go back quick to Shanghai, that's the safest place for now. Pay at the desk."

The orderly put Ranjit's shirt back on and brought him a cup of hot tea. As Eddie helped him drink, he said, "Do you think you can travel, Ranjit? We can take the night steamer back."

Ranjit smiled weakly, "After this, I would even ride a cow out of here, man."

Chapter 13

1903: England -- Children of the Missions

The tall, young man boarded the second class carriage at Waterloo Station in London. As he closed the door behind him, shutting out the chill December air with its smell of coal steam and soot, and made his way down the carriage to his compartment, he felt a sense of relief to be getting out of London. It was the twentieth of December, five days before Christmas, and he had in his suitcase presents for his grandmother and his sister Margaret, chosen with great care at one of the ladies' boutiques in Oxford Street. He had twelve days off from his studies at Guy's Hospital: twelve days of invigorating sea wind, log fires, plenty of Gran's great cooking and all the spoiling a man could wish for. As he settled down to his newspapers for the two and a half hour journey to Bournemouth, on the south coast of Hampshire, James Hopkins was as contented a man as any in England. Outside his carriage window snowflakes started twirling down from the darkening sky.

*

By the time he unlatched the gate to his grandmother's cottage two streets from the cliff in West Bournemouth, everything was blanketed by an inch of snow. In the early winter night, he could see a chink of golden orange light between the curtains, felt the warmth of the sitting room before he put his hand on the brass door knocker with its gaping lion's head. He had his key but wanted to see the joy on their faces when one or other of them answered the rap.

"James! Oh dear James! Granny, he's here!" Adorable Margaret, three years younger, all blonde curls and sparkling grey eyes.

He put down his suitcase and grabbed her in a bear hug just as Granny Hopkins bustled out of the kitchen, wiping her plump hands on her blue apron, all fond smiles. He grabbed her too, and for a moment the two women had no breathing space, locked as they were against the tickly wool of his coat.

"How clever of you, James, dinner's just done to a turn," Granny Hopkins said as he released her. "You go up to your room and have a wash. We'll eat in ten minutes. Maggie, do set the table, dear." And she was gone, back to the kitchen.

The smell of shepherds' pie filled his nostrils and he sighed pleasurably as he climbed the stairs.

*

After dinner, he took a crumpled envelope out of his jacket pocket.

"Letter from Pater," he said, hating to deliver the news. "They are staying on another two years."

He handed the envelope to his grandmother. Disappointment showed in both women's faces.

"And I was so hoping they would make it home in the spring. What's keeping them this time?"

"They've got souls to save, Gran. Apparently the mission is busier than ever since the Boxers were squelched two years ago. That's sort of the green light for full steam ahead."

The senior Hopkinses had been at the Macau mission for the last twenty-five years. The school they started under the auspices of the Church of England's London Missionary Society had succeeded, despite the opposition from the Roman Catholic Portuguese. Both children were born there, growing up within the confines of the mission grounds. They had been repeatedly sick with the miasma of the swamps and inlets of that part of south China until Granny Hopkins had stomped her little feet and insisted that they remain with her on the second of their holidays back to England. So from the age of fourteen, James, with eleven-year-old Margaret, had been under the care of their widowed grandmother in the sublime seaside town on the south coast of Hampshire, and thrived.

"Hell's bells, I am so disappointed," Margaret sniffed. "Mama's health hasn't been that good for the last several years."

"He has put a time on it, yet again, but he says with the increase in missionaries from both England and America, he has the chance to leave the place in capable hands. He just needs to settle them in," Granny Hopkins transcribed from the letter. "Oh dear, I do worry so. But at least you won't be going back, will you James, after you finish your training?"

James laughed. "Have no fear, Gran. Fourteen years in that swampy hole is more than enough to put me off. No, I shall wheedle my way into a general practice in London after I have served my internship."

"Wouldn't you like to specialise, James?" Margaret asked, herself halfway through a teaching diploma at the local college in Lansdowne.

"I don't think so, Margaret. That just means more years committed to study. Well, it's not settled yet. I admit, after our early deprivation in Macau, I am absolutely certain I don't want to be poor ever again. So yes, I may specialise and then work in a group practice in Harley Street."

But before the words were barely out of his mouth, he felt a twinge of something he could not put a name to. *Love? Hate? Nostalgia? Guilt? It is always to do with the Chinese.* He had left them behind, but they had not left him, impinging into his psyche whenever he was off guard. He was haunted by memories of his first amah, who remained with the family through all their struggles, and of the kitchen boy cum mission factotum, with his dangling queue and wicked sense of humour. The amah had died three years after their return to England. The kitchen boy was still at the mission, missing his teeth now, Pater had said. Cantonese was as natural to James and Margaret as English and the ghosts resurrected themselves unbidden from time to time.

Now Margaret gazed at her brother fondly. So clever he was, and so handsome. Even as a prepubescent girl living in Macau, she had despaired of ever meeting a suitable boy to marry, a boy like James. Not one of the traders from the various companies setting up in Hong Kong or Canton, nor any of the unwed missionaries, was attractive to her. Not that any of them were young enough. She had felt condemned to be an old maid in Macau, tied to the holy apron strings of the London Missionary Society of the Church of England. Then at last, Granny, bless her heart, had saved them from that beastly mosquito-infested, stinky swamp. And Papa had the temerity to suggest that she should return once she qualified as a teacher! *Oh dream on, Pater, as James would say, dream on. Never! Not in a million years.* Not all the prayers in the Bible could induce in her a love of the "Celestials", what with the men's long pigtails and the ridiculous feet of the poor girls. But that was their culture, wasn't it, and they should be left to their own.

Even as children she and James could see the futility of their parents' work. But not so the parents. So few successes for so much expanded energy and sacrifice. No, they were blind in their love of conversion, obsessed by the mammoth challenge of civilising the Chinese through Christianity. Maybe so, but she had seen some instances of what she would call civilisation amongst the gorgeous silks the merchant men took into the holds of their ships. Bolts of such exquisite beauty and colour. And their tea! Surely a nation that discovered tea wasn't that backward? Surely a country capable of such creations had a modicum of civility? Well, whatever. Not for her the missionary life and she was grateful she had an ally in her brother.

And just the other day, she had met Patrick, who was a year ahead at college. Now there was a man!

1904: Berkeley, California

Dexter Hauptman studied the Chinaman eating at the next table in the student refectory in Berkeley. He had noticed him before, of course. Chinamen in Med School at Berkeley stood out like sore toes. Sore toes that longed to be shod in solid American shoes, and to go unnoticed, but alas, there were no such possibilities for their kind. Not with their slope eyes and their queues. But this one, and most of the others on campus, had cut their racial brand off, another attempt at anonymity, poor bastards. Though he knew these were not poor; they were the scions of the wealthy.

The wealthy that had treated his parents and all their fellow missionaries with cool, decorous scorn. Who had looked down their pinched little noses at the teachings of the Lord, pointing out politely that the ways of the ancient sages – KungTze, Lao Tze, Mengtze – and a host of others had guided their society for two and a half thousand years and more.

"And so, *Levelen Howman*," they had always said at the end of a discussion, "does that not tell you we have no requirement of your Jesus teaching?"

But they had requirement enough for everything else that America could offer: the universities, the technologies, the open, clean spaces. His parents had spent the last twenty years of their lives in China, feeding the poor, trying to convert them with wheat buns and gruel. They ran an orphanage for abandoned girl babies, but worst of all, they subjected their own children to the poverty and diseases of that God-forsaken country. Only to be hacked to pieces at their mission house in Tongzhou, fourteen miles outside of Beijing just before the siege. The wisdom of the ancient sages had obviously nothing to say about sparing innocent children. And if he had not left nine months earlier for university, his remains, too, would have been left to the dogs somewhere...

Hongyun looked up, aware he was being scrutinised. He stared back at Dexter and smiled slightly, uncertain of what was passing through the mind of the American with deep blue eyes. They were the same blue eyes as those of David O'Malley. The American's scrutiny was blank, seeing yet unseeing. What was he thinking about? His gaze had not shifted. Perhaps he wasn't looking at him at all, just daydreaming, and he was merely in line of sight. Hongyun nodded and widened his smile. The blond American blinked, tore his eyes away and returned to his food. From the titles of the books beside him, Hongyun deduced that he, too, was a medical student, though two years his senior, and remembered seeing him in the corridors.

The American finished his meal, emptied his glass of milk and rose to walk away. Hongyun observed his mannerisms, his casual, confident movements, and made a note of them. That would be how he must act, casual and confident, as if this land was his too. As the American passed Hongyun's table, he bumped into the unoccupied chair opposite, which in turn jolted the table, causing Hongyun's glass of orange juice to spill.

He looked down at Hongyun and walked on without a "beg your pardon", without a word, but with a look of such cold contempt that Hongyun was shocked to his very being. He had seen contempt since his arrival four years ago, had witnessed casual disregard for his person, but never such hatred. What was with this man? He did not have a cruel face; indeed, it was rather an open one with wide spaced eyes, a clear brow and, as Westerners went, he was attractive. But... then, why?

That fleeting look spoilt the meal for Hongyun, so he finished his juice and went back to the frat house.

*

Hongyun had seen Virginia only four times since she rejected his proposal of marriage. He knew she was avoiding him and only attended family functions which were impossible to escape from. He knew she made excuses not to come to the regular dinners at the Sarginson home and suspected the elders had cottoned on to the split in their friendship, but were too genteel to inquire. He had managed to get Zhou Yu to increase his allowance by five more dollars a month which he was saving towards a car. The little nest egg was growing steadily in a special account at the bank. That would be the ultimate: to drive an automobile, to show Virginia and the other scornful Americans that he had made it, that he was someone to reckon with.

It didn't take him long to realise that his love was not for Virginia, but more with the idea of becoming American. From the newspapers he read, he knew he did not want to be part of the up-heaved Chinese landscape for a long while. No matter. Right now he had to concentrate on building his base to be more ready for the next girl who might come along. But by heaven, he was still smarting from stung pride and one day... one day... he would show Virginia just what she had missed by rejecting his proposal. He'd show her, *by jingo*, as the Americans would say. He'd show her.

*

Hongyun applied himself assiduously to his studies and was lauded by several of his tutors, especially the Christian ones. However, he was not a Christian. His years at the mission had passed tolerably because he attended chapel and learnt the hymns, but he remained untouched in spirit. Neither did he pay any attention to the teachings of KungTze or Lao Tze; life on the Suzhou farm did not include any active reference to the sages. And he had not the curiosity to find out. Sunday services with the Sarginsons, who remained active in their congregation, had not forged any friendship for him with people his own age. The older ones were solicitously kind, but it was his peers he wanted to cultivate. And now, in his second year at med school, he decided to increase his scant social circle by participating in activities on campus. And it was here that he came across that blond American again in the tramping club.

Dexter Hauptman was surprised to see Hongyun at a meeting one evening. The Chinaman was sitting alone by the sidelines, listening to Horace Gilmour explain the course of action for the next outing, a Saturday at Yosemite. There were around twenty men present. Most had been members since the beginning of their university life. The Chinaman was so obviously at sea in this group of tough, outdoorsy men that Dexter almost felt sorry for him. He looked delicate, deathly yellow-white amongst the tanned, ruddy young men, most of whom wore sweaters, knickerbockers and long white socks and boots. The Chinese was in his suit, his arms crossed across his chest, his legs stretched out with ankles crossed, trying to appear nonchalant, but, to Dexter's mind, only succeeding in looking uncomfortably out of place.

Henry Gilpin, Dexter's room-mate, elbowed him in the ribs, his head indicating Hongyun.

"How do you think he'll do, Dex? That yellow pansy?"

Dexter followed his eyes, and shrugged with a scowl. "He probably won't last the distance. Looks as winsome as a girl."

Hongyun had to ignore their disparaging whispers. The sting of that cold, hateful look from the blond American in the refectory the other week washed over him yet again. How often had he ruminated on it! He forced his attention back to Horace Gilmour but before long his eyes wandered round the gathering, looking for a friendly face, but all were intent on Gilmour. He started feeling silly. He realized he had to get suitable clothes for the outdoors.

*

The cost of clothes, boots and walking poles dug somewhat into Hongyun's savings, but he was committed to the course. It would be good exercise and he had noticed some level of cordiality towards him amongst one or two members of the club. During the journey from Berkeley a congenial fellow took the seat next to him and offered his hand.

"Hi, my name's John Kemp. New to this, are you?"

He shook John Kemp's hand in gratitude at being noticed, at being talked to first without having to make any effort. The joviality amongst the trampers was reassuring. Yes, he had done the right thing joining up. The big blond and his companion from the meeting cast him a derogatory glance as they made their way to the rear of the bus. Hongyun refused to let that spoil his day. He was determined to enjoy the tramp.

This was his second time to Yosemite. The first was with a group from the Sarginsons' church three years previously when he was still courting Virginia. Or at least he thought he was courting her. Now, of course, he knew better. She was just being kind, following orders from the Sarginsons.

On that occasion, they had not gone too far as there was a preponderance of women in the group, but had stopped by a river for a picnic. This time, the prospect of tramping with like-minded men his age excited him.

*

The morning was crisp and clear with the mist thinning between the trees when the chartered bus off-loaded them at the entrance of Yosemite. The vastness of the meadows, coloured by wildflowers of every colour against the backdrop of bluish mountains beyond, exhilarated him. He stopped to gaze with wonderment. Not in the four years in America had he seen this expanse of tall grass and wild flowers.

His group started walking up between the sequoias and he ran to keep up. Hongyun saw John Kemp's red-checked shirt disappearing up a small rise. He decided John was the best to follow, being the only man who had talked to him properly. But as he approached, he saw Kemp had banded up with several others, amongst them the tall blond and his friend. He dropped back, suddenly shy, and was soon bypassed by the remaining trampers, all chatting amiably without a break in their determined progress. They barely glanced at him. All he could do was follow as best he could though he noticed the distance between them increasing. He checked his pocket watch. Within an hour, they were about a quarter of a mile ahead. He was furious at his own lack of fitness which soon extrapolated into resentment of his fellow trampers. There was no question of turning back. He had to carry on, but was left further and further behind. No one looked back for him.

By midday, he saw they had come to a lunch stop at the top of a high rise. Shading his eyes against the sun, he could see they were all in a congenial mood amongst a copse of pine trees and his bile rose further. He was hungry, but realised he could not spare time to eat. The risk of being left further behind was greater than ever. Before he had gone two hundred paces, he was confronted by a shallow ravine and realised his group must have gone down it before pushing upwards onto the other side to where they were now lunching.

His heart sank. He could not turn back as they had arranged to meet the bus at another entrance on the other side of the park, a distance of some five miles. He sobbed as he descended down the stony side, gripping onto bushes to prevent losing his footing. Soon his hands were bruised and cut from the sharp brambles. He could hear loud, boisterous shouts from the other trampers. As he strained to see them, he missed his traction and fell, tumbling all the way down to the bottom.

"Aaagghhh!" he screamed. A streak of pain splintered his right ankle. He rolled to a standstill on his back and blacked out.

*

"How is he?" John Kemp's voice was close amongst the chatter of others and Hongyun opened his eyes. To see the blue of the Blond's above him.

"His ankle's broken," the Blond murmured.

He propped Hongyun up to a sitting position.

Horace Gilmour swore. "Damnation! Now we've got to figure how to get him outta here. I did think he was too green to come on this one."

Hongyun stared up into the ocean-blue eyes above him, imagining the wash of the sea in them. As he sank into his agony, he was aware of another overwhelming feeling, one he had never experienced before, unexplainable in his present sorry condition. But it was the effect of the closeness of the Blond: of his beautiful, clear eyes gazing into his own, of his breath on his face, the scent of his fresh sweat and the strength of his arms around him. His heart catapulted, surmounting the hurt from his ankle and the cold that was creeping through him in the shade of the ravine. Then he became conscious of John Kemp and another man tying a splint onto his broken ankle. It felt better. Horace Gilmour gave him a couple of tablets with his bottle of water.

"This will help dull the pain," Horace said grimly. "You guys go ahead. We'll have to prop him up between us."

The other trampers retraced their path, clambering up.

"Might be easier to carry him, Horace," the Blond said. "This is too steep."

"Yeah, right Dexter. Will you do the honours?"

Without a word, the Blond swung Hongyun like a sack of rice across his broad shoulders. John Kemp picked up Hongyun's pack and walking cane and the group made their way up the incline. At the top of the rise, Dexter lowered Hongyun to his feet.

"Aaghh!" Hongyun yelled as his broken ankle met dirt. Immediately Dexter's arm clutched him, holding him upright so he could stand on his one good leg.

"It's a long hike. What shall we do?" Horace asked.

"He's no weight. I'll carry him," Dexter said. "But if it gets too much, perhaps you or John can take over." And he crouched down in front of Hongyun. "Okay, Chinaboy, hop on."

Hongyun climbed onto Dexter's strong back, aware of the thrill that coursed through him as he clung onto his strong neck, inhaling the sweet smell of his tanned skin; as he marvelled at the soft, golden curls at his nape. He realised he had become besotted with the American. Who despised him. He closed his eyes and prayed: prayed to be spared the bittersweet nectar of the forbidden love he was falling into.

Chapter 14

Summer 1906: Dunedin

A Hong Kong postmark. Zhou Yu ripped open the envelope. Eddie. And in English instead of his preferred Chinese. He read the letter slowly, his lips moving as he walked up his garden path. Eddie was not a frequent correspondent but at least he never used his family as a sounding board for bad news. Unlike Hongyun, whose infrequent letters always had the unnerving ability to lessen any good news with the negative and, more often than not, ended up with a disguised demand for more money. Eddie never asked for money, neither did Emily, nor Alex. They seemed content with what they were given and now that Emily had a paid job, she refused any offer he made.

In his careful script, Eddie wrote that he was leaving his secure job at Swire's Hong Kong and taking ship for Singapore that night. *That means he is there already. Damn! Why didn't the boy allow me some room for discussion?*

He opened the door to the delicious smell of pork frying in ginger and soy sauce. The additional comforting aroma of steaming rice wafted over him. It was Emily's week-end off from Seacliff and she had earlier dropped into the warehouse on her way home, laden down with shopping. She always cooked enough food to tide them over for a couple of days while she worked at the asylum as a live-in nurse. By Monday morning, he would also be assured of a well-scrubbed house. *Blessed daughter, what would I do without you?* he thought at sight of her at the stove.

She turned round at the sound of his footsteps. "Hello, Pa, has it been a good day, then?" She spoke in Chinese, their language at home.

"Yes," he replied as he sat down at the kitchen table laden with plates and bowls of vegetables, diced, sliced and chopped, ready to be fried, steamed or boiled. He knew they were from old Wong Kiok though the market gardener was now nearly seventy. Zhou Yu fluttered Eddie's letter to get Emily's attention. "Eddie's in Singapore."

"What? Why? I thought he was happy in his job in Hong Kong. When did he go?"

"The very evening he posted this letter. So he's there now, I think. And he gives no reason. Just says he wants to try someplace new, something new. It's that Indian friend of his, Ranjit. He seems to be the one with ideas. They're travelling together."

Zhou Yu poured himself a cold cup of tea from the jug and smiled at his daughter's back. The sight of Emily always filled him with pleasure. She carried herself with an air of graceful authority. The faded European dress printed with blue flowers she wore was one of several she had brought back, custom-made, from Shanghai. Four years on, they still fitted well.

I must insist she allows me to buy her some new clothes soon, Zhou Yu thought. Emily's wages at Seacliff did not afford too many personal extravagances. He knew her spare money went to supplying her mother with regular treats. Not that Horowhai would notice whether the shawl she had on was new or not, nor whether the bun she ate was filled with cream or not. She was so out of it, hardly acknowledging Emily herself, though the girl swore she was aware of her. Thinking of Horowhai now saddened Zhou Yu. Her illness had blighted Emily's life as surely as if she had cut off her daughter's arm.

"I won't leave Seacliff as long as Mama's alive, Pa," she had insisted when pressed one evening, "so please don't ask me again. And as for marrying, how can I even think of it right now?"

"Wiremu's still hanging out for you, Emily," Alex had teased then, but was instantly silenced by Zhou Yu with an annoyed "SSHHH!"

Zhou Yu didn't want to risk any possible regressive behaviour coming through with that Maori-American boy. Wiremu's father had left with the whaling ship when the boy was six, and hadn't returned. Who knew what scars that would have left on young Wiremu? Nothing much was known of this man's family or background and he was rough! Zhou Yu had seen him on the wharf. And look at the damage all that kerfuffle up in Pita Hohepa's village had done to poor Horowhai. No, no more Maoris in the family. *Let's stick to what we really know.* Well, thank God the young man himself had abandoned nursing and gone off on an Australian whaler, so was not often around. Zhou Yu hoped he would stay away, set up house in Sydney or something; be somewhere safe with someone safe. And let Emily be safe – from him.

If Emily was drawn to Wiremu, she made sure she kept it to herself.

*

Alex came home soon after. He had been studying catechism at the house of the Reverend Salmond in town. Big and gentle with a wry sense of humour, Alex had, three years before, decided that the church was for him. His namesake and mentor, the Presbyterian minister, Alex Don, had taught him the virtue of converting Chinese and had groomed him for mission work in China. It had taken Zhou Yu a long time to realise what the wily man was up to when he offered to take little Alex under his tutelage all those years ago when Eddie and Emily were in Shanghai. The arrangement had kept Alex in Dunedin as consolation to his mother, but Zhou Yu was furious that missionary work would be Alex's future. By the time he found out, though, it was too late. His youngest son had been totally brainwashed.

"Pa, I am at one with the Reverend Don," Alex, at age fifteen, had argued one evening. "You have to admit, a huge chunk of that population needs bettering. I've seen them, remember, when you took me back to visit?"

"They surely do need to improve, but who is he, or you, to say that they need Christianity? They need food, better living conditions, education for their children, and that includes girl children – so you see, I'm progressive. Who are Christians to say Chinese need that foreign religion to be better people? Better in what? And for what? The Chinese in Panyu where Don went only want a better way of life, but that does not necessarily mean Christianity. Put food in their belly and you will see instant betterment, my son."

"Why are you so against Christians?" Alex had challenged.

"I'm not against Christians. I just don't want religion used to manipulate people. Don't forget what I was dragged into, my brothers and I. If it wasn't for that Hong Xiuquan and his belief he was God's Chinese Son and Jesus' younger brother, my own brothers would be alive today. We fought a twenty-year war with the excuse of Christianity. Now I abhor it."

"Pa, Hong Xiuquan was wrong and totally misguided. Times are different now. Christian missionaries are feeding the poor in China, are sincerely caring for them and not leading them into any kind of rebellion. And look, Pa, even after so many of them were massacred by the Boxers, they are still going in. Doesn't that show true faith? True love of their fellow men? Even Chinese?"

"Alex, I'll tell you what it shows – true arrogance, that's what it shows. How dare they say their way is the only way to enlightenment? We Chinese have been enlightened for five thousand years longer than Christianity has existed. And ours was an enlightenment of philosophy, of a way of honouring all that is above that we might know how to treat those below. And none of the "eat this of my body, drink this of my blood in remembrance of me" rubbish. That's spiritual cannibalism. Or have you forgotten what was done to your mother's mother?"

"Pa, that was not Christianity. That wasn't done in the name of Christ! It was an old forbidden tradition."

"Enough, Alex, enough! I don't want you apostatizing in China."

"Pa, you forget, your Aunt Meng was a missionary and you loved her."

"She was a teacher, first and foremost, Alex. True, that lot of missionaries gave her the life she wanted. They filled a need then. But, Alex, times are different now. We fought and killed each other for twenty years under Taiping Tiankuo – Kingdom of Heavenly Peace. Ha! There is no heavenly peace. The peace you make here on this earth, in this life, is the only piece of heaven you can expect to get. It is peace on earth that is heavenly. Enough said; I don't want you going to China, not as a missionary anyway."

Alex had quietly left. And now, this evening, he had quietly come in, in time to commune with his tiny family, to eat of his beloved sister's cooking... and to show his father what love of Christ can bring to their household. His faith was unshaken.

*

Six days later, a weeping Emily stood at the door of Zhou Yu's office in the warehouse.

"Mama died in the night, Pa. I found her this morning."

Zhou Yu had jumped up to take her into his arms but even as he comforted his grieving daughter, relief slowly flooded his being. *At last that yoke is shattered. Now Emily is free.*

"I will arrange the funeral," he said as he released her. And he called to one of his workers to find Alex, who was playing cricket with his old school friends. "Do you want to come with me or go home to rest?"

"I'll come with you, Pa. I want her to have the best we can afford."

"Of course, Emily, nothing but the best for your mother." But inwardly Zhou Yu was unhappy. The cost of a funeral at the high end would take up the past year's savings. He was hoping to buy Emily a new wardrobe for her new life. No matter, it had to be done. Emily wouldn't have it any other way.

*

All of Zhou Yu's friends, including Edward and Emily Rose Hats and a few Pakeha neighbours, came to pay their respects at the funeral held in Alex Don's small Chinese Community Church in Walker Street. Zhou Yu knew their sympathy was laced with relief for him. And, at the end of the day, there was enough money left over to buy Emily a black wool dress and bonnet for her mourning.

That morning, at the last minute before they closed the casket at the funeral home, he had placed the shoebox with Arel's head on Horowhai's chest.

"You can both rest in peace, now," he whispered.

In death, Horowhai's resemblance to her mother Arel, as Zhou Yu remembered her, was striking. Her cheeks and eyes were deeply hollowed, her lips taut and, in late middle age, her

103

hair was grey and thin. The pretty girl he had fallen in lust with all those years ago was no more. Silent tears rolled down his face as he said a final prayer under his breath.

*

Eddie's letter arrived a month later, upsetting Emily and Alex with its lack of remorse.

"Don't be angry with him," Zhou Yu had said. "He took the brunt of your mother's mental decline at an early age. But he's not unsympathetic, merely glad that she has left her earthly body for a better place." He then added, "And he wants a better future for you away from Seacliff, Emily."

"You can work at the hospital in town, Em," Alex had suggested.

"I want to apply to the medical school. I want to be a doctor," she said, looking at her father, uncertain of his reaction.

"A doctor!" Zhou Yu exclaimed. Then pride suffused his face. "Of course, Emily, you will be a wonderful doctor. And I will support you!"

"Well, that will certainly put you out of Wiremu's league now," Alex couldn't help saying with a chuckle.

Zhou Yu kicked him under the table. "She was always beyond his league."

"Will you marry again, Pa?" the recalcitrant boy now asked.

"I *am* married, you forget," Zhou Yu replied.

Of course, Yung never intruded into Alex's life. Unlike his brother and sister, he was spared holidays on that Suzhou farm. Yung was a hazy figure recessed in his short past.

Now, Zhou Yu's thoughts turned to Yung. She had not replied to any of his letters since he last visited. He wondered if her lover, that furniture maker, was still there, where he himself should be. *But that life is dead now, dead and gone, like Horowhai,* he thought as he gazed at his very alive children before him at the table.

"Well, that makes two doctors in the family, with big brother Hongyun in America," Alex now said.

"Yes, and I am very proud, especially of you, Emily, because in truth, I don't really know what Hongyun is up to. But of you I am always sure."

"Thank you, dearest Pa."

*

But the university was adamant a Chinese woman would not be admitted, to medical school or any other faculty. Zhou Yu enlisted the help of Edward Hats and, reluctantly, also that of Alex Don to plead her case.

Each separately wrote:

'This young woman was born and raised in this country of an immigrant Chinese father and a Maori mother. She has nursed at Seacliff for the last several years and is highly thought of by her superiors in that institution. She has also had the best of education at the most prestigious private school in Shanghai owned and operated by American missionaries. Surely there is no reason to keep this excellent young gentlewoman subservient in the lower orders of auxiliary nursing?

In our dominion, we are sorely in need of well-trained doctors. The native community, with which Emily Zhou also identifies, needs doctors. She can work with them and the betterment of their lot must surely be of benefit to our country. I humbly urge you to please reconsider your opinion and accept this unusual and highly intelligent young woman into your great halls of learning. Once you interview her, you will be of like mind.'

*

Emily herself wrote to the Dean and Vice-Chancellor.

'Sirs,

I have seen the plight of the Chinese people whilst schooling in Shanghai and realised what good medicine could do to help them. I returned to see that the lot of the Maoris can be much improved with better health care too. I am seeking the privilege of the training your medical school can offer me that I might be of service to them, my mother's people. And even though my father's race, the Chinese, are much prevented from advancing in so many ways, at least New Zealand can offer to those already here the right to a better quality of life through better medical care. I hope that you will entrust me with the training to be of use to these two communities.

I was privileged to study the various sciences in Shanghai which were taught in the American curriculum, and which was not accorded to most of my gender. Please be assured, my previous education will not fail me at university. I enclose my school and examination reports.

Your humble servant,

Emily Zhou Mei Ling.'

And by spring, Emily found herself amongst the first year intake.

*

That Same Year: Suzhou County

Hongyun's last letter had filled Yung with great sadness. She sat before her sewing machine, turning the handle with her right hand as her left guided the red cotton fabric through the feeder. She was making a dress for the neighbouring Liu family's daughter as a favour. It would be the girl's fourteenth birthday soon and the dress was for a photograph. A matchmaker had found a suitable boy for Xing Lan; a boy whose successful commercial family also owned a much bigger farm on the far side of the county. The Lius had always been generous with their recommendations which brought steady work for Feng Wen Kai, the carpenter who had replaced Zhou Yu in Yung's life.

As the machine burred its way through the seams, she ran over in her mind the contents of Hongyun's letter. He, who had always told her everything, he who could not keep a secret from her for want of trying, had now confided that he was in love with an American fellow medical student: *a man!* Two years ahead of him in studies, though of the same age. And he was distraught. In America, he had said, such love would be condemned, careers ruined, the culprits imprisoned. What was he to do?

But is your love returned, son? Is it a reality or just in your imagination? Even if it is real, would you risk imprisonment? And how much is this affecting your studies? She wondered what she could do, who she could confide in. Certainly not Zhou Yu. Not him who had flung them from his life. He might even cut off Hongyun's allowance.

Serves him right that the native woman is a committed lunatic. Serves him right.

When she consulted Feng Wen Kai, she found him unperturbed.

"Why aren't you shocked?" she demanded.

"I've always suspected it in him," replied the good man.

"But you never said anything!" She felt betrayed, felt Hongyun betrayed.

"What good would it do to bring it out unnecessarily? I hoped he could ignore it and get on with a normal life. I don't know too much about it, wife, but I don't think it is something you could advise out of a boy. However, I have heard that from ancient times, there were men who could go with both sexes. Perhaps he could resolve it that way."

Yung started weeping. She saw the empty years ahead, devoid of grandchildren. "He said it could destroy his life if he were found out."

"Wife, there is nothing we can do, is there? An ocean separates us. We can only hope nothing will come of it. Does he say his love is returned? Anyway, when he comes back to China, he might get over it."

"It matters to me!" she shouted. "You ask is his love returned? He didn't say, but the American's parents were missionaries massacred in the rebellion of the Righteous Harmonious Fists. His Christian faith alone would condemn it. The murder of his parents condemns Hongyun. I think my poor son is baying at the moon."

Feng sank into contemplation. He had no real place on the farm, being a de facto husband, a de facto boss, a de facto father. He had no authority over Hongyun; none, certainly, over Yung. He was there by her grace – and Zhou Yu's. But this now was home: there was no place else he could go, nobody else he wanted to be with but her. Now all he could offer was some feeble advice and consolation.

They were interrupted by Lao Chun, the local mail and general goods carrier.

"*Taitai* Yung, there is a letter from *Xin Xi Lan*!" he shouted from the front door and was invited in for a cup of tea before going on his way.

She snatched the envelope from him and prised it open with her forefinger.

'Yung,

I know this means nothing to you, that we mean nothing to you. Yet, somehow I feel the need to impart sad news concerning my life at present. The mother of my children, the native woman as you call her, is gone from this wretched life. She had spent the last eight years in a mental asylum and died last month. Emily, who had been nursing her from the time she returned to New Zealand, has now been accepted into the university to study medicine. That is my sole piece of happy news.

I have not heard from Hongyun for several months. I hope he is well as I know he writes you more frequently than he does me.

As I told you and your man Feng when I was last at the farm, he can stay on there as long as he wants. As long as he is there for you, I can be more assured of your wellbeing and for that I thank him. Please do believe me; I worry about your welfare. Let him know of my gratitude. I know how I have failed you and Hongyun, but hope I am making up for the past, at least where he is concerned. Money is all that he wants of me. And if you need help on that front, I shall do my best to oblige.

I do not know if I will ever live in China again. Neither am I certain about what to do with the farm. Therefore I will wait till I am sure of Hongyun's future intentions and those of the other children. Rest assured, whatever happens, you have the legal right to be there for the rest of your life, and, by extension, your man Feng to whom I send my salutes.

Keep well,

Zhou Yu

Dunedin 9th month 1906'

So the native woman is dead! Good. Good. Good.

*

December 1906: The Crown Colony of Singapore

"What shall we do for Christmas?" Ranjit asked Eddie as they hunched over a lime toddy at Malingam's curry hut on Katong Beach. The small remains of their south Indian dinner – a sweet and sour coconut fish curry, a vegetarian vindaloo for Ranjit and a goat one for Eddie, and turmeric rice – sat on large sheets of banana leaves in front of them. Eddie called out for the young boy lurking nearby to take them away. They had eaten with their hands, Indian style, and had washed them in cold water in the bucket by the hut. Now the boy came with another tin bucket into which he swept the leftovers. Eddie sniffed the taint of the pungent curries on his right hand.

He and Ranjit had joined the police force a week after their arrival in the growing port city. Both young men wanted a change from their sedentary jobs at Swire's and found the tiny police department in Singapore was hiring. Now their basic training was almost over.

Ranjit, though Hindu, had always gone along to the Christmas celebrations held at Swire's in both Shanghai and Hong Kong. Eddie, reared in the Methodist faith of the Shanghai mission school, observed the holiday.

Now Eddie looked at the moon casting its reflection on the sea as he enjoyed the cool evening breeze, oblivious of the chatter of other diners.

"I don't know. What is there to do but join the party in the mess?"

"Well, we could attend that and then go to the rongeng hall," replied Ranjit, whose craving for female company well exceeded Eddie's.

The rongeng hall was the local dance centre near the police compound where one bought chits to dance with the girls. It was a very recent establishment but with the increasing immigration of single males from different parts of Asia, a need had arisen for some places of recreation. Rongeng was strictly a no-touch, sedate Malay walking dance and the music was, to Eddie's mind, too repetitive and simple to entice. The entire duration of the dance consisted of couples facing and walking each other backward and forward with little twists of their hands in time to the music. It required absolutely no skills and, in his opinion, was a complete waste of time and money. He had much preferred the waltzes and Scottish dances introduced by the British bosses at the Swire parties. They had such wonderful music with a lot of swing and lilt. But now here they were with the Singapore police and the few English officers had nothing planned for the local men except a low-key party – if they so wanted.

*

The force was composed mainly of former sepoys, some Malays and, till Eddie showed up, no Chinese. Policing was not a profession any self-respecting Chinese would go into willingly. It equated to spying and brought to mind the activities of the imperial secret police in China. Now the problems of triads were rapidly escalating in the colony. Extortion, prostitution, gambling and opium smuggling, with the resultant murders, were on the rise. When Eddie, taller by head and shoulders over the local southern immigrants, showed up at Police Headquarters, he was instantly corralled. His fluency in two Chinese dialects and English made him a golden find. It didn't matter to the hierarchy in the force that Mandarin and the Suzhou dialect were not spoken amongst the Chinese of Singapore, who spoke Cantonese, Fukien and Teochew – any dialect but Suzhou. Certainly the gangsters had absolutely no intention of learning English.

"We might get lucky and be on duty Christmas Day," Eddie now said. With his mother dead, he wondered whether he should stick around or return to Dunedin. He could take over the business and ease things for the old man. More than anything, he missed Emily.

"You're always spoiling it for me," grumbled his friend. "Here I am, hoping to get married soon to someone, somewhere, and here we are in our sorry bachelor state. I can see some pretty Indian girls around here, though they are of the dark Tamil variety."

"I thought your parents would pick you a bride from your own caste."

"Most surely they will. Just joking, man. But I need some fun; you get my meaning, Eddie?"

"I get it, but I'd rather be out on duty," Eddie said, finishing his toddy.

Chapter 15

1908: Loss in the Humidity

Eddie and Ranjit, now eighteen months into their sojourn in the colony, were patrolling the Chinese quarters on the western side of the river. The short rows of rickety, Chinese shophouses lining dirt streets carved out of the jungle, were common all over south Asia. Their covered verandas suited the rainy seasons. The fronts, which were boarded up at night, were used as eateries or shops. Poor vendors hawked their wares from baskets under the verandas. The second floors were sleeping quarters for the owners, workers and their families and whichever itinerant immigrant could pay for the space of a pallet.

A healthy stench of rotted vegetables, urine, fish and river mud hung ripe in the humidity. Small plots of pepper vines, taro, and banana trees had been hacked out of the jungle. Between these, wooden cottages with sloping roofs thatched with *attap*, dried palm leaves, to facilitate the rain run-off, clustered together. Narrow dirt tracks meandered between them and eventually led to the main dirt road if one followed them long enough.

The built-up areas were noisy with barely a let-up till ten each night when the pedestrian traffic dried up. The hawkers would then drag their portable stalls home to some other side streets or to solitary huts in the pepper plantations. Here toads croaked, night insects shrieked and mosquitoes played havoc with their malarial bites.

Then the shops would shut and the gambling dens behind them open. Mah-jong was the favourite game and played with high stakes. But fan-tan, a betting game with cubes and buttons, and many different card games were played. Whatever the game, it was the stakes that mattered. A desperate hope to gain a month's wages with the throw of a dice. For many single Chinese men, gambling was the only diversion after a hard day's labouring, and as these dens were also places for friendship, they were substitutes for families.

Then there was opium.

The colony police turned a blind eye on gambling and opium, and only intervened when there was an uncontrollable fight or when someone was killed. The colonial government, the Malay sultan and the *temenggong*, or chief minister, obtained half their income from opium, thereby all encouraged its legal importation from India.

*

The British administrators and wealthy businessmen from many nations lived on the other side of the town, beyond the flat commercial area that had been created from the swamp. A hill in the centre of the island had also been sacrificed for this and it prospered instantly. Now each day, Parsis, Armenian Jews, Arabs, Chinese and Malays from every island in South-East Asia intermingled with British and Dutch for trade and barter. Beyond, interspersed by jungle, pepper and gambia plantations, sugar cane and taro fields, the rest of the transient population of Singapore, mostly Chinese from the southern region and Tamils blackbirded from southern India and Sri Lanka, toiled and sickened their way in the humidity of the mangrove swamps along the coast.

The mangrove trees grew to great heights in the tropics with their roots snarling above water at low tide – high enough to hide pirates, the scourge of the seas around Singapore. Their swift skiffs lunged out at passing smaller vessels. They worked in teams, pirates from some boats lassoing the unfortunate ships to a standstill as others boarded. The crews were quickly despatched with machetes or krises and entire vessels would be emptied of cargo within a couple of hours. The large British and Dutch steam ships puffed in and out of port unmolested, but the owners of smaller vessels, all from neighbouring islands, were now demanding greater surveillance along the coast and stricter anti-piracy laws.

*

113

By working undercover as a trader for the first year, Eddie had mastered the various southern dialects. The previous day, he had learnt about an especially valuable pirated cargo of opium that would be disposed of in the small settlement of Kampong Lembok, set apart from the Chinese area by dense jungle and thick coastal mangroves. They had ascertained Kampong Lembok was where many pirates got rid of their contraband.

Today, Eddie and Ranjit were to meet up with the rest of the harbour police at the western side of the river to ambush the pirates and their clients.

"I wish you hadn't learnt their lingo, Eddie," Ranjit complained as they made their way in. "This is too dangerous and I must keep myself in one piece for my bride-to-be."

"Sorry," replied his friend close behind him. "I have no stomach for this either. Let's hope they don't put up much of a fight."

"Do you think we'll have enough men?"

"I certainly hope so, or our goose will be cooked."

"Right when we're leaving. Bloody fool, you are, Eddie, bloody fool."

"Yes, bloody fool I am, sorry," Eddie replied, oppressed by the presentiment he had woken up with that morning. Today was going to be a disaster, he knew it.

*

This was to be Ranjit's last week in Singapore. His parents had, indeed, found him a suitable bride in Delhi and he was to sail the following Sunday for Bengal on a British trader. With his friend leaving, Eddie planned to quit the force and head up north for further exploration of Penang and Siam, after which he would be happy to sail for home. Zhou Yu had expressed a desire to see him take over his business and Emily had pleaded in all her letters. Alex, she had informed him, was going to join the missions in China. She wanted a family reunion before Alex departed.

*

And now they waited, steaming in the dense undercover of the jungle. Nearby, the mangrove roots were beginning to show up through the ebbing tide. Eddie had learnt rendezvous time

114

was five-thirty that evening, giving the pirates and their customers time for a quick exchange of opium and money before the sudden tropical darkness of evening. They had come an hour earlier ahead of the merchants and each man was scratching every exposed part of himself as mosquitoes launched their revenge for being disturbed. Insects screeched and hummed in deafening cacophony. Nobody spoke as they held guns at the ready, and their uniforms soaked up the perspiration that coursed down their faces.

Soon, low Fukien voices came through the mangroves as others drifted, muffled, from the jungle side. They heard a couple of sampans sidle up between the giant roots and men crawled ashore. The merchants appeared from the thicket opposite where Eddie, Ranjit and several others were crouching. The rest of the team of twenty police were on the other side of them.

The police waited till all the contraband opium was unloaded before they pounced. The receivers were putting the large square packets, wrapped in brown oiled paper, into woven baskets which would be lugged out on the ends of flat bamboo posts. The Sikh sergeant blew a shrill whistle and his men jumped out, confounding the criminals. However, the twenty policemen were not enough to apprehend both cargo and pirates. A great melee ensued. The pirates bandied machetes and cleavers. The opium merchants carried knives in their belts. The police had pistols. Three pirates dropped from gunshots. The police chased their retreating cohort, firing into them and producing screams of pain. Ranjit, Eddie and a couple of ex-sepoys stayed behind to arrest the merchants and seize the contraband goods.

Just as Eddie was retrieving a packet, a small cleaver slashed the air.

"*Loo see ahh!* You die!" shouted the attacker with a hate-reddened face. He snatched the packet from Eddie as his cleaver connected with Eddie's right hand.

"Ahhh!" Eddie grabbed his hand as pain flashed white in his eyes.

"Eddie!" Ranjit cried, running over, then gave chase to the retreating culprit, who had pushed through the thicket with the rest of his cronies. He returned to find Eddie crouching on the trampled undergrowth, moaning. Eddie had his right arm up and blood was streaming down to his elbows, bloodying his knee before dripping onto the vegetation.

One of the sepoys knelt beside him and wrapped his injured hand with his own handkerchief.

"Very much loss of blood, Eddie," he sympathised.

"Can you walk?" Ranjit asked.

Eddie nodded through his grimace. Now the other policemen were returning. They gathered up the strewn packets of opium, and carried them out of the jungle the way the merchants had intended – slung on the ends of their bamboo poles. They left the dead where they lay as a lesson to others. Ranjit and the sepoy helped Eddie limp out, his injured hand crudely bandaged and secured high to his head with his belt to minimise further blood loss.

*

The British doctor at General Hospital was a thin man with a fine-veined, red face. He removed the entire small and ring fingers down to their proximal phalanges, as well as the distal phalange of the middle finger. *Damned shame, waste of a decent hand,* he thought grimly as he cut and sutured, glancing at the chloroformed sleeping man on the gurney. He could not place the ethnicity of the boy. He was Chinese, yet there was some other tint that refused to come to mind. Curly hair, as big as a European, dark skin, flattish nose, full lips. Not bad looking in his police khakis.

"Could be a lot worse, young man," he told Eddie when he emerged from his ether fug. "It's not pretty, but you'll manage quite all right. You'll have to learn to hold your pen differently, though."

*

Ranjit sailed on Sunday, his handsome, moustachioed face beaming as he waved goodbye to a very depressed Eddie standing on the wharf, his right hand thickly bandaged and the entire arm in a sling.

"It will be good to get married, Eddie," Ranjit had said contentedly the night before as they ate their last meal together at Malingam's. "You shouldn't leave it too long. After all, your assets are daily diminishing," he chortled, indicating the bandaged arm in its sling.

Now, Eddie, overwhelmed by remorse, waved back to his friend. Ranjit was right. He was now nearly twenty-six and his prospects of getting a wife and family together seemed as distant as the stars. He was still in uniform but intended to quit when his hand healed. Till then he was on desk duty. Now he watched the departing steamer being replaced by a blank future looming up at him, unrelenting, misty, and bleak as the snows in Shanghai winters.

May 1908: *Dunedin*

"So much of my life seems to be spent on wharves," Eddie commented to a tearful Emily, as they stood beside their father, waving Alex goodbye at the wharf.

The young missionary was waving his red scarf in a wide arc in order to be seen, his face a maze of complicated emotions. He was weeping with his fear of returning to China, alone, doing God's work, so far from home.

The Reverend Alex Don, his face set in an emotion Zhou Yu could not fathom, was waving too. He stood several feet away from the Zhou family. Zhou Yu could not bring himself to speak to him this evening. Don was not forgiven for brainwashing young Alex into a missionary life, in China or anywhere else. Zhou Yu looked across to the other side of the minister to Edward and Emily Rose Hats, his oldest friends in the country. The motherly Emily Rose was sniffling and wiping her plump face with a green handkerchief. Since Horowhai was committed to Seacliff Mental Hospital all those years ago, she had relished the role of being Alex's surrogate mother. She, too, was not speaking to the Reverend Don today.

When the steamer was well out past Port Chalmers heading towards Tairoa Heads, the group turned slowly back to town. Emily gripped her father's hand tight as she looped her other arm round Eddie's. They took leave of their friends with Zhou Yu ignoring Alex Don's goodbye.

Zhou Yu felt his heart had been gouged out from within. He was losing his youngest child to a China that he knew had essentially not changed much from the time of his own youth, when, with the Taiping rebels, he had rampaged across that very southern part, converting the peasants to the twisted version of Christianity expounded by rebel leader Hong Xiuquan. They converted and died. And there was no Kingdom of Heavenly Peace to receive them as promised.

As he walked between his two older children with his head bowed, Zhou Yu could only reminisce about his own bitter loss to that crowd. His gallant eldest brother, Captain Zhou Yun, fought ten years for Hong Xiuquan, only to be executed in the public square of Suzhou. His middle brother, the comedic Ying, had his throat pierced with a spike defending the ancient capital of Nanjing. His father, Fengyi, left alone and broken-hearted, was soon to be addicted to the cursed opium.

Now Alex was going headlong into that terrain. Zhou Yu knew the countryside would be every bit as poor as when the rebellion was raging, the people as addicted, if not more. And Alex would soon be promising them, yet again, heaven on a stick. *At least it would not be a sword this time, thank God, thank God. Damn Don! He calls himself our friend. Friend indeed. Damn Don!*

"Darling Pa, please don't be so sad. He'll be all right. Reverend Don promised he'll be safe. China's good now for missionaries." Emily hugged him as she took her leave to return to university to collect her books.

"See you at home, Em," Eddie waved.

The men wandered slowly home as Emily walked purposefully towards the medical school on the other side of town. As they approached their house, Zhou Yu stopped short with a groan. At their low wooden gate, Wiremu O'Neil was about to leave when he saw them approaching.

"*Kia ora*, Mr Zhou. I was in port and thought I'd call on Emily," he said, his smile dying at Zhou Yu's sour look. "Well, on all of you, actually." He handed a large brown bag to Eddie. "I got some souvenirs for you," he finished lamely.

"You better come in, then," Zhou Yu said to Eddie's relief.

Since his return from Singapore, Eddie had been well aware of Zhou Yu's antagonism towards Wiremu, a feeling he was disinclined to share. Like Alex, he thought their father unreasonable. This was the first time he was meeting Wiremu and he instantly liked the half-caste. Wiremu seemed to have inherited the best of both Maori and European features. The fact that his whaler father took off soon after his sixth birthday probably helped him stay on the straight and narrow path of his very pious mother.

"No one more pious than a converted sinner," Zhou Yu had once commented when they were discussing Wiremu and had instantly felt ashamed. He just wished the man would disappear. Yet here he was, with gifts for the family that he himself could not possibly accept.

*

The pleasure on Emily's face when she entered the kitchen thirty minutes later plunged Zhou Yu's heart into an abyss. He looked on glumly as she welcomed Wiremu with too much warmth. He refused to start preparing their meal. He did not want Wiremu staying to eat with them.

But Emily was saying, "I'm about to cook dinner, Wiremu. You must dine with us and tell us about all your adventures."

She was bringing out the contents of Wiremu's peace offering... and sighing over them. A lovely purple wool shawl, ribbons, a coral brooch. A rakish red cap for Alex which now went to Eddie. And for Zhou Yu a bottle of bourbon.

Yes, true to form, bourbon from the son of an American whaler. Damn. Damn. Damn.

He became aware of Eddie smiling conspiratorially at him with eyebrows lifting and knew whose side Eddie was on.

As the evening progressed, Zhou Yu grew more and more morose. What with Alex's departure – how he was missing his boy already – and across the table Eddie and Emily were hanging on to every word the handsome Maori was spouting. And the glow on Emily's face! The coquettishness that he had never before seen in her. *Oh God, don't let it be, please, don't let it be.*

He poured his fifth glass from the bottle of bourbon.

Chapter 16

1910: Alex in China

Alex stared out the train window chugging him from Shanghai to Suzhou. He had been in Shanghai since June, arriving in Hong Kong just before the start of the hot summer monsoons. The mild heat of Otago summers had not prepared him for the steamy cauldron of Hong Kong. The memories of his first trip ten years previously in the winter filled his twenty-year-old heart with anxiety. But he had made a promise to his father that he would visit his wife Yung on the Suzhou farm as soon as possible. Yung had not mattered a jot to him in New Zealand; his daily activities had washed her into the backdrop of his father's life. But since setting foot on Chinese ground, she loomed large. Large and angry. Large and spiteful. He closed his eyes, whispered a soft plea, begged for the courage to face her rage.

When he opened them, the faces ogling him tried his patience once more. He still could not get used to the rude stares and comments. He knew he did not blend into this landscape: he had a darker skin, wild curly hair and large, round eyes. His father's Chinese features did not tamper with his visage. And his six-foot frame made him an uncomfortable target for rude finger-pointing. Well, here at least, they were speaking the Suzhou dialect he could understand, but the uncomplimentary comments only emphasised his feeling of alienation.

*

At last the train glided into the station and his fellow travellers pushed and jostled each other out onto the platform. He waited till they had vacated the carriage before getting up to follow. From the overhead luggage rack he took down his brown leather valise, a present from Zhou Yu, and stepped onto the platform to be accosted by several scrawny rickshaw drivers, their eyes hungry for the trade from this big foreigner. His father had instructed him to take a public cart to the small town near their home and from there a rickshaw to the farm. But he felt too tired to change the mode of transport and decided to hire a rickshaw for the entire ride. He had been in China for six months now and was able to hold his own in bargaining.

"I am a poor scholar," he always said, which was true: he was a scholar of Chinese and the Bible. "So this is what I can pay," and they always accepted his coins.

*

As the rickshaw approached the farm, his stomach started convulsing.

I need not fear her, he told himself, *she is as she is and I am not in her life. I will leave tomorrow morning.*

As he passed the family rice fields, he could see that Yung was a good manager. The farm was in pristine condition and the few workers seemed better fed and dressed than many he had passed on the way.

She came to the door when the rickshaw peddler rang his bell. Her face showed no welcome as she stared at him walking towards her. Behind her Feng Wen Kai stood, his expression unreadable in the shadows. She expected him. Alex had written to her of his intentions from Hong Kong a month previously. He stopped three feet away from her, dropped his case and bowed, holding his clasped hands on his chest.

"*Ni hao*, Mama Yung," he said softly.

She nodded. He detected a fluttering of her eyelids, a quiver in the corner of her mouth, but no sound came. At that point, Feng Wen Kai inched past her. He had aged much in the ten years since they last saw each other. The older man smiled warmly.

"*Ni hao*, Alex-ah." He took Alex's large hands in his calloused ones.

Then he picked up the valise and ushered Alex into the house. Yung had, meanwhile, disappeared inside.

*

121

That evening at dinner, he brought out the small present Zhou Yu had given him for Yung. It was a pendant of the koru, the fern significant to Maoris, carved from whale bone. She looked at the soft, polished ivory curves in disbelief, and Alex sighed. It was as Zhou Yu had warned him: being Chinese, she would not appreciate a lowly bone carving hanging on a slim leather thong. "But explain to her the history of this place, the whaling station and whales caught in these waters, and that my good friend Tauwhire, who is a good carpenter like Feng Wen Kai, carved it especially for her. The koru signifies new birth, fresh awakenings, you know that. So tell her that. It is more a souvenir of New Zealand than any piece of gold that I could buy."

But she was not impressed. Emily and Eddie had warned Zhou Yu that a reminder of New Zealand was the last thing Yung would want. None of them could understand their father's reasoning for the gift. But when Alex withdrew a thick wad of high denomination Chinese money from his shirt pocket, Yung's expression lit up. This she could understand; this she could appreciate.

Feng Wen Kai was very pleased with the solid penknife Alex produced from his trouser pocket.

"Pa thought you might like it," he said shyly. "The blades are very sharp," he demonstrated each blade and attachment. "This one is for opening bottles and this one is a can opener," he ended feebly when he realised that, out here in the countryside, bottles with tops and cans of tinned food were hardly ever come upon.

But the old man was very pleased with the wonder of a western pen knife in all its intricacies.

"Thank your pa very much for me when you next write," he said and spent all evening releasing and shutting each blade into its slot.

From Emily and Eddie there was a woollen shawl for Yung and a meerschaum pipe for Feng which Eddie had managed to procure on his stopover in Sydney on his return to New Zealand. He had bought two, one intended for his father and the other for himself at a later stage. Now Feng was given his.

"I know that your mother died," Yung spoke at last. "Tell me about it."

Alex did not wish this intrusion into his own pain, knew her question was not out of sympathy but of a venial desire to gloat. But he decided to humour her and throughout dinner, answered her questions, though as briefly as possible. Then just when he had exhausted himself, she surprised him by the outpouring of grief that she had harboured during all those years of separation from his father. For the first time, Alex wakened to the other side of his father's life, as told by this woman now aged; his father's wife of the last thirty years, with whom he had lived for only one and then left for a country nearly ten thousand miles away. As he listened to her dry-eyed account, his innate compassion rose from deep within the boundaries of his fear and crossed its barrier from his dead mother to her. He stretched his hand out to take hers. This simple gesture from the gentle young man broke the floodgates and she sobbed with heart-wrenching anguish.

With tears in his own eyes, Alex rose, knelt beside her and took her into his strong young arms. She buried her face in his chest and for the first time since he met her, Alex felt his soul meet hers, and a feeling akin to love and its accompanying peace washed over him.

*

With the new understanding between them, Alex had agreed to stay an extra week with Yung and Feng.

On his return to Shanghai he checked into a spartan room at the YMCA situated in a crowded narrow lane near Nanjing Lu, one of the main city streets. Here, people remained out late on the streets in summer. And this evening, as Alex sat down to pen a letter to his family, the noise from outside his open window made it difficult for him to concentrate. He swept back his curly hair, wiped the tears from his eyes and began the story of Yung's confession. With this new appreciation, he recognised her bravery, her stalwart strength, her loyalty, and in knowing her thus, saw a side of his father which deepened his understanding of the old man. Within his youthful expectations, Alex began to recognise universal love and with it, the fullness of his own dual culture: so different, one from the other, yet so alike in their differences. And it was with this knowledge that he felt he had grown into the heart and mind of his ministry. He knew now what he was meant to do.

Chapter 17

Summer 1910: Dunedin

Emily had just sat the examinations of her third year in medical school and this evening returned from the hospital where she worked during the summer holidays. She entered the kitchen to find her father sitting hunched over a cup of tea with a letter in his hand. Alex! She thrilled to see the Chinese postmark on the envelope beside him.

"He's going to Shandong," Zhou Yu said as he looked up. He was pale but cheered up at sight of her.

She knew from the warmth in the kitchen that he had been home awhile. He was beginning to relegate the running of the business to a reluctant Eddie. But she also knew that Eddie didn't really want to remain in New Zealand for too long. Returning as a grown man, he was still not impressed with Dunedin.

In his quiet way, Eddie seemed to harbour a deep need to move about, to reach out for new adventures into the unknown. She had often wondered how her elder brother, with that morose inner streak, could actually fancy himself an explorer, yet he had done a fair bit of travelling and was determined to do more.

She had listened, wide-eyed, to his adventures in Tsingdao with Ranjit, ending with the latter being stabbed in the back. His account of the pirate ambush in Singapore with the loss of his fingers had made her ill with post-drama worry. And he had confided that he was about to persuade Zhou Yu to give his blessings for his departure. He was confident of a job in Penang, the capital of the Presidency of Straits Settlements, which included Singapore and Malacca.

"I've also heard the golden temples of Siam and Rangoon in Burma are amazing. Then there's the biggest reclining golden Buddha and the emerald Buddha in Bangkok. I've simply got to see them, Em."

"I can't understand where you get your adventurous nature from, Eddie. Why do you have to go? You can make a good life here at home."

"A good life here? Ha!" He shook his head in disbelief. After some consideration, he added, "Well, I suppose my audacity would have come from Pa, what do you think? I mean, he ran off to fight in that Taiping rebellion and then came to Australia and here finally."

"They were things he had to do, not *wanted* to do, Eddie."

"Anyway, I like it out there, you know, Em? There's something that pulls me to that region. Don't know what, can't explain it. Filthy, swampy, mosquito-infested holes they are, really. With pythons that can swallow you whole after crushing you into a soft, long pulp." Now he was enjoying her squirming. "But I like it out there. Besides, Pa should be happy that I am looking out for a wife, carry on the Zhou name."

"Are you?"

"Sure, there have been proper settlements of Chinese for hundreds of years. There are lots of Chinese women in Malaya. The ones in Penang have a reputation for beauty. And the food is much better there. After the East, who can stomach the crap here? Honestly, Em, Dunedin stultifies me. It offers me nothing but bad memories. The racism here is still too difficult and I'm not going to get married in China and live apart from my wife and children like Pa did with Mama Yung and Hongyun."

"What about the business?" Emily felt him slipping away.

"He can sell it. It's a decent size now and there are new migrants who would buy it, or he can sell it to any of the old ones who want to expand their holdings. He doesn't need to hand it over to me and certainly not to Alex. No, Em, I cannot stay just to run the business. I can build one for myself in Malaya. There's more scope out there for Chinese. Besides, he's got you and that's the most important thing to him. You are his angel child, Em. You and Alex. I somehow am rather dispensable in the patriarchal love stakes."

He looked at her with a repressed smile. She started to protest but he silenced her with a hand. "Don't think I don't know it, Em, don't think I don't know it."

She remained quiet, pondering. Then she said, "Perhaps you were born too soon, before he could settle down properly with Mama. He said he only brought her out of that *marae* to save her, but you came along too soon. Yes, Eddie, now that I think of it, that's the reason. You chained him to her. Then by the time I arrived, he was inured to the idea."

Eddie nodded. "Anyway, I missed out on both of them. So I'm glad you're here, Em. You and Alex will be the comfort of his old age. But I'm out of here as soon as I can. I know you'll look after them both... and Wiremu." He smiled at her affectionately. "Think you'll marry him?"

"It would upset Pa too much, Eddie. I won't have that. As long as Pa lives, I shan't marry Wiremu."

"Em! That could be many years. What about your own happiness?"

"I am happy, Eddie, just knowing Wiremu loves me and I him. God will decide how things will turn out. Besides, I will have my own work to do. I'll soon be a doctor, remember?"

Eddie squeezed her hand affectionately. "You are a living miracle, Em, do you know that?"

*

October 10, 1911: Shandong Province -- Tsingdao

Alex, now twenty-one and beginning the second year of his ministry, stood gazing out the window of the YMCA hall. China had been declared a republic that morning. The foreign Qing Dynasty was at last over after three hundred years.

Megaphones proclaiming the wondrous news were all over Tsingdao and, as Alex knew, other cities and towns all over the country. Outside in their own courtyard and in others around the city, thousands of firecrackers were blasting acrid smoke. Brilliant fireworks were shooting up high into the night sky.

For months, the missionaries had been discussing the future of China without the Manchus. For forty-seven years, China had been ruled unofficially by Cixi, the Empress Dowager, and the real power behind the Dragon Throne. Cixi had died three years previously in 1908, leaving Emperor Xiantong, reign name of the twelve-year old Puyi, as head of the vast, crumbling, empire; rotted from within by warlords, poverty and opium and ravaged from without by the confederacy of eight foreign powers.

The old saying that China would be destroyed by a woman had proven true. Cixi had seized and held power for forty-seven years, playing puppet master within the Forbidden City. But she had not been strong enough to stand up to the foreigners, had vacillated between them and the Boxers, and had finally allowed the foreign powers to bring China to her knees, ripe for disembowelment by their superior military and naval strength.

The missionaries agreed that there would be little peace in China for a very long time. The firecrackers of this day, the tenth of October – Double Ten as they would soon shorten it to – were really the sound of portents to come.

"The worst thing about disunity in China is their penchant for finding scapegoats," James Wilson from Cincinnati said as he stood watching beside Alex at the window.

A short, bitter chuckle came from behind them. "Yes, and in the last century, missionaries and their converts filled that role."

Alex turned to the speaker who was Richard Dempsey, a Californian. Dempsey tamped his pipe and lit it. The smoke wreathing around his greying moustache made him squint, despite his glasses. Dempsey was one of the survivors of the fifty-five-day siege of Beijing. Though Alex had tried to lure stories out of him, he had been reluctant to talk about the siege, or the slaughter of missionaries and their Chinese converts.

"Best to let the dead bury the dead, son," he had said each time. "Look to the future, umm?" But there was a certain look in his eyes that refused to be buried.

Alex turned back to the window. His thoughts drifted south to Dunedin, where Emily had two more years to go before graduating, where his father was holding out against selling a part of his business to an old friend who already owned a couple of restaurants and wanted something new for his China-born third son to work at...

To Eddie, who was somewhere in South-East Asia looking for a new life or a good wife, whichever came first, his last letter had said.

A woman passed by the window, a cleaner in the kitchen and one of the Y's converts, who reminded him of Yung, thereby turning his thoughts to that peaceful farm in Suzhou county. Their last letter had been positive. The troubles in the towns and cities had not reached them, though Feng Wen Kai had developed a truculent cough which refused to go away. *Please God,* he prayed, *please keep them safe from any hostility*

He asked of the two older men, "Do you think it'll be safe enough to go inland? Brother Huan wants to bring some bibles and exercise books to the little school in his village."

"Best wait a day or two, Alex, see how long this celebration will last. One can never tell when a peaceful demonstration can turn into a riot at times like this," Dempsey advised.

"Look at Brother Matthew," Wilson said, indicating with his chin.

In the courtyard, a young man in a grey gown had laughingly cut off his queue with a pair of sharp scissors and was lining others up to do the service for them.

"Liberation, at last, from this bondage," he was saying.

"But look," Alex chuckled. He pointed to an old man haranguing the crowd. "Old Lao Gu is not having a bar of it."

"Years of repression do succeed in brainwashing people. Lao Gu's never had his hair cut, he's had that queue for over sixty years under pain of death. He can't trust anything after all the turmoil his generation's lived through, poor devil."

"This is not the end of turmoil in China, Alex. I can bet my month's tobacco allowance there will be no peace in this country for at least another hundred years."

"Why do you say that?" Alex asked, turning round to Dempsey.

"They've never had peace at any time in their history, not for long anyway. It's too large a country, with too many different factions, too many different people, too many languages and dialects. You've been here long enough to see how feisty they can be, under their subservient demeanour. No, Alex, there will not be peace here for a very long time."

"Richard is right, unfortunately," Wilson said, nodding. "We'll see a lot more unrest yet."

Alex sank into his own reverie. They were right. China was no different now than in his father's days of the Taiping Rebellion. It was the Chinese curse to be born and to die in bloody continuum. *That's why there are so many of them – the mill of fate needs a never ending supply of grain to grind.*

*

Uncertain Lives

The young teacher stood at the door of the two-room school as he watched his neighbour, Huan Tse Tung, approach with the towering dark foreigner beside him. Huan had left the village five years previously to work at the beer distillery owned by the hated Germans. Tsingdao Beer. The name galled him. The Germans might have used the name of the port as a brand, but to his mind that only heaped insult on injury.

The approaching foreigner was not the first one he had seen since his father was executed thirteen years ago up on that spirit hill close by. That hill, which, since that fateful day, nobody would ascend needlessly, certainly not at night; the souls of the executed might decide to pay a haunting. Much as the dead were venerated, the villagers preferred their ghosts to keep distant. And they all made sure of this by burning much paper money with offerings of food every year at *Chingming*, All Souls' Day. They wanted their dead to protect them, but to remain unseen.

Feng Hua had been to Tsingdao once, when he had accompanied his mother's cousin, Uncle Li Quang, to buy provisions for his sundry store. There, he had taken time to wander about the narrow streets, away from the dreaded, wider foreign-patrolled routes, to hunt for some candied haws for his mother. Then he saw them. The two dark foreigners. One the colour of soy sauce with wavy hair and a clipped beard, like those who policed the port, and the other looking not too much different from this one now approaching – the curly hair, the same skin tone. He remembered his rage when he saw them pass, talking and walking like all damned foreigners, like they owned the land. And he had taken the small knife from his belt and plunged it into the Indian's back, then run away, so frightened was he by that unthinking, rage-filled action. He had wiped the knife clean of blood on a rag by the side of the dirt street. Had boasted of it to his uncle on the way home, when his fear of being caught had vanished in the safety of the countryside.

Now this big foreigner was smiling at him as he transferred the heavy sack from his shoulders to the floor.

"*Ni hao,*" the foreigner said.

The children clustered noisily around, greeting Huan Tse Tung.

"What have you brought for us, Huan Laoshi?" they chorused.

"*Ni hao,* Xiao Hua," Huan smiled as he, too, shucked his burden. "Hey, children, Brother Alex and I have brought you books and writing sticks and brushes and inks."

And damned bibles, thought Feng Hua to himself. *They won't feed us, but the rest will be useful.* He forced himself to smile.

He was taken aback by the foreigner's fluency in *putong hua*, Mandarin, used by the more educated, and by his polite kowtows.

Now Huan introduced him. "Brother Alex is from a far-away country called *Xin Xi Lan* and his father was born Suzhou."

"Suzhou!" everyone shouted in surprise. "Does that mean he is Chinese? He doesn't look Chinese!"

Feng Hua and Huan turned to Alex, waiting for his explanation. It came rather tersely. "My mother was a native of *Xin Xi Lan.*"

The giggles from the children no longer fazed Alex. It was all part of his life here now.

Feng Hua turned to Huan, who was unloading the contents of the two sacks neatly onto the small teacher's desk. "I've never heard of *Xin Xi Lan.* Where is that? Is it one of the countries stealing our land?" he whispered.

"No, it's not. It is a colony of the English, though, far to the south near New Gold Mountain where our Guangzhou brothers go to dig for gold."

"This one's not like other foreigners."

"No, he's actually very kind, very understanding and he speaks our language almost perfectly. He's a missionary."

"My father killed missionaries," Feng Hua insisted, belligerent.

"Please, Xiao Hua, those times have gone. I live amongst them and believe me, their intentions are honourable."

"You are easily bribed," Feng Hua accused under his breath.

Huan sighed, "No, not easily bribed, but I find reasoning easier than you do."

"Well, I don't want the bibles," Feng Hua insisted as he flicked the three offending tomes with his right hand.

"Why not just use them as a philosophical guide?" Huan suggested.

"We have our own philosophers."

"Be open, Xiao Hua. We are a republic now, and it is time to go out into the rest of the world, to test what we are as a nation. We shall be strong again, on the same terms with the West. No longer will we be despised."

Feng Hua sneered and turned to the noisy class. The foreigner was proving to be a big hit with the children. *Damn him.*

Chapter 18

Winter 1912: Berkeley -- Dr Victor Zhou Hongyun

Hongyun parked his black Model T runabout by the kerb fronting his apartment house, and clipped the canopy into place on the windscreen. He left the locked car in its usual parking space and hurried up the short walk to the front door. The large, double-storey Victorian building, painted white with blue-trimmed windows and front door, was divided into four self-contained apartments. He had taken the lease of one on the second floor as soon as he had finished his internship at the General Hospital. By careful saving and the extra five dollars he got from Zhou Yu each month, he was able to pay for his car in full as a graduation present to himself. It had cost six hundred and eighty dollars with all the additions. The pride he felt each time he cruised it around town, drawing attention from the crowds he passed, made up for all the slights he had encountered in America. He no longer cared whether the looks he attracted were of envy or admiration. He was a doctor, with an American name which he had asked the university to pen into his degree certificate, and with his new salary, he was able to move into a more salubrious neighbourhood.

Now he undressed quickly, showered, put on fresh clothes and rushed into the small kitchen to prepare dinner. Tuesday evening was his time with Dexter, a weekly tryst of stolen bliss. They had to meet in his apartment, to keep secret from Dexter's blonde wife and three blond children. To keep secret from the entire world.

As Hongyun put two pieces of T-bone steak under the grill and started to toss the salad, he heard Dexter turn the key and enter with his medical bag and a large tome under his arm. He always brought these. The importance of a professional visit was an important part of Dexter's façade.

The big American's blond hair was beginning to silver at the temples though his face, at thirty-three, was still fresh and unlined. The clear light of his blue eyes usually thrilled Hongyun but this evening they were shaded, deeply troubled. Hongyun rushed up eagerly to kiss him full on the mouth.

"What's wrong?" Hongyun asked as Dexter held him away. But before Dexter could reply, Hongyun moved to the refrigerator and brought out two bottles of beer. He uncapped them, handed one to his lover and took a swig of his own. "What is it?"

Dexter sat down on the plump, striped sofa and gulped his beer, his Adam's apple moving with each swallow. He could not bring himself to speak and kept his eyes averted.

Hongyun waited, leaning against the writing desk by the wall, watching his handsome friend's face flit through a dozen dark emotions. With each, his heart sank further. He could guess what the problem was: there was always only the one problem, but he refused to acknowledge the doubt that now sprang up.

The odour of burning meat rushed him to the grill. With a gloved hand, he grabbed the tray of blackened, smouldering steaks and dumped them into the sink.

"Well, that's dinner," he muttered aloud and walked back to Dexter. He sat down beside him. Timorously, he took the large hand in his more delicate one. Even in this uneasy situation, their difference in size pleased him. He always took pleasure in their clutched hands. Dexter's, large and pink, strong and square with blond hairs and his, ivory-toned, long-fingered, almost feminine by comparison. Dexter let his hand remain still, unresponsive and Hongyun knew what he was trying to say, once he found the courage, the voice. So they sat for a long time, with Dexter taking quiet sips of his beer. Hongyun's was still on the kitchen bench where he left it during his rescue of the burning steaks.

"Esther found out," Dexter finally whispered.

"How?"

Dexter shook his head. "Damned if I know. I never say anything at home." He turned to face Hongyun. "Do you? Do you speak of us, of me in any way?"

Hongyun shook his head, gazing into the middle distance as he tried to think of any occasion when he might have let slip a word, a phrase that might have revealed their relationship. The only thing he was ever adamant about was keeping his Tuesday nights free and Dexter had also done the same. But it had not always worked out, of course, what with their full hospital schedules and Dexter's family commitments.

"What did she say?"

Dexter cupped his face in his hands. "It was the most awful row. She screeched through every gamut of emotions. She threatened to expose me, ruin me, before she realised that it would also ruin her. She called me all sorts of names. I never thought she even knew such."

"What about the children?"

"They're okay; they were already in bed. Thank God for small mercies."

"What will you do, Dexter?" Hongyun prayed for the inevitable not to be spoken.

"What we've always agreed on, Victor: to stop seeing each other if we were ever suspected." Dexter turned a reddened face to Hongyun.

Hongyun withdrew his hand. He looked towards the kitchen, his eyes hardening, his lips setting into grim lines.

"I'm sorry, I'm so sorry," Dexter muttered.

"It's all right for you. You have a marriage to fall back on, children. The pillar of your society, you are. And now, no more of your Christian bloody guilt," Hongyun spat.

"We can still be friends," Dexter said lamely. "We've survived so much together."

"Yes, I'll never hear enough of that damned earthquake when you rescued me from under the rubble of the frat house. Nor how you carried me out of Yosemite that first weekend tramping," Hong Zhou Yun said bitterly. "I suppose next you'll say I owe you my life."

Dexter shook his head, hurt. "I'll never say that, Hongyun. You know our kind of love is forbidden. We'll both be ruined, imprisoned even. And in my case, there are others to consider. I don't want to lose my children. They're all the family I have now."

"And your Christian beliefs," Hongyun countered. "You'll no longer feel guilty for loving a heathen man, for fucking a heathen man." He spat again.

"And that, yes," Dexter whispered, his head bowed. Then he began to weep, his shoulders shaking as he covered his face.

Hongyun knelt before him, removed his hands from his face and kissed him fervently. After a moment, Dexter returned the kiss through his tears. He gasped and moaned as he opened his mouth to receive Hongyun's tongue. His large hands held Hongyun's head, kneaded his ears, his hair, moved down to his crotch.

Thus, with their juices mingling, they made love, grunting with surging, angry, hungry lust until both burst with agonising release.

Hongyun collapsed, Dexter's heaviness pressing on him, securing the length of him fast to the rug beneath. Dexter's breath panted hot into his ear, Dexter's large hands imprisoning his own.

"'How can I let you go?" Hongyun whimpered.
Silence from above.

Hongyun lay there long after he had grown cold. Long after Dexter had let himself out of the flat, leaving his key to the apartment on the writing table. He remained so till the tears dried up, till he could weep no more.

*

Dexter blew his nose and gave his face a final wipe of his handkerchief. His face set into a resolute expression as he left the Victorian mansion. He decided to walk the three miles home. The evening was turning very cold. He wrapped his scarf tighter round his neck, pulled his derby lower down his forehead and set off into the west wind. He was determined this would be truly the final time he had to go through with this. He had tried twice before.

He hated what Hongyun represented: the people who had belittled his father with airs of their own perceived cultural and historical superiority. The people whose malevolent minions had finally slaughtered his family.

He hated all that Hongyun stood for, yet had been enmeshed all these years by the adoration of his dark sloe eyes and their deep physical connection. How could something so vile, so sinful, so completely against all that he believed in, be so deeply enthralling?

The first time he tried to escape by marrying Esther, the daughter of one of his uncle's close friends and a fishing companion. Esther with her pretty face, her prim, ladylike manners, who knew where she stood, where *they all* stood, where every cog in their lives fitted. Esther provided him comfort and two lovely daughters before finally birthing Roddy, who completed their perfect family. Esther, with her big clan of relatives who always rallied around for all the important occasions of American life. No, his life was here, out here in the open with Esther and the children. His children who reminded him of his younger brothers and sisters killed by Hongyun's Chinese. No. NO! Hongyun must not, *must not* intrude, must no longer be the dark presence hovering in the shadows where, at times of sanity, he dared not peek. For he knew that was where damnation sat and brooded.

Esther had not discovered his secret. He had lied. How well he had lied! He hated himself for this sin, but it meant the bigger one would be erased. What did the Bible say about deceit? He could not remember.

1912: London -- Christmas holidays

James Hopkins left his surgery in Harley Street after bidding his receptionist and partner, William Hanson, a cardio-vascular surgeon, the best of the season. He was returning to Bournemouth to spend the few days of the Christmas break with his widower father and his sister Margaret and her family. At thirty-one, James had matured into a more considerate man than he had been at medical school. He had decided to specialise in osteopathy and, what with one thing or another, none of which he considered his own fault, had still not married. Hence, the annual Christmas trip back to the only family he had in the town where his father was born.

This Christmas promised to be a dull, wet one. The temperature was not cold enough for snow and in its place fell rain that dampened everybody's mood. Anyway, Margaret would make sure their father's house would be cheery and her own would have all the warmth and fragrance of baking they had enjoyed in Granny Hopkins' time. Margaret, with her mild-mannered school-teacher husband Patrick and their two boys.

Pater, whose sad eyes filmed over with memories of his mission days in Macau. Who was always banging on about the Chinese, his fellow missionaries, and most of all, Joan, James' mother, his partner-in-ministration in the name of the Lord. Pater, who put the plight of the Chinese before his own children. Who always insisted they polished off their small meals of rice because their heathen brethren just outside their mission walls would give their eye teeth to have such food.

And stick-thin Mater who was always too tired, at the end of each day, to minister to him and Margaret and whose ectopian pregnancy made any more children impossible. *Thank God for that; no more little Hopkinses to suffer for their parents' zeal.*

She had never fully recovered from that operation that had nearly killed her in the backward hell-hole of swampy Macau. And no sooner had they stepped back on English soil than she died.

Now he, James, was going to have to relive those days, because he had to stay with his Pater for the holidays. Granny Hopkins' cottage, which Pater inherited five years ago, had the spare room Margaret's house lacked. His Pater who had lost all heart with the death of his partner-in-crime and his own worsening macular degeneration needed James' ears to rant to.

I'm growing too hard, James told himself as he settled into the warm first class compartment. *I should get married, but to whom?*

Lady Veronica, Sir Peter Flavell's daughter and heiress who was his most ardent admirer, had finally flounced off after waiting around for eighteen months. He had understood that eighteen months of being stood up or left in the middle of whatever fashionable restaurant or party while he was in the operating rooms at St Thomas' was too much for any woman to endure. But she had taken her revenge by marrying Sir John Arkins, his professor at the London Medical School. At least he was available. Why wouldn't he be? He was a semi-retired boffin. But he was also independently wealthy from his family's slate business in Wales and he had time.

Chapter 19

February 1912: Penang-- Spring Festival,

In the small bathroom of his rooming house, Eddie doused cold water over himself to rinse off the soapsuds as he whistled the tune of 'A Happy Wanderer' remembered from his school days. This evening he had been invited to a New Year's dinner at the home of Chan Koh Fong, a prosperous businessman in town with *a daughter!*

Eddie had begun to feel the desperation of a single man at a time when all respectable men were married and safe from the temptation of brothels in seedy lanes. Then out of the blue, one of his colleagues at the Town Hall where he worked as Chief Clerk announced he had found a suitable match for him.

He had then met with Chan Koh Fong and his *taitai* a few times, had had their circumstances explained to him and, in turn, had satisfied them with his family background.

That his English was impeccable and he was fluent in several dialects of Chinese, particularly Mandarin, spoken and written, had put him in a class well above the rest of the Chinese in Penang.

That he had a brother who had graduated as a doctor in San Francisco induced exclamations of "Whaaa!" That his sister was studying medicine at university produced incredulous questioning as to how that was possible, a girl studying to be a doctor? That he had grown up in a prestigious American mission school in Shanghai and that his father was a successful immigrant in a British dominion secured him such a favourable place in Chan Koh Fong's esteem that he was left wondering why he'd had to wait this long to be snapped up.

But as he combed his curly hair in front of the small mirror in his bedroom, he knew why. With his deeply tanned complexion, his curly hair and unusual height, he did not fit the bill of an average Chinese. He was half-caste and the Chinese did not like to marry their daughters to such. Who knew what the progeny would be like? Who knew what abnormalities he carried in his blood and bones? Besides, his missing fingers presented a sinister hint at an unsavoury past. He had heard it whispered by those not in the know that he was perhaps a triad fugitive.

*

Eddie arrived at the Chan townhouse, one in a row fronting the paved granite courtyard of the Chan clan temple in the better part of Georgetown. Large, elongated red lanterns hung on each side of the door on the veranda, the good luck character painted in bold black calligraphy on each. He rapped the bronze lion-head knocker. Soon a high female voice approached. A middle-aged woman opened the door, took one look at Eddie and burst into an excited smile.

"*Ayah,* you must be the foreigner come for dinner. Come in, I will announce you."

Eddie entered, handing her the red parcel of fruit and nuts he had brought. She shuffled, dragging her flip flops, through to the interior, which, as Eddie discovered, was a high, bright courtyard open to the sky. A living/dining area filled with large, dark rosewood furniture lay behind it. Steps leading to the upstairs quarters were on his right along the corridor. The courtyard itself had a granite slab floor sloping gently to a shallow drain on the south side for the rain runoff. Pots of orchids, bougainvillea and wide-leaved rubber plants were placed tastefully on metal shelves along the wall opposite the stairs. In the comparative darkness of the dining room, a figure rose to greet him.

Chan Koh Fong, a plump man with an alert though kindly face, had, like overseas-Chinese everywhere, cut off his queue. His grey, thinning hair now lay flattened on his round head. His short, clipped, western moustache gave a debonair finish to his red brocade jacket and black trousers. Beside him, also rising to her feet was his equally plump wife, in a long, straight-cut gown of deep green silk with red piping along its inch-high collar and short sleeves. Her pleasant face would have been pretty in

141

youth. Between them was Eddie's colleague who had orchestrated the potential marriage. This Chan Wei Hing was a member of the Chan clan and a cousin to Chan Koh Fong. He introduced his wife, a pretty woman from Amoy, and their two boys aged nine and eleven who kowtowed obediently. All exchanged New Year greetings with polite bows.

After a round of *moutai jiu*, the sorghum wine prized by Chinese but personally dreaded by Eddie, Chan *taitai*, his prospective mother-in-law, tottered out onto the open courtyard on her bound feet and shouted upwards, "Daughter, it's time to come down."

A sullen voice answered, "I won't be long."

Eddie's heart was a-flutter. This was it, this was serious; *this* was his future in the making.

He had been delighted with the photograph Chan *taitai* proudly showed him at their first meeting. Now he waited with a thumping heart and a slight, nervous smile on his lips as footsteps made their way along the wooden corridor upstairs. Soon beaded silk slippers appeared in view under a pink brocade gown. With slow deliberation, the feet descended. He looked to Chan Wei Hing and his wife, both of whom beamed at him. He stood up as Chan Chingling appeared in full form, catching his breath.

Here was a girl of remarkable beauty. Her high forehead, large almond eyes deep-set above high cheekbones, a slightly hooked nose over a wide mouth and strong chin were all set off in an oval face. She wore her hair coiled at the base of her neck. Now she kept her gaze on him as she approached, fearless. Haughty.

"My daughter, Chingling," Chan said, looking up at Eddie with an anxious smile.

The girl flicked her fan as she bowed. When she straightened, Eddie detected a flicker of an emotion he could not decipher at the corner of her lips. *Scorn?*

"Sit, daughter, have some tea before dinner is served," her father ordered.

*

The maid who had shown Eddie in made the rounds refilling everybody's wine cups and brought Chingling a small glass of cold tea. She accepted it with hauteur and looked straight at Eddie, one corner of her lips twisting upwards as she raised her chin. Eddie knew, as he looked at her, the battles he would have to fight in the future. As everyone waited for him to speak, his head spun with indecision.

It is not too late to pull out, but do I want to pull out? Out of this gorgeous creature's life? What would I be missing?

A beautiful wife who had enough education to be able to read, write and calculate. He had been assured she could keep a sharp eye on the servants, run a neat house and ensure well-cooked meals on the table each day. And her feet were unbound. And… best of all, she came with a dowry handsome enough for a house without borrowing from the bank. But oh, the scorn from those eyes. What else lay behind them?

This is what happens when you marry a rich man's daughter, he thought.

He tried to stare her down as all eyes passed between them, to and fro, to and fro. All waited for one of them to say the first word.

Finally, without taking his eyes off her, he said, "Chan *Lao Yeh*, your daughter is truly beautiful."

Relieved laughter erupted around the table. Chingling smirked, and passed scornful eyes coldly over him.

The servants brought out special dishes to honour the New Year. Chicken braised in succulent black mushrooms, chicken steamed in rice wine, a Beijing roast duck complete with pancake wrappers, julienned carrots and spring onions and sweet, black sauce. Longevity noodles. Fish in its entirety steamed the Cantonese way, garnished with sprigs of spring onions and laced with sesame oil and seeds. Hot soup served in a lovely china tureen with pork, water chestnuts, gingko nuts and ginseng, and roast pork with crispy crackling. It was the best meal Eddie had eaten since arriving in Penang. Then for dessert, an elaborate seven fruits and rice cake, multi-layered, pink, green and white. Finally, an assortment of sweet candy on a frilled glass platter found its way to the centre of the table. And all the time the brandy and *moutai* wine flowed.

Eddie could not take his eyes off the gorgeous stuck-up girl sitting opposite him at the round marble-topped table. The longing in his gaze was noted by everyone who passed congratulatory smiles to each other. The two Mrs Chans started planning the wedding party. Chan Koh Fong's relieved expression went unnoticed by Eddie. Whatever thoughts Chingling had of the whole set-up, she nailed them under her haughty demeanour.

Chapter 20

July 1st 1914: Rumbles From Across the Sea.

Wiremu stood up as Emily entered the small tea shop at the corner of George Street. His whaler had docked two days ago. The envelope he left in her letterbox immediately he came ashore was sealed with wax in order to deter Zhou Yu from opening it. He was only too aware of the old Chinese's antipathy towards him, but after Emily's explanation of her parents' difficult relationship, understood Zhou Yu's predicament.

Now, as he watched her serene approach, he wondered at his amazing luck to be loved by this glorious woman, a recently qualified doctor. He deeply regretted missing her conferment the previous month. He was harpooning whales in the southern ocean, in towering seas straight from hell and covered in blood all over, frozen to his bones in icy winds. Covered in whale blood that formed a skin of red ice all over him. The job made him feel contaminated. He was Maori, and he was killing whales, sacred to his people. But the money had tempted him. He needed the money to win Zhou Yu's approval, to raise himself in the old man's eyes. To be worthy of Emily. Now he was ready to leave that unholy life. The money was no longer reason enough to stay because Emily had assured him she could not hurt her father for all the money in the world – as long as he lived. And she had added that she would then marry him even if he were poorest man in the world. *Well, Zhou Yu won't live forever.*

"Em, dear heart," he whispered as he took both her hands in his rough ones and kissed her on the cheek. After all these years of courtship, she still had the power to make him quiver. "I've missed you badly." He held her at arms' length to appraise her. "You look wonderful."

Emily had matured into a head-turning beauty. Her figure had filled out slightly and her cheeks were smooth, honey-coloured. She wore her long hair in a chignon under her stylish felt hat, its wide brim complementing her large sloe eyes to perfection. The unseasonal cold wind blasting into Dunedin this early July brought her out in a russet coat matching her hat, under which the deep blue of her dress peeked out. Her happiness at seeing him was evident in her wide smile.

She sat down on the chair he pulled out for her and peeled off her kid gloves, one finger at a time, as her eyes flirted with him. Wiremu resumed his seat. He could not take his off her. Zhou Yu, that disapproving old codger, was not stinting with her wardrobe. *She's mine, she's said so, darling wahine. Her pa might as well stop showing her off; she's not interested in anyone but me. But who am I to deserve her? Me, a rough, bloody whaler, and she a doctor. Oh Em, what do you see in this Maori boy, eh?*

"You look so tired, Wiremu," she was saying. "Talk to me."

"Yah, I am exhausted, Em, and sick of it all. I wanna come ashore now, I'm ready."

"What do you want to do, Wiremu, when you come ashore?"

"Marry me," he pleaded, taking her hand, aware of several pairs of eyes turning their way, cold, disapproving. But they could be damned, he was going to touch her all he wanted.

"No, not as long as Pa lives, you know that. Please, don't ask me again."

"I could kill him," he jested and quickly regretted the joke as he saw her reproving look. "Just joking, Em, you know that. Sorry."

"What job will you take on shore?" she asked.

"Perhaps I'll go back to nursing, at your hospital." He chuckled at the thought. "Then we'll really have to hide our relationship, you being a mighty doctor an' all."

She smiled but as she gazed at him, the conversation with her father the evening before came into her mind, killing her happiness...

*

"What do you see in that Maori boy?" Zhou Yu had asked for the umpteenth time. "Daughter, you are not suited for each other. I can find you a good match in Melbourne through my friends or better, one from China. A doctor, qualified in America, like Hongyun. I am sure there is a suitable boy from amongst his Chinese friends in Berkeley. Even if you have to live there, I would prefer that than for you to be here in this… in this… aberration with Wiremu." He thumped his fist on the table.

She had lowered her head, silent.

"You are not sleeping with him, are you?"

No sooner was that out than Zhou Yu clamped his hand over his mouth. Emily stared at him, at this outburst from her circumspect Pa. She shook her head, eyes moist.

"I'm sorry to ask such an unbecoming question, but I am so relieved you are not. I don't want you to have the life I had with your mother, Emily. I want only happiness for you. You deserve it more than anybody I know, daughter. And I want to be able to leave this world knowing that you have a husband to care for you. But that Wiremu is not the one. Not the one, Emily. You do not know how they live, but I do, remember? We are a world apart… a world apart."

And he shuddered with the recollection of his final days at Pita Hohepa's village. He looked across the table at his daughter then turned away at the pity in her eyes.

*

Now, in the crowded café, Wiremu had a change of mood.

"The papers are full of news about that assassination of the Archduke Ferdinand in Sarajevo. There could be a war any day now," he said.

"I pray not. Wars are such a dreadful waste of life, achieving nothing."

"If there is a war, New Zealand will have to fight for England and we will have to take part. Those would be orders."

Emily stared at him. The previous night's confrontation with her Pa still lay heavy on her mood and now Wiremu was bringing up the topic that was rife amongst her colleagues at the hospital. Rife all over town and country.

"I will join up if there's war, Em," Wiremu was saying.

"No! Please don't, Wiremu."

"It will be my duty, Em, like every other man in the country. We are part of England, remember?"

"You are not, I am not. You have no English blood in you. It is not your war."

"I am a British subject and a Maori warrior. I will fight," Wiremu reiterated, surprising himself with the force of his statement. Then, suddenly sad, he murmured, "My ma's dying. She's got tuberculosis."

"Oh, Wiremu, I'm so, so sorry. Shall I go to see her?"

"If you want to but she's had Doc McKenzie for years now. He put her into the sanatorium but they reckon she won't last a month. So, it's one more good reason to come ashore. I wanna spend as much time with her as possible. I reckon I shall get a job at the sanatorium, to be closer to her, like you did with your ma at Seacliff."

Emily said nothing. *What a restless, unforgiving place the world is. We humans are so fragile, so cruel to each other, so unforgiving of each other. Oh Lord, please don't let there be a war.*

"So you must not think of joining up," she said.

"How're your bros?"

"Alex is working with the YMCA in Shandong, that province in the north that is ceded to the Germans. He seems happy there. Eddie married a while back. She's very beautiful but a terrible tyrant. Poor Eddie is having a rather hard time. Apparently, she has a tongue like a whip."

"Ouch," Wiremu grinned. "Any baby coming?"

"No," Emily giggled. "She crosses her legs whenever he's near, so he says."

And Wiremu roared with laughter, picturing the scene. Heads turned again in their direction. Emily giggled. That's what she loved about him; his attitude to life, his bigger than life personality, his warm brown eyes and cheeky grin. His honest approach to his world. Yes, that's what she would tell Pa next time he demanded to know what she saw in Wiremu.

1914: Shandong, China

"It's amazing, isn't it, that an event so far away would cause ripples in this country," James Wilson remarked over dinner at the YMCA.

"Well, the Brits are not letting the Kaiser walk all over Belgium," Richard Dempsey, his Californian counterpart, replied. He slurped at his spoon appreciatively. "At last, cook has managed to make a creamy soup."

"Well, they grow the corn in this province, there's no excuse for not making decent corn soup," James said. "But I guess you mean they've learnt to make it the American way."

Alex, at the opposite side of the table, smiled. He had never tasted creamed corn soup till he came here and he could understand why the Americans loved it. Cooked in a stock of chicken bones and sieved, it was nutritious and heart-warming. Chinese soups were much of a kind: lumps of vegetables and bones in stock of some sort.

"What do you think Woodrow Wilson will do if there is war in Europe?" he asked Dempsey.

"Keep out of it, if he has any sense. Why get involved in something that distant?"

"He'll be in a quandary raising an army to fight the Germans when there are so many German immigrants in the States."

Alex now asked, "Why should the Chinese be concerned?"

"Because of the Germans' occupation of Shandong. They'd desecrated this province, see? This is the Province of Saints to the Chinese. Confucius, Mencius, Lao Tzu; all those sages were born here. This is sacred land and the Germans defiled it. They hadn't been benevolent administrators either. Those Krauts ruled with fists of iron," Dempsey answered.

"And they pillaged coal from all the surrounding areas and shipped it away, using Chinese slave labour," James Wilson added. "Then when the Boxers started retaliating, they came down so hard on the general populace, they will never be forgiven."

"Nor forgotten. These people have the memory of elephants." Dempsey again.

"So going back to Chinese interest in the war in Europe, they will see it as a way of getting back at Germany. And for them to weigh up to the European powers."

"How can the Chinese help?" Alex asked.

"They're determined fighters, as you must know. So if they are armed, they will go. And if they help the Brits win, they may have some say in the return of Shandong. And a cessation to British demands on the ceded territories," Dempsey explained. "That's what Brother Huan tells me, anyway."

"The Japanese are equally harsh on the local population. They won't surrender Tsingdao easily now they've got it. They need coal even more than the Germans," Alex said.

"Yes, whatever happens, China wants to be embroiled. It's her way of regaining face – to be fighting alongside the Allies in Europe," Dempsey concluded as he mopped up the last of his corn soup with a piece of steamed bread.

"They'd be fighting under terrible conditions so far from home, without any chance of furlough," Alex remarked. He reminisced on his own lack of furlough. He'd been in China five years now. He had hoped to go home for a visit, but the YMCA was an American organisation and he was not really under their auspices. They had welcomed his involvement but he was acting on his own and, apart from his food and board, he was not paid, unlike Richard Dempsey and James Wilson. He had come to China on his own, or rather on Alex Don's congregational pocket, and he would have to fund his own passage home. He knew his father would be more than glad to pay for a one-way ticket but he needed a return, to continue his ministry in China.

Alex had always felt more his father's child than his mother's. Horowhai's deteriorating mental condition meant she had little interest to impart any aspect of her culture to her children. Alex, like his elder siblings, had little knowledge of the daily lives of Maori. He was Chinese, with a strong English colonial influence.

Emily's affectionate letters, regular and frequent, came in the same envelope with his father's. Eddie's correspondence was sporadic and Alex Don's infrequent.

Alex Don was having his own problems with his church elders and congregation and was about to transfer to Auckland, way up north. Having launched young Alex onto his favourite mission in his own career, Don now seemed content to let him muck along on his own—to sink or swim.

His last letter, received eight months previously, had said, 'I know that you, more than any young man in my entire acquaintance, will follow your heart and calling. God will show you what to do when the time comes. You have fortitude, my boy, and courage. They won't fail you.'

What is my calling? Alex had asked himself then. *To teach and convert? I feel such a fraud. They are the ones who have something to teach me, something far more relevant to this life than I have. Oh Lord, show me the way.*

When the time comes, when the time comes, he heard in the back of his head.

*

1914: Penang-- Double Ten Day

Eddie looked around the large marble-topped table at Fuzhou Restaurant, the best in Penang. His father-in-law, Chan Koh Fong, was hosting the dinner to celebrate the third anniversary of the founding of the Republic. His own head was already in a fug, having consumed copious amounts of the French brandy that Chan was so fond of.

I swear the old man's keeping half the brandy region in France afloat, he thought, as he gazed languidly round at his newly acquired in-laws. Earlier, he had gone with old Chan to the clan temple near their house to burn joss sticks to the Chan ancestors and to pray for the future of China and the Republicans. Long may they reign and may they never have another lot of sodding emperors inflicted upon them, *ommimotofo, ommimotofo*, amen.

Eddie felt comfortable with his relatives by marriage. Old Chan Koh Fong was an understanding father-in-law, a good man to have on his side. The other men were a friendly bunch of moderately successful businessmen who looked, rather sycophantically, to old Chan for guidance in most things, he

151

being the most successful of them all. He seemed to know all manner of tricks in his dealings with the Malays and Indians around the place.

And he was most relieved and thankful that Eddie had taken Chingling off his hands.

"Truth be told, Eddie-ah," he had confided late one night, when he was well plastered with brandy, "truth be told, you did me a great favour. Ha! That daughter of mine had been a problem that only increased with the years. Beautiful she is, but that mouth of hers! Well, sure, you know by now, right? The poison from that lovely mouth drove me to this," he indicated his glass, swivelling the golden liquid inside. "True, believe me, Eddie-ah, I will forever be grateful to you. You know why I gave you that house? Free of loan from the bank, ah? Just so you won't have any excuse to send her back!"

And he roared with delight at the young man's grim face.

"Take my advice, Eddie-ah, take my advice. Get her knocked up and she'll be too busy to nag. Anything on the way yet? Oh why need I ask, uh? Ma would have been the first to be told... no, to be yelled at. Haha! Then Ma would've yelled at me! That follows every time in our house, have you noticed, uh? Give me the British, the Indians, the triads, any of these, any time, than Chingling in a bad mood. Ahh, well, Eddie-ah, she's your problem now, boy. Good luck to you, and good riddance for me!" And he had laughed till he choked on his spittle.

Eddie had left then, reluctant to return home, but knew there would be hell to pay if he didn't. Chingling would be there waiting in their living room, no matter the hour. She would look austerely at him, and without a word, sniff him for evidence of any house of pleasure he might have gone to that night. On pay day, she would rifle his pockets for the brown envelope with his wages. She kept the money to manage the household with and doled out sufficient for him each day to buy his lunch and coffee at the eateries near the Municipal Offices. After the first month, Eddie had persuaded the chief accounts clerk to separate his pay: one envelope for his wife to find and the other he kept locked in his desk at work.

She had been suspicious when she counted the smaller amount of money. "Where is the rest?"

"There were expenses to be taken out, you know, like when I travelled to Butterworth last month?"

"Surely the government should pay for that?" she demanded. She was not stupid; not Chan Koh Fong's daughter for nothing. And she could count, alas.

Tonight, on Double Ten Day, Eddie mulled over what he had read in the *Straits Times* that morning. The war in Europe was worsening. The first trenches had been dug in the Western Front of France and every side was feeding more and more troops into the campaigns. The British were preparing to send their armies to someplace called Ypres. They were calling on the Dominions – Australia, New Zealand and Canada – to send troops. And tonight, for the first time, he was glad that Alex was in China, safe from it all, safe from recruitment.

After his own foray with the Harbour Board Police in Singapore, and here was his digitless hand to show for it, Eddie was definitely not on the side of any British call-up. Thinking of Singapore, his thoughts went to Ranjit in Delhi, who had returned to college and was now a qualified civil engineer and the unhappy father of two girls.

"The worst curse you can give a man, Eddie," he had written in his letter after the second birth, "is to bless him with many girls. Now I must work that much harder for their bloody dowries, man."

I wouldn't mind a girl, Eddie thought, *a girl like Em.* Fat chance. That damned ice queen was keeping him out of range with her strident voice and crossed legs. *I wonder how long her beauty will last with that dreadful temper, that awful character. Nothing's good enough, no one is ever good enough. No, better I don't have a girl. I can't bear another Chingling. And with my bloody luck, it would be a Chingling and not an Emily.*

*

1914: Berkeley -- Christmas Day

Hongyun sat in the staff cafeteria of the hospital, reading the *San Francisco Chronicle* over a belated breakfast. The front page was filled with reports of the Christmas Truce between the Allies and the Germans on the Western Front. Both sides had mutually agreed to cease shelling each other and to enjoy

Christmas. There were photos of men from both sides meeting in No Man's Land, the land between the trenches, drinking and smoking together, even kicking a ball around.

As he perused the news, his mind wandered to Dexter, who worked at the Medical School and who had successfully avoided him for the last two years. It was the second anniversary of their separation this Christmas. While he had frequented Dexter's usual haunts, even going as far as wandering the corridors of his unit, Dexter had managed to evade him. Till this morning, in the car park. And Dexter had pretended not to see him, had escaped through the nearest door. That hurt. He had nursed the feeling all morning, punishing himself. Now his attention shifted to the newspaper before him. He wondered what Woodrow Wilson would do. The Allies were calling, pressuring America for help. But the president would not commit US troops to a cause not theirs.

I'm sick of all this, Hongyun thought, *I shall be glad to go home and see Ma in the Chinese New Year.* This would be his first time home since he left ten years ago. He had been too busy studying and, upon graduation, working. Till two years ago, it was Dexter who had inadvertently kept him in Berkeley. He had been afraid he would lose Dexter if his back were turned. Now there was nothing to keep him.

Ma's getting old; I must see her before she goes. And Uncle Feng's ill. Must go, must go.

February 1915: Suzhou County

Hongyun entered the farm gate and was astonished to see a big, curly-haired foreigner waiting at the front door. As he walked towards him, the man turned into the house and called out. Yung came running.

"Son, oh son, it is so good to see you home. So good, so good." She wept as she embraced him. He held her tight, his hand stroking her back as he looked over her head to Alex who stood just inside the door, a shy smile on his earnest face. Then Uncle Feng tottered up behind, and held onto Alex's arm as he called out his greeting.

How old they both are, Hongyun thought. He released his mother and walked with her towards the house. He bowed to

Uncle Feng, noting his bald head, the wrinkled, dry skin, the pouches under the tired eyes, the stoop. Then he looked at Alex who had extended his hand. Hongyun clasped it as he studied his half-brother.

"I hadn't expected to see you here," he said flatly.

"Coincidentally, I too thought it was time to visit. Imagine my surprise to know you would be home. They've been living for this day. Thank you for coming."

"It is not your place to thank or not thank me, surely?" Hongyun replied coldly.

Alex was taken aback at this rebuttal. He had hoped Hongyun would be kinder, after all these years. He was a doctor. In Alex's unsophisticated mind, that meant a generic kindness.

Now the old couple led them into the sitting room where the housekeeper was bringing in a kettle of hot water. Lao Ma, the old one Hongyun grew up with, had died. Her replacement, SongSong, bowed to Hongyun with a respectful smile. This was the doctor from America. The master come home. She poured hot water into the teapot on the side table and brought the tray of cups and pot over, with a plate of rice biscuits already set on it.

"Well," said Hongyun looking around. "Nothing has changed, Ma?"

"Only that we are so much older, son, but you, you look wonderful. Doesn't he look wonderful, Alex-ah? Doesn't your big brother look wonderful?"

Yung grasped both men with each hand and looked from one to the other, her face red, snotty, her thinned lips quivering through her tears, her greying hair dishevelled.

Alex nodded, smiling, quiet. He held Yung's hand comfortingly. Hongyun tolerated his mother's excessive emotions, his own smile repressed.

*

After dinner that evening, Hongyun said, "Alex, walk with me," and led the way outside into the frozen cold. "Now, what's your game?"

Alex stood stupefied. "Game?"

"Yeah, what's your game? Why are you here? What business have you here with them?" Hongyun's tone was belligerent.

"I don't know what you are talking about, brother," Alex murmured. He started to walk away, hands in pockets, out through the gate and down to the paddy fields, his curly hair lifting in the breeze.

Hongyun trotted after him. "They are very fond of you, I can see that. What did you do? Why should they be?" He caught up with Alex, grabbed him by the sleeve of his jacket.

Alex turned slowly. "Hongyun, why are you angry with that? You haven't been back for ten years. From what Mama Yung told me, you had money enough to buy a beautiful car, to live in a gorgeous apartment. Why didn't you come back earlier to see them? You knew Uncle Feng has been very sick for a long time. You knew China's been through great unrest all these years. Weren't you worried for them?"

"So you took advantage of my absence? Is that it? You ingratiated yourself into my place?"

"No, I did not. I see them when I can afford to travel down. I know they appreciate that. What have I to gain? What are you accusing me of?"

Hongyun stood staring up at him. He studied the guileless face towering above his. He could find no fault. He hated to see there was no fault.

Finally, he said, spitefully, "Perhaps you want the farm."

"What?" Alex could not believe his ears. "Why would I want the farm? The farm belongs to Pa. Why would I want it?"

Suddenly, Hongyun felt ashamed. He continued staring at this big man, so naïve, so uncomplicated, for as long as he could hold his gaze. Then he dropped his eyes and arm. "I'm sorry." He turned and walked away.

Alex called out through the deadening dark. "You are hurt."

Hongyun hesitated and Alex caught up with him.

"Want to talk about it?"

Hongyun paused, shook his head. No, he would not reveal himself to this stranger, this man so closely related, yet a million miles apart in character.

Chapter 21

*April 1916: The Journey of Ten Thousand Miles and More --
Shandong Province*

"Brother Huan is signing up for the Chinese Labour Corps," Alex
announced at dinner.

"Like half the young men in Shandong," James Wilson said.
"They've been queuing up at the old German silk factory down
by Chong Hua Lu since morning. That's been converted into an
enrolment and medical barracks."

"I've seen enough war and killing to last me the rest of my
life," added Richard Dempsey. "I can't imagine all these men
volunteering to get blown up."

Alex studied his companions. Richard Dempsey had
survived the siege of Beijing. James Wilson had spent his first
years at the Y in Macao in comparative safety before coming up
to Tsingdao after the defeat of the Boxers in 1901. The service
time both had done in China totalled to more than Alex's age.

Now Alex reasoned, "I can see the very poor ones going
because of the financial help to their families, but why the ones
within our compound? They are so much better off here."

"Alex, they have no comprehension of what awaits them
over there. I tried to tell Brother Matthew yesterday. I showed
him the newspapers from home. They look on it as a patriotic
duty, to help China get recognised as a sovereign nation on the
international stage. They hope that the fine principles the Allies
are fighting for in Europe will eventually be applied to them.
This war is China's chance to right some of the wrongs foisted
on them by the eight foreign powers. As to their safety issues,
possibly they think they would be protected by their own
karma. They may be Christians, but their innate heathen beliefs
still lie within them," Dempsey reasoned.

"And the Chinese have never been afraid to die for their principles," Wilson said.

"No, you're right there, James. They never have," Dempsey agreed.

"How many are going?" Alex asked.

Dempsey shrugged. "Who knows? But the Chinese do things in big numbers, and they are recruiting in the south as well, in all the ports – Shanghai, Fuchien, Guangzhou. So who knows?"

"How will they get across to Europe? They have to cross two oceans and another continent, whichever way they go."

"Yes," James Wilson said as he picked up a second helping of steamed bun and turnip pickles with his chopsticks. "The logistics would drive me mad, quite frankly. But they are building a lot of ships down in Shanghai for the war effort. They'll probably send the volunteers over on these when they do the delivery voyages."

"China may as well be actively involved. With all they have lost this would be their big chance to gain reparation. The Boxer Indemnity is on hold meanwhile," Dempsey continued.

"Yes, but the tariffs on everything have been rounded up to a neat 5%. And I hear the Allies have mortgaged the timber forests down south. The poor sods." Wilson put down his chopsticks and wiped his mouth with his handkerchief.

"Can they do that?" Alex asked.

"They can't but they do. You do know that since the Europeans, particularly the British, came to China they have systematically raped the country. We Americans bring mostly our faith, education and trade, but the others came to plunder," Dempsey went on.

"The Church of England does good work here too, Richard. Morrison did a wonderful job spearheading the missions nearly a hundred years ago, and they continue doing a great job," Wilson said.

"It seems whichever way, the Chinese cannot win," Alex summarised. *These are my Pa's people, yet I am speaking of them as though they are a separate entity altogether. What am I really?*

*

The next morning, as Alex was teaching English to a class of boys, he glanced out of the open window to see the school teacher from Brother Huan's village entering their compound. Feng Hua waved to him.

"Why are you here?" Alex asked in Chinese out the window. "Oh, don't tell me, you've come to volunteer for the Labour Corps?"

"Yes, I am on my way to the old silk factory. I thought I would stop by to say hello to Brother Huan," Feng Hua replied.

"Well, you will need a lot of patience and some lunch. I hear the queues are very long. Ask Brother Huan to give you buns and tea. Good luck."

That evening Feng Hua was back, squatting in the compound under the bauhina tree talking to Brother Huan. Alex strolled out to join them.

They rose at his approach.

"All done?" Alex asked.

"Not yet, I must go back tomorrow, but I will be early this time."

"And I shall go with him," said Brother Huan.

"What do you need to do to get accepted?" Alex asked as he sat down on a bench.

"Be healthy and strong. They take care of everything else. They issue us essential clothes and some equipment for travelling and use in Europe," Brother Huan replied, having checked up on the requirements the day before. "I think they will use us in different ways, according to our skills. We will be paid over there and our families here will get allotments."

"Why do you want to go such a long way to help in a war that's not yours?"

"But it is ours," Brother Huan replied. "It is the only way we can regain our pride and our own nationhood from the foreign powers. By participating, we will show the Allies what we Chinese can do, are prepared to do. What sacrifices we are capable of making to earn back that which was taken from us: our self-respect, our honour. So, Brother Alex, this is also a Chinese war, believe it."

"And I want to go because I want to kill Germans," Feng Hua declared.

"Why? What have they done to you?" Alex asked.

And so it was that Alex was the first and only foreigner to be told the story of Feng Hua's father's execution, so many years ago, on that hill outside their village, when he was a little boy of six. As he listened to Feng Hua's narration, another window opened in Alex's mind. One he peeked in and saw the endless reasons for hatred that humankind was capable of and he became afraid for the first time in his life.

*

That night, before he went to bed, Alex wiped the mucus from his nose as he penned a letter home.

'God willing,' he wrote with teary eyes, 'if it be His will, I would find it my duty to go to France to minister to these, the poorest of the poor, who are driven by the sins of the West to salvage their nation's honour by dying in a war not of their making, so far from home.'

*

Back in Dunedin, Zhou Yu shrieked as Emily read the letter to him. He butted his head repeatedly against the parlour door, pounding it with his fists. And cursed Alex Don for sending his youngest son so far away to satisfy his own godforsaken ideals.

As Emily looked on, her own grief, buried so many months with Wiremu's departure for Europe as part of the Native Contingent, welled to the surface. This war, for which none of them owed any dues, was now taking her baby brother. That Alex was volunteering to travel with the Chinese Labour Corps without coming home for a last goodbye broke her heart. She studied his photograph, received six months ago, hanging on the wall beside one of Eddie and his bride on their wedding day.

The sepia photograph showed the mature Alex in Chinese clothes, his round youthful cheeks angled now, his smile tinged with sadness. His wisdom, apparent even as a young boy, had at last fully manifested itself in his soft, round Maori eyes. *You're so beautiful, my darling Alex. Return safely home to us. Pa needs you in his growing frailty. I need you. Come home safe to us. Oh Lord, how I hate this useless, useless war. Thank God Wiremu survived Gallipoli, but where is he now? His last letter mentioned France. Another hell, another hell. Oh, Wiremu, my love, stay alive.*

160

*

In the blistering heat of August, Alex looked back from the gangplank, hemmed in by young men from this part of north China on their first leg to France. Each carried a tote bag stuffed with Government Issue clothes, GI items of daily use in France and some personal effects from home. Each wore a tin bracelet on his left wrist with his number engraved on it. A khaki cap sat on each head. Matching shirt and trousers. They had all been deloused in the Going Away Shed a couple of hours earlier, their uniforms still damp, the smell of disinfectant enveloping them. Silently they made their slow way up the gangplanks and into the bowels of the beautiful, converted liner, the three-funnelled *Empress of Asia*, only four years old. She would take them across the Pacific to British Columbia. Most, like Alex, turned to look back to the wharf but few had anyone to wave goodbye to. They had come from villages a long way outside Tsingdao, this port of departure. Their loved ones could not afford to come to see them off. But for Alex, Richard Dempsey, James Wilson and several Chinese staff of the Y were there to wave a sad goodbye. To him, to Brothers Huan and Matthew and their friend Feng Hua.Sad, tight gestures from the two aging missionaries. They knew what he was going into. They had assured him of their fervent prayers for a short, safe war.

As Alex looked back ashore from the second level deck, he thought of the other time he was on a ship leaving his family at the dock in Dunedin. Then, it had been with trepidation tinged with youthful excitement. This time fear gripped his heart. As he thought of his family, a hopeless loneliness descended upon him.

"I am afraid too, Brother Alex," Huan said at his elbow. The three friends were standing by his side.

"My mother will receive my allotment. That will help her while I kill Germans," Feng Hua said, mustering up a brave voice.

"How long will it take to get to France?" asked Brother Matthew.

"I'm afraid I don't know. It depends on so many factors. We have to traverse two big oceans and a wide continent," Alex replied as he looked around the crowded deck. Few were talking; the reality of the dangerous future was now coming home to them. Indeed, some were fingering prayer beads as they gazed at the receding shores of their homeland.

The *Empress of Asia* carried over 2,500 passengers and crew. It had been refitted with the necessities of a war transport carrier. The cabins of peace time had been converted into bunk rooms and were sparse and clean. Bathrooms and toilets were ample along the corridors but it was the canteens that made the Chinese happiest. The kitchens were staffed by cooks from Shanghai and Singapore. And here, in large pots, was more food than most of them had seen in their entire lives. As they lined up eagerly for their first meal on board, the mood changed to one of conviviality. They had the luxury of soups, with rice and noodles and the kind of dishes many had never encountered before. Even the YMCA brothers were in awe and Alex cheered up considerably.

"This is going to be a wonderful voyage," Brother Huan said with a wide grin.

*

On the second day, the second mate came on deck to see Alex. "Good morning, you'll be Alex Zhou, the New Zealand missionary?"

"Why, yes," Alex replied, happy to be able to speak English so soon.

The young man handed him a folded note. "From the captain, sir. He'd be happy if you can join him at his table from now on."

"Why?"

"For meals, sir. He's extended you an invitation to eat with him for the voyage. It's a great honour to be asked, Alex. May I call you Alex?" said Officer Paul McInnes.

Sure enough, that was what the note said. Alex jumped at the chance instantly. "Please tell him I'm most honoured myself, to be asked."

*

The Western fare of the captain's table soon banished Alex's guilt at this special treatment. He had not realised how much he missed chops, steaks and puddings all these years he had been in China.

162

"You're lucky to be transported by the *Empress*, Alex," Captain Robinson told him one day. "This is a damned decent ship. Many others put the Chinese in quarters just above the cargo holds, if not in the holds themselves. This is a new ship and, God willing, once the war is over, will go back to what she was built for: carrying paying passengers. Hence we've just put in bunks where beds used to be. Yes, you are fortunate. Happy with your bunk? Want a cabin? I can get you a cabin."

And before Alex could protest, he was marched to an officer's cabin a deck above. Luckily his fellows from the Y bore neither grudge nor envy for his special treatment.

"'After all, Brother Alex, you are one of them, so it is only right that you eat with them. No, you must enjoy yourself with your own kind," Matthew assured him.

With this, Alex was reminded once more that in spite of his paternity, he was, and always would be, a foreigner. But he enjoyed the camaraderie of the friendly crew who were informative on the progress of the war and most afternoons he played cards or deck games with whoever was off-duty.

*

After a voyage of two weeks, the *Empress of Asia* arrived in the mist of early autumn at Vancouver. Captain Robinson shook Alex's hand warmly and sent him down below decks to his Chinese.

"You'll stay at William Head while you wait for the Canadian Pacific trains, Alex. It's a long journey, but not too uncomfortable. And the scenery is spectacular. On the other side, you'll board another ship for Calais. Good luck, young man. God go with you and pray for this damned fracas to end soon."

*

William Head, twenty-five miles outside Vancouver, had hastily constructed barracks to quarantine the new arrivals from China. The number of trucks and long hours getting the Chinese from the wharf to the barracks exhausted everybody and exacerbated the tempers of their military guards. Murmurings of discontent spread, especially since they had been given no food since they left the ship. Some ingenious souls had managed to squirrel a few buns from the cafeteria that morning. But the majority mooched about, nursing their hunger pangs and uncertainty in this new land where they were treated with brusque officiousness and a heap of contempt.

"Why are we fenced in by barbed wire?" Feng Hua had asked for everyone.

But Alex did not wish to voice his darkest thoughts as to the reasons why.

By late morning the next day, a minor official of the Canadian Pacific Railway came knocking.

"You the missionary from the Y?" he asked as he looked around at Alex's unkempt companions, wrinkling his nose at the odour of the over-cramped barracks.

"Yes," Alex replied. "I'm Alex Zhou."

"What the hell? I thought you were from New Zealand. You don't look like a Chink. Why have you got a Chink name?"

"My father's Chinese," Alex replied tersely.

"Well, what the hell. I'm telling you that you guys will be leaving tomorrow morning, first light. The box cars are being coupled to the engines as we speak. Now, since you seem to be in charge, I want you to get this clear to your Chinks. They will not be allowed to get off the train at any stop, get me? Not till they reach the East Coast. We won't have any Chinks doing a runner in the prairies."

The hair on Alex's neck bristled with suppressed rage. During their mealtimes on the *Empress of Asia*, Captain Robinson and the officers had told him how dreadfully Chinese workers were treated in the building of this mammoth railroad. How one Chinese died for every mile of track laid. They got the dirtiest and most dangerous jobs and were paid $1 per day out of which they had to pay for their food and equipment. The white labourers, meantime, were paid from $1.50 to $2.50 per day with food and lodgings thrown in. The Chinese lived in tents or box cars, winter and summer, cooked their rice in the open and died of scurvy because they could not afford vegetables or fruit.

"Have you heard of a Chinaman's chance?" the second mate, Paul McInnes, had asked.

Alex had shaken his head.

"It originated with the building of the railroads. It was always the Chinese who were sent in to lay dynamite to blast out the tunnels. A lot were deliberately blown up whilst the Europeans were laying bets on their chances of survival." Now he, Paul, shook his head. "I don't mind admitting, Alex, there are times when I don't like my race."

Then, Alex had felt the despair of his father's people seep through his bones, holding his heart fast. And now, looking down at the pale face of the company clerk, his lips curled with disdain.

"I shall inform them of this, your company's decision, because I hope it is not your own, sir. For a more despicable one I have yet to hear of, this treatment of your fellow men."

The man stared a moment at him before his face reddened, but carried on. "Well, the other thing you are to know is that provisions will be given to them to last till they get to the next town, which will be three days. So they must ration themselves, because there will be no more till then. Good day to you."

He stalked off, followed by the astonished eyes of Brothers Matthew and Huan who had understood enough of his accent to know of the abysmal journey ahead.

"Shall we pass the word, Brother Alex?" Huan asked. Alex nodded. He was too distressed to relay this news to the gathering men.

Oh Lord, give them strength to overcome such hatred. What have they done to deserve this?

*

The siren went at three the next morning. The Chinese woke up to loudspeakers blaring in the cold morning fog. Headlights from the look-out posts shone full beam as they stumbled out of their barracks with their tote bags. Confusion set in. Alex, Matthew and Huan translated the orders from the loudspeakers as they were hustled onto trucks.

"I need to pee," grumbled Feng Hua as he climbed into Alex's truck. Matthew and Huan went into separate trucks to act as translators. Several more volunteers from the Y had also spread themselves thus.

"I'm afraid we'll have to wait till we get to the railway station," Alex said. But during the twenty-five mile ride, the men took turns to urinate into the darkness out the backs of the trucks.

At the railway station, brown paper parcels tied with string were relayed from soldier to soldier from trucks to the entrance. As the Chinese disembarked, they were each given one before they could proceed onto the platform. They balked at sight of the box cars as they streamed into the station.

"They are treating us like cattle," Feng Hua pronounced.

"Yes," Alex said. "But there is nothing we can do about it now, Xiao Feng."

They were hustled down along the platform and counted into the boxcars. Alex could not see to the end of the train. As the boxcars filled, he saw there was only enough room on the floor for sitting. Ventilation slats six inches deep, man-high, ran the entire length of each car on both sides.

"What will they use for toilets?" Alex asked the sergeant in charge.

"There are squat holes at the corners of each car. But you tell them they cannot be used when the train is idling at a station."

Alex, Matthew and Huan announced the message repeatedly up and down the platform as the mass of men were processed.

"There is also a barrel of fresh water in each one," the sergeant shouted as Alex moved away.

A guard approached Alex. "You're the missionary from the Y? You can travel with us in the front. That will be more comfortable for you."

Alex hesitated as he watched the Chinese mount the box cars. When the cars along the length of the platform filled and were locked from the outside, the train shunted down further east to enable empty cars moving in to be filled.

"Thank you, but I will travel with them," he replied.

The entire train was loaded and ready to leave by noon. Alex was the last one to get on. He walked along the length of the platform to bless his fellow travellers in the Shandong dialect.

"God go with you. We will see each other at the other end."

"You speak their lingo well," said the sergeant. "You grew up in China?"

Alex, heartsick, pretended not to hear as he climbed on. The metal bar slammed into place.

As soon as the train picked up speed, Alex's companions opened their parcels to find two loaves of brown bread, and a half pound hunk of cheese in each. They stared at the contents in dismay, their noses wrinkling at the odour of the cheese.

"That is made from milk, so it's better than it smells," Alex told them, "but don't forget they are to last you three days."

"But how can we eat this stinking lump?" asked one.

"You take bites out of it with the bread. Wash it down with water from that barrel. Let's hope the next parcel will be better."

"Alex-ah, this is much worse than prison."

"Yes, it is. Let's pray the ship at the other end will be better."

*

But the journey was much, much worse than a prison. As soon as the train picked up speed, the loud clatter of the wheels chugging along underneath them filled the box cars with ear-shattering roars. The men cramped within shook and shivered with the swaying of the seemingly fragile contraptions they were cooped up in. Alex looked around at his travelling companions. Their grim faces visible in the dim light from the slat windows conveyed the fear of animals being transported to slaughter.

They suffocated in the heat that built up during the day with the sun beating down on the metal boxcars. At night, they froze with the chill of the prairies and mountains. All the time, the intense vulnerability to the elements.

"Alex-ah," his closest companion asked one night, his teeth chattering, "When will this journey to hell end? If I freeze anymore, I shall become an iced carcass. All this would be in vain."

"You'll warm up soon enough when morning comes," said the quivering man beside him. "Then they can deliver us like baked crabs to the ship at the other end."

*

At the second station, soldiers patrolled the length of the train and the drivers and guards were changed. The train shunted forward slowly as more food parcels were handed out and the water barrels in each car replenished

As other doors were noisily slid open, Alex heard the loud voices of approaching guards.

"You smell that lot? Shit! That's what those stinking Chinks pong of. Bloody shit. They're worse than pigs."

The metal door of Alex's car grunted aside. He made his way to the front and was greeted by the startled ruddy faces of several guards with rifles slung over their shoulders, dispensing food parcels from a huge cart. Another stood by with a water pump, ready to hose down the inside of the cars and replenish the water barrels in each. The travellers clambered down for the few minutes to stretch their legs. It was the only time they got a glimpse of the beautiful wilderness of Canada.

"How can such a beautiful country produce such cruel people?" one of them muttered to Alex.

How, indeed, Alex thought to himself.

"If you treat us like pigs, we will smell like pigs. And in this case, we are given less consideration than pigs," he said, calm despite his own disgust of them. Without another word, he put his hands out for the parcels and passed them along to the rest of the men. Huan worked beside him.

"Hey, where did you come from? You ain't one of them?" an astonished guard asked.

Alex knew there was nothing he could do to elevate the position of his charges and chose to ignore the question. He would not give them quarter for gossip in their comfortable barracks.

*

The train took two weeks to reach Halifax on the east coast. By the time they were let out, all, to a man, were weak, sick and dehydrated. Several were dead on arrival and their bodies hauled out and loaded onto a truck. Those alive were too ill to show much concern for their fellows. But at sight of this operation, Alex struggled up to the truck.

"I am their pastor. I need to see who they are," he told the soldiers. "Their deaths must be recorded for their families. And I want to say a prayer for them."

The soldiers looked at him, wrinkling their noses at his close proximity.

"Look, padre, these are going to be processed. We'll get their identities from their wrist bands and inform the authorities at the other end. What are you doing here anyway? They're just a pack a' heathens. Now, we've got lots to do. Scram, okay?"

They shoved him away. Alex stumbled back to rejoin Huan and the others; to be whistled and shouted into trucks that would take them to their huts miles away from port.

*

At the makeshift camp, they were again put into newly-built Nissen huts, half-round, barrel-shaped constructions, fifty men in each sleeping on ground sheets, in the plains outside the port. These too were surrounded by barbed wire and guarded. Here, there were cooks in several hut-kitchens and potatoes and vegetables were on the ready in large pots.

"Well, at least we can fortify ourselves for the next stage, Brother Alex," Matthew said when he saw the food. Alex nodded in silence. Like everybody else, he was much weakened by the horrendous journey and diet of bread and water with the occasional lumps of cheese. After the initial food allotment, cheese was not always included.

*

By the end of a week, the process they went through at William Head was repeated, this time into the holds of several troopships and converted passenger liners.

On his troop ship, Alex was not singled out for preferential treatment. But by now, he had seen enough of his fellow travellers' despair not to wish for any.

All, to a man, suffered severe sea-sickness, compounding the illnesses already present from the train journey. Their excretions, both fore and aft, turned the cramped, airless conditions into a living hell. As the voyage progressed into the countless days and countless nights, his companions succumbed into deep silence occasioned by delirious moans and cries of pain.

"Brother Alex, I think some have passed on," a stricken Huan whispered in English.

Alex looked over the heads of his neighbours in Huan's direction. In the dim light from the small portholes he could see several men near Huan slumped over, looking like they had given up the ghost, with closed or open vacant eyes, mouths agog and dribbled-on chins. *Now I know the conditions African slaves were shipped to America in,* Alex thought as he fought his rising bile. *Lord, please let this nightmare end quickly.*

"We must be certain, Brother Huan. If they are, we must tell the guards when they bring us food," he said, still in English.

But the men revived, and it was some days later before the first body had to be evacuated for sea burial.

"Please let me pray for this soul," Alex begged of the guards as he helped hand the corpse over. "He is one of the Christians from our mission."

Reluctantly, the guards allowed him out of the hold, holding their breaths till they were well away from the opening. Alex heaved himself out and followed them three flights up and along the narrow corridors till they reached the open deck. As he stepped through the heavy metal door, the sudden cold, salty air overwhelmed him, sending him staggering. He grasped the door for support. A guard grabbed his sleeve.

"You're not one of the coolies, what is your role here?"

"I'm their pastor and this poor man was amongst many converts going to the war."

"But you are not Chinese," the guard insisted.

"Half Chinese," Alex gasped. "I was born in New Zealand."

The other guards had let go of the dead man and were now listening with expressions of interest.

The first man said, "You are the worse for wear, pastor, why don't we let you stay on top? We can find you a bunk with the crew."

Every cell in Alex's being shouted in agreement. He looked at the dead man, now lying crumpled on the deck, covered in vomit and excrement and wet from the spume.

"Let us bury him first, while I think about it."

The guards produced a length of heavy chain with which they bound the dead man's ankles as Alex, supporting himself with an arm wrapped round the rail, closed his eyes and prayed. At the end, he bent to sign the cross on the dead man's forehead with his right thumb. At his nod, one guard clipped the numbered wristband from the corpse before the four men picked up the body between them and consigned it over the rail into the waves.

"Well, pastor, what's it to be? Bunk or hold?" the first guard asked, his face puckered against the wind and spume.

"I thank you, but I cannot, with all due consideration to my fellows below, accept. I shall go below. How long before we reach port?"

"Another six days, pastor. We expect our British escorts within the next four. There are torpedoes closer to Europe. Sure you won't come above?"

"No, thank you. But if I can come up to pray for the deceased each time there is a burial, I would be grateful."

"Look, pastor, let's have a cup of tea or some grog before you go down below."

And with that, the men escorted Alex down a flight to the mess.

*

The remaining six days over swelling seas saw a further two deaths before they reached the port of Boulogne-Sur-Mer on the French coast. The Chinese climbed slowly out of their holds, their pale faces squinting against the light, grey though the afternoon was. Most had barely strength enough to hold themselves upright as they were marched down the gangplanks and onto the waiting trains to trundle them the thirty-eight miles south to Noyelles-Sur-Mer, in the Somme, the base camp for the Chinese Labour Corps. They were deposited outside the town and divided by their registered numbers into camps of five hundred men.

Brothers Matthew, Huan and Feng Hua were in the same camp as they had enrolled together. Here too, barbed wire surrounded each camp with one guarded gate. The same barrel-shaped Nissen huts awaited them.

"Look sharp, now, you lot, you have an hour to settle in before work begins," the British lieutenant told them in strangely garbled Mandarin-sounding words.

"Alex-ah, what in a pig's arse is he saying?" one Chinese squeaked.

Now the Englishman noticed Alex, who rose to his full height from his weary slump and said, "Why don't you speak English and I will translate for you? Even I can't understand you."

"What are you doing here? Who are you?"

"If you have time to study your papers, you will see my name down there as the add-on from the YMCA in Shandong."

The lieutenant flicked through his thick book of passenger lists. "Ah, got it here. Reverend Alexander Zhou, Chaplain, New Zealand." He looked up with new respect at Alex who had now drawn nearer.

"God, man, you look bloody awful. Could you please step aside, sir, I will take you to your quarters."

"I am to be quartered separately?" Alex replied as he looked round at his weakened companions.

"Yes, sir, you are to be housed with the officers in town."

Before Alex could interject, Huan said in Chinese, "Brother Alex, you must go with him. If you get sick or die, you will lose the reason you came in the first place."

He turned to the crowd around and saw the general assent.

"You have proven yourself one of us by suffering with us on the journey through Canada and the second ocean. Enough, I say. You must be strong for us from now on. Go with him, Brother Alex. We will not think less of you."

"All right," Alex said as he turned to the young lieutenant. "Surely they can rest awhile before being put to work? They've had a rotten six weeks. Look at them."

"This is a war, Reverend. Our men have had nearly three rotten years. None of us can rest awhile, certainly not these coolies. They will be taken down to the wharves to unload supply ships. When they come back at sundown, they will find provisions in the kitchens. They cook their own meals."

At the look of consternation on Alex's face, Brother Huan reassured him, "We will be all right, Brother Alex. We are Chinese, born to endure remember?"

Chapter 22

January 1917: Dunedin -- A Father Destitute

Eddie stepped off the steamer at Dunedin to be greeted by Emily and Zhou Yu. His father's silver hair and fragility splintered his heart. Deep sadness welled up in Zhou Yu's eyes as he hugged his number two son.

"I have missed you, Eddie, don't think I haven't," he whispered in Chinese.

"And I you, Pa," replied Eddie as he looked at Emily over Zhou Yu's shoulder.

A month ago, Emily had written the fateful letter to bring him home. He was to be here to comfort their Pa whilst she herself went to Europe.

'As I told you of Alex's involvement with the Chinese Labour Corps and his being in France for the duration of the war, I feel I must now do my duty, hateful though I feel it is. Both Wiremu and Alex are putting their lives on the line. So Eddie, I can be of far greater use over there with the Medical Corps and at the same time be closer to them. I want you home to look after Pa. He needs you now; he is broken-hearted over Alex and my going. God willing, we will all return safely. Maybe you are allowed to bring your wife?'

As he read Emily's letter, Eddie's feelings had been mixed. He chuckled drily over the irony of the last sentence. Here was the chance of legitimate escape from his beautiful harridan but the reason for him returning home, the absence of his brother and sister, dampened his spirits.

From all the news, he knew the Western Front was a murderous place. Thousands were sacrificed fruitlessly each month. There were more stalemates than the bowls of rice he consumed each week. So, with Chingling's sharp protest ringing in his ear, he had jumped on the first available ship out of Penang for Singapore and from there had taken a vessel Sydney-bound. And now he was home, having trans-shipped from there.

"When will you leave?" he asked on the bus from the wharf.

"In a week's time. I'm so glad to be able to spend some time with you before I go, Eddie. I shall leave with an easier heart, knowing Pa's got you here."

"I did tell her I can manage," Zhou Yu protested.

"I just don't want you to be alone, Pa," Emily said, clasping his hand.

*

Zhou Yu turned in early after dinner that evening.

As Eddie stood by the kitchen sink drying the plates his sister handed him, he asked, "When was the last time you heard from Wiremu?"

"Three months and five days ago," Emily replied, her expression a misery.

"Is he still alive?"

"Oh, Lord, don't say that, Eddie! He is alive; he's got to be alive." After some hesitation, she added, "I would have heard otherwise."

"Who would the War Office notify now that his mother's dead?"

"His Aunt Marama. And I would be the first person she would tell. So he is alive, please God."

"Poor Em. What you're bearing is far worse than my predicament. I merely need to shut my ears against Chingling and ignore her. How is Alex?"

"He's suffering with the Chinese labourers. Poor Alex, he's just got to participate in others' agony. There's his last letter." She tipped her head towards a thick envelope on the sideboard.

The letter was written on coarse lined paper. Sentences had been blacked out. That there was the need for such censorship must mean the authorities did not like his description of conditions at the camps.

"I promise one of the first things I will do is to seek him out. Seek them both out. Actually, Wiremu would be easier to locate,

174

as he is with the Pioneer Maori Battalion. Alex, however, could be anywhere over the many CLC camps. He was talking of going out to the trenches where most are working."

"Oh God," Eddie moaned.

He took Emily into his arms as she dissolved into tears, up to her elbows in the sudsy water of the basin.

*

A week later, Eddie and Zhou Yu, amidst scores of other weeping families, waved Emily off from the wharf. Both Zhou Yu and Emily had been in tears on and off for the whole week before her departure. Eddie had stood by, a helpless witness to this grief, unable to feel the emotional force behind it. He understood his own sadness, his analysis of their separation, but compared to his father and sister, he felt he was merely audience to a play whose tragedy was insufficient to rip him apart, even as it was ripping the players before him apart.

Have I built a wall around myself all these years? Do I not feel because I am afraid of feeling too much, afraid of being hurt yet again? So different am I to my family... except for Hongyun. Yes, I am like Hongyun after all. We've both isolated ourselves behind our own walls. How is Hongyun?

"How is Hongyun?" he now asked his father as they sat at the kitchen table, Zhou Yu red-eyed and disconsolate, over a cup of green tea.

"Well, I suppose. I haven't heard from him for six months or more. But he must be all right, otherwise I would have heard. At least he won't be going to war."

"How do you know?"

"He's too selfish, too self-centred to put himself in danger for others."

"But he's now an American citizen. He might get drafted."

"He's a doctor. If he gets drafted, he'll be safer than the fighting men. I have less fear for him."

"Em will be safe too, Pa. She'll be working at a proper hospital, not in the field, especially as she's a woman."

"Em has a mission to find Alex and Wiremu. Who knows what peril she'll put herself into?" Zhou Yu replied as he studied

Eddie, seeing his deeply tanned skin, his wavy hair clipped short.

Of the three New Zealand children, Eddie had more of the Chinese look in him. It was his slanted eyes, large though they were, and his high cheekbones that bespoke his Oriental blood.

"Are you happy in Malaya?" Zhou Yu asked.

Slant Eyes nodded with a half chuckle. "Yes, Pa, I'm happy enough, I guess. I've a good job in the Civil Service with decent prospects, a nice house fully paid for, and an understanding father-in-law and all his clansmen. I don't feel lonely, if that's what you mean. I miss you all, but I guess I fill my days over there well enough."

"You don't speak of your wife."

"Ha, well, there is nothing positive to report there."

"What about children?"

"Pa, she won't let me touch her. We sleep in different rooms. And quite frankly, I can't be bothered anymore."

"You can always come home, you know. The business is there waiting."

"Pa, for the last time, I won't live in New Zealand. I was so miserable here, remember? There is much less discrimination in Malaya and that is spread evenly throughout the Asian community. A Chinese can do well there. It's an open frontier. And the food is so much better. I like it there, Pa. Sell the business or wait till Alex comes home. I don't want it."

"It's always the eldest son who takes over a family business," Zhou Yu finished lamely.

"Your eldest son is Hongyun and he's certainly not coming here. Alex will return home though. He was happier than either Em or me in this godforsaken place. The business could be his day job."

Zhou Yu shook his head. "No, I feel in my bones that Alex has discovered his life's work. He will live his life in China, ministering to the poor, and heaven knows, there are plenty of them. I will leave him the farm. He will get his income from it."

"What would Hongyun say about that? He was born and raised there. What about Yung?"

"What about her? She will live out her days in control of it. Don't you know, Alex made peace with her years ago?"

"I heard something like that, but I didn't know it went that far." *Good old Alex.*

"Yes, Alex is truly God's child, Eddie. I only pray God will protect him in this instance." And another tear rolled down Zhou Yu's cheeks.

Eddie held his father's hands as his own eyes moistened. And through his tears he thought, *Perhaps I am not as dead as I feared.*

*

Spring 1917: Berkeley

Hongyun studied the article in the *San Francisco Chronicle* over his morning coffee. *Call up time,* he thought. *Shall I or shall I not?*

Woodrow Wilson had volunteered America into the fray. Registration centres were being set up all over the country to draft young men into the European war and medical personnel were joining up by the dozens every week.

Curtis Novak, an anaesthetist at the hospital and Hongyun's sometime lover, had responded to the call up.

"It's all right for you, you're third-generation American, but why should I risk getting blown up for this country?" Hongyun had defended himself one evening.

Curtis looked at him, long-lashed brown eyes incredulous.

"Victor, you owe it. This country gave you everything you've got."

And Victor Hongyun had looked up stubbornly.

"I've also suffered a great deal of prejudice here, and my people have already given a lot to build this country, unrecognised, un-thanked and despised for their efforts. Died for their efforts. Besides, men like us cannot be open here, being what we are. How would we survive in a military situation? That I would like to know."

"Men like us cannot be open anywhere. But that is beside the point, Victor. Our country is going to war, we do our bit. I'm registering tomorrow."

And he had. So had Mark Denby, also in his year at Med School. And Gene Hicks, and Will Treanor, both general surgeons. And, and, and. The hospital was going to be short-staffed. He should stay. But the way they had looked at him, especially Curtis, who had not called for several days now, made him feel left out. His father had written to say that both his sister and youngest brother were at the Front. Had asked of his intentions.

And he had assured the old man of his intention to stay put. But the next letter from New Zealand held a tinge of disappointment. He was being compared to Alex. *That naïve do-gooder.* That raised his heckles, especially as his mother Yung had also sung Alex's praises for going off to minister to the Chinese Labour Corps. The next day he saw Curtis in the hospital canteen.

"I'm registering, Curtis," he said on impulse.

Curtis' face lit up. "I hoped you would, Victor. That's really raised you in my good books." He squeezed Hongyun's arm.

Encouraged by this gesture, Hongyun begged, "Curtis, I... I was wondering if we could make dinner tonight, please?"

Curtis hesitated a moment, then said, "Sure, why not? I'll cancel tennis."

*

Curtis Kovac, a small man of twenty-eight with a shock of wavy black hair, large, brown eyes, and full sensuous lips, entered Hongyun's apartment to be assailed by the aroma of his favourite Chinese dish. Sweet and sour pork. Hongyun always cooked this for him when he came to dinner. This, and his soya sauce chicken which, as always, was accompanied by a variety of sautéed vegetables with garlic.

Garlic was a main component of Curtis' diet. Both his Italian mother and paternal *nagyanya* frequently incorporated it in their pasta and Hungarian dishes. But he was always careful not to eat it before work or a social occasion. The Anglos did not like the stink, as one nurse told him one day. She was lovely, that Sarah Holmes, and he had asked her out to a movie. But he could not resist a forkful of his mother's famous spaghetti con vongole in passing on his way to pick Sarah up. That ended the romance before it had really begun. However, an evening with Victor Zhou Hongyun was always perfect. Good garlicky food followed by great sex without any preliminaries.

178

Victor could be a problem if they were stationed together in the war. Curtis was comfortable with either gender. Victor, however, was totally homosexual; he was nothing if not consistent, and dangerously needy. That very emotional lack of Victor's had put Curtis in an occasional quandary with several stand-off periods in the last eight months of their year-long relationship. Victor considered consorting with the opposite sex a betrayal. It was all or nothing with Victor. *It will be a dilemma, all right, in the army.*

Hongyun wrote home to his mother of his joining up. Her reply, worry-filled, tear-smudged, arrived a week before he sailed. His father, Zhou Yu, sent his blessings and praise, calling his action "unselfish and not quite what I expected from you", which made him fume.

*

Hongyun's unit of the American Expeditionary Forces Medical Corps was taken by train to New York, the gathering point of military personnel from the entire country, where they boarded the waiting military carrier immediately. They were the first of the American forces to be shipped out. There were three other vessels apart from Hongyun's. The mood on board the troop carrier was light as the young doctors from Hongyun's unit mixed easily with officers from the other divisions. A day out of New York, the weather turned. Early morning fog surrounded their ship as it steamed silently through the cold waters of the North Atlantic.

"We've got to be on the lookout as we enter British waters," one of the engineers told them. "Apart from their U-boats patrolling the area, the Huns are mining the seas. Keep your life jackets handy."

*

Hongyun, like every other man on board the carrier, did not know what to expect. That the numbers would be great had been proven to them from the time they boarded the train in San Francisco. It was brought home to them in New York as they piled, all two thousand of them, into each troop ship.

He found Curtis on deck smoking a cigarette.

"We are just one of three at the moment," Curtis said, indicating the carriers. "There'll be dozens more coming into

179

operation. I hear the commitment is for several hundred thousand men, maybe a million, depending on how long the war continues for."

"Are you scared?" Hongyun whispered as he gazed at the hazy horizon.

"Not yet," Curtis replied, his face grimly set. "I know conditions will be hell. Ten hour shifts under bombardment if we're unlucky. I've been reading up on all the sickness and diseases we will encounter, apart from the broken bones and spilled guts. Victor, the only consolation we have is that we will be saving lives, not destroying them. What about you, are you scared?"

"Petrified, actually."

*

They were escorted in convoy by a British destroyer from Portsmouth to the large ship-building city of Saint Nazaire in the Bay of Biscay. The other two ships went further up, to Brest and Boulogne-Sur-Mer. At Saint Nazaire, they had two days to wait for trains to transport them north. Two days to spend in the bars of the port. Two thousand, five hundred footloose young men with money leaping from their pockets made a huge, cheerful impression on the war-weary port. Prostitutes turned up in force, from teenagers to middle-aged women and older, many who, till the war, had worked in city factories and on farms. Nearly three years into the war, they had to resort to the oldest trade in the world to feed their families. In port, the wine ran out, the beer ran out, the coffee ran out, but the women kept coming in.

"All we can get in exchange for cigarettes and chocolate," said one of the sailors.

Or whatever they could buy at the PX on board or pilfer from the mess.

*

The second night, Hongyun was coming out on deck for a smoke when he glanced down to the grille iron gate of the wharf. Curtis was in a small group of soldiers chatting up some women who were comparatively young. Their outfits had seen better days. He watched them all stroll off, arm in arm, laughing, past the long line of sheds into the dark town. He

180

grabbed the railing in mounting rage. Curtis was up to his old tricks, the ambivalent bastard. Since they had been on board, they had snatched three unsatisfactory quick connections in the ship toilets. And now he was going for a knee trembler in some dark alley with a French whore. *Damn him. Damn him. Traitor!*

*

Early August 1917: Paris

Waves fifteen feet high swamped the ferry transporting the medical unit and part of the British 2nd Army to Calais. When it finally docked on the French coast, hundreds of troops, soaked to the skin, emerged from the bowels of the ship followed by jeeps and trucks carrying military arsenal into the gloom. The rain they left with in Dover had followed them across the Channel and now they marched to the trains waiting nearby on tracks specially laid for the war. They filed in, cold, wet and reluctant.

James Hopkins and his fellow officers settled into the first-class compartments. He looked out the window, past the rivulets of rain, to the darkening town. He was returning after his second furlough and the thought of the carnage on the Front made him grind his teeth. On this trip, he was taking young Michael Ladrow, fresh from the operating rooms of St Thomas' Hospital. Lady Ladrow, Michael's mother, had personally entrusted her only son to his care the week before when she invited him to tea at her home in Chelsea.

"I would feel so much more at ease, James darling, if I knew you were keeping an eye on him," she had pressed, her violet-blue eyes beseeching him in a face still free from the devastation of time.

"I promise to do my best, Lydia," he had said, falling, as always, under her charm, as he remembered their short relationship of a few years back. She had just then lost her husband of twenty-two years and he was on hand to comfort the bereaved beauty. He had taken an interest in her son who was in his last year at university.

Now he gazed across at the young man with an uxorious smile. Michael had inherited his mother's beautiful eyes, but the wavy black hair and aquiline nose came from his Irish father. Like his father, he was tall and lean. Lord Ladrow's ancestors had made their fortune in Northern Ireland when they went across with Cromwell and stayed to farm the huge swathes of seized land. They later progressed into industry at the start of the Industrial Revolution; the Ladrows were always a step ahead. Peter Ladrow had met Lydia Montieth at a supper party, fallen in love with the debutante and married her. Only Michael had graced their successful marriage.

This young doctor, remarkably unspoiled and ingenuous, was heir to millions back in Belfast. Michael could have gone into the family's huge business, but chose instead to pursue medicine. Lydia had once explained that on her side of the family there had been an uncle who was a missionary doctor in China. Perhaps that was where he got his altruistic nature from, she had sighed, as they finished a cigarette between them in his bedroom.

Looking at him, James felt a twinge of regret that he had not married and perhaps sired a son just like this one. *And now he is my responsibility,* thought James.

"Feeling okay?" he asked.

The young man nodded with a little smile, but his eyes told another story.

There had been too many reports of carnage and he, Michael, had actually worked on some of them at St Thomas' hospital. But like all aristocrats, he had felt it his duty to sign up, to subject himself to horrors that would surely remain with him all his life. For who could ever forget what he had seen in the operating theatre? How much worse it must be in the field. But he could not feel easy, staying safe in England when fellows his age were being blown up in the trenches. When many of his schoolmates were having their feet, festering with trench disease, amputated, or were dying from typhus, dysentery, cholera and heaven knew what else. No, he would never be able to hold his head up high, or look himself in the mirror, if he did not volunteer to do his bit. His bit for God, king and country, even though some factions of his father's people were rumbling against the king's men and demanding independence. But then his mother was a king's woman and he was born in London; an Englishman by birth as were his early ancestors in Cromwell's England.

Chapter 23

October 1917: The Rumbling Earth.

There were other YMCA missionaries in France and Belgium dispersed in other camps all over the Front, in ravaged villages and towns close to the lines. From there they would visit the Chinese labourers. They had set up canteens and drop-in centres where the labourers could come for help. These lay missionaries, joined by Chinese student volunteers from Paris, worked as translators between the British and French for the Chinese. Hospitals for the CLC had been set up separate from those of the regular army. Attempts were made by Chinese youth associations from the French capital to promote literacy but these failed dismally because, after a hard day, the last thing on a labourer's mind was to study another language.

Feng Hua's group came back from one of these, chortling.

"Imagine having to say, 'Excuse me, but can you tell me where the hospital is' in English? If I needed to go to hospital, I wouldn't be in a fit state to ask, would I? Dumb clods. They have no idea what it's like for us, spoilt rich boys as they are."

*

Six weeks after their arrival, Alex was on his routine visit with his flock after dinner. At such times, the men might work up enough energy for a game of cards, talk or, for the literate ones, attend to correspondence. He held his second letter from Emily, stationed at a hospital on the Belgian border with other medical personnel from the Allied forces. It had not taken her long to discover his whereabouts at Noyelles-Sur-Mer.

She had also found Wiremu with his Pioneer Maori Battalion.

'He is not too many miles from here, on the other side of Ypres. But that might just as well be on the far side of the moon.

I do worry so; they are in such a dangerous position. Dissatisfaction is rife amongst them because this battalion has been turned into a labouring one. All, to a man, feel insulted, that they might perchance die as common labourers when in fact, they had volunteered to fight as soldiers. This is an insult to their *mana*, as you can appreciate, Alex. And all this is due to some fracas with their officers in Gallipoli. Our boys should have their own New Zealand commanders, but apparently here, as in Gallipoli, they have to take orders from the Brits who have little appreciation of New Zealanders' work. On the happy side, they have been able to blow up nineteen German bunkers through subterranean tunnelling. The holes created collapsed in the ensuing rains and now have formed large crater lakes. So that was a small triumph for their efforts. I hope your labourers are much better treated, Alex. At least they knew what they signed up for. Dear brother, be safe; please do not put yourself in any danger. Keep your ministering in the base camps.'

But as he read her letter several times over, Alex knew it was an impossible ask. A whole division of the Chinese had been ordered out to dig more trenches. They were to leave for the Front in droves from the following day onwards. An intended total of forty thousand of them, from all the ports and factory towns, were to be spread right across the west. To dig, to fill, to set up mines, to deactivate mines, to bury the dead, to put up thousands of rolls of barbed wires, to cut through thousands of yards of barbed wires. And to possibly die.

Oh God, he prayed, *keep them safe, keep me safe, for I must go. All over the Front, from one group to the other. Dear Lord, let this be over soon.*

Now Matthew was talking. "I must confess, I am truly grateful to have my particular skill, Brother Alex. I know how selfish it sounds, may the Lord forgive me, but I must stay alive for I am my widowed mother's only son. At least the tank workshops are safe. Brother Huan and I will minister to the ones remaining here. Don't you worry, Alex, I will pray hard for you and all those going." He stopped, studied Alex's despondent face and added, "You are fearful, Brother Alex. I can see it."

"Yes, Matthew, I am afraid. My fear is no less than the others and because they have no choice, I must not exercise my prerogative. I will go."

"Then the Lord go with you, Brother Alex."

*

The next morning, Brother Huan came to the officers' barracks as Alex was finishing his porridge and bread. His tote bag, packed and ready, sat beside him.

An orderly showed Huan in. He hesitated at the door of the mess hut. Confronted by so many uniformed officers, he felt intimated indeed. Their silent stares further unnerved him. He floundered. He swiped his cap from his head, looked around for Alex, who came forward immediately.

"What is it, Brother Huan?"

"I have come to walk with you back to our camp, Brother Alex. I need to talk about Feng Hua. Please take your time. I will wait till you finish."

Alex resumed his breakfast, but as quickly as he could he joined Huan at the door. He slung his belongings over his shoulders, waved to the officers he had befriended and followed Huan out into the cold dawn. A wind was getting up, threatening rain.

"What about Feng Hua?"

"He has stolen a gun to shoot Germans with. That's why he was so quick to volunteer for the trenches in the first place. To get close to them."

"He probably won't be able to get that close to them, Brother Huan, there must be quite a distance between the two sides."

"Brother Alex, I know Feng Hua. I grew up with him. He even knifed an Indian once in Tsingdao when he was only eleven. You are the only foreigner he doesn't hate. Believe me, I know him."

Something tickled Alex's memory.

"Tell me about that incident, knifing the Indian."

"Well, the Indian and a friend were strolling down a market street, and on the spur of the moment, Feng Hua stabbed him in the back."

"What was the friend like?"

"Actually, Feng Hua told me that when he first met you, you reminded him of that man."

"That was my brother Eddie. Because of that incident in Tsingdao, he never got to Qufu. His friend Ranjit is now safe in Delhi."

"Well, Feng Hua is a hothead. And if he wants to do something, he will do it, regardless. He's waited so long to avenge his father, he'll find a way. I am so afraid for him, Brother Alex."

"Brother Matthew told me last night that he feels compelled to stay alive for his mother's sake. Surely Feng Hua is in the same situation?"

"He has made provisions. If he dies, his mother will be looked after by his uncle who has been a surrogate father to him. That's why I know he'll go through with it."

"Would he be happy killing just one German? A life for a life?"

"There were six Germans at his father's execution. So he wants to take at least that number, probably many more."

"I'll talk to him, see what I can do."

Then the rain heaved down. They had to run to reach the CLC camp where their part of the forty thousand men were being herded into convoys of trucks. The headlights beamed into the thickening rain. Alex and Huan, soaked to the skin, searched for Feng Hua from truck to truck, calling his name. He was nowhere to be seen.

"We had an argument last night and again this morning. He knew I was going for you. So he hides."

"I promise I will keep an eye out for him, Brother Huan. That's all we can do."

"I'm coming with you, Brother Alex. I may be the only one who can stop him."

"What about your work here with Matthew?"

"He will manage, especially since the Y is sending more people out. And the student volunteers are useful when they want to be."

Then lightning filled the sky, followed by such claps of thunder that they jumped and clamped their hands tight to their ears.

*

The trucks rumbled slowly along the broken road north-west to Ypres. Visibility ahead was less than a hundred feet. The storm accompanied them all the way. They cringed with each slash of lightning, each roar of thunder. Sheets of rain hammered the canvas awnings mercilessly, saturating the men at the open rear, suffocating those in the interior.

"This is a very bad omen, Brother Alex, this storm. We say it is heaven crying."

"Hey, remember you're Christian now, Brother Huan," Alex said, though the Reverend Dempsey's oft-repeated remark that beneath their thin Christian skins the Chinese remained heathens surfaced in his mind.

"The heavens are crying because of so much death," Huan persisted.

Alex rubbed Huan's shoulders as he stared into heaven's tears. Christian though he himself was, he silently agreed.

*

They reached the battleground around Ypres an hour later than expected in late afternoon. They had passed through bog with soldiers, horses, donkeys and drays so buried in the quagmire that they were barely discernible. The city itself was in a state of devastation.

"The fighting is so close, Brother Alex," Huan whispered as they passed through.

Already, they could see ruins of churches and public buildings, shelled to their skeletons, standing sombre. The steeple of a huge church was half blown away, its remaining fragment rising beseechingly skyward. They passed through street upon street with, on both sides, the rubble of apartment buildings that would house their occupants no more. These same occupants now paused in the rain, most unprotected from the deluge, as their trucks passed, looking on with faces mute beyond comprehension. It was obvious food was in short supply.

At least today's storm had kept the bi-planes from the skies. Alex remembered the first time they saw these huge, wondrous machines droning past overhead on his third day at Noyelles-Sur-Mer. Many of the Chinese had ducked low, covering their heads and yelling in fright till they had passed into the distant sky.

"They are ours, thank God, just doing reconnaissance. You can be grateful for that," the sergeant had told Alex. "Hopefully those boys will help us end this war quickly. But as many as we put up, the Huns do the same. So it's stalemate, yet again."

"Is that all they are used for?"

"No, mate. They are our spies in the skies, and now with both sides producing them, they are also fighters. With mounted guns."

"How accurate would that be, when they are flying at such speed?"

"Accurate enough to go down in flames very regularly."

And as they approached the fighting front, Alex knew those planes would be over them much more, delivering both help and death from the skies. He shivered as he thought of the multiple ways those on the ground could be affected.

Mercifully, the camps were on slightly higher ground but, all around, Alex could see the hopelessness of the terrain. His truck was one of a hundred that stopped at Camp One. The others kept on trundling further down the line to drop off their human cargo.

Now the orders were to throw their belongings into the huts and look sharp for duty. Divisions were formed, each with a senior coolie in charge, selected from amongst themselves, who was to be responsible for their work unit. Alex and Huan translated to as many as they could. The orders were relayed down. And all the time, they searched for Feng Hua in the grey-black sea of desolation.

"Well," Huan remarked bitterly, "at least here they don't fence us in with barbed wire, not like base camp. Ha, nothing to steal here, no goods, no women, eh? We're safe from nothing here."

Then a shattering roar stopped them in their tracks. The fighting at the lines had started up again. The sky lit up with continuous explosions. They heard screams, real or imagined, from a long way off. Carnage had come to meet them face on.

Stop this horror, stop this horror, Alex prayed as he followed Huan in his search for the errant Feng Hua, shouting his name.

"Here I am," said a calm voice behind them at the eighth hut along.

"Thank goodness," Huan gasped, "are you all right?"

"Of course I am all right, and I intend to stay all right till I am satisfied." He looked towards the bright sky eastwards, his eyes glinting in the spasmodic bursts of light.

"Feng Hua, please do no such thing," Huan pleaded.

"Feng Hua, will you share our hut? Over there." Alex pointed to the Nissen hut where he and Huan had deposited their equipment.

"Sure," replied Feng Hua, "it makes no difference."

He followed them back, walking jauntily despite his obvious fatigue, his own bag slung on his back.

*

A young lieutenant picked his way through the rain and fetched up to Alex. The exhausted man was no older than he.

"I hear you're the Kiwi non-combatant accompanying this group of coolies."

"Yes, I am their pastor from the YMCA," Alex replied.

"My name's Jarvis, sir. I'm in charge of this division. Have they chosen their section leaders?"

"Yes, it was done, but surely they can eat and rest before working? Can they start tomorrow?"

"Yah, that's fine. Coolie canteens are over there. They can't dawdle over their meal, though. Not enough room. So it's chuck down and beat it out of there. Tomorrow, they are to hike towards the line over there, thirty degrees north-east. I'll give them their orders before they leave and let's hope this sodding rain ceases by then. I'm to take you to the officers' hut. Follow me?" And he marched off.

Alex grabbed his gear, yelling to Huan who was already nodding, having heard everything.

"I'll be back with him tomorrow morning. Good luck," he shouted.

They squelched past the coolies' mess and kitchens, one hut after another, like rows of giant sausages; past laundry buildings, shower rooms and toilets, work-shops, stables with snorting, wet horses and mules and water-filled drays tilted on their sides. The field hospital was to the left of the officers' barracks. It was large and of the same structure, half a mile from the coolie huts. These semi-permanent buildings were constructed of solid timber framing covered with strong canvas. Compared to the half-barrelled Nissen huts, they exuded an air of stability.

"This is the officers' mess. I bet you're ready for some hot nosh. It's not posh, but it's filling and after a stint in the trenches buried in mud, this place is heaven, take it from me."

The heat of the room swiped Alex like a slap from a hot towel. The smoky interior was lit by paraffin lamps, and crowded with men between shifts. They had climbed out of their dirty wet fatigues and were all dressed in clean though un-pressed khakis. Many were smoking, with beer in front of them.

Those men who had finished their meals were taking time out for some quiet chat before turning in. Others were queuing in front of the servers.

"This way," Jarvis said as he led Alex towards the rows of cooks behind the pots.

"Heaven be praised! Wiremu!" Alex pounced on the man two in front of him in the queue.

Wiremu turned round. His face lit up as he returned the hug. "Hey, cousin! God! Em told me you were in Noyelles-Sur-Mer. What are you doing here?" Wiremu turned to the other Maoris in front of them. "Hey fellas! Meet Alex, my girl's baby brother. He's come to look after the Chinese coolies."

The Maoris, already interested in the reunion, greeted Alex warmly.

Alex could see they must have just returned to camp, such was the fatigue on their faces, such the sag in their once-upright lean bodies.

"They wanted forty thousand Chinese on the Front. So I came," he said.

"Yeah, they would be welcome reinforcement, I tell you, Alex. We are going down like flies," Wiremu continued as they shuffled along with their trays.

Alex turned to Jarvis. "Have you met?"

Jarvis shook Wiremu's hand. "Of Pioneer Maori Battalion, right?"

"Yeah, the slaves in battle fatigues," Wiremu replied caustically.

From Jarvis's embarrassed silence, Alex sensed friction.

"Well, now that you've got your mates, I'll see you later, Alex," said Jarvis before moving on to another table.

"Not that it's his fault," Wiremu said as they sat down to eat. "Misgivings happened way back in Gallipoli and his higher-ups insisted our skills be relocated elsewhere and not used in fighting Huns. I guess we take our resentment out occasionally. We make it known we are fighters, warriors, not damned labourers."

"Where do you sleep?" Alex asked.

"We've got our own huts. Way down after the whities', way down. By the way, heard from Em? She's working very, very hard. If she wasn't anti-war before, she certainly is now. And she *was very anti-war*, as you know. Should've listened to her," Wiremu said, bitterly. "Thought we were fighting for God, king and country. But here we are, shot at from every bloody angle an' dropping from every conceivable disease man's ever known – as bloody labourers. Friggin' Poms. Friggin' Frogs, friggin' bastard Huns." He stabbed at his food with a ferocity Alex had never seen in the good-natured Maori.

Wiremu rubbed his bleary, red-shot eyes and looked at Alex. "We're moving back to the Front tomorrow. We stay twelve friggin' hours on duty, night and day, before coming back here to wash, eat, sleep. Then it's back to more of the same. Five days on, two off, sometimes one, like now."

"What do you do?" Alex looked round his table.

"What your Chinese will be doing – digging trenches, bringing in the dead and wounded, laying barbed wire, all the dirty work."

"But that's not exclusively just for you and us, surely? The Brits and French must do their fair share of that?"

"Casualties have been so high, they want to concentrate their boys on the fighting and leave us to do the labouring."

"Keep safe, Wiremu. Do you have a pastor here?"

"We do, sort of, an English chaplain. But it's good you are here, Alex, you can do for us."

The other Maoris concurred. "Yeah, Alex, we'd be happier, having you minister to us, or bury us."

"Pray God, not the latter," Alex murmured. Turning back to Wiremu, he said, "Will you be writing back to Em?"

"When I am not too tired. Or heartsick, or just plain friggin' sick."

"I'll write. I'll tell her you are here and that you are well. I'll send her your love."

"You do that, *ehoa*, you do that, my friend."

*

The rain eased off the next morning as the Chinese coolies squelched their long way to the front lines, muttering, praying, clutching their totes under their arms. The Maoris were also starting early in a different direction. Alex saw Wiremu amongst them. He walked up to the group from home.

"*Kia ora*, hello," he greeted them. The tired smiles returned were warm.

"At least the rain's stopped," said one.

"Aye, and the shelling for a while," said another.

Alex looked towards Wiremu but realised that the man whom he had always considered a friend was actually avoiding him. Hurt, he turned to the first Maori.

"We're heading north-east with Lieutenant Jarvis. Which way are you going?"

"Back where we were yesterday, about a couple of miles west of where you're going."

Alex decided not to be put off by Wiremu. He walked up to him.

"Wiremu, are you all right?"

"Yeah, don't you worry about me, Alex boy, I'll be okay. You take care." And he and the group of over two hundred men slouched off, dragging their exhaustion behind them.

But Alex knew Wiremu was not all right, yet felt helpless in the face of the man's depression. He could only write to his sister. He could only lie.

Chapter 24

1st November 1917: The Gates of Hell -- The Western Front

Alex walked rapidly, a huge tote on his back, along the fields leading to Polygon Wood where he knew Huan and Feng Hua's group was working. For several days now they had been cutting the remaining tree stumps that were left from the second Ypres battle on the 26th September, working the perimeter of the devastation, sawing the trunks into beams and planks for sapping and supports. The brown-grey battlefield was heavily ridged and littered with bog holes of freezing water from the last downfall. Barbed wire lay careless and twisted, testament to the carnage only five weeks before.

Huan was the first to spot him. "Brother Alex, you should not be coming here. The enemy will start shooting soon."

Alex looked towards the German lines on the higher ground of the ridge beyond. The afternoon was dull, the temperature made worse by the intense, wintry east winds. Alex, huddled in his army overcoat, his hands in thick mittens and a knitted hat pulled down low on his forehead, strode towards Huan. About two hundred yards away, other Chinese, alongside round-helmeted British soldiers, were lugging stretchers towards ambulances waiting on firmer terrain. *More dying and dead,* he thought, watching the hurried pace.

"I thought I'd come to see how you are, as you didn't come back last night."

"We had to stay. Did you hear the firing last night? We thought it would never end. The enfilade fire kept us in the trenches. Alex, that place is one step from hell." Huan indicated the trenches with his chin.

"Has the water drained away much?" Alex asked, referring to the week after they arrived in October when the entire length of the trench was filled eighteen inches deep in muddy water. He had seen the shivering men crouching in them, soaking wet, mud-covered, many patched-up wounded, most looking ill. The stench had horrified him.

Lieutenant Jarvis, his guide, had said grimly, "Dysentery is a regular visitor, I'm afraid, Alex. And all the diseases that produce it."

"This is clay, Brother Alex. We are all rotting here," Huan was now saying.

Alex nodded and breathed a sigh of relief as Feng Hua approached them. If the Chinese men had any surplus flesh on their bones before, they had lost it now. Work in the trenches was so much harder and so much more terrifying than in the safety of tank and munitions factories or the docks of Saint Nazaire or Brest.

"*Ni hao*, Feng Hua, how are you?" Alex called out. He opened his tote bag and brought out cold boiled potatoes and small lumps of boiled meat. "Here, take these and distribute them amongst the others. You must be starving."

"That we are, ravenous," Feng Hua agreed as he and Huan bit into their share. Then Feng Hua took the tote bag and left to distribute food to the other workers. Alex gave him a kitchen knife, before remembering to add, "Bring that knife back. I promised the cook I will return it."

As he watched Feng Hua's retreating back, Alex asked Huan, "Is he behaving? Any more ideas of killing Germans?"

"You were right to ask for that knife back. He had been saying lately that a knife would be a better weapon. He's not sure about the gun. 'Too conspicuous,' he said. Besides he isn't really sure how to use it and he hasn't more bullets," Huan replied, his face gaunt and lined, his stooped body belying his twenty-eight years.

Just a week ago, he had confided to Alex, "I wish I had remained in Ypres with Brother Matthew. God forgive me, but I wish I had. I don't know how long I or any one of us can retain our sanity here. This was not what we signed up for, Alex, this danger of death, this exposure to so much gunfire."

"No, it isn't. They have violated the contract of the Labour Corps."

"Can anything be done, Alex?" Huan asked, tears rolling copiously down his hollowed cheeks. The few around listening began to crumble before his eyes.

*

The next day, Alex had sought out Lieutenant Jarvis. "I need to speak to the commander of this offensive. It's General Gough, isn't it? Where can I find him?"

"What about, Pastor?" Jarvis sensed trouble.

"What the Chinese are made to do here goes against the terms of their contract. They did not sign up for this kind of work. The agreement was that their labour would be used in towns, cities, factories, dockyards and work away from the front lines. Not this, Jarvis, not this. I want to see the General about it."

"First of all, it isn't General Gough who's in charge of the Chinese. It's Lieutenant Colonel Fairfax and I don't know where the hell he is," Jarvis had scoffed through his own fatigue. "Sorry, old chap. We all want to see Gough. We all want this confounded war to end. But we can't always have what we want, can we? Not as long as the blasted Huns keep on the way they do. Until we defeat them, we need every man jack to do the best he can, agreement or no agreement, contract or no contract. Now, please go away. I really need to sleep."

And he had turned his back on Alex.

*

Now, standing in the ruins of the woods, Alex's eyes followed Feng Hua who was hopping from man to man distributing largesse. "So he hasn't changed his mind, even after seeing the actual sight of the enemy?"

"No, Brother Alex, he had been training back in China for just this day. He had been preparing himself since he was six years old."

"God help him. I can't imagine such unrelenting pain," Alex said, looking further afield. "I shall go say hello to Lieutenant Jarvis. Where is he?"

"See there? Over there by the ambulances," Huan pointed.

"I hope you can all return to camp tonight."

"Brother Alex, please go back to camp. The wind is blowing our way. That means we might get gassed anytime soon. Please

195

don't stay long here. The shooting will start soon, and the grenades," Huan yelled after him.

And sure enough, no sooner had Alex reached within shouting distance of Lieutenant Jarvis than a huge explosion made them all leap. Alex looked back and saw the Chinese workers flat on the ground, arms over heads. After some minutes of quiet, they started getting to their feet, their fronts covered in mud. No one seemed to be hurt.

"Get away, will you?" the Englishman yelled. "We don't want unnecessary deaths here. Your men are okay."

"Will they be coming back tonight? They were supposed to have their rest day today."

"I know. I shall send them off a bit earlier. The new roster will come in tomorrow morning."

"Is it true that the Germans may release the poison gas tonight?"

"Yep, that's why the men are issued with those masks."

"But my men are not." Alex said, appalled by the exclusion.

Jarvis looked guilty. "Look, there aren't enough, right? Soldiers have first call. Now blast off, will you, Reverend? Just go!"

Jarvis waved Alex off. Another explosion sent him scurrying back towards base. The stretcher bearers, already scrambling hard, hastened their pace. Soon the ambulances roared off, belching smoke, passing Alex on their way to Ypres.

*

When he got back to the mess hut, Alex poured himself a hot mug of tea, sat down and reread Emily's latest letter, delivered by an ambulance on its way to the battle zone. She had been ill, she said, but he was not to worry. Just a minor touch of the 'flu that plagued Europe every winter.

'What worries me so much is the increasing number of desperately ill soldiers coming here. Our facilities are stretched to the limit and they are now making semi-permanent hospitals out of the huts that the soldiers live in. We seem to be burying more than we are healing. And among the wounded are so many of our own boys. Each time an Anzac is brought in, I pray it isn't Wiremu. Your last letter said he was well, but Alex, I know you. If he truly were well, you would have quoted a quip or two from him. And you didn't. You are not telling me the whole truth. This is the third year for Wiremu. I fully expect him to be unwell, in either mind or body. So darling, please don't spare me the truth in your next letter.

'Now to lighter things. We have had a change of personnel, amongst whom is a very charming doctor of Eddie's age. He actually spent his early years in China as his parents were missionaries in Macao. He was born there. He tells me he has fond memories of that place, though I suspect he's colouring them pink on my behalf. He is an orthopaedic surgeon so you can imagine how useful he is. Under his tutelage is an extremely blue-blooded young surgeon who is just as lovely. I must admit I do enjoy their company hugely as I am the only female doctor here.

'That's not to say the other people around are not. A fresh contingent of nurses from Canada has now joined us, widening the topics of conversation even more. As I write this, I seem lighter in spirit. Does that mean I'm happier, more optimistic or resigned to the impossible situation? How I hate this dreadful war! How I wish it to end!

'On a happier note, Pa is more relaxed with Eddie now. He is reconciled to him living in Malaya forever. But he lives in fear of a telegram from Defence, concerning any one of us. Oh, I have forgotten to mention Hongyun is also here with the US Army. Pa couldn't say where they are, but sooner or later, they will come to this theatre of war, I am sure. Talk is of the next big battle in Cambrai. It will be most desperate and the Allies are putting in hundreds of tanks for the very first time. They are just waiting for the main American reinforcements to arrive. If you ever hear the name Victor Zhou, that would be Hongyun. He has taken an American name since his naturalisation.

'Dear Alex, please take care. I worry so much for you. Just remember, you are a pastor, not a soldier or a labourer. Promise me you won't be a brave idiot. I enclose a letter for Wiremu.

All my love, Em.'

*

The next day, Alex checked in with Lieutenant Jarvis.
"What do I do to travel over the border?"

"Why? What are you about?"

"I want to visit my sister at Hoogestadt. She's a doctor there. Can I travel with one of the ambulances? I've been on the Front for more than two months now and I thought that as she's not that far away, I want to visit."

"Alex, old chap, you are a pastor of the Y and frankly not under our jurisdiction. You don't seem to grasp that. You came to be with your coolies but seem to have taken over their burden. Go wherever you wish, just don't be a bloody fool."

So Alex hung around for the next ambulance and squeezed in between the driver and his fellow attendee in the cab. They negotiated their way through bogged land till they hit the road which was surprisingly intact. The friendly natter of the two para-medics made the journey of twenty-three miles to Hoogestadt painless.

At the converted alms house hospital, Alex hopped down eagerly. "You need my help with your stretchers?"

"Nah, go on, Padre. Go to your sister. You'd be a sight for sore eyes, I betcha."

The long dark room filled with rows upon rows of the bloodied and mutilated in bandages and casts awed Alex, toughened though he had been since his arrival at the Front. Most of the patients lay quiet in their cots, but a few moans erupted from time to time – and from time to time, desperate coughing resounded through the chill air. The smell of antiseptic, musty bodies and urine hit his nostrils. Several nurses moved about amongst the bandaged men, their white veils pristine in the gloom.

"Yes? Are you looking for someone?" came a Scottish voice at his elbow.

He looked down at the short nurse who had come up to him unnoticed. The authoritative tone and red stripes on her lower sleeves told him she must be a sister of the ward.

He smiled. "I'm looking for Emily Zhou. I'm her brother."

The petite woman broke into a warm smile. "Aye, and you are Alex, mightn't you be? Emily has told us so much about you and we were hoping you'd visit someday. She's in the operating theatre at the moment. Why don't you go to the kitchen and have yourself a cuppa tea? You might even find a biscuit or two in the tin. I'll tell her you are here. Might be a while though, Alex, there are several poor bairns for her to work through."

"They must be happy you call them bairns, Sister Fiona," Alex smiled into the kindly face as he read her name tag.

"And so they are, the age of them, Alex. It fair breaks my heart each time. I'm Catholic, you know, and I pray the Blessed Virgin looks after her boys on the Front. You go along, I'll tell Emily. Stay in the kitchen, it's warmer and you'll be out of the way."

The pot of tea simmering on the wood burner came out a deep brown into Alex's mug. Milk and sugar were luxuries now, so he was content to sip the hot, bitter liquid on its own. The ginger nuts in the tin were welcome as he had not had anything to eat since breakfast. He sat at the well-scrubbed wooden table and took out his pocket Bible to read while he waited with a pumping heart to see Emily.

It was three hours before she emerged. He had been tempted to explore the outside but hated to miss her. Now she scampered through the long ward towards him.

"Oh, Alex, darling. Oh, it's been so long, so long."

He hugged her tight for as long as they both wept. He kept nuzzling her hair through her grey theatre cap. "Oh God, Em, how I've missed you. I've missed you so much," he whispered through his tears. They continued holding each other till Emily broke away. She held him at arm's length as she studied his thin face and curly hair, now speckled prematurely with grey. He was only twenty-eight.

"How long has it been, Alex? Over eight years? Eight years since we were together! Oh, how I've missed you. And now look, you are greying!" She stroked his hair with a sad smile. "But you are a man, now, darling, and what a man!"

"And you, Em? How are you really?" He studied her lovely face, devoid long since of its New Zealand tan. Her large, sloe eyes were edged with fine lines at the corner, the naso-labia lines beginning to form down her cheeks, just like Pa's. She looked terribly tired.

"You need a rest, Em. Can you get away for a week or two?"

"Well, I did have a holiday two months back when I went to London. But I am due for another break next month. But oh, I *am so-o glad* to see you. Now at last, I can report to Pa that you are truly well, if not half-starved! Come, let's walk about a bit before it gets dark. I want to show you the medic huts."

Their breaths puffed mists into the wintery air. Emily clutched his arm tight as they strolled across the field to where several huts stood side by side.

"How's Wiremu?" she asked.

"I don't really know, Em. He's totally exhausted and, like all of us, has a festering rage. He's angry about their whole division being used just for hard labour. Apparently, that's how the American army is using their Negro volunteers too. So the Maoris regard their treatment as second class and degrading. And frankly they are right. They signed up to fight as soldiers."

"How is his health?"

"He'd been hospitalised with typhus, but he got over that. He seems all right. Not great, but he's still standing. To tell the truth, Em, the stuffing's been knocked out of those men."

She nodded silently. Then as they approached the hospital hut, a tall Englishman emerged in a blood-soiled white coat over army fatigues. He broke into a joyous smile at sight of Emily and, as Alex looked down at his sister, he realised this was no ordinary acquaintance in her life. Her exhaustion had disappeared in an instant, her face shone radiant.

"Oh, James, meet my baby brother Alex," Emily beamed. "Alex dear, this is James Hopkins, the orthopaedic surgeon who's not long joined us."

As he shook the firm hand, as he gazed into the other man's warm eyes, clarity dawned upon Alex. *This is Emily's salvation. Wiremu will not survive the war.* And with this vision, a deep sadness enfolded him.

*

In the cold of that bitter November, the third battle of Ypres raged on, neither side winning much ground even though many thousands died. As Alex wandered around his camp on his return from Hoogestadt, he was sickened to the heart to see the increasing number of dead trundled off by truck to the cemeteries, and the wounded men and horses in transit to hospitals and veterinary clinics. He wondered what happened to the animals when they were beyond salvation.

"Wonder no more, Alex," Jarvis told him one night over dinner, indicating his plate.

Alex looked down at his stew, then slowly picked up his knife and fork. "This is war after all," he murmured. "I suppose they were the basis of our protein all along?"

"Right on," Jarvis replied. "The camps have to use them regularly. That's when we find ourselves on short rations. It keeps the locals supportive; they love horsemeat."

*

In their hut, Huan looked down at the deadly-looking curved knife Feng Hua was sharpening with a welt of leather.

"Where did you get that?" Huan whispered.

"Stole it," replied Feng Hua, with an air of satisfaction.

"Please, don't do it, Xiao Hua, please."

"Why not? I will be doing a great service to the British by killing Germans. Fewer for them to worry about."

"How will you do it?" Huan asked, but of course, he already knew. Feng Hua had outlined his plan for him several times. He only needed an appropriate weapon. He only needed to be rostered into the trenches on a moonless night.

Chapter 25

The Roll of Tanks: Cambrai

Alex knew from Matthew's letters that there would be a massive campaign soon not too many miles from where he was outside Ypres. Matthew wrote in Chinese, so his letters were not censored. The powers-that-be obviously thought that should any fall into German hands, they would not bother sending them to Berlin to be translated.

'For weeks now, our men have been sent all over the forests preparing huge bundles of brushwood which we have to tie up and load onto rail trucks. The army calls them fascines and they are to be used as improvised bridges for the tanks to roll on over the trenches. Each weighs about a ton, so heavy they are. So you can imagine the size of each – about nine feet long and six high. The pace of work is back-breaking as you can guess, Alex, and goes on day and night. They labour in the forest by day and by night, they tie the cuttings up into fascines. We have never known how painfully numbing cold is.

'The building of tanks too goes on day and night. I swear by my ancestors, my hands are screwing on rivets even in my sleep. The only good thing is that we riveters and mechanics are paid two francs a day, so that is more to save for home, and our families, too, get an increased allotment. Ours is a much safer job as we have to remain here to not only build the tanks, but also to repair them. So we have tank hospitals on the ready. I very much pity our brothers who lack the skills that would preserve their lives. And they are paid only one franc a day. I question myself, how unfair is life? They are very afraid and I do God's work by praying with them. Many have converted already, you will be pleased to know. At least if they die here, they will do so in the bosom of Jesus.

'Day and night, there is so much amassment of soldiers from all over the place. We have never seen so many soldiers, not even during the Boxer rebellion. Alex, I think this is the battle to end all battles. We have over four hundred tanks going on flatbed trucks and trains to the battlefield under cover of night. On arrival they will be heavily camouflaged until the day of the battle. So secretive is this operation and no wonder. We must win this next battle.

'But the worst news is that those unskilled amongst us are to go with the Army. Thousands of them. They are to help unload and mount the fascines on top of the tanks. Many have left already, but more men are arriving from China. You told me in your last letter there are new people in your camp. So they must be sending them all over the Front as they arrive. From what the soldiers talk about, I know our men must also do very dangerous work, like yours are. They will have to pick up bodies, plant mines, clear the used barbed wires and do all the horrible things under heaven that our ancients would rage against.

'Alex, the morale here, from the British to our own men, is lower than a scrape of the earth. We drown in despair and sickness. Like you, we also have a high rate of accidents. Alex, when will these atrocities end? I hear the Germans are losing as many as the Allies. What good does all this do, whoever wins? Their countries will be devoid of young men; they have lost the flower of their generation. How will they rebuild? I weep Alex, every night I weep, as we all do. God help us. God help us all.'

And in Alex's mess, the British could talk of nothing else but the next big strategy in the south-east. Some units were being readied to move. The road to St Quentin rumbled with trucks, jeeps and the clip-clop of cavalry day and night. *Truly it will be a battle to hell and back,* he thought as he watched.

*

Alex had been trying to find Hongyun since Emily told him of their brother's presence on the Western Front. He started writing letters to all American military bases and hospitals in the region. Knowing nothing of Hongyun's unit, he was aware he was stabbing in the dark but nevertheless grew increasingly despondent with the return of each letter. *I must find him, for Pa's sake. Hongyun might be too busy to write him of his whereabouts.*

*

Huan had come to him one day after his return from Hoogestadt.

"Alex, Feng Hua now has a knife. We must try to prevent him from going to the trenches. That's where he will start."

So Alex had approached Lieutenant Jarvis with the problem.

"But he's intent on killing Huns only, right? So I say good-ho! Kill on! I shan't do anything about that, Alex. We need all the help we can get. Sorry, old boy." And he had slumped away, his khakis all the worse for mud and grime.

Dejected, Alex had gone back to Huan.

"There's nothing the British will do, Brother Huan. And nothing we can do either. Let us pray for his safe return from this endeavour."

And they had both gone down on their knees in the muddy field as the sky turned grey and sleet started to pelt down on them.

*

On the 21st of November, the jubilation of the British in their camp toasting the victory at Cambrai heartened Alex and his CLC men. At last, the end was in sight.

"And it's those wonderful tanks that won the day, Alex," Jarvis said, with an arm around his shoulders as they drank in the mess. "They can tear up and roll away miles of barbed wire, allowing the infantry and cavalry to push through. With this battle, we can beat the Huns and go home soon. You better tell that Feng whatever-his-name to hurry up. Soon there won't be any Huns left for him to kill."

A few days later, however, the news turned sour as the Germans quickly recovered from their defeat of the 20th and were defending their Hindenburg Line with renewed ferocity. They had also come up with bullets that could pierce through steel. The three hundred and twenty-four tanks deployed were either destroyed or damaged so badly that they had to be abandoned or taken back to tank hospital.

Now, amongst the tank drivers there was a new sickness – carbon monoxide poisoning. The gas filled the interior of the tanks, killing the men inside them. This, coupled with the usual battle fire, produced so many casualties that the cemeteries nearby filled to capacity and extended into the fallow fields.

Matthew wrote, 'We are now working as hard as ever repairing the damaged tanks and their long guns. Three hundred of our workers are burying the dead as they come in. Alex, this kind of work is not meant to be. Meanwhile, of our own men who went to Cambrai, four hundred and sixty-five were killed and many injured. Our dead are buried without ceremony at one corner of the cemetery, away from the soldiers – for racist reasons, I personally feel. We are very insulted by that, but it is to be expected. It is no worse than our not being allowed into the villages in case we molest their women or steal their possessions. I ask you again, what kind of world is this, my brother?'

What kind, indeed? Alex thought as he read on.

'Still that conflict continues and each day, more and more shattered bodies return, both of men, horses and tanks. I pray God for patience and fortitude and that He forgives what is happening here. And for me to forget when it is finally over. Oh, the nightmares we have in our huts. Moans all through the night. But now I must bid you goodnight, Alex. My shift begins tomorrow at six in the morning and it is now past midnight. God grant you peaceful sleep. Be safe. My good wishes and prayers to Brother Huan and everyone else.

Your brother in Christ, Matthew.'

By the time the soldiers on the Front received family letters rejoicing about the victory of Cambrai, the conflict was over with a loss of over forty-four thousand dead on the Allied side.

*

Christmas 1917: The Golden Army of the West: Field Hospital

Snow swirled gently down, settling on the already impacted ground. The landscape visible in the light of the half moon was a forlorn expanse of grey shadows of human occupation. Tents,

205

Nissen huts, wooden stables, huddled close together, darkly lonely except for silvery moonlight on their roofs and dim gold-orange lantern light from doorways and windows. Army and medical personnel flittered between them, silent but for the occasional 'Merry Christmas' wished upon each other. And as if in response, an odd neigh or snort resounded from the stables.

Inside the medical staff mess hut, one of the largest in the camp, Hongyun sat alone at the table watching the other doctors and nurses dance in tight embrace to gramophone music. The singing duo, Violet Lorraine and George Robey, crooned to the sentimental strains of 'Till we meet again'. Brightly coloured balloons and streamers and fluttering candles in the centre of tables provided a party atmosphere.

Care parcels from home were spread out on the tables around. Earlier, Curtis had come into their sleeping quarters with a large pack of hand-knitted socks from his grandmother, a photo of his family's Thanksgiving get-together, and presents of every sort from various members of his large family. His happiness was curtailed by Hongyun's morose expression.

"That bad, uh?" he said.

He sat down beside Hongyun on his cot and gave him a squeeze on the shoulder. Hongyun was one of those who did not get a care parcel, at Christmas or any other time. He was without family in America and one of his host parents, Mr Sarginson, had passed away before the war started, leaving his widow in a rest home in San Francisco.

Hongyun had gone to see her before leaving but her worsening dementia had proven the journey wasted. His mother Yung would not know where to send anything to him in Europe. So now he sat, isolated from the merry-making of his colleagues. *I should have put myself on roster duty. This is a total waste of time.* And he got up to leave. He looked round for Curtis, found him laughing amongst a group of para-medics at the far end of the mess and decided not to bother saying goodbye. He walked the five hundred yards to the hospital huts, his hands in his coat pocket, cap low on his forehead.

The doctor on duty, Jordi Hyatt, who was writing out a post-op report, looked up when he entered the main surgical hut. "Hi, Victor, why aren't you with the rest? Take a break, man."

"Don't feel festive, Jordi. Thought I might make myself useful. Any new admissions for OR?"

"Been quiet for the last half hour," Jordi replied. "Here, have some of these." He handed Hongyun a box of Belgian chocolates. "Imagine, folks back home pay a ton for these chocs and we're just on the border of the country that makes them."

"I imagine it would be difficult for your family to give you a gift voucher to send off for them."

"Oh by the way, this came for you an hour ago, courtesy of Nurse Angela." Jordi handed him an envelope with the frank of the British Army.

Hongyun turned the brown envelope over. Alex Zhou! *Alex is here in this hell.*

What is he doing here? He ripped open the envelope.

"Good grief," he said as Jordi looked up, "my kid brother is here, not twenty miles away, and my sister too. Oh God."

"I didn't know you had siblings, Victor."

"Half siblings. Same father, different mother. They were born in New Zealand. I only met them when I was thirteen." He carried on reading as he filled Jordi in. "I hated the bastards, and bastards they are too. My mother was the proper wife. Theirs was a native slave."

"Where's New Zealand?" Jordi was from the Mid-West and ignorant of world geography, despite his education.

"Some godforsaken place near Australia. He tells me he's with the YMCA here, looking after the Chinese labourers. Trust him, stupid do-gooder. She's with the medics at Hoogestadt."

"A nurse?"

"No, like us, a doctor. She's the bright one."

"That's great, Victor, you've family here fighting the same fight. That's more than can be said for most of us."

"I don't give a damn, actually, Jordi. They mean nothing to me."

Then the sirens of approaching ambulances cut short Jordi's next question.

"There seems to be many of them. Might have to grab some of the revellers," Jordi yelled as he dashed outside. Other doctors and nurses were already pelting past them.

*

They worked through the night. Men came in with feet stinking in heavy muddied boots, uniforms so covered in slime that they had to be scraped before the nurses could access the buttons. Many arrived in time to be pronounced dead and were taken in trucks to another section of the camp for processing before burial. Many were British, with some Canadians at this end of the trenches. But lately more and more Americans were beginning to come in as they got into the fighting.

As Hongyun worked on them, he was glad he was a doctor and not a soldier. *What a damn waste, damn waste,* he swore as he amputated a foot here, an arm there, patched up cracked skulls and ribs, sutured torn flesh and muscles. It was becoming a mantra to him. He wondered where they got so many young men from. Surely these warring nations would soon run out of cannon fodder. Well, they were now tapping into the American forces. That's where the new cannon fodder was coming from. Fresh young men volunteering to be killed in foreign fields far from home. He hated it, hated the waste of everything in this goddamn war. *How far away is bloody Alex? Which part of the radius of fifty miles is he in?*

*

1917: Hoogestadt -- Christmas
The kitchen and dining area of the alms house hospital had been turned into a party room by the enthusiastic young nurses. Sweet, sentimental wartime songs, especially composed to hearten the troops, played on the gramophone. The cooks had managed to get a large chunk of horsemeat. "A fine rump," Ted, the chief cook, had pronounced before roasting it with the potatoes, carrots and parsnips the garden had yielded. The nurses had blown up the few coloured balloons the kindly army chaplain, Father Donahue, had donated and were sharing the puddings, tarts and precious Christmas cakes from home. The remainder of some prized family wine still maturing in its small oak barrel had been relinquished by a neighbouring farmer, Jean-Paul Losette.

The personnel were taking turns to come into the dining room to eat and partake of the Christmas conviviality. The festive food was served to the wounded well enough to eat and, earlier, Father Donahue had donned a red surplice to distribute simple, handmade presents bought from the villagers, eager to supplement their income, to the patients, ringing his small bell as he made his way round the wards.

Emily, held tight in James Hopkins' arms, turned slowly with him in the centre of the room to the music, her eyes closed, tiredness banished to the back of her mind. His masculine scent thrilled her. Tonight, in freshly laundered khakis, he smelled of Knights Castile soap. She allowed herself to meld into him, aware of the warmth spreading in her groin and the dizziness in her head. She was in love with him as much he was with her. That much she knew. Tonight she had given up fighting her feelings, had stopped reminding herself of Wiremu each time James looked at her. Had deliberately stoppered up the bottle of guilt.

"I love you," he whispered into her hair.

"Yes," she murmured, nodding imperceptibly, "and I you, my darling."

His grip tightened even more. "Marry me when this war is over?"

She could not bring herself to answer. Now the vision of Wiremu sprang up between them, unbidden, unwanted, demanding. She hesitated.

"What's wrong?" His voice betrayed his gentle concern.

"Let's wait a while. It's such a long war."

"Then why wait? Precisely because it is a long war, why wait? Let's get married as soon as possible, live this confounded war out together, darling." He tilted his head back to look at her. Now the others were looking their way, smiling, knowing. In the drab, fear-generated atmosphere of the hospital, everyone was sensitive to nuances in the air.

Emily shifted her gaze from him only to let it fall on Father Donahue, who raised his cup with a smile and a wink. Beside him, Sister Fiona was beaming at them.

This was the first time Emily and James had been together sharing a proper meal and a drink in the four months since he arrived. *How I love you, James, God help me, I want to marry you, but what about Wiremu?* She now looked back at him.

"Tomorrow, my darling, I will give you my reasons. But please, let us enjoy tonight. Tonight is all we can be sure of," and, in front of everybody, she kissed him full on the mouth. Such a kiss as she had never experienced before, not even with Wiremu, the only man in her life since her return from China so many years ago. She felt herself disappear into him as tears coursed down her face. She knew whatever future she would have was here with James. So they held each other, oblivious of the world around them, for the longest period they would both later remember of holding each other, body and soul together... that Christmas... while out in the trenches not thirty miles away, hundreds of thousands of young men cried for home in the mud, as snow drifted down on them.

Chapter 26

February 1918: The Curse of Love Divided

Hongyun was driven up to Alex's hut as more snow fell from grey skies on the destroyed countryside. His jeep kept getting into ruts after they left the main road and by the time they arrived at the British camp, the driver was cussing roundly through his cigarette, his mood as foul as the weather. Once in, they had enquired for the whereabouts of the Kiwi pastor and were pointed in the direction of Alex's billet. It was a little before noon and the chance of finding him was good as the sentry at the gate had seen him that morning.

"Will you be long, Doc?" Sergeant Bill Brown asked. "It won't take me two ticks to deliver this mail and do the errands for the Captain."

"I hope not, Sarge, once I've found him. There won't be much to say."

"You're lucky you got family here, Doc, but on the other hand, I oughtta be thankful I haven't. Wouldn't want my kid brother in this mess, no sir."

Hongyun jumped off and entered the officers' #9 hut. Alex's bunk was at the far end and he was sitting at his desk with his back towards the entrance. *Strange, I'd recognise him anywhere,* Hongyun thought as he approached.

The bleak light from the window fell on the letter Alex was writing. So intent was he on the task that Hongyun was standing beside him a full minute before he looked up, and nearly jumped out of his skin.

"Oh, God! So I finally found you!" Alex leapt up. His arms reflexively reached out to hug Hongyun, but the indifferent look on the other's face made him lower them. "How are you?"

"I am as you see. How many letters did you write before one got to me?"

Alex laughed. "A dozen, I think, could be more. Lost count. Where are you based?"

"Poperinghe; we have base hospitals there. But we will probably get moved, depending on where the fighting is," Hongyun replied, sounding nonchalant.

"Emily is at Hoogestadt," Alex volunteered.

"That's close," Hongyun remarked, his eyes drifting toward the half-finished letter.

As he studied his older half-brother, Alex wondered why Hongyun had bothered to visit. He did not seem interested in any of his news. He followed Hongyun's glance. "I'm writing home to Pa. And Mama Yung. Just to let them know we are safe."

Now Hongyun noticed the sealed envelope with its familiar address and the English word "China" at the bottom. He felt a pang of jealousy. "Yes, I should write more often but never quite know what to say to Pa. Ma understands but somehow the old man is so judgemental." He cast a challenging look at Alex.

"Well, he is entitled to his opinions, brother, don't you think? Anyway, it's nearly lunch time. Care to join me?"

*

Playing with the horsemeat stew on his plate, Hongyun said, "How do you put up with this crap? Our catering's so much better at Poperinghe. When Britain and France are running out of steam, we, the conquering heroes, have brought all the good stuff from bounteous US of A. What exactly are you doing here, anyway? Do you work alongside your guys?"

"No, I don't do the labouring, if that's what you mean. But I help them with their daily problems back at camp, conduct services for the converts and try to extend the Christian line of hope and salvation to those that aren't of our faith. They live in great fear of dying here. But Hongyun, these men have such incredible fortitude. Most of the time, *they* prop me up. Tell me, are you in any danger yourself?"

"Not yet. We'll probably have to go out into the field before too long, though. That should be a lot of fun."

"Why did you sign up? I never thought you'd care enough."

"Don't you just sound like Pa! What did he say now, that he didn't think I had it in me!" Hongyun scoffed. "Wretched man, what does he know about me?"

"You're his son; I suppose he can read character as well as any," Alex replied quietly. He found Hongyun had put him off the simple stew he was eating but forced himself to finish it. He would never throw food away at any time, and certainly not now.

"How's Emily? Why did she come to this godforsaken conflict?"

Reluctantly, Alex filled him in with Emily's love story, leaving out James Hopkins' recent entry into his sister's life.

"Think this Wiremu fella will make it through?"

Alex shook his head slowly, his empathy for Wiremu overpowering him. "I don't think so. I think he's come to the stage of surrender, you know? The British are not treating the Maoris well in this war. I can't help feeling his spirit is broken. And from what I've seen, men die when they've lost that will to live."

"Poor bastard."

"And you, why did you come?" Alex looked across at the handsome face of his half-brother; smooth, seemingly untouched by the war. His khakis pressed.

"You would never guess in a million years," Hongyun replied with a sardonic smile.

"Tell me, I'm too tired to play games."

"For my lover," Hongyun whispered as he leant close across the table, looking around to make sure nobody in the crowded mess was listening.

"She's a doctor too?" Shake of Hongyun's head. "A nurse?" Another shake. "A French woman?"

Hongyun burst out laughing, then moved close to Alex's ear and whispered, "*He* signed up."

Alex stared at him, uncomprehending. Hongyun studied the tired, innocent face and shook his head. *Where has this guy been?* He decided to put him out of his perplexity.

"I like men."

And Alex's mouth dropped. "Is that possible? Is that allowed?" he whispered.

"Not allowed, so don't you go blathering on, baby boy. Keep mum." Hongyun lit a cigarette, offering Alex one. Alex took it, his hand shaking as his brother lit it for him.

At that moment, hell blew its door wide. A deafening blast from outside rumbled the mess. Everyone dived under the trestle tables. Screams of pain came from outside and grew in intensity. When the firing had stopped, they rushed out, Alex and Hongyun amongst them. Soldiers, Chinese coolies and ambulance crews working further down the fields closer to the front lay shattered. The ambulances were fire-lit, smouldering wrecks. Bodies lay scattered everywhere in the blackened landscape.

By the time Alex and Hongyun arrived, some men on the perimeter were picking themselves up. Others writhed and moaned in agony. Body parts were scattered around, the mud taking on a sinister reddening colour as blood pooled in the clay soil. Sirens rang out; horses whinnied in panic, kicking at their constraints in the stables. Shouts came from all directions with the pounding of feet as men ran past them with stretchers.

Sergeant Bill Brown came panting up to Hongyun. "That's some blast from hell, Doc," he panted. "Any more to come, d'you reckon?"

Hongyun shook his head, shrugged. Alex was already ahead, and had reached the field where many Chinese lay.

"Whaddya wanna do, Doc? Stay and help or go back to base?" Sergeant Brown asked.

"There is a hospital here, right? I'm sure they could use me. Why don't you check that formality out while I go down and lend a hand?"

"How the hell did they get that close?" Bill Brown asked.

"They must've got longer guns now, that's how. Trying us out for range practice."

The Chinese labourers on lay-by rushed past with stretchers to pick up the dead and wounded. Sergeant Jarvis stomped up to Alex.

"Tell your men to hop onto that truck, get digging graves. As soon as we've identified these, we'll bury them," he ordered, his face grim.

Alex saw Huan amongst the group of helpers.

"Thank God you're safe. Where's Feng Hua?"

"There, he's all right." Huan pointed at a stretcher bearer.

"How many men have we lost?" Alex asked as they both laid an unconscious soldier onto a stretcher.

"There were at least three hundred on duty in this field. Too early to say, Brother Alex."

*

Hongyun stayed till the next day, operating well into the night. The triages were soon overloaded, but more ambulances had come and began to take the excess wounded off-site to hospitals in and around Ypres.

Alex stopped by the operating hut and, from the doorway, watched Hongyun work. This was the Hongyun he had not seen before, the serious eyes over the surgical mask, the steady hands in blood-stained gloves moving confidently over broken body parts. *I must write Pa about this. He should know what Hongyun is capable of. He can be proud of him.*

*

James Hopkins marched down the lane towards the town of Hoogestadt, his hands stuffed deep into his army wool coat, collar turned up, cap down over his eyes. His breath curled white in the frosty air as snow swirled down on him. He had a couple of hours free before checking in for theatre duty. It was Michael's shift till then.

True to her word, Emily had stolen a half hour away from work on Boxing Day and, in tears, explained her moral conundrum of Wiremu. She had begged James for patience, for time till she could see Wiremu and sort things out between them. That was two months ago now, and she had not been able to see Wiremu.

"Write to him. You know where he is, write."

"No, James, I can't. I've got to see him face to face."

"Is it possible for him to come to see you? When he's on furlough?"

She had shaken her head. Of course Wiremu could have visited and James knew it was Emily who was putting off that day. She, who was so brave in so much, was afraid of facing Wiremu, afraid of going back on her own word to him. James

215

had been furious and backed off: backed off to try to be out of love, backed off to mend his pride. He was being put in second place to a common colonial soldier. And he now needed to walk off his steam in the flat, ravaged countryside.

Sister Fiona had whispered to him a few days into the New Year, "We can make a room ready as married quarters, James, anytime." To which he had smiled lamely.

In his angry moments, not even young Michael Ladrow could cheer him up. He had tried reasoning with himself, had asked himself why he should be involved with a Chinese woman. He had left all that behind when he was sent home from Macau more than twenty years ago. Didn't he hate the Chinese for being the cause of his parents' neglect of him and Margaret? Hadn't he sworn he would have nothing to do with them again? Bloody hell, why was he hung up on a string by one then?

And damn that native Wiremu. But Emily was herself half New Zealand native. And that was another thing: she was secretive about her mother. Why? What was she hiding? Yet here he was, damn it, besotted. For the first time in his life, he was truly in love. Not the infatuation with a beautiful socialite, but with a woman so assured of her own being she did not need the artifice of cosmetics, perfume or fashion. Emily moved with an inner calm borne of her humanity. She knew her place in the universe. Perhaps she knew his too?

*

One evening, Michael had come across him smoking outside their hut and in his misery he had confided his reservations to the younger man.

Michael had been a thoughtful listener, and stayed quiet till James had finished. Then he said in a steady voice, "I have heard it said that children of China missionaries usually have an abiding affection for the natives their parents ministered to. That the country gets under their skin despite the Celestials' poverty, their heathenism, their intricacies. Perhaps it is a challenge too difficult to be let go. The fact that they cannot overcome such insurmountable problems means it's a test for them forever. Maybe that's Emily's hold on you, James. She represents that challenge, do you think? You love her, yet you despise her race."

And he had nodded slowly. "You could be right, I possibly do despise the Chinese, though I know I have no right to."

"And you want to marry her, James, but think awhile. Would she be of use to you back in England?"

"What do you mean?"

"Socially. She's not even white, is she? I can't imagine Mummy's crowd welcoming her into their fold, can you?"

James pondered before answering with some derision, "To be honest, Michael, I don't think Emily would want to be with Mummy's type of women."

"What other type is there, James?"

"Ah, Michael, that shows how sheltered your world really is. Emily is a colonial, yet is even outside of that system. She would, I know, prefer to be with ordinary working people. She would hate England."

"What will you do then, if and when she agrees to marry you?"

"I've thought hard about it. I shall go out to New Zealand."

"Oh God, James, are you serious?"

"As can be, Michael. I don't think England will mean that much to me without Emily."

And Michael had left him, shaking his head.

*

And now he walked on. But not twenty minutes later, a convoy of Red Cross ambulances roared past him, on the way to Hoogestadt alms house, now their hospital. He turned and ran back.

James arrived to find the place in an uproar. There were five ambulances in all, each with six wounded men. Michael and Emily worked among the other personnel, unloading the stretchers whose occupants were divided into the main hospital and the medic huts. Everyone moved with frantic precision. Emily and Michael were a well-matched team: Michael was supervising those going into the medic huts while Emily controlled the emergency inflow. As he trotted up, James could hear the soft moans of the wounded and shouted instructions being bandied about. Then suddenly Emily uttered a shriek. He ran to her. Sister Fiona was already holding her by the shoulders as Emily bent over a wounded Anzac with a pool of blood on his torso.

She looked up as James approached, her face tear-streaked.

"Wiremu," she uttered, unbelieving.

James looked down with horror at the man. Wiremu was unconscious, with a large gash above the right temple. The blood was widening on his stomach. James stared at Emily, who was beginning to recover some composure.

"Get him into the operating room," she ordered.

Sister Fiona led the way. Emily strode briskly in with them, followed by James. He wanted to see the outcome of the operation, yet was aware of his unworthy hope of a negative result.

Wiremu had sustained injuries too severe to survive. He died as James and a weeping Emily worked on his abdomen. He had multiple gunshot wounds to his liver, spleen and a greater part of his bowels. They could see the spread of the smashed organs. And the bleeding refused to stop. Within five minutes of being loaded onto the operating table, Wiremu stopped breathing. It was then that Emily burst into wails of such hopeless pathos that neither Sister Fiona nor James could touch her. She collapsed weeping over Wiremu's body as the other two stood helplessly by. The assisting nurse had already absconded.

"Let us see to the others, James. Leave her be a while," Sister Fiona whispered.

Then a Maori soldier entered searching for Wiremu. He was directed to Emily slumped over his body. The man took a look at Wiremu from the entrance, then approached Emily.

"Doctor, I know you are his *wahine*, I have seen your photo in his Bible. I am Corporal Jack Hohepa from his division. Before you send him to the grave, may I say a *karakia* for him? It is our way, to say a prayer for our dead."

Emily gazed at the ravaged face of this soldier, old before his time, his entire body covered in mud and slime. She nodded and moved aside for him. With both hands, Corporal Hohepa took some water from the basin nearby and washed Wiremu's face and arms with sad reverence. Then, with his face uplifted, he closed his eyes and with raised hands intoned a prayer so moving, so heartfelt, that Emily wept afresh. When he finished, Corporal Hohepa brought himself up straight and saluted Wiremu.

"Farewell, my brother, may your journey home be swift and light. Today, a mighty totara has fallen in the forest of Tane. *Kua hinga te totara i te wao nui a Tane.*"

As he took his leave, he said, "Doctor Emily, if you have occasion to write to your Pa, please tell him I am the grandson of Tai, from the village outside Oamaru. Pita Hohepa was my grand-uncle. Please give him our regards. We never forgot him." And he was gone.

Emily stared at his retreating back and, from the recesses of her memory, retrieved the information from her father's story of his time at Pita Hohepa's marae. Then she remembered who it was who had gone against a discarded tradition and had her grandmother Arel's head smoked as a keepsake for her own mother, Horowhai.

*

James did not have a free moment till well after midnight. From the time he left Emily to her grief, he had performed seven amputations. Six were battle wounds but one was a trench foot. All thoughts of Emily and Wiremu were blanked out as he, Michael and other surgeons worked round the clock.

After a quiet lull around Christmas, the fighting had renewed. The trench casualties from diseases mounted with the freezing cold. Emily had talked of the hospital in Ypres since Alex's first visit to Hoogestadt, and had visited with him, Alex, at the Chinese camp in Noyelles-Sur-Mer where there was also one. She had told James that Alex was ministering across the field camps for a stretch of fifty miles along the front. Casualties, dead and wounded, mounted into the hundreds of thousands with each offensive as the war dragged on. Emily had been worried sick for her brothers and Wiremu all the time he had known her. And now Wiremu was dead. She was free. James hated himself for the elation that crept into his heart.

The next morning, he saw Emily, with red puffy eyes, standing at the kitchen table eating a bowl of porridge.

"Have you been up all night?" he asked gently as he held her, gazing into her exhausted face.

She nodded. "You?"

"Yes, and there'll be more today too, from what the radio says. There's renewed fighting east of Ypres. Our troops are trying to reclaim the mile or two that they lost in the last offensive. Winning or losing a yard at a time as boys go down like flies." *A dance of death macabre*, he thought to himself. He saw she was distracted beyond caring. "You must rest, darling, get some sleep before the next onslaught."

Emily whispered, "I've released Wiremu's body for burial. I must write to his aunt, she'll want a letter from me. It was good I was with him at the end. She'd like that... yes...she'd... like that."

James took her up to her room. Coming downstairs, he said to Sister Fiona, "Please let her sleep on, Sister. As she is, she'll be hopeless working anyway."

"She wept through the night, James, as she worked. It's a wonder she's still standing. Don't worry; she can sleep till the heavens fall down, I'll see to that. And you make sure you do now." She stumbled off to give that instruction to the day crew before tottering to her own bed.

Chapter 27

He who pursues revenge digs two graves

There were now greatly increased numbers of German troops all along the Front. Upon learning of the latest development, Alex told his Chinese that Russia had pulled out of the war. The Russians were having their own revolution. The Czar and his family had been executed in some obscure place none of them had ever heard of. So the Eastern flank of the German army was now free to concentrate on making their lives even more untenable.

He wrote to Emily and Hongyun separately with the same message.

'We're all very sick. Of course you know the diseases are inflicting as much damage as the physical wounds. My men are so dispirited; their nerves so stretched to breaking point that they succumb to every germ around. The only thing they are spared is trench foot. Not too many seem to get that. But their dental hygiene, never good to begin with, is dreadful now. Doctor Lewis here tells me bad oral hygiene poisons the entire body. But how can my poor Chinese put that together with the rest of their suffering? How I pray for all this abomination to end soon.'

To his fellow missionaries back at the Y in Tsingdao, he wrote,

'Alas, you were only too right. After all these months here, I am convinced certain men are created by the Devil for his own purpose. With so much carnage around I cannot help but think that the powers ordering this death and destruction are reaping for Satan. Damn them to hell. God forgive me, but I grow angrier by the day as I see the futility of it all. I only pray I will be able to bring back my flock as intact as He would allow.'

To his father and Eddie, he was slightly more circumspect as to the tragedy. But he could not help adding, 'From my studies of *The Romance of the Three Kingdoms* or the *Warring States Period*, I know that never in the Chinese history of wars was there ever so much butchery as what we are witnessing here. These European nations are stripping each other of their young men. There are fresh stories of old men and young boys being now drafted to fight. I pray that isn't true.'

And in Dunedin, safe on the far side of the world, Zhou Yu once more cursed Alex Don for brainwashing his youngest son with his missionary zeal.

*

Brother Huan came to see Alex one evening when he was praying with a separate group of newcomers.

"Our group is going on trench duty tomorrow morning, Brother Alex, and we have been told it will be for at least six days before our next rest. The weather is clearing now with spring and Feng Hua is ready."

Alex put down his Chinese Bible and said quietly, "I will come down with you, Brother Huan, down to the trenches."

Everybody gasped. Huan held up his hand, "No, no, you must not. You do not know how horrible it is. To be there even for a day, Alex, will destroy your soul. Alex, Feng Hua must make his own destiny. You have done your best. I only came to tell you so that you will be prepared for whatever comes next."

"Nevertheless, I will go," Alex replied, his voice strangely calm to those listening.

"Oh heaven forgive me, I should not have told you," Brother Huan wailed.

"I shall be all right. I need to be with him at his time."

*

At dawn, Alex, with a canvas pack of necessities on his back, ran to catch up with Brother Huan's labour group of two hundred men. Huan had given him a set-out time of ten but he knew that was too late an hour for a work team to leave camp. So he had woken up at seven but, even so, now found them to be three quarters of a mile ahead. He soon caught up with the straggling, work-worn men dragging their feet along the battle-scarred earth. Only Feng Hua, wearing a look of maniacal

222

determination, had a zing in his step, despite his deteriorating health. He seemed to be already there, his knife at the first German throat.

For weeks Feng Hua had been living in an alternating state of feverish anticipation and disappointment. The winter had not produced many fine days or nights. The much-needed moon had been obscured most of the time by heavy clouds and he had not been lucky enough to be rostered for trench work when it was fine. He always kept his well-honed knife in his belt when he was sent to labour, but the opportunity for him to creep into enemy trenches never arose. Since their arrival at the Ypres front, Feng Hua's will to fulfil his mission had pulled him through a bout of cholera and dysentery. He had also survived shrapnel wounds to his back and legs.

When Alex visited him on these occasions in hospital, all Feng Hua could talk about were the killing opportunities he might have missed during his recuperation.

"I fear for him, Sergeant Jarvis. I'm sure his mental health is deteriorating. Is there any way we can get him transferred back to factory duties at Noyelles-Sur-Mer?"

"Not a hope, old chap. The superiors have too much to worry about to be interested in one Chinaman going gaga in the trenches. They would tell us to just point his nose in the enemies' direction and prod him onwards."

Now Alex walked beside Feng Hua for the two miles to a new part of the trenches. Like the others, this area was on low, boggy ground with the Germans holding the dryer high ridge about four hundred yards away. As they approached, the sound of shelling boomed their welcome. Activity behind the trenches was intense as always. Men with stretchers were running to and from waiting ambulances. Huge tangles of barbed wire were strewn across the destroyed land. The miasma of the unburied and the irretrievable body parts rotting in the mud swamped them. The fear of the labourers was palpable. Many started praying under their breaths.

Feng Hua, too, was praying.

"*Ommimotofo*, Lord Buddha, give me the first opportunity as soon as possible. Allow me the revenge my father's spirit cries out for. *Ommimotofo, ommimotofo.*"

Alex saw he was fingering his prayer beads wrapped loosely on his left wrist together with his identification band as his eyes scanned the ridge. His knife was wrapped in a dirty rag wedged into his belt.

"You bastards certainly took your time," a red-faced, pockmarked sergeant ran up to them. "Anybody here speakie Englishie?"

Another shell explosion; the British were returning fire. They all ducked involuntarily.

"Well?" asked the sergeant as he righted himself.

"Yes," Alex and Huan replied simultaneously.

"Well, you are to go over to that part fifty degrees north." He pointed in the direction. "Start digging away from the existing trench. Then start laying wire fifty yards closer to Jerry lines. They've got to push as much of the existing wire forward as possible. Chop, chop!" He pelted off but after a few steps turned back and shouted, "Hey, you the New Zealand chaplain for this lot? I've heard of you."

"Yes," Alex answered, turning round.

"Don't go in there, mate. They need you for later."

"Thank you. But they need me now." And Alex continued walking.

"Suit yerself," cussed the sergeant as he ran off.

*

Alex and the Chinese ran the last hundred yards in a crouching position to minimise their exposure to sniper fire, dodging the strafing bullets. When they reached the trench, each jumped in with relief. The soldiers in there moved to make room for them.

"Great now that these Chinks are here. Let's set them to work," one said. "Hey, you speakie Englishie? Get moving over there, and there and there." He pointed to the points all along the dug-outs.

Alex jumped in after Huan who was interpreting for the Limey. The coolies took a swig from their water canteens before beginning work. All of them were already covered with mud.

The walk boards were slippery, oozing mud and blood from the ground below, and were barely discernible. The inexorable stench slapped Alex in the face as he hunkered down and made his way towards the soldiers. They all tied kerchiefs to their faces. The coolies ran along the walk boards further down to begin digging several channels towards the German lines with shovels nearly as long as themselves.

Feng Hua was the first in one of the channels. "I'll go as close towards them as I can," he muttered, "just watch me, Pa, just watch me. I'm not afraid, Pa, not afraid. I shall avenge you, yes, yes. Soon. Soon."

Huan was filled with despair as he watched him. He knew his old school friend was numbering his days in this hell. As the guns blazed near them, sharp and deafening, he knew all he could do was pray. So he did, as each man around him did. They prayed as they dug, prayed to see home, to see family, to be back on the farm in one piece, where the allotments and their accumulated pay would make a better life for them all.

Alex tried to befriend the soldiers around but most were too sick and exhausted to be interested in conversation. Half of them had been on the Front for several months without furlough and most had festering wounds. Many were feverish. Many more had heads or parts of torsos and limbs wrapped in dirty bandages. The reek of rotten flesh remained moribund in the trench.

Cigarette smoke drifted around. "Got to smoke, mate. Helps still hunger pains and the smoke goes in part to mask the pong. You can buy a ciggy for a ha'penny from Jones over there. They're a bit sodden, but better than nought, aye?"

By nightfall they had dug through the fifty yards of frozen soil and their teams began to split sideways to form the fighting trench. Alex had gone back to Huan, and taken up a shovel to help.

"I think I will make it tonight," Feng Hua came up to them, his eyes gleaming through his exhaustion.

"Perhaps not tonight, Feng Hua. You should rest. What strength would you have to crawl over No Man's Land?" Alex replied.

"But the moonlight will be good tonight," Feng Hua insisted. "I've waited so long for moonlight."

"All the better for them to see you with?" Alex said.

Feng Hua looked nonplussed. "Maybe you are right, Alex-ah. So I waited for nothing. Tomorrow I will not work as hard, conserve my strength."

"And pray for the moon to be hidden," added Huan.

"Oh yes, I will pray. You are right, Alex-ah. My Pa will hide the moon. He wants revenge."

*

That night, by the light of the moon, they ate their lumps of boiled horsemeat and bread to the sounds of scurrying rats round their feet. They could not sit down; the freezing water had risen with the newly dug trenches, obscuring the walk boards and they stood six inches deep in the odorous sludge. They leaned against the wooden supports eating their cold rations in silence – too exhausted to care about the rats, or to mind the stench which now seemed a part of them.

"The only fat things I see here are these rodents," Huan murmured.

"Well, they certainly have a lot of food. So many unburied dead out there," replied Alex.

But Huan was now looking out at teams of soldiers crawling up ladders onto No Man's Land. "What are those soldiers doing?" He whispered.

"I think they are reconnoitring or bringing back bodies for burial," Alex replied as he too looked.

"They will be shot," Huan whispered.

And as though by command, a long line of bullets strafed the ground followed by short cries as they hit their targets. Now the soldiers were scampering down, pulling the injured and dead after them.

"See, Feng Hua, aren't you glad you didn't attempt to go over tonight?" Alex asked.

"Yah, it's too bright," the recalcitrant agreed.

Feng Hua's teeth chattered loud in the cold. Alex and Huan, though shivering, were not so adversely affected.

"Are you all right?" Alex asked. "Do you have a fever?"

"Yes, Alex-ah, I always have a fever. But tonight it is slightly worse. I think I am over-tired and also excited about tomorrow night."

"And frightened too?"

"Yes, very much frightened too." Feng Hua's voice dropped away.

"Don't do it, Feng Hua. Your Pa will understand. He would rather you live and look after your mother in her old age, than die here in the mud. Those Germans who ordered his execution are not the ones here. You would be killing young men your own age who had nothing to do with China."

"I have prepared a long time for this day," Feng Hua remained obstinate.

"If you were killed, your mother would not be able to visit your grave, nor feed your spirit at Chingming. Be kind to her. Don't do it." Alex peered into the gaunt face in the moonlight. He saw the eyes glistening in the silver shadow; the mouth gripped thin. He looked down sadly at his lump of bread. There was nothing more he could say.

*

The next day, the coolies made good progress along the parallel trenches. Alex noticed Feng Hua digging his part heading towards the German-held ridge. He could see what the distraught man was up to. He would make his exit from out of his own digging that night, closest to the ridge. Throughout the late afternoon, Feng Hua kept looking up at the clouds and Alex's gaze followed his upwards. It looked like Feng Hua would get his wish. Cumulous clouds were gathering.

By nine o'clock, the moon was behind clouds.

"Well, here I go," Feng Hua whispered, "wish me good fortune." And he climbed up the ladder.

"God go with you, Feng Hua," Alex whispered as he watched the determined man crawl away.

As Alex and the others peered over the top, they could see his black form heading towards slight depressions in the destroyed ground. He stopped every so often, as if testing to see if he had been noticed. Meanwhile, on the far side of the old trench, British soldiers were running around picking up bodies whilst some crept further away, heading up the ridge. A hail of indiscriminate fire followed them, except this time, under cloud cover, they were able to work on gathering up the dead whilst their group who were reconnoitring sprinted away in a half crouch.

Alex's gaze returned to Feng Hua and he was surprised to see him crawling much further up the ridge. He must have taken advantage of the action on the other side and sprinted, but now in the lull, was once more creeping on his belly. In a trice, the shadow was gone.

"Oh Lord, Brother Huan, Feng Hua's disappeared."

"Down into enemy lines?"

"Must be. I was watching him but he's gone now."

"Oh, pray with me now, Alex, pray with me now. I cannot bear it otherwise."

So Alex, Huan and the Christians gathered around and prayed, standing ankle-deep in worm-crawling, rat-slithering, freezing mud.

*

It was close to midnight before Feng Hua slipped over the top of their trench. The moon was now high in the tempestuous sky and clouds scudded rapidly across it. He startled them in their snatched, upright sleep.

"I'm back," he said, triumphant.

Nobody made a move. All waited for him to elaborate. "I killed over fifty of them," he went on. "As silent as a cat, I was. Came up from behind, held them by their mouths as I slit their throats. Then I released them so softly, their companions didn't notice the difference between the living and the dead."

"Now I hope you are satisfied, Xiao Hua," whispered Huan in the dark. "No more, okay?"

"Oh no! I'm going out every night that I can. I have courage! I know what to do now."

"But you've killed fifty for the six who oversaw your father's death, Feng Hua. Surely that's revenge enough?" Alex now reasoned.

"No. I know what I'm doing, Alex-ah. Don't talk anymore. I need to sleep."

*

The next day, Sergeant Jarvis came around. He had been overseeing another group of labourers further west. As he stopped to talk to Alex, Feng Hua came up, encrusted with mud and blood from head to foot.

"Tell him, Alex-ah. Tell this sergeant what I did last night. He should be pleased there's fifty less Germans to shoot at us."

Alex studied the boastful face of the Chinese, but hesitated to impart this piece of information.

"What's he saying, Alex?"

Reluctantly, Alex replied, "He killed fifty Germans last night. Crept up the ridge under cloud cover and slashed fifty throats."

Jarvis turned to Feng Hua with a look of surprised approval. "Did he now? Well, that's wonderful. Tell him that."

So Alex translated and Feng Hua made a mock salute, grinning.

"Tell him I will continue as long as I can," said Feng Hua.

Upon this translation, Jarvis turned back to Alex, "He's just given me an idea, Alex. Tell him we can use him. He could probably help our cause."

"How?" Alex asked, hating what he knew would be coming.

"He can reconnoitre for us. Take note of their positions; let us know how many men and guns there are up behind that ridge. Maybe even lob a grenade or two on his way out. Think he can do that? He looks bright enough."

Alex shook his head. "I'd rather he doesn't endanger himself any more than he has to. He's an only son."

"Yes, but he's hell bent on carrying on." Jarvis became impatient as he looked at the placid pastor. "He might as well be really useful."

When Alex explained this latest bit, leaving out the grenade part, Feng Hua drew himself up with pride and thumped his chest.

"Tell the sergeant I can count the guns and draw him the places of the big guns. And I will go back tonight, even if it rains."

And he did. That night and the night after, through the sleet of spring, while Alex and the other Chinese prayed for him. On each return, he gave Jarvis positions of the long guns and boasted of the many throats he slit.

"I'm sure the Germans must be puzzled, Alex-ah," he chuckled, tired, yet so very satisfied. "They must be wondering who the phantom throat slitter is, since it is not a tactic of true soldiers. Yah?"

And with the information, the British were able to push through more effective measures of silencing the long guns. But it was not forever. With each advantage came more disadvantages for both sides, and once more another stalemate ensued with many thousands more lives wasted. The bodies rotted, the stench increased and half the men went slowly mad.

*

At the end of a shift, Jarvis told Alex, "Tell your men to go back to base, but your Feng Hua wants to remain. Do you think he can make it? He looks positively maniacal."

Alex translated. Feng Hua was adamant about remaining.

"I can keep on, Alex-ah. I have my father's courage and he's watching over me."

"Feng Hua, please take this rest and when we return next week you will be of even greater and better use. Don't worry."

So Feng Hua, now assured of his place in the British line, reluctantly agreed to return to rest with the others. But he pained everybody so much with his stories of bravado, which most of them thought were exaggerated, that they took to avoiding his company and slept with their pillows over their heads.

*

As Alex listened to Feng Hua, he feared for the security of the man's mind. It was not just his incessant boasting but the feverish gleam in his eyes and the way he kept repeating his words, his stutters increasingly worse.

He might have been gassed, Alex thought. *Yet the others were not affected by this gibbering.*

He wrote to Brother Matthew in Noyelles. 'I fear for our friend's mental and emotional state. He is rapidly declining and I can only watch hopelessly, uselessly, as he plunges deeper into his private nightmare. I can get no help from the British because their own men are also quagmired in this desperately corrosive situation. What is one mad Chinese coolie amongst hundreds of thousands of British men slowly losing their sanity,

230

lives and limbs in this useless, cruel war? At least I am grateful a big number of you are moderately safe in your factories. You told me some are talking of remaining in France should they survive the war. For the life of me, I cannot understand why.'

Chapter 28

Reunion: Chateau-Thierry.

After the bitterly cold spring, the Germans renewed their offensives and started the march towards Paris, rolling their tanks and cannons towards the French capital after taking on the British and French armies in Somme and Lys. In spite of the reinforcements from the Russian front, they had not managed to gain very much ground and now, with the Americans in the arena, were pushing for new advantages.

*

Hongyun's field medical corps had to relocate with the advance of 27,500 marines of the US Army's 3rd Division towards the town of Chateau-Thierry. The Germans had to be stopped before they could cross the River Marne. Casualties in the previous Somme and Lys offensives had been so severe that, like every member of the medical corps, Hongyun was buried up to his elbows in surgery. He had had no time to sort out his private life with Curtis.

In the months since they landed in France, Curtis seemed to have developed a life of his own independent of his relationship with Hongyun. They did not share the same quarters in this new location. In their time off, Curtis usually had recreation planned which did not include Hongyun and, from the occasional group talk, Hongyun surmised he was consorting with the local French and Flemish women in what was left of the villages and towns.

He's deserting me, deserting us. The mantra broke repeatedly through Hongyun's consciousness as he tried to concentrate on his work in the surgical units. *He is like Dexter, bi-sexual. Why can't I be like them? Life would be so much easier.*

232

But he knew he wasn't like them. He was true. True to himself at such harrowing times when he needed to have someone true to him, to be with him: an alien in this alien land – in a war that destroyed both body and soul, and not of their making.

One foggy dawn, he was coming off duty after operating all night; the casualties of the salient at Chemin des Dames were still coming in by ambulance loads. He spotted Curtis walking away from another medical station. The triage tents covered a square mile on the ravaged land, blighting the spring green of the few remaining trees around what had once been fertile fields. Red Cross ambulances were making turn-around trips. Trucks carried the repaired wounded to Calais to be shipped to England or on to Paris and other safer cities in the region to convalesce. Horses, mules and tanks were tended to in stables and workshops on the outer perimeters of the Allied encampment.

Now Curtis, head bowed, was tramping to one of the canteens near their barracks. Hongyun ran to catch up.

"Curtis! Wait for me!"

The anaesthetist turned around, exhaustion lining his olive-skinned face. He had a shadow of bristles and looked as crumpled as a sack turned inside out.

"Hey, Victor, what's up?" Curtis carried on walking, hands in the pockets of his bloodied khakis.

"I just want to see you, it's been a while. How have you been?"

Curtis' neutral demeanour had disarmed Hongyun, vacating his mind of all his intended speeches.

"I'm okay, fella, just overworked like everyone, right? What do you want to see me about?"

Hongyun was stumped.

"I... I thought we might get some rec time together, go somewhere..." He fumbled about, feeling drained and hopeless; helpless in the face of Curtis' indifference.

"Here? It's at least twenty miles into Chateau which is probably shot to hell by now, and in case you need reminding, the war's still on." Curtis carried on walking. "Look, Victor, I'm doggone tired and I just wanna feed and rest up, okay? I don't know about your roster, but I'm on again at six, so bye!"

And he walked on, picking up his pace just a little, but sufficient enough to leave Hongyun standing, staring after him as he walked away in the lightening morning mist.

After a moment's hesitation, Hongyun followed but chose the second canteen. He, too, needed to eat and sleep. He, too, was going back on duty at six that evening, if not before.

*

Late spring in southern England in 1918 was refreshingly beautiful. James had persuaded Emily to visit with his family on their joint furlough and now they were on the bus going through the New Forest. Both sat silent, hands clasped, as they allowed the peace of this ancient forest's spring green to wash over them. James had deliberately chosen this mode of travel instead of taking his usual train, so that Emily might be persuaded to like England, and be happy to live there with him. Though he was fully prepared to immigrate to New Zealand if she so wished, as a last resort, he was an Englishman after all with a lucrative practise in Harley Street to return to after the war.

*

It had taken her months to get anywhere past her grieving of Wiremu's death. James knew her sorrow was heavily overlaid with guilt. She had intended to break gently with Wiremu when they next met, but death had intervened instead. Subsequently, torn between grief and relief, she could not allow her love for James free rein. She had written to Wiremu's aunt with her personal condolences and, in the same post, had informed her father and Eddie.

As she licked the envelope addressed to her family, she was almost tempted to add, 'And now you don't have to worry about Wiremu and I being together. He has solved your problem for you.' But she could not recriminate her father for this. He was not to blame. She only hoped his relief would soften his feelings for the dead Maori. So instead she had added the information about Corporal Hohepa, ending with 'They still remember you well in that marae.'

*

In Dunedin, Zhou Yu received the news with mixed emotions. He was relieved, but the sadness that overwhelmed him was inexplicable. In his mind, the deaths of Arel, Horowhai and Wiremu fused together in one big, explosive emptiness that dragged him deep into its void. He took to his bed. Eddie returned home from the office to find him under the blankets in a foetal position, his face set in stony silence, his eyes staring at something beyond the physical four walls of his bedroom – staring within himself.

"Pa, what's the matter?" Eddie asked.

No answer. Eddie touched his shoulder but Zhou Yu neither moved nor looked up at him. After a while, Eddie went into the kitchen to find Emily's letter lying open on the kitchen table. He read it and started to ponder about the effect it obviously had on his father. But Eddie, with his straightforward approach to life, could no more fathom his father's angst than he could his own wife's aversion to him. Unlike Emily and Alex, he had not been privy to Zhou Yu's last days at Pita Hohepa's marae.

He made a cup of tea and took it to his father. Zhou Yu was in the same space as when he left him. Eddie put the cup on the bedside table and shut the door, leaving his father in the darkening night.

So much death. All those deaths. What is it all for? Where is God in all this? Zhou Yu wept deep within himself. *"Ying, Yun, my dead brothers. General Li... all those innocents, so many millions killed to no avail. Now, so many millions are being killed. To no avail. Oh heaven, I am so tired of all this... so tired.*

Zhou Yu did not rise from his bed till well into the next afternoon. He took himself down to the shops, but avoided going to his warehouse. He bought some fresh vegetables and then walked towards the wharves where Southern Ocean Fisheries had a walk-in shop for the locals. He chose a large blue cod and plodded home. He intended to cook his son a good dinner that night. He intended to celebrate the living.

"This is a great dinner, Pa. Thank you."

Eddie looked at his father across the deep platter of cod steamed in soya sauce and sesame oil, cooked whole the way

Zhou Yu liked it – the way the entire family liked it. The cod's upturned eye popped up at him in its blank stare, the green of the spring onions enticingly fresh against the grey skin of the fish, the white flesh peeping through the diagonal slits Zhou Yu had made across its body. *The fish cooks quicker that way*, he had once explained. And they had all followed his example. A plate of egg omelette done with young sliced onions and a bowl of fresh, stir-fried greens completed the meal with its usual rice and soup.

No doubt about it, Eddie thought fondly, *Pa's a great cook.*

Then his thoughts wandered to his mother Horowhai, dead now all these years, and he shook his head in reflex. She wasn't much of a cook, and in his early years his father's cooking filled the family most nights. He studied Zhou Yu silently. There was something on his father's mind that was begging to get out. Eddie decided to wait for the old man to speak while he enjoyed his repast.

Finally, when nothing was forthcoming, he said,

"I saw Mr Hats this afternoon. He's retired from Land and Survey, you know? He asked after you and Em and Alex. He said Mrs Hats and her group of ladies are knitting socks like mad for the boys at the Front."

Zhou Yu nodded, distracted. "I shall visit them one day soon," he said.

Halfway through the meal, Zhou Yu said, "This war reminds me of the one I fought in all those years ago. The Taiping Tian Guo. It has the same futility, the same loss of lives for no winnable cause."

Eddie nodded, waited for him to continue.

"When I got that letter yesterday, and I notice you've read it, I was not overjoyed that Wiremu is dead. On the contrary, I felt desolate. Yes, desolate. Yet you know, somewhere, a relief that he is not around to scare me where Emily is concerned. But desolation, that was what affected me so much. And suddenly, the reliving of that other war when I lost my brothers. When I myself took part in so much futile killing. I didn't think it would affect me still, but yesterday... I knew... yesterday, that I would go to my grave with it."

"Pa, your war was long past."

Zhou Yu shook his head slowly. "It's my survival, you see, Eddie. Why I lived when millions died. I live with that guilt. My brothers deserved life much more than I. Ying was so clever, so original, so very comical. My father adored him because he was the image of our mother in so many ways. He was the reminder of their wonderful marriage, and that was a rare thing in those days. And Zhou Yun was so brave, loyal, so very handsome. You would have loved them both, Eddie, loved them both. Yet they died and I lived. That news of Wiremu made me realise how useless my life has been. I couldn't even be a good husband, not to your mother and certainly not to Yung. Certainly, I was a very poor son."

"No, Pa! You have lived well, made something of yourself here in spite of all the difficulties. You are a kind and good man, Pa. Please, don't think otherwise."

"Have I been a good father, Eddie?"

"Oh yes, Pa, the very best. We all – Em, Alex and I – think you are the best."

"I'm glad of that," Zhou Yu said in a whisper.

As Eddie studied his father eating his dinner in slow motion, with a droop of the head, a stoop of the thin shoulders, he saw the fragility in the old man that he had not noticed before. Zhou Yu was now seventy years old. His hair was greying over his still handsome face, but it was a face lined with deep sadness and uncertainty.

If ever there is a picture of contrition, this is it, Eddie thought. *I hope he's not sick. I wish to God Em and Alex would come home soon.*

*

James took Emily by cab to his father's house, now his. His father had died of pneumonia when James was serving his second term in France.

'It is a mercy he passed when he did, dearest James,' his sister Margaret had written after the funeral. 'His mind was most delicate and his lungs were drowning in fluid. Please don't grieve over-much. He wouldn't have liked that...'

Now, as he showed Emily into the house, he felt a rush of tears, regretting that he was not even able to attend the funeral. His father's presence was still around. His pipe in its rack, a tin

237

of tobacco beside it. Margaret had tidied the house up, but, as she informed him in her letters, had left Pater's possessions where they were for James to sort out, being closer to Pater in his last years and all.

He saw that she had recently dusted the place and left a bucket of coal by the fireplace, already set, in the drawing room. Emily watched him as he moved solemnly about reacquainting himself with his father's possessions.

After a while he turned to her.

"Welcome to my home, my darling," and took her into his arms. She felt his tremble through her woollen army coat. "Let's rest awhile and have a cup of tea before going over to Margaret's, shall we?"

He led the way to the kitchen and lit the gas stove. There was already water in the whistling kettle. A blue cake tin sat on the table. He opened it and smiled at its contents – a lovely fruit cake, topped with slices of almond and cherries under a white card. It read 'Welcome Home' and was signed with crosses and noughts and a flourishing M.

"Such luxury at this time. She must have saved and scavenged for the ingredients to make this cake."

"Then let's take it over to share it with them," Emily suggested, making James smile at her generosity.

*

As James showed her around the house, Emily could not help but feel the sadness absorbed in the walls. She studied the photographs in simple black wooden frames on the walls of every room. Scenes of the mission in Macau, of James and his sister at different ages with their parents in the courtyard, all wearing Chinese clothes. Others with Chinese servants and converts. The simple church that stood next to their compound, on the other side of the low wall. Street scenes. Nostalgia gripped her.

"Were you happy back here?" she now asked.

"Happy? Yes, I suppose I was. Relieved, more like, to be honest. Margaret and I were just so relieved to be always clean and fed when others over there starved. I suppose that's happiness. But we did miss the parents."

He had told her how quickly his mother had died once they were back on English soil. The illness that had dogged her for years in Macau finally had let rip with a vengeance once she quit that place. Yet, here Mater was, as a young woman with fine hair tugged up into a simple chignon, her high, laced collar clasped with an ornate brooch. Soft wide eyes, well-fringed, a mobile mouth. A sweet study in sepia, she gazed limpidly out of the photograph at Emily.

"That's coral, that brooch. It's a family heirloom. Margaret's got it now," he whispered as he bent down near her ear to look at it.

"You look very like her, James. You've got her eyes and mouth."

"Yes, and Pater's nose!" he chuckled.

"It's a good, strong nose, darling. Shows character," Emily assured him with a caress on his cheek.

"And here is Pater," he said, pointing to an old photograph.

The young man staring out had a resolute moustache, but the rest of his face showed a humanity that Emily was beginning to see more and more of in the war-torn regions of France and Belgium: a face of suffering, of an understanding of the sadness of the human condition.

"He was a good man, I know it," she whispered.

"Yes, he was," James replied, close to tears once more.

*

July 1918: the Decisives

A large group of off-duty Chinese labourers, newly converted, were seated around Alex listening to him read from the translated Bible. As the war dragged on, more and more members of the Chinese Labour Corps arrived to swell the numbers and many began going to his regular after-dinner prayer meetings. As Brother Huan explained to Alex, they found it hard to evoke their own saints in this mutilated foreign landscape. Christianity seemed a closer fit in their present lives. Besides, with so many more being sick or killed, it was a comfort for them to know Alex was beside them, on the ready with his prayers and solace. So with the continuation of the war, the numbers of converts in Alex's camp grew.

During these meetings, a discussion would usually ensue after an explanation of the text just read. Then he would answer the pertinent questions the Chinese asked about the Allied countries and he would end each session with a prayer for everyone's safety.

Now he looked across at Feng Hua, seated at the back of the group. Feng Hua, though a regular attendee, refused to be converted.

"Your Jesus preached love and turning the other cheek, Alex-ah. No way could I love the Germans, and I certainly am doing the opposite of turning the other cheek. But I will come to your prayer meetings. I find they ease my headaches quite a lot," he had once told Alex.

And the headaches were increasingly frequent, leaving Feng Hua with a frenetic look which oftentimes would be accompanied by erratic rambling speech. Feng Hua was still creeping over to the German side most nights, still counting slashed throats. But his information for the British effort was beginning to prove unreliable.

One night, as he shared a cigarette with Alex, Sergeant Jarvis remarked, "Your man can be a bit worrying sometimes, Alex. He seems not to recognise us on occasions."

"I must beg you to stop using him for reconnoitring, Sergeant. He's putting himself in too much danger, but he feels you sanction his activities and won't stop."

"Ha, d'you think he wants to stop? Sanction or no?"

"Could he be putting your own men in jeopardy?

"You know, Alex, this is a moot point and a very worrisome one. I shall order him to stop going over for this very reason."

"That would be a great relief, Sergeant. I confess he drives me to distraction with worry."

*

The next day saw the start of another roster for Brother Huan's group. Feng Hua had already left the night before, contrary to Huan's orders. Feng Hua had lost his temper when told to wait till morning to leave with the group.

240

"The conditions are excellent tonight for my work. Why should I wait for you lot? Besides, the British need my help."

And he had flounced off, his knife tucked under his belt, his rations in his canvas rucksack.

*

Emily had sent Alex a letter from Bournemouth in early June.

'Darling Alex, I am now having a much needed rest and will remain in this lovely sea-side town with James for the whole of my furlough. I have agreed to marry him once the war is over. I see no rush, especially since I have not told Pa about him yet. I know Pa's always wanted me to marry back into the Chinese, but can one really choose the path one's heart must follow? Dear Alex, you've met James. He is right for me, isn't he? I know he is. With the distance of time between Wiremu's death and the end of the war, which, God willing may be quite soon, I shall be able to begin life with James. But I must question myself whether I really want to live in England. From his sister Margaret's reaction when we met and, I must admit, the doubt still persists, I am not sure whether I can be happy here. England no longer feels as strange as when I first visited, but Pa is back in New Zealand and with Eddie in Malaya and you in China, then I should be closer to you all. That's why the end of the war would be a good time to wed. It gives me time to consider all the options.

'James and I will be transferred to the Marne upon our return to France. The Germans are hoping to push through to Paris and out to the coast.

'I pray for your safety, Alex. Please be careful, darling. Stay safe. Let us go home together when it is all over.'

Since then, Alex had planned to travel further south to minister to the Chinese labourers working around the Chateau-Thierry salient, fifty-four miles from Paris. Jarvis had told him that over thirty thousand Chinese had been located in that area to help with the build-up of troops. As usual, they were the luggers of cannon, buriers of mines and auxiliaries in transporting the dead and wounded from the battle. They worked on repairing damaged tanks, assisted in the stables and buried the dead, **often without the protection of masks against the gas.**

This trip would also afford him time to scout Emily out, which, hopefully, would not be overly difficult. He took Brother Huan aside the morning they were leaving for their shift.

"I will probably be gone for at least three to four weeks, Brother Huan. I have to leave it to you to see to our people. Will that be okay?"

"Yes, Brother Alex. I will try my best to do your job and mine. But hurry back for Feng Hua's sake. There is nothing I can do to help him. I feel in my bones a disaster will soon happen."

"Not much I can do either. God give you strength."

*

Alex hitched a lift with one of the French trucks transporting more men southwards on the Epernay road. The countryside they passed, miles in from the battlefields, seemed almost untouched though the roads were much rutted and broken. The soldiers he travelled with were weary and shell-shocked and had no energy to spare for small talk. All sat looking into the near distance, smelling of old sweat, their rifles between their legs, silent in their own reverie. Alex's mood matched theirs – he could not bear light banter at this stage of the war, especially as his French was not that sharp.

But even so, snatches of sombre conversation reached him. He picked out certain words of sufficient interest and got an English-speaking soldier to translate. The US forces were already in the Chateau-Thierry region. More than three hundred thousand men with all their well-equipped back-up had been there since May, skirmishing with the Germans.

"We are too few now, *mon Père*. Our forces are totally demoralised, and you know, there has been talk of mutinies happening in our army. But it is very, how you say, hush hush? Quiet, *oui*? So we now wish for our American friends to dig us out of this long *merde* of a hole. *Oui*, Monsieur, we now rely on our American friends."

Hongyun! Will he be there too with the medical units?

Since they last met, especially since he watched him work in the surgical triage, Hongyun had occupied Alex's thoughts considerably. He felt he had something intangible in common with his half-brother and was sorry the latter's visit had been so short. The older man had left the morning following the attack without saying goodbye and Alex had heard no more from him. Though he had written a couple of times, his letters were never answered. Nor were they returned to sender.

*

Alex arrived on the outskirts of Chateau-Thierry a day later. The entire countryside around the Marne was crawling with the Allied forces. Though the British, US and French divisions were all encamped miles apart from each other, he could see a lot of inter-related activity between them. The Allied Front stretched for forty miles. The truck dropped him off at the American camp before trundling on further down the line.

Alex presented his papers to the guards at the gates.

"Far from home, then, Pastor?" the young corporal asked as he looked at Alex. "You be one of their natives?"

"You can say that," Alex replied tiredly. "Can I find Doctor Victor Zhou here, I wonder?"

"Ask at one of those Red Cross tents over there."

Alex strolled past frenetic activity of men, horses, mules and vehicles to reach the huge Red Cross tents. Gun carriages were being readied with long guns clipped to them. Teams of soldiers were cleaning their own weapons, talk muted and sombre amongst them. Ambulances puttered between the medical triages. Alex approached a para-medic.

"Where can I find Dr Victor Zhou?"

The para-medic took a second to remember. "Tent Six, over there." He pointed south.

Alex peered in at the entrance. He asked a nurse coming out.

"Is Doctor Victor Zhou in there?"

She pointed to a group of blue-scrubbed figures around an operating table. "You can't go in there. Medical personnel only."

"When will he be free?"

She gave a shrug.

"Can you get word to him that his brother's here?"

At this the nurse gave him a sharp look.

"Wait here," she said and went into the interior.

Alex's eyes followed her to a figure with his back turned to the entrance who looked up at her interruption. Hongyun turned round and gazed at him awhile before going back to his work. The nurse returned to Alex.

"He will be along soon. Wait here," she said, and walked away to another tent.

*

It was thirty minutes before Hongyun emerged, followed by para-medics carrying his latest patient out on a stretcher.

"What brought you here?" Hongyun asked as he approached, removing his mask.

Alex smiled. "And it's good to see you too, brother. Actually I came to minister to the Chinese labourers, find Emily and then you, in that order. But you somehow bounced up first. How are you?"

"As you see." Hongyun was tired, thin and his usual brusque self. "By the end of this confounded war, I and all the others here will be the most experienced general surgeons in the United States. In fact, every damn medical personnel will be amongst the most experienced, whatever in his field. Where are you staying? Where's Emily?"

"I hoped you'd tell me. I suppose I can doss down at the pastors' barracks for the night? As to Emily, I don't know. She's probably with the British medics. But where is that? That would be where the Chinese labourers are too."

"She might not necessarily be with the Brits. We're in all this together here. How long has she been in this region? I would have heard of a New Zealand woman doctor if she were right here. So you might like to go further. The Brits and French have hospitals further inland in other towns. Anyway, ask around, you found me after all. Try the Red Cross admin tent over there."

Hongyun started back into his tent. Then he turned around.

"The base offices are over there, left of the Red Cross. Ask for a billet. Meet me at Canteen 1 tonight around 7. We can eat together."

*

"I suppose you know that Uncle Feng died eight months ago?"Hongyun said over dinner in the mess.

244

Alex shook his head. He had not had any mail from China for a while now. The last was over a year ago when Yung told him of Uncle Feng's decline – he was suffering from tuberculosis. He looked down at his boiled salt beef dinner.

"How is Mama Yung?" he now asked.

"Well, she's lonely and growing older. She's seventy now. The farm must be getting too much for her."

"Will you return to China after the war, Hongyun?" But Alex knew even as he asked what the answer would be.

"No, I don't reckon I will, certainly not anytime soon. Look, I am a surgeon, why should I rot on that farm? I have a life in California."

"I would think your mother would be reason enough?" Alex replied softly.

Hongyun said nothing as he sat back and contemplated his youngest sibling long and hard with unblinking eyes.

Chapter 29

July 18th. The Battle of Aisne-Marne

Thru the night winds, wet and dreary
Word goes on to Chateau-Thierry
Ghostly phantoms hear the call –
Gather those who gave their all.
Private L C McCollum

The American preparations were stealthy and secretive. After seeing the damage done to the British and French troops since the beginning of the war, General Pershing was in no mood to warn the Germans with the usual artillery bombardment.

"We can't keep beating out the same old tune if it doesn't work. Your boys have gone down like flies, therefore I want to minimise the damage to ours. We'll change the key and tempo for this one."

And it had been brilliant. The US Expeditionary Forces woke up one early morning and in the dark walked behind their long lines of rolling barrage fire, synchronised with seventy-five long guns, into the town of Torcy by 5.30 a.m., taking the Germans by surprise. Here they engaged the defenders in hand to hand combat and triumphed. Three hours later, Belleau Woods, with its stumps of shell-shot oak trees and surrounding trenches, was captured. The US forces, both Army and Marines, aided by the heartened French, then charged northward into Bois de Givny and drove the Germans down Hill 193 into the village of Givny itself. Two hours later, another flank of the US Expeditionary Forces took the area south of Soissons. Within a day, they had broken the spine of the Germans. But, despite General Pershing's efforts, over sixty-three thousand young

American men were dead or wounded… and the injured and the smashed kept coming in.

That night, General Pershing said a silent prayer for them even as he lifted up his glass of bourbon to toast their success in the quiet of his office.

*

The field hospitals increased exponentially all along the Allied cantonments. James and Emily found themselves transferred to a stately *manoir* conversion on the outer perimeter of Chateau-Thierry. Meanwhile, Alex had trekked over the many miles of destroyed woods and trenches, past temporary graves, blown-up bunkers and a million coils of barbed wire, and trod over earth festering with body parts too small to salvage before he fetched up on their doorsteps.

Along the way, he found Chinese labourers spread all along the entire Allied occupied ground. Most had been in the trenches for over a year now, with no furlough allowed as there was no way of controlling them outside the war zone. So they remained in their barracks and tents, imprisoned in the area, and spent their rest days listening to cannon fire, smelling the putrefaction of the dead as they played mah-jong and cards and fought each other due to nerves frayed beyond their ability to cope.

"When will it all end, Brother Alex-ah?" they asked him.

"I think it will be soon, from all the talk I gathered along the way. The Germans are now desperate. I am sure it will be over before too long. Take heart."

But as he looked at their skeletal frames and disease-ravaged faces, he wondered how many would survive to see the end.

He tried to set up prayer meetings, tried talking to different gatherings, but was met with such weariness that he knew he was wasting his time now. The Chinese here had reached the end of their wits. The kingdom of Jesus' heaven meant nothing when they had seen such hell on earth inflicted by Jesus' followers on each other.

"Apart from the physical illnesses and disease, we are also suffering from the dysfunction of minds and hearts, Alex-ah," one group leader told him over an American cigarette – one from many packets Alex had managed to beg from Hongyun for them. "Last month one of our men killed a fellow worker over a gambling debt. We punished him with severe words, but the French authorities shot him for murder."

The informant, Swee Lin, chuckled humourlessly. "Imagine, executing one man for killing another… in this place! Where is the justice, tell me? We had punished him already, but that was not enough. The French wanted to make an example of him, to control us. Control us! What in heaven's name did they think they could achieve by shooting him? Haven't they seen enough of death already? You tell me, Alex-ah. Where is their God in all this?"

Alex, at the end of this lengthy journey, himself stretched to beyond his own capacity to cope, was in tears as he listened. *Where, indeed, is God in all this? These are Christian nations killing each other. Swee Lin is right; they are, all of them, right. Where is God in this?*

"As time drags on, I feel even the spirits of our ancestors have lost their way through this morass. They cannot find us through all the blood, all the poisoned air. So we are unprotected. We die, Alex-ah. We die each day, every day, so far from home that our ancestors' spirits cannot find us to take us back."

*

The *manoir* sat tranquil, other-worldly, surrounded by several acres of woods at the end of a quiet, poplar-fringed side road on the way to Epernay. It was also large enough to have a convalescence wing. Alex announced himself at the reception desk in the elegant hall. The young nurse on duty took a pitying look at his dirty, ragged appearance and shot off up the wide staircase to the second floor.

"Dr Zhou is resting between shifts. But I'm sure she wouldn't mind being disturbed for you, Chaplain," she informed him on her return.

Within five minutes, Emily was rushing down stairs.

"Alex! Oh Alex! You've come!"

He looked up to see her running down closely followed by James. She flung herself into his arms, crying and laughing with

248

relief, as she buried her face into his chest. Alex collapsed into her, hugging her tight as he looked across at James watching them and knew this was the home Emily had sought all her life. He nodded and smiled at the Englishman as his eyes brimmed with tears.

*

Two days after he arrived at the *manoir,* they were all astonished to see Hongyun stride across the lawn where they were enjoying a cup of comfrey tea in the afternoon sun.

Hongyun's khaki shirt was tucked neatly into his tan slacks, his black shoes polished to a mirror shine. Alex, James and Emily stood up as he approached, Alex grinning his welcome. Emily had her hands over her mouth, her eyes wide with a mixture of joy and disbelief. James stood back as he watched all three. He knew about this elder half-brother.

"I had a couple of days off, so I thought I should visit," Hongyun told them.

He stood a few feet away looking at each in turn before finally resting his eyes on Emily. His right hand clutched a small bunch of white daisies. "Here, I bought these for you."

Emily smiled. She stepped up to him with open arms and he let himself walk into them.

"I've hoped for this moment a long time, my brother," she whispered as she kissed him. Slowly, his arms went round her and he nuzzled her left ear.

Then Alex approached and Hongyun extended an arm around the younger man. As James watched, he knew their tears were washing away the torment and hurt of their collective earlier lives and he allowed himself to weep his own tears of joy for their sake.

*

Alex rested a week with Emily and James at their hospital before leaving to finish his ministering work on the front.

A month later, back at their own camp in Ypres, Alex found Brother Huan and his group in a state of paralytic shock in the Chinese barracks. They wandered around, despair on every face which turned to relief when they saw him.

"What's the matter?" he asked.

"They are going to shoot Feng Hua," Brother Huan wept.

249

"They? The British?"

All nodded.

"What happened? Why are they going to shoot him?" *God help us, it's happening here too?*

"He killed Sergeant Jarvis and another soldier."

"What? When?" Alex's head swam. He had to sit down.

"He was out of his mind, Brother Alex. I think it was over a disagreement of some sort, I'm not sure what, but he became enraged and pulled his knife on the sergeant. Then when another soldier tried to stop him, he was also killed. He is now in the lock-up, over there." Huan pointed to an old concrete building near the stables.

"Oh God, what is all this for?" Alex hunched over, his elbows on his knees, his face in his trembling hands.

The others stood around him as they waited for him to recover.

"You must save him, Alex, he cannot die now. We hear the war may end soon. The enemy's out of resources. He must return to his mother," Huan said, clutching Alex's shoulder.

Alex stood up. "I shall see the commander, but I must see Feng Hua first."

He walked out towards the jail, watched by the despairing men.

*

The lock-up was bigger than it looked from the outside. Apart from the main area, where a sergeant on duty sat behind a desk, there were four cells on each side of a corridor about five feet wide.

The closest cell held two doughboys who looked distracted and in a dirty state of dishevelment.

"Chinaman's in here, down the corridor, last cell on the left," the sergeant said as he led Alex down the cold, dark corridor.

Feng Hua was lying on his cot in a foetal position facing the wall. As Alex stood by while the sergeant unlocked the cell, Feng Hua turned round. He sat up immediately.

"Alex-ah, you must get me out of here," he cried and scrambled up as Alex entered.

"How are you coping in here, Feng Hua?" Alex put a hand on the Chinese's shoulder and led him back to sit on the cot.

"I am very frightened. I know they are going to kill me."

Alex lit Feng Hua a cigarette. "Tell me what happened."

"In truth I cannot remember, Alex-ah. I cannot remember. All I can think of is the bloody knife in my hand and two soldiers dead in front of me. Then other soldiers captured me, hit me, see? They hit me with their guns. And then Huan and the others rushed to us, shouting, shouting. Everything was so bad, so confusing. I cannot remember. But it was my knife and it was in my hand."

The gashes on Feng Hua's face appalled Alex. He had obviously been butted with a rifle several times. The wounds had caked dry and the rest of his face was black and blue. His right eye was closed over and his lips were puffed and cut. His front teeth and an eye tooth were missing. Nobody had tended to his wounds. His hands, too, were badly bruised. Feng Hua had been left to fester in his pain.

"I think my ribs are broken. There is much pain there."

"Let me look," Alex said and helped Feng Hua raise his shirt.

The bruises extended from the top of his rib cage down to his abdomen and hips. He had been punched or kicked. Anger welled up in Alex.

"When did all this happen?" he asked.

"I cannot remember, but it must be, maybe, ten days ago. I cannot remember. Get me out of here, Alex-ah, please. I need to see my mother."

Suddenly, Alex realised that Feng Hua's speech was more stable than it had been for a long while. *Maybe the beating has knocked his delirium out of his head.*

"I'm going to see the camp commander to get you released. Just stay strong, Feng Hua. All right?"

"Yes, Alex-ah, I will stay strong."

*

Major Tom Ainslie was at his desk. He had been in charge of that area of the camp for the past several months. Now he looked up when Alex was announced.

"Ah, Alex, thank God you're back. You're a sight for sore eyes, old boy. Sit, sit. I can guess what you've come about."

251

Alex took the proffered chair opposite the major, and sat for several minutes to compose his thoughts.

"You are not seriously going to shoot him, are you, Tom?"

Ainslie shrugged his shoulders. "What can I do, Alex? He killed two of my men. Knifed them in front of many witnesses. My hands are tied, old chap. We were waiting for you to return, seeing you are his chaplain, before we have the trial. I want you to interpret fully what's going to happen to him."

"But there are mitigating circumstances, Major. I must be allowed to explain. Surely that will help him?"

"I have been told he's a half-wit, and I now know of his exploits behind enemy lines."

"Surely that's to his favour? He saved many British lives."

"Alex," Tom Ainslie lit up his pipe and took several puffs before he continued.

"The man was on a killing spree. Huan told me his history. He was out for revenge, and rightly or wrongly, Sergeant Jarvis encouraged it, thinking it would help our cause. He had trained himself to be a killer even back in China. I suppose, in the end, it clouded his mind and he couldn't tell the difference between a Brit and a Hun. Sorry, Alex, the board will not let him off."

*

The trial was as expected. As Feng Hua, filthy in the clothes he was arrested in, bruised all over, stood handcuffed and slumped in front of the board of six officers, he was found guilty and condemned to die by firing squad three days after the trial. Alex had pre-warned the whole Chinese camp on what to expect. They had gone into mourning and wanted to visit him. Alex had to plead for this privilege. So they went in groups of ten, one group after another to extend their solace standing outside his cell.

"I shall pray for you, Xiao Hua," Huan said, as he held both Feng Hua's broken hands in his own. "To our Lord Jesus, that He saves your soul."

With angry tears, Feng Hua retorted, "It is your Jesus' people who are killing me. How can you even mention *him* and my soul in the same breath?"

*

That final evening, Alex brought some extra horsemeat dumplings and bread together with a glass of root beer from the officers' mess to Feng Hua.

"So, is this my final dinner, Alex-ah? I was told this is the Western rule. But I cannot eat. My stomach hurts too much with the fear of death."

Alex studied Feng Hua awhile, listened as he started on about his father's death and his desire for revenge. As he talked, Alex recognised the signs of his delirium returning. The reality of the situation was now reverting Feng Hua into that recess of his mind where few could reach. Alex sat and listened into the night. When he realised that dawn was approaching, he interrupted the condemned man's rant.

"You must write a last letter to your mother, Feng Hua, while there is still some time left."

Feng Hua stopped and looked at him, coherence returning to his battered face. He thought awhile as tears welled in his eyes.

"As you see, Alex-ah, my hands are too broken for me to hold a pen properly. You write for me."

Alex waited with the pad on his knees, his pen poised, as Feng Hua composed his thoughts.

Feng Hua looked down on the pad and began.

"My respected mother, may the spirits of our ancestors be with you, especially the spirit of my beloved father. May he be with you as you read this letter." He quivered and started weeping. Mucus dripped unchecked from his nose. His eyes remained on the pad.

"Soon, I will be able to meet my father again after so many years. I will be able to tell him, as I tell you now, that I have honoured his spirit, that I have revenged his death so many years ago. I have killed hundreds... no, Alex, make that thousands, of Germans. The British are going to execute me in an hour from now." He paused and looked at Alex, then to the window where the rays of the summer morning sun shone through. He stared out at the light as he dictated on. "Not for killing Germans, which they liked, but by mistake for killing two British soldiers. Mother, forgive me for not returning to you. Forgive me for not being the best son for you. Please remember me at Chingming. When you pray at Father's grave, pray for me too. Include me in your offerings to him that I will not be a hungry ghost.

"Your son. For all his lack of piety, still your son, Mother.

Feng Hua."

Alex wrote in careful, well-formed Chinese characters, wiping his nose from time to time with his sleeves, brushing the tears from his cheeks. At the end of the letter, he penned the date: 29th August 1918.

"Shall we pray, Feng Hua?" he asked softly, hoping the answer would be different this final time.

"No, Alex-ah. Since you pray to your Jesus God, I will not want to pray with you. I will speak to my ancestors now."

"Then allow me to pray."

And Alex knelt by Feng Hua's feet. He put his hands on the condemned man's knees, bowed his head, and prayed fervently in English as his tears dripped onto the cold concrete floor.

"Forgive me, Lord, for I have failed in my duty to this poor man. I beseech you to grant him courage as he walks to his Maker, though he knows not that is you. Forgive all the killing in this war and let peace come quickly. Please grant me the fortitude to see this tragedy through. Please receive the soul of Feng Hua as his hour approaches. Amen."

He looked at Feng Hua as he got to his feet. The Chinese had his eyes closed, his lips quivering, his entire body trembling.

Footsteps sounded along the corridor and stopped outside the cell. The key turned and three soldiers entered. Feng Hua opened his eyes, stared at them as the actual horror hit home.

"Alex-ah! Alex-ah!" He shot up, clutching Alex's arms.

"It's time, Reverend," one of the soldiers said. He walked towards Feng Hua with a short rope. His companions, too, stepped forward.

Alex held Feng Hua steady as the soldiers tied his hands behind his back. Feng Hua was now gibbering.

"Alex-ah, I am so afraid. So afraid. I don't want to die. Alex-ah, tell them, tell them!"

He started wailing as the soldiers half dragged, half carried him down the corridor and out into the clearing behind a brick wall. Alex prayed as he walked behind Feng Hua, his right hand firm on Feng Hua's shoulder.

In the clearing, three soldiers stood by, their rifles on the ready. Beyond it, Brother Huan and a large group of Chinese waited – sombre, silent, still. Feng Hua started to shriek. The soldiers dragged him to the wall. One put a white blindfold on him while another pinned a square of white cotton on his chest. Then they forced him to kneel on the ground. Alex went down on his haunches beside him and clutched his shoulders.

"Feng Hua, die with your honour intact. Raise your head. Be proud."

"Alex-ah," Feng Hua turned his blindfolded face towards his friend. "Promise me. Go to my mother. When this war is over, go to my mother. Tell her I died well. Promise me."

"I promise, my brother, I promise. Go with God."

Before Alex could reach the perimeter where the Chinese stood, three shots rang out. A collective moan rose from them. Alex turned. The body of Feng Hua began its slump to the ground, the white patch on his chest reddening.

Brother Huan and several others walked rapidly to Feng Hua's body. They had brought a stretcher with them.

"We will bury him, Alex. We will make the first offerings to him to send him on his way home."

Chapter 30

November 1918: The Aftermath

It was said that the last shot was fired at 11 a.m., on 11th November 1918.

*

Out in the trenches, the Chinese were at work repairing the wooden supports when suddenly a realisation dawned on them.

"Why is it so silent, Brother Alex?" Huan asked Alex at noon.

Alex shook his head. "The Germans have been retreating for several weeks now. The tide is turning."

"So it will end soon?"

"I pray so, Brother Huan."

Then the sound of horses galloping close drew their attention. Shots rang in the air. Groups of the cavalry were riding all over their salient, shooting into the air with their pistols, their whoops of joy carrying in the wind to all.

"It's over! It's over! We can all go home!"

And soon, all the soldiers in the trenches climbed wearily up into the destroyed landscape and started their slow, silent walk back to their encampments.

*

But in all the hospitals, in both fields and towns, the wounded did not stop coming in. And in the cemeteries all over the Western Front, the burying continued. It was now not the fighting that was killing the troops, but a mysterious illness with all the signs of a virulent influenza. It had begun the year before but, as the months progressed, so had this illness, striking without impunity. Nobody knew how it started but everybody blamed the dreadful diseases and inhuman conditions suffered by all on the Western Front. And it was spreading through Europe.

In their *manoir* hospital, Emily said, "At least New Zealand is far away from all this carnage. Let's pray they will not get the contagion."

"But the troops are going back, Emily. They are the carriers, surely?" James replied.

"No, I don't want to believe that. With better food and conditions and the sea air, they will fight it. And right now, we don't know if the disease is airborne."

"It is airborne, my love," he reasoned softly.

"No! NO! It mustn't be. After all we've been through, we must survive this, we must!"

*

"The Allies need you all in the CLC to clean up the land after this, Brother Huan," Alex said. "Of course they will still pay you till the last day. Is that all right?"

"We are here, we are alive, that will be the best job of all," replied Huan. "The darkness is over. What about you, Brother Alex? Will you stay with us and return to China?"

Alex looked at the sad, young-old face of his friend. He took a while to consider.

"I will go home first, Brother Huan. I haven't seen my father for more than ten years. That is my immediate duty now and I can go with my sister on the New Zealand ship. But most certainly, I intend to return to China. I promised Feng Hua that I will see his mother. I have a letter to deliver, remember?"

"Well, we have at last proven our worth to the foreign nations, Brother Alex. We have proven we are a people in our own right, with our own self-respect and they must let us have our sovereignty back. Now China can rebuild herself as a nation." Huan's pride shone on his face.

"I pray you are right, Brother Huan. But what this war has taught me is the cold treachery of men in power. I hope you won't be disappointed. Truly, I do."

"When will you go home?"

"I don't know as yet. My sister will do her best to find a berth for me on the ship she will be on. Now, I will try to see our American brother and consider what else from there."

*

The American troops were not going home as yet. France and Belgium were severely damaged and President Woodrow Wilson wanted their troops to remain to help with the clean-up.

After six days of hitching rides from American camp to American camp, Alex finally found Hongyun in a field hospital along the route to Soisson. The entire camp was preparing to move on. Ambulances were transferring the last of the sick and wounded from field hospitals into those in towns and cities and the medical personnel was in the final stages of cleaning up.

Alex walked into Number 3 Operation Unit to find Hongyun tidying up surgical instruments.

"Are you leaving?" he asked his elder brother.

"As you see, kid, we're packing up and heading to Paris for a bit of R and R. Then it's home, sweet home. What about you? Staying on with your labourers?"

"I'm catching up with Emily. She's going to get me a berth on a boat home. It's been years since I last saw Pa so we're planning a reunion before Eddie leaves for Malaya."

"Lucky you," Hongyun remarked, his expression as flat as his voice.

Alex saw the desperate fatigue on his face. Hongyun's hair was speckled with grey and his eyes were deeply shadowed. Alex did a quick calculation; of course, Hongyun was now forty and into early middle-age.

"I've an idea, brother, why don't you hitch a ride too and come home to New Zealand with us? Pa would love to see you and we'll all be together as a family."

"Alex, Alex, how can I? First, every berth on your ships will be taken with your own Anzacs. Second, the paperwork will be too complicated. I'm a Yank, remember? A Chinese Yank. Can you imagine the headache that will give the racist bureaucrats on both sides – war or no war?"

He paused to study Alex whose shoulders were collapsing by the minute and softened his tone. "Look, let this whole darn thing settle first. Then I may book a passage from San Fran. But right now, what I need is a long break and to get back to Berkeley. There's the possibility of setting up private practice with a group of medics from here. It will be a shoo-in with all the experience we've accumulated. That's my first priority, I'm afraid. Sorry."

Hongyun carried on clipping up the surgical boxes as he talked, pausing now and then to look at his younger brother. Alex looked lost and forlorn. He moved to put a comforting hand on Alex's shoulder.

"Look, why don't you wait a bit? There's a truck going out of here after lunch. I'll get them to drop us off at Emily's and I can say goodbye properly to her."

*

"You must stay till tomorrow, at least," Emily insisted after her initial surprise at seeing both brothers walk into her ward together. "James and I are getting married. So you must stay. And that's an order, Captain!" she laughed, noticing Hongyun's rank.

*

They had the wedding ceremony in the main entry hall with everybody able to stand or sit up in a wheelchair attending. James looked assured and handsome in his officer's uniform. Emily wore a simple blue woollen dress with an army jacket over her shoulders. Alex made a hollyhock posy from a bush he found in the garden and stuck mistletoe randomly into her hair. She giggled, delirious with joy.

"Happy at last, Em?" he asked softly.

"Perfectly, darling Alex, just perfectly happy. Especially since you and Hongyun are both here. We've all come through safe."

The Anglican chaplain attached to the hospital, the Reverend Joseph Cavendish, blessed the couple and then a party of sorts was held with the lean provisions of the aftermath being all there was to eat and drink. However, the happiness on every face made up for the lack. The war was over and for Emily, the time for burying tragedies had at last come. Wiremu was at rest in the soil of Flanders freeing her to finally start a new beginning with James.

*

"And we'll soon be home," Alex murmured in her ear as he bent to kiss her.

259

Postscript:
The Treaty of Versailles was signed on the 28th June 1919 between the Allies and Germany. Because both Britain and America needed Japan's support to form the League of Nations, Japan was allowed to retain Shandong Province as an incentive. Thus China was once more betrayed by the Western powers. China refused to sign the Treaty.

I dedicate this book to the memory of all those who died in the First World War, from all sides, but especially to the Chinese Labour Corps, the unsung heroes who helped make the Allied victory possible. And also to those thousands of Chinese railroad workers, much mistreated and maligned, without whom the great railways of Canada and the United States of America would have cost much, much more. I remember them.

Thank you for reading this book. I truly hope you have enjoyed it. If so, please find the first book in this trilogy, **MEMORIES IN THE BONE**, of the Chinese Diaspora on your favourite e-book site or as a print copy from retailers. The final book is in progress.

Memories in the Bone

Synopsis

In the crumbling days of the Qing Dynasty, a failed peasant-scholar styles himself God's Chinese Son and Jesus' Younger Brother to lead the biggest uprising against any emperor in Chinese history.

Caught up in this tumult leading them into battle, death and exile are the three sons of the Zhou family from Suzhou. Zhou Fengyi, the patriarch with his own ghosts to overcome, struggles to hold his family together as he lives in fear of what he witnessed as a twelve-year old.

A young Zhou Yu and his brothers join the rebel army and Yu quickly excels as a fearless warrior. When he is forced to flee after watching the execution of his eldest brother, Captain Zhou Yun, his father smuggles him into the Shanghai sanctuary of his missionary sister, Aunt Meng who hides him. She eventually secures him a passage on a ship headed for Australia.

Zhou Yu forges a new life in Australia, striking it rich in the gold fields. A run with the law over a white woman has Yu sailing to Otago, New Zealand. After a sojourn home to marry and father a son, he returns to New Zealand to escape the poll tax and finds solace in a Maori settlement. But his warm relationship with the Reverend Pita Hohepa and his Aunt Ngaire, and the slave girl Horowhai does not protect him from memories of his murderous past. Meanwhile his wife and baby son wait in China for letters to arrive.

The Reverend Pita Hohepa struggles to reconcile the old world of the Maori with his new Christian beliefs, representing a people divided between the old Aotearoa and the new white New Zealand. Auntie Ngaire, his aunt, an ancient Maori princess, hangs on to the old ways regardless of the hurt inflicted on others by her own desires in her dying days.

As their lives unfold in the dangerous, tumultuous years of 19th Century China where foreigners stoop to the lowest to gain large concessions of Chinese soil, a passionate story of the Chinese Diaspora emerges; and the reasons why so many left their Motherland to suffer the hardships, racism and indignities to eventually become men of substance in the alien lands of the very foreigners who carve up their own.

Memories in the Bone is a stirring story of love and trust betrayed; of honour lost and regained.

Reviews for Memories in the Bone

"…a believable and intelligent read…" -- 4 Stars, Forward Clarion Reviews.

"Phipps is a graceful writer, particularly adept at describing places and events with vibrant and keenly observant details." -- Blue Ink Review.

"Phipps delivers an engaging story…The author's clear passion for the historical material definitely comes through." – Kirkus Review.

To further your interest in Chinese culture and history,
THE MING ADMIRAL: A CHINESE ODYSSEY is available on
Create Space and Kindle.

The Ming Admiral: A Chinese Odyssey

A synopsis

China 1382

A new emperor has been on the throne since 1368 and proceeds to cleanse the empire of the supporters of the previous Muslim Mongol dynasty. The village of Kunyang in Yunnan is destroyed and its young taken into slavery. Out of this chaos, an exceptionally gifted boy born with a recessive gene, grows to become the right hand man of the founding emperor's third son, the Warrior Prince Zhu Di, helping him take the throne from the mandated heir, his nephew, the Emperor Jianwen.

As the Emperor Yongle, Zhu Di makes the dusty frontier town of Dadu his new capital, calls it Beijing, builds the Forbidden City and moves the entire court north to the edge of the desert. He instigates the writing of world's greatest encyclopaedia and builds the Great Treasure Fleets which will ply the seas, bringing all nations they encounter under the thrall of China in the first instance of gunboat diplomacy. The Emperor's drive, however, comes at the cost of those closest to him. His oldest friend and ally, ZhengHe, is not only forced to endure indignity and suffering at his hand, but also is rewarded with greatness as Grand Admiral of the Treasure Fleets.

Eventually, Zhu Di commits his greatest crime against humanity with the execution of two thousand concubines and the eunuchs suspected of cavorting with them. This forces ZhengHe into a dangerous political alliance and it is only with the death of Zhu Di that there is reconciliation.

Reviews for The Ming Admiral

"… a wonderful read …. this is a wonderful book that is a true testament to the author's strengths in writing such a well-organized and complex tale in the genre of Chinese historical fiction.' 5 Stars – Red City Review.

"Mee-mee Phipps has done credit to her heritage by bringing this story to life." Miles Hughes, author of The Coconut War, Catalan, Richmond Road.

"Phipps' attention to details brought 14th Century China so alive for me I could smell the spices in the market places." Tom Ryan, author of The Field of Blackbirds.

I would love to have your opinion on these books. I can be contacted by email at: meemee.f.phipps@gmail.
Website : www.meemeephipps.com
I also run a monthly blog: meemeephipps.blogspot.co.nz and you can find me on FaceBook:
https://www.facebook.com/meemee.phipps
and Twitter: https://twitter.com/meemeefrancesph

www.ingramcontent.com/pod-product-compliance
Lightning Source LLC
Chambersburg PA
CBHW051554030726
47592CB00001B/287